D0344828

MARCH TO
THE STARS

MARCH TO THE STARS

DAVID WEBER
JOHN RINGO

MARCH TO THE STARS

This is a work of fiction. All the characters and events portrayed in this book are fictional, and any resemblance to real people or incidents is purely coincidental.

Copyright © 2003 by David Weber & John Ringo

All rights reserved, including the right to reproduce this book or portions thereof in any form.

A Baen Books Original

Baen Publishing Enterprises
P.O. Box 1403
Riverdale, NY 10471
www.baen.com

ISBN: 0-7434-3562-1

Cover art by Patrick Turner

First printing, January 2003

Library of Congress Cataloging-in-Publication Data

Weber, David, 1952-
    March to the stars / by David Weber & John Ringo.
        p. cm.
    ISBN 0-7434-3562-1
    1. Life on other planets—Fiction. 2. Space warfare—Fiction. I. Ringo, John, 1963-
II. Title.

PS3573.E217 M354 2003
813'.54—dc21

2002034184

Distributed by Simon & Schuster
1230 Avenue of the Americas
New York, NY 10020

Production by Windhaven Press, Auburn, NH
Printed in the United States of America

10   9   8   7   6   5   4   3   2   1

This book is dedicated to Sergeant First Class (later Sergeant Major) Miles Rutherford. Who took a slacker jerk and turned him into a decent soldier. Any similarity to characters or events in the books is purely coincidental.

MARCH TO
THE STARS

PROLOGUE

The body was in a state of advanced decomposition. Time, and the various insect analogues of Marduk, had worked their way with it, and what was left was mostly skeleton with a few bits of clinging tendon and skin. Temu Jin would have liked to say it was the worst thing he'd ever seen, but that would have been a lie.

He turned over one of the skeletal hands and ran a sensor wand across it. The catacomblike tomb was hot and close, especially with three more team members and one of the gigantic Mardukans packed into it with him. The heat on Marduk was always bad—the "temperate" regions were a fairly constant thirty-five degrees—but in the tomb, with the remnant stink of decomposition (not to mention the smell of the unwashed assholes he'd arrived with), it was like an antechamber to Hell.

One that was already inhabited.

There was no question that its occupants had been Imperial Marines. Or, at least, people with Marine nano packs. The trace materials and surviving nanites were coded, and the sensor practically screamed "Imperials." But the questions were how they had gotten here . . . and *why* they were here. He could think of several reasons, and he liked the stink of all of them even less than he did the stench in this room.

"Ask them again, geek," Dara said in a tight voice. The survey team leader choked for a second—again—then hawked, spat, and finished by blowing out his nose on the floor. Marduk was hell on his sinuses. "Talk gook. Make sure this is all there was."

Jin looked up at the towering Mardukan and ran the translation through his "toot." The tutorial implant, lodged just inside his mastoid bone, took his chosen words, translated them into the local Mardukan dialect, and adjusted his speaking voice to compensate.

"My illustrious leader wishes to ensure, once again, that there were no survivors."

Mardukan expressions were not the same as those of humans. Among other things, their faces had fewer muscles, and much of their expressiveness came from eloquent gestures of their four arms. But the body language of this Mardukan was closed, as well. Part of that might be from the fact that he was missing one arm from the elbow down. Currently, there was a rather nice prosthetic hook in its place, razor-sharp on both sides. So Dara had to be either stupid, arrogant, or both to ask, for the fifth time, if the Voitan representative was lying.

"Alas," T'Leen Targ said with a sorrowful but cautious sweep of his arms (and hook), "there were no survivors. A few lasted a pair of days, but then they, too, succumbed. We did all we could for them. That we had been only a day sooner! The battle was great; your friends warred upon more Kranolta than the stars in the sky! They stacked them against the walls of the city and cut them down with their powerful fire-lances! Had our relief force but been sooner, some might have survived! Woe! But we were too late, alas. However, they did break the power of the Kranolta, and for that Voitan was and is eternally thankful. It was because of that gratitude that we interred them here, with our own honored dead, in hopes that someday others of their kind might come for them. And . . . here you are!"

"Same story," Jin said, turning back to the team leader.

"Where's the weapons? Where's the gear?" Dara

demanded. Unlike the commo-puke's, his toot was an off-the-shelf civilian model and couldn't handle the only translation program available. It was loaded with the local patois used around the distant starport, but handling multiple dialects was beyond its capability, and Jin's system couldn't cross load the translation files.

"*Some* of that stuff should have survived," the team leader continued. "And there were supposed to be more of them at the last city. Where'd the rest of 'em go?"

"My illustrious leader asks about our dear friends' weapons and equipment," Jin said. The communications technician had had fairly extensive dealings with the natives, both back at the distant starport and on the hellish odyssey to this final resting place of the human castaways. And of them all, this one made him the most nervous. He'd almost rather be in the jungles again. Which was saying a lot.

Marduk was an incredibly hot, wet, and stable planet. The result was a nearly worldwide jungle, filled with the most vicious predators in the known worlds. And it seemed that the search team—or assassination team, depending on how one viewed it—had run into all of them on its journey here.

The starport's atmospheric puddle-jumpers had flown them to the dry lakebed where the four combat shuttles had landed. There was no indication, anywhere, of what unit had flown those shuttles, or where they had come from. All of them had been stripped of any information, and their computers purged. Just four Imperial assault shuttles, totally out of fuel, in the middle of five thousand square kilometers of salt.

There had, however, been a clear trail off the lakebed, leading up into the mountains. The search team had followed it, flying low, until it reached the lowland jungles. After that it had just . . . disappeared into the green hell.

Dara's request to return to base at that point had been denied. It was unlikely, to say the very least, that the shuttle crews might survive to reach civilization. Even taking the local flora and fauna out of the equation, the landing site was on the far side of the planet from the starport, and unless they had brought along enough dietary supplements, they would starve to death long before they could make the trip. But unlikely or not, their fate had to be known. Not so much because anyone would ever ask, or care, about them. Because if there was *any* shred of a possibility that they could reach the base, or worse, get off planet, they had to be eliminated.

That consideration had been unstated, and it was also one of the reasons that the tech wasn't sure he would survive the mission. The "official" reason for the search was simply to rescue the survivors. But the composition of the team made it much more likely that the real reason was to eliminate a threat. Dara was the governor's official bully-boy. Any minor "problem" that could be fixed with a little muscle or a discreetly disappearing body tended to get handed to the team leader. Otherwise, he was pretty useless. As demonstrated by his inability to see what was right in front of his eyes.

The rest of the team was cut from the same cloth. All fourteen of them—there'd been seventeen . . . before the local fauna got a shot at them on the trek here—were from the locally hired "guard" force, and all were wanted on one planet or another. Aware that maintaining forces on Class Three planets was difficult, at best, the distant Imperial capital allowed local governors wide latitude in the choice of personnel. Governor Brown had, by and large, hired what were still known as "Schultzes," guards who could be trusted to see, do, and hear nothing. Still, there were those special occasions when a real problem cropped up. And to deal with those problems, he had secured a "special reaction force" composed of what could graciously be called "scum." If, of course, one wanted to insult scum.

Jin was well aware that he was not an "official" member of the Special Force. As such, this mission might be a test for entry, and in many ways, that could be a good thing. Unfortunately, even if it was an entry test, there was still one huge issue associated with the mission: It might involve fighting the Marines. He had several reasons, not the least of which was the likelihood of being blasted into plasma, to not want to fight Marines, but the mission had been angling steadily that way.

Now, however, it seemed all his worry had been for naught. The last of the Marines had died here, in this lonely outpost, overrun by barbarians before their friendly "civilized" supporters could arrive to save them!

Sure they did, he thought, and snorted mentally. *Either they wandered off and these guys are covering for them . . . or else the locals finished them off themselves and are graciously willing to give these "Kranolta" the credit. The only problem at this point is figuring out which.*

"Alas," the local said yet again. He seemed remarkably fond of that word, Jin thought cynically as Targ gestured in the direction of the distant jungle somewhere outside the tomb. "The Kranolta took all their equipment with them. There was nothing left for us to give to their friends. That is, to you."

And you can believe as much or as little of that as you like, Jin thought. But the answer left a glaring hole he had to plug. And hope his efforts never came to light.

"The scummy says the barbs threw all the gear into the river," he mistranslated.

"Poth!" Dara snarled. "That means it's all trashed. *And* we can't trace the power packs! Even trashed, we could've gotten something for them."

What an imbecile, Jin thought. Dara must have been hiding behind the door when brains were given out.

When a body is looted, the looters very rarely take *every scrap* of clothing. Nor was that the only peculiarity. There was one clinging bit of skin on the corpse before him which had clearly been cut away in an oval, as if to remove a tattoo after the person was dead . . . and there were no weapons or even bits of weapons anywhere in sight. For that matter, the entire battle site had been meticulously picked over to remove every trace of evidence. Some of the scars from plasma gun fire had even been covered up. The barbarians, according to the locals' time line, could not possibly have swept the battlefield that well, no matter how addicted to trophy-taking they might be, before the "civilized" locals arrived to finish driving them off.

The last city they'd passed through had also been remarkably reticent about the actions the objects of the search team's curiosity had taken on their way through. The crews of the downed shuttles had apparently swept into town, destroyed and looted a selected few of the local "Great Houses," and then swept out again, just as rapidly. According to the local king and the very few nobles they'd been permitted to question, at least. And in that town, the search team had been followed everywhere by a large enough contingent of guards to make attempts to question anyone else contraindicated.

All of that proved one thing to Jin, and it took a sadistic, snot-filled idiot like Dara not to see it.

The bodies had been sterilized.

Somebody wanted to make *damn* sure no one could determine who these Marines had been without a DNA database. The dead Marines' toots were already a dead issue, of course. Their built-in nanites had obediently reduced them to half-crumbled wreckage once their owners were dead. That was a routine security measure, but the rest of this definitely went far beyond "routine." Which meant these particular people were something other than standard Marines. Either Raiders or . . . something else. And since the locals were covering for them so assiduously, it was glaringly obvious that all of them *hadn't* died.

All of which meant that there was a short company—from the number of shuttles, Jin had put their initial force at a company—of an Imperial special operations unit out there wandering in the jungle. And the only reasonable target for their wandering was a certain starport.

Lovely.

He pushed aside a bit of the current corpse's hair, looking for any clue. The Marine had been female, with longish, dishwater blond hair. That was the only thing about the skeletal remains which would have been recognizable to anyone but a forensic pathologist, which Jin was not. He had some basic training in forensics, but all he could tell about this corpse was that a blade had half-severed the left arm. However, under the cover of the hair, there was a tiny earring. Just a scrap of bronze, with one ten-letter word on it.

Jin was unable to keep his eyes from widening, but he didn't freeze. He was far too well trained to do something so obvious. He simply moved his hand in a smooth motion, and the tiny earring was ripped from the decaying ear, a scrap of skin still dangling from it.

"I'm not finding anything," he said, getting to his feet as he willed his face to total immobility.

He looked at the native, who returned his regard impassively. The local "king" was named T'Kal Vlan. He'd greeted the search team as long-lost cousins, all the time giving the impression that he wanted to sell them a rug. For T'Leen Targ, though, it always seemed to be a toss-up between selling them a rug and burying them in one. Now the local scratched his horn with his hook and nodded . . . in a distinctly human fashion.

"I take it that you did not find anything," Targ said. "I'm *so* sorry. Will you be taking the bodies with you?"

"I think not," Jin replied. Standing as they were, the team leader was behind the local. Jin reached out with his left hand, and the Mardukan took it automatically, another example of acculturation to Terrans. Jin wondered if the Marines had realized how many clues they were unavoidably leaving behind. Given who they apparently were, it was probable, for all the proof of how hard they'd worked to avoid it. As he shook the Mardukan's slime-covered hand, a tiny drop of bronze was left behind, stuck in the mucus.

"I don't think we'll be back," the commo tech said. "But you might want to melt this down so nobody else finds it."

In the palm of the native's hand, the word "BARBARIANS" was briefly impressed into the mucus.

Then it disappeared.

CHAPTER ONE

"It's a halyard."

"No, it's a stay. T'e headstay."

The thirty-meter schooner *Ima Hooker* swooped close-hauled into aquamarine swells so perfect they might have been drawn from a painting by the semimythical Maxfield Parrish. Overhead, the rigging sang in a faint but steady breeze. That gentle zephyr, smelling faintly of brine, was the only relief for the sweltering figures on her deck.

Julian mopped his brow and pointed to the offending bit of rigging.

"Look, there's a rope—"

"A line," Poertena corrected pedantically.

"Okay, there's a line and a pulley—"

"T'at's a block. Actually, it's a deadeye."

"Really? I thought a block was one of those with cranks."

"No, t'at's a windlass."

Six other schooners kept formation on *Hooker*. Five of them were identical to the one on whose deck Julian and Poertena stood: low, trim hulls with two masts of equal height and what was technically known as a "top-sail schooner rig." What that meant was that each mast carried a "gaff sail," a fore-and-aft sail cut like a

9

truncated triangle with its head set from an angled yard—
the "gaff"—while the foremast also carried an entire set
of conventional square sails. The after gaff sail—the
"mainsail," Julian mentally corrected; after all, he had
to get *something* right—had a boom; the forward gaff sail
did not. Of course, it was called the foresail whereas the
lowest square sail on that mast was called the "fore
course," which struck him as a weird name for any sail.
Then there were the "fore topsail," "fore topgallant," and
"fore royal," all set above the fore course.

The second mast (called the "mainmast" rather than
the "aftermast," for some reason Julian didn't quite
understand, given that the ship had only two masts to
begin with and that it carried considerably less canvas
than the foremast) carried only a single square topsail,
but compensated by setting a triangular "leg of mutton"
fore-and-aft sail above the mainsail. There were also
staysails set between the masts, not to mention a flying jib, outer jib, and inner jib, all set between the
foremast and the bowsprit.

The seventh schooner was different—a much bigger, less
agile, somehow unfinished-looking vessel with a far deeper
hull and no less than five masts—and, at the insistence
of Captain Armand Pahner, Imperial Marines, rejoiced in
the name of *Snarleyow.* The smaller, more nimble ships
seemed to regard their larger sister with mixed emotions.
No one would ever have called *Snarleyow* anything so
gauche as *clumsy,* perhaps, but she was clearly less fleet
of foot, and her heavier, more deliberate motion almost
seemed to hold the others back.

All of the ships carried short-barreled cannon along
their sides. *Snarleyow* mounted fifteen of them to a side,
which gave her a quarter again the broadside armament
of any of her consorts, but all of them carried a single,
much larger cannon on a pivot mount towards the bow,
as well. And every single one of them had ropes everywhere. Which was the problem.

"Okay." Julian drew a deep breath, then continued in
a tone of massive calm. "There's a line and a pu—block.
So why isn't it a halyard?"

"Halyard hauls up t'e sail. T'e stay, it hold t'e pocking mast up."

The Pinopan had grown up around the arcane terminology of the sea. In fact, he was the only human member of the expedition (with the exception of Roger, who had spent summers in Old Earth's blue-water recreational sailing community) who actually understood it at all. But despite the impression of landsmen—that the arcana existed purely to cause them confusion—there was a real necessity for the distinct terminology. Ships constantly encounter situations where clear and unambiguous orders may mean the difference between life and death. Thus the importance of being able to tell hands to pull upon a certain "rope" in a certain way. Or, alternatively, to let it out slowly, all the while maintaining tension.

Thus such unambiguous and unintelligible orders as "Douse the mainsail and make fast!" Which does *not* mean throw water on it to increase speed.

"So which one's the halyard?" Julian asked plaintively.

"Which halyard? Countin' t'e stays'ils, t'ere's seventeen pocking halyards on t'is ship. . . ."

Hooker's design had been agreed upon as the best possible for the local conditions. She and her consorts had been created, through human design and local engineering, to carry Prince Roger and his bodyguards—now augmented by various local forces—across a previously unexplored ocean. Not that there hadn't, as always, been the odd, unanticipated circumstance requiring last-minute improvisation. The fact that a rather larger number of Mardukan allies than originally anticipated had been added to Roger's force had created the need for more sealift capacity. Especially given the sheer size of the Mardukan cavalry's mounts. *Civan* were fast, tough, capable of eating almost anything, and relatively intelligent. One thing they were *not*, however, was petite. Hardly surprising, since the cavalrymen who rode into battle on their backs averaged between three and three and a half meters tall.

Carrying enough of them to sea aboard the six original schooners had turned out to be impossible once the revised numbers of local troopers had been totaled up. So just when everyone had thought they were done building, they—and somewhere around a quarter of the total shipbuilding force of K'Vaern's Cove—had turned to to build the *Snarleyow*. Fortunately, the local labor force had learned a lot about the new building techniques working on the smaller ships, but it had still been a backbreaking, exhausting task no one had expected to face. Nor had Poertena been able to spend as much time refining her basic design, which was one reason she was ugly, slabsided, and slow, compared to her smaller sisters. She was also built of green timber, which had never been seasoned properly and could be expected to rot with dismaying speed in a climate like Marduk's. But that was all right with Prince Roger and his companions. All they really cared about was that she last long enough for a single voyage.

Although she was scarcely in the same class for speed or handiness as Poertena's original, twin-masted design, *Snarleyow* was still enormously more efficient than any native Mardukan design. She had to be. The nature of the local weather was such that there was an almost unvarying wind from the northeast, yet that was the very direction in which the ships had to sail. That was the reason for their triangular sails. Their fore-and-aft rig—a technology the humans had introduced—made it possible for them to sail much more sharply into the wind than any local vessel, with its clumsy and inefficient, primitive square-rigged design, had ever been able to do. Similar ships had sailed the seas of Earth all the way up to the beginning of the Information Age, and they remained the mainstay for water worlds like Pinopa.

"Now I'm really confused," Julian moaned. "All right. Tying something down is 'making fast.' A rope attached to a sail is a 'sheet.' A rope tied to the mast is a 'stay.' And a bail is the iron thingamajig on the mast."

"T'e boom," Poertena corrected, wiping away a drop of sweat. The day, as always, was like a steambath, even with the light wind that filled the sails. "T'e bail is on t'e boom. Unless you're taking on water. T'en you bail it out."

"I give up!"

"Don' worry about it," the Pinopan said with a chuckle. "You only been at t'is a few weeks. Besides, you got me an' all t'ose four-armed monstrosities to do t'e sailing. You jus' pull when we say 'heave,' and stop when we say 'avast.' "

"And hold on when you say 'belay.' "

"And hold on *tight* when we say belay."

"I blame Roger for this," Julian said with another shake of his head.

"You blame Roger for what?" a cool female voice asked from behind him.

Julian looked over his shoulder and grinned at Nimashet Despreaux. The female sergeant was frowning at him, but it slid off the irrepressible NCO like water off a duck.

"It's all Roger's fault that we're in this predicament," he replied. "If it wasn't for him, I wouldn't have to learn this junk!"

Despreaux opened her mouth, but Julian held up a hand before she could retort.

"Calmly, Nimashet. I know it's not Roger's fault. It was a joke, okay?"

Despreaux's frown only underscored the classical beauty of her face, but it was dark with worry.

"Roger's . . . still not taking Kostas' death very well, Adib. I just don't . . . I don't want anybody even *joking* about this being his fault," she said, and Poertena nodded in agreement.

"T'e prince didn't maroon us here, Julian. T'e Saints an' whoever set t'at pocking toombie on us marooned us." The diminutive armorer shrugged. "I guess it wasn't very pocking punny."

"Okay," a chagrined Julian said. "You've got a point. Roger has been sort of dragging around, hasn't he?"

"He's been in a funk, is what you mean," Despreaux said.

"Well, I'm sure there's some way you could cheer him up," Julian suggested with an evil grin.

"Oh, pock," Poertena muttered, and backed up quickly. After a crack like that the fecal matter was about to hit the impeller.

"Now this is a mutinous crew, if ever I've seen one." Sergeant Major Eva Kosutic said, joining them. She looked from Despreaux's furious face to Julian's "butter-wouldn't-melt-in-my-mouth" expression and frowned. "All right, Julian. What did you say this time?"

"Me?" Julian asked with enormous innocence but little real hope of evading the consequences. The sergeant major had an almost miraculous sense of timing; she always turned up just as the action was hottest. Which come to think of it, described her in bed as well. "What would I have said?"

Now he looked from the sergeant major to the fulminating Despreaux, decided that coming clean offered his best chance of survival, and shrugged with a repentant expression.

"I just suggested that there might be a way to cheer Roger up," he admitted, then, unable to help himself, grinned again. "I guarantee I'm right. God knows *I've* been more cheerful lately."

The sergeant major rolled her eyes and crossed her arms.

"Well if that's your attitude, you'll damned well be less cheerful for a while!" She looked at the three noncoms and shook her head. "This is a clear case of His Evilness' finding work for idle hands. Poertena, I thought you were supposed to be conducting a class in rigging."

"I was trying to get Julian up to speed, Sergeant Major," the Pinopan said, tossing a length of rope to the deck. "T'at's not going too good."

"I've got all the stuff loaded in my toot," Julian said with a shrug. "But some of the data seems to be wrong, and the rest just seems to be hitting and bouncing. I mean, what's 'luff' mean?"

"It's when the sail flaps," Kosutic replied, shaking her head. "Even *I* know that, and I *hate* sailing. I guess we should've known better than to try to teach Marines to be sailors."

"We don't really need them, Sergeant Major," Poertena told her. "We've got plenty of Mardukans."

"We need to work on our entry techniques, anyway," Julian pointed out. "We've been engaging in all these open-field maneuvers, but when we take the spaceport, it's going to be mostly close quarters. Whole different style, Smaj. And we haven't really done any of that since Q'Nkok."

The sergeant major frowned, then nodded. She was sure Julian had come up with that because it was more fun than learning to sail. But that didn't mean he was wrong.

"Okay. Concur. If we wanted sailors, we should've left you on the *DeGlopper* and brought Navy pukes. I'll talk the change over with the Old Man. If he approves, we'll start working on close combat techniques for the rest of the voyage."

"Besides," Poertena pointed out gloomily, "we might need them before t'en. I've never seen a place like t'is t'at *didn't* have pirates."

"And then there's the 'fish of unusual size.' " Julian chuckled and gestured out over the emerald waters. "So far, so good, right?"

"Don't laugh," Despreaux muttered. "I read that log. I do *not* want to tangle with something big enough to bite a boat in half, even a small one."

"Well," Kosutic said, with a tug on her earlobe. "If worse comes to worst, we can always give Roger a pocket knife and throw him at it."

"Ooooo!" Julian shook his head. "You haven't even *met* one of these little fishies and you hate them *that* much?"

Prince Roger Ramius Sergei Alexander Chiang MacClintock, Heir Tertiary to the Throne of Man, turned away from the creaming waves to look across the shipboard bustle. The sergeant major had just broken up the huddle around Julian, and the four NCOs were headed in four different directions. He took a moment extra to watch Despreaux make for the fo'c'sle. He knew his depression was beginning to affect her, and that he needed to snap out of it. But the loss of Kostas was the one wound that would not seem to heal, and he'd had too much time to think about it since the frenetic haste of getting all seven ships built had eased into the voyage itself. For the first time in what seemed forever, he wasn't engaged in frantic efforts to train native troops, fight barbarian armies, build ships, or simply hike through endless jungle. For that matter, nothing was actively attempting to kill him, devour him, assassinate him, or kidnap him, and a part of him was distantly amazed to discover just how much having that respite depressed him. Having time to think, he had learned, was not always a good thing.

He supposed he could pull up the list of casualties on his implanted toot. But there wouldn't be much point. When they'd first landed, the Marines of Bravo Company, Bronze Battalion of the Empress' Own Regiment, had been just so many faces. And the officers and crew of the Assault Ship *DeGlopper*, long since expanding plasma, had just been blurs. But since some time after the pilots of the shuttles had brought them to deadstick landings on this backward hell, some time between the internecine fighting that had erupted at the first city they'd visited and the furious battles with the Kranolta barbarians, the Marines had become more than faces. In many ways, they had become more than family—as close as a part of his own body.

And each loss had been like flaying skin.

First the loss of half the company in Voitan, fighting the Kranolta. Then the constant low-level seepage as they battled their way across the rest of the continent. More good troops killed in Diaspra against the Boman, and then a handful more in Sindi against the main Boman force. The ones who fell to the damnbeasts and the vampire moths. And the crocs. The ever-be-damned damncrocs.

And one of those fallen had been Kostas.

Kostas. Not a Marine, or even one of the Navy shuttle pilots. Not one of the Mardukan mercenaries who had become welded to the Bronze Barbarians. Roger could, to an extent, justify their losses. The entire purpose of Bravo Company, and of the mercenaries, was to protect the once lily-white skin of Prince Roger Ramius Sergei Alexander Chiang MacClintock, and they'd all known it when they signed on. But that wasn't Kostas' purpose. He was just a valet. A nobody. A nonentity. Just . . . Kostas.

Just the man who had stood by Roger when the rest of the universe thought he was a complete loss. Just the man who, thrown the responsibility for feeding and clothing the company on its march, had taken it on without a qualm. Just the man who had found food where there was none, and prepared sumptuous dishes from swamp water and carnivores. Only the man who had been a father figure to him.

Only Kostas.

And not even lost to enemy action. Lost to a damn croc, five meters of rubbery skin and teeth. One of the innumerable hazards of the damned jungles of Marduk. Roger had killed the croc almost immediately, but it had been too late. He'd killed dozens of them since, but all of them were too late for Kostas. Too late for his . . . friend.

He hadn't had many friends growing up. Even as the least little scion of the Imperial Family, Roger had faced a future of power and wealth. And from the youngest age, there had been sycophants aplenty swarming around the prince. The innumerable Byzantine plots of Imperial City had sought constantly to co-opt one self-absorbed prince. And from the time he was a teenager, it had been Kostas—cautious, mousey Kostas—who had helped him thread the rocks and shoals. Often without Roger ever knowing it.

And now, he was gone. Just . . . gone. Like Hooker and Bilali and Pentzikis and . . . gods. The list went on and on.

Oh, they'd left a few widows on the other side in their wake. They'd made alliances when and where they could, even passed without a ripple in a few places. But more often than not, it had been plasma guns and bead rifles,

swords and pikes and a few thousand years of technical and tactical expertise, blasting a swath of destruction a blind man could track because they had no choice.
Which created its own problems, because they scarcely
needed to be leaving any bread crumb trails behind them.
Especially when they already knew they didn't face only
"casual" enemies on the planet. True, there were more
than enough foes who had become dangers solely because
they felt . . . argumentative when the company had needed
to cross their territory, but beyond them, Roger and the
Barbarians faced the sworn enemies of the Empire and
the Imperial House.

The planet Marduk was, technically, a fief of the
Empire of Man. In fact, officially it was personally held
by the Empress herself, since it had been discovered a
few hundred years before by the expanding Empire and
promptly claimed in the name of the House of
MacClintock. For over a century, the planet had been no
more than a notation on a survey somewhere, though.
Then, early in the reign of Roger's grandfather, plans had
been advanced for the Sagittarius Sector. Settlers were
going to be sent out to the planets in the region, and
a "new day of hope" would dawn for the beleaguered
poor of the inner worlds. In preparation for the projected
wave of expansion, outposts had been established on
several of the habitable planets and provided with bare-
bones starports. The Imperial government had put some
additional seed money into establishing a limited infra-
structure and offered highly attractive concessions to some
of the Empire's biggest multistellar corporations to help
produce more, but by and large, the planets in this sector
had been earmarked strictly as new homes for the "little
people" of the Empire.

Roger supposed the plans had spoken well for his
grandfather's altruistic side. Of course, it was that same
misplaced altruism and his tendency to trust advisers
because of what he *thought* their characters were that
had created most of the problems Roger's Empress Mother
had been dealing with, first as Heir Primus and then as
Empress, for longer than Roger had been alive. And it

had also been an altruism whose hopes had been frustrated more often than not.

As they had been in the case of the Sagittarius Sector project.

Unfortunately for Grandfather's plans, the "poor" of the inner worlds were relatively comfortable with their low-paid work or government stipends. Given a choice between a small but decent apartment in Imperial City or Metrocal or New Glasgow or Delcutta and a small but decent house in a howling wilderness, the "poor" knew which side of their bread was buttered. Especially when the howling wilderness in question was on a planet like Marduk. For one thing, even in Delcutta, people rarely had to worry about being eaten.

So, despite all of the government's plans (and Emperor Andrew's), the sector had languished. Oh, two or three of the star systems in the area had attracted at least limited colonization, and the Sandahl System had actually done fairly well. But Sandahl was on the very fringe of the Sagittarius Sector, more of an appendage of the neighboring Handelmann Sector. For the most part, the Sagittarius planetary outposts and their starports had discovered that they were the designated hosts for a party no one came to. Except for the Saints.

One of the less altruistic reasons for the effort to colonize the sector in the first place had been the fact that the Cavaza Empire was expanding in that direction. Unfortunately, the plan to build up a countervailing Imperial presence had failed, and eventually, as the Saints continued their expansion, they had noticed the port installed on the small, mountainous subcontinent of Marduk.

In many ways, Marduk was perfect for the Saints' purposes. The "untouched" world would require very little in "remedy" to return it to its "natural state." Or to colonize. With their higher birthrate, and despite their "green" stand, the Saints were notably expansionist. It was one of the many little inconsistencies which somehow failed to endear them to their interstellar neighbors. And in the meantime, the star system was well placed as a staging point for clandestine operations deeper into the Empire of Man.

Roger and his Marines were unsure of the conditions on the ground. But after their assault ship/transport, HMS *DeGlopper*, had been crippled by a programmed "toombie" saboteur, they had needed the closest port to which they could divert, and Marduk had been elected. Unfortunately, they had arrived only to be jumped by two Saint sublight cruisers which had been working in-system along with their globular "tunnel-drive" FTL carrier mother ship. The presence of Cavazan warships had told the Marines that whatever else was going on here, the planetary gover-nor and his "locally" recruited Colonial Guards were no longer working for the Empire. That could be because they were all dead, but it was far more likely that the governor had reached some sort of accommodation with the Saints.

Whatever the fate of the governor might have been, the unpalatable outlines of the Bronze Barbarians' new mission had been abundantly clear. *DeGlopper* had man-aged to defeat the two cruisers, but she'd been destroyed in action with all hands herself in the process. Fortu-nately, the prince and his Marine bodyguards had got-ten away undetected in the assault ship's shuttles while she died to cover their escape and conceal the secret of Roger's presence aboard her. *Un*fortunately, the only way for the Marines to get Roger home would be to take the spaceport from whoever controlled it and then capture a ship. Possibly in the face of the remaining Cavazan carrier.

It was a tall order, especially for one understrength Marine company, be it ever so elite, shipwrecked on a planet whose brutal climate ate high-tech equipment like candy. The fact that they'd had only a very limited win-dow of time before their essential dietary supplements ran out had only made the order taller. But Bravo Com-pany of the Empress' Own was the force which had ham-mered fifteen thousand screaming Kranolta barbarians into offal. The force which had smashed every enemy in its path across half the circumference of the planet.

Whether it was turncoat Colonial Guards or a Saint carrier wouldn't matter. The Bronze Barbarians, and His Highness' Imperial Mardukan Guards, were going to hammer them into dust, as well.

Which didn't mean all of the hammers were going to survive.

Armand Pahner chewed a sliver of mildly spicy *bisti* root and watched the prince out of one eye as Kosutic approached. She was probably going to suggest a change in the training program, and he was going to approve it, since it had become abundantly clear that they were never going to make the Marines "real" sailors in the short voyage across the Northern Sea.

They were just about on the last leg of the journey they had begun so many months before, and he couldn't be more pleased. There would be a hard fight at the end. Taking the spaceport and, even more important, a functional ship would take some solid soldiering. But compared to the rest of the journey, it ought to be a picnic.

He chuckled grimly to himself, not for the first time, at how easily and completely a "routine" voyage could go wrong. Assuming they got back to report, this would definitely be one for the security school to study. Murphy's fell presence was obvious everywhere, from the helpless saboteur secreted within the loyal ship's company and driven to her suicidal mission by orders programmed into her toot, to the poor choices of potential emergency diversion planets, to the presence of Saint forces in the supposedly loyal system.

Once they'd reached the planet's actual surface, of course, things had only gone downhill. The sole redeeming quality of the trip was that they had left Earth guarding what was surely the weakest link in the Imperial Family. Now . . . he wasn't. The foppish, useless prince who had left Earth had died somewhere in the steaming jungles of Marduk. The MacClintock warrior who had replaced him had some problems of his own: the most serious of them, a tendency to brood and an even more dangerous tendency to look for answers in the barrel of a gun. But no one could call him a fop anymore. Not to his face, at least. Not and survive.

In a way, looked at with cold logic, the trip had been enormously beneficial, shipwreck, deaths, and all. Eventually, the old prince—unthinking, uncommitted, subject to control or manipulation by the various factions in the Imperial Palace—would probably have caused the deaths of far more than a company of Marines. So the loss of so many of Pahner's Barbarians could almost be counted as a win.

If you looked at it with cold enough logic.

But it was hard to be logical when it was *your* Marines doing the dying.

Kosutic smiled at the company commander. She knew damned well what he was pondering, in general, if not specifically. But it never hurt to ask.

"Penny for your thoughts, Captain."

"I'm not sure what his mother is going to say," the captain replied. It wasn't exactly what he'd been thinking about, but it was part and parcel of his thought process.

"Well, initially, she'll be dealing with disbelief," Kosutic snorted. "Not only that we, and Prince Roger in particular, are alive, but at the change in him. It'll be hard for her to accept. There've been times it seemed the Unholy One Himself was doing the operational planning, but between you and me, the prince is shaping up pretty well."

"True enough," Pahner said softly, then chuckled and changed the subject. "Speaking of shaping up, though, I take it you don't think we can turn Julian into a swabbie?"

"More along the lines of it not being worth the trouble," Kosutic admitted. "Besides, Julian just pointed out that we've gotten awful shabby at close combat work, and I have to agree. I'd like to set the Company to training on that, and maybe some cross-training with the Mardukan infantry."

"Works for me," Pahner agreed. "Despreaux took the

Advanced Tactical Assault Course," he added after double-checking with his toot implant. "Make her NCOIC."

"Ah, Julian took it, too," the sergeant major said. Pahner glanced at her, and she shrugged. "It's not official, because he took it 'off the books.' That's why it's not in his official jacket."

"How'd that happen?" Pahner asked. After this long together, he'd thought he knew everything there was to know about the human troops. But there was always another surprise.

"ATAC is taught by contractors," Kosutic pointed out. "When he couldn't get a slot for the school, he took leave and paid his own way."

"Hmmm." Pahner shook his head doubtfully. "I don't know if I can approve using him for an instructor if he didn't take it through approved channels. Which contractor was it?"

"Firecat, LLC. It's the company Sergeant Major Catrone started after he got out."

"Tomcat?" Pahner shook his head again, this time with a laugh. "I can just see him teaching that class. A couple of times in the jungle, it was like I heard his voice echoing in my head. 'You think *this* is hot? Boy, you'd best wait to complain in HELL! And that's where you're gonna be if you don't get your head out of your ass!' "

"When in the Unholy One's Fifth Name did you deal with Sergeant Major Catrone?" Kosutic asked. "He'd been retired for at least a decade when I joined the Raiders."

"He was one of my basic training instructors at Brasilia Base," Pahner admitted. "That man made duralloy look soft. We swore that the way they made ChromSten armor was to have him eat nails for breakfast, then collect it from the latrines, because his anus compressed it so hard the atoms got crushed. If Julian passed the course with Tomcat teaching it, he's okay by me. Decide for yourself who should lead the instruction."

"Okay. Consider it done." Kosutic gave a wave that could almost have been classified as a salute, then turned away and beckoned for the other NCOs to cluster back around her.

Pahner nodded as he watched her sketching a plan on the deck. Training and doctrine might not be all there was to war, but it was damned well half. And—

His head jerked up and he looked towards the *Sea Skimmer* as a crackle of rifle fire broke out, but then he relaxed with a crooked, approving grin. It looked as if the Marines weren't the only ones doing some training.

CHAPTER TWO

Captain Krindi Fain tapped the rifle breech with a leather-wrapped swagger stick.

"Keep that barrel down. You're missing high."

"Sorry, Sir," the recruit said. "I think the roll of the ship is throwing me off." He clutched the breech-loading rifle in his lower set of hands as the more dexterous upper hands opened the mechanism and thumbed in another greased paper cartridge. It was an action he could perform with blinding speed, given the fact that he had four hands, which was why his bright blue leather harness was literally covered in cartridges.

"Better to miss low," the officer said through the sulfurous tang of powder smoke. "Even if you miss the first target, it gives you an aiming point to reference to. And it might hit his buddy."

The shooting was going well, he thought. The rifles were at least hitting *near* the floating barrel. But it needed to be better, because the Carnan Rifles had a tendency to be in the thick of it. Which was a bit of a change from when they had been the Carnan Canal Labor Battalion.

The captain looked out at the seawater stretching beyond sight in every direction and snorted. His native Diaspra had existed under the mostly benevolent rule of

a water-worshiping theocracy from time out of mind, but
the few priests who'd accompanied the Diaspran infantry to K'Vaern's Cove had first goggled at so much water,
then balked at crossing it when the time came. So much
of The God had turned out to be a bad thing for
worship.

He stepped along to the next firer to watch over the
private's shoulder. The captain was tall, even for a
Mardukan. Not as tall or as massive as his shadow
Erkum Pol, perhaps, but still tall enough to see over the
shoulder of the private as the wind swept the huge
powder bloom aside.

"Low and to the left, Sardon. I think you've got the
aim right; it's the motion of the ship that's throwing you
off. More practice."

"Yes, Sir," the private said, and grunted a chuckle.
"We're going to kill that barrel sooner or later," he promised, then spat out a bit of *bisti* root and started
reloading.

Fain glanced towards the back of the ship—the "stern"
as the sailors insisted it be called. Major Bes, the
infantry commander of the Carnan Battalion—"The
Basik's Own," as it was sometimes called, although any
resemblance between the human prince it served and
the harmless, cowardly herbivorous *basik* was purely
superficial—was talking with one of the human privates
assigned to the ship. The three humans were "liaisons"
and maintained communications via their Terran systems.
But unlike most of the few remaining humans, these
were still uncomfortable around Mardukans, and the team
leader seemed particularly upset about the quality of the
food. Which just went to show that humans must be
utterly spoiled. The food which had been available since
joining the army was one of the high points for most
of the Mardukans.

"I like the food," Erkum rumbled discontentedly
behind him. "The human should keep his opinions to
himself."

"Perhaps." Fain shrugged. "But the humans are our
employers and leaders. We've learned from them, and

they were the saviors of our home. I'll put up with one of them being less than perfect."

There was more to it than that, of course. Fain wasn't terribly introspective, but he'd had to think long and hard before embarking on this journey. The human prince had called for volunteers from among the Diaspran infantry after the Battle of Sindi. He'd warned them that he could promise little—that they would be paid a stipend and see new lands, but that that was, for all practical purposes, it.

The choice had seemed clear cut to most of the Diasprans. They liked the humans, and their prince perhaps most of all, but things were happening at home. The almost simultaneous arrival of the Boman hordes and the humans had broken the city out of its millennia-old stasis. New industries were being built every day, and there were fortunes to be made.

As a veteran officer of the Sindi campaign, Fain was bulging with loot to invest, and his family had already found a good opportunity, a foundry that was being built on the extended family's land. A tiny bit of capital could see a handsome return. In fact, he could probably have retired on the income.

Yet he'd found himself looking to the west. He hadn't known what was calling to him at the time. Indeed, he hadn't even begun to understand until days after he'd volunteered for the expedition. But some siren song had been pulling him into the train of the humans, and he'd found the answer in an offhand comment from one of those same humans. Fain had made a pronouncement about the status of "his" company, and Sergeant Julian had cocked his head at him and smiled. "You've got it bad," the NCO had said.

And that was when Fain had realized he'd been bitten by the command bug.

The command bug was one of the most pernicious drugs known to any sentient race. To command in battle was both the greatest and most horrible activity in which any adult could participate. Any good commander felt each death as if it were his own. To him, his men were his children, and holding one of his troops while he died was like holding a brother. But to command well was to know that whatever casualties he'd taken, more lives would have been lost under an inferior commander. And Fain had commanded well.

Handed a company out of the gray sky, he'd taken them into the most complicated environment possible— as outnumbered skirmishers on the flank of a large force—and managed to perform his duty magnificently. He'd lost troops, people he'd known for months and even years. But he'd also been in a few other battles, both before and since, and he'd known that many more of those people would have died under the commander he'd replaced. He'd kept his head, been innovative, and known when and how to cut his losses.

So when the choice came, to give up command and return to a life of business and luxury, or to take a command into the unknown, following an alien leader, he'd taken only a moment to decide. He'd sent most of his accumulated funds, the traded loot of four major and minor battles, to his family for investment, raised a true-hand, and sworn his allegiance to Prince Roger MacClintock and the Empire of Man.

And, to no one's amazement (except, perhaps his own), most of his company had followed him. They'd follow him to Hell.

Most of his troops were aboard the *Ima Hooker* with Sergeant Knever, but there was also a small detachment here on *Sea Skimmer*, and today was one of its twice-weekly riflery drills.

Fain made it a point to supervise those drills in person, because he'd learned the hard way that good marksmanship was an important factor in the sort of warfare the humans taught. The Carnan Rifles' entire battalion had gradually segued into a rifle skirmisher force, following the lead of its most famous captain, and with skirmishers, excellent marksmanship was paramount. They were supposed to get out in front of conventional forces and snipe the leaders of approaching formations. They had to be able to hit something smaller than the broad side of a temple to do that job, and the Carnan Rifles were proving they could do just that.

Well, most of them.

Then there was Erkum.

At almost four meters in height, the big Mardukan dwarfed even his captain. Mardukans generally ran to three meters or so, from their broad, bare feet to their curved double horns, so Erkum was a giant even for them. And, except mentally, he wasn't slow, either, despite his size. Fain had seen him catch spears in flight and outrun *civan* for short bursts.

But he couldn't hit a *pagathar* with a rifle at ten paces. If it was headed straight for him.

At a walk.

Erkum had attached himself to the captain before that particular weakness became apparent. Before, in fact, Fain had been anything but a junior pike NCO. But everything seemed to have worked out. Erkum protected the captain's back, and that wasn't long-range work. As long as Fain's enemies came within five meters or so, the hulking private could usually hit them. And even if he hit them only with the butt of his weapon, they tended to stay down. More than that, he had acquired what was probably the perfect tool for his chosen spot.

The weapon was more cannon than gun. It was the brainchild of the same inventor who'd come up with the standard Mardukan rifle, and it used metallic cartridges similar to the ones developed for the bolt action rifles that had replaced the Marines' bead rifles as their sophisticated ammunition ran out. But its barrel diameter was nearly three times that of the standard rifles, and it fired "semi-automatically." A barlike magazine protruded vertically from the top of the weapon. It held seven short, stubby cartridges, each as long as a Mardukan hand, and as each round was fired, the bar slid downward to expose the next cartridge to the firing mechanism and hammer. The weight of the dropping "magazine" both cocked the weapon and brought the next round into position.

It had been originally intended as a quick-firing swivel

gun to mount on the schooners' bulwarks as an anti-sea monster defense, but in the end, it had been replaced for that function by the pintle-mounted harpoon cannons. As part of its original design concept, however, it had been designed to fire either buckshot or conical slugs, and Erkum carried a pair of reloads for each ammunition type on his person at all times.

The breech-bar reloads were a meter long by themselves, and could be lifted by a human only with difficulty. Erkum, on the other hand, reloaded one-handed, and fired the rounds as fast as he could pull the trigger. Of course, being near his line of fire was rather unhealthy. But it was a decent weapon for a combat-environment bodyguard. Even one who couldn't hit a mountain if it was falling on him.

Unfortunately, he had the damnedest time admitting his lack of marksmanship.

"These youngsters, they don't know how to hit nothing," the big Mardukan growled. If he were a season older than most of the recruits and privates, Fain would have been astonished.

"It's okay, Erkum," the captain said, knowing what was coming. "Really. They're doing fine."

"They need to be showed how to really shoot," Erkum rumbled, taking the semiportable cannon off his back.

"You don't have to do this," Fain muttered. But although Erkum was easy to control in most areas, he was inordinately proud of his lack of skill with the damned gun.

"None of you *biset* could hit the side of a temple!" he yelled to the riflemen lining the rail. "I will now show you how it is done!"

The gun had a double shoulder rest with a lower support/stock that rested on the hips. It was held and "gross" aimed with the lower false-hands and "fine" aimed with the upper true-hands. Now the private shouldered the weapon, dropped in one of the magazine bars, and opened fire.

The gun really was a small cannon, and emitted the smoke level of one. But even with the smoke, the slow-moving shot could be tracked visually as it lofted through the air and fell beyond the barrel. The private wasn't able to use that information to adjust, however, because he'd already triggered two more bruising, smoke-spewing blasts from the weapon during its time of flight.

Fain coughed on the stinking cloud of smoke and tried not to laugh. Judging by the splashes, the rounds were falling all around the barrel and even tracking far enough off to be a hazard to the longboat that had dropped the target. None of them, however, were coming within a reasonable distance of the barrel itself.

He glanced over his shoulder at a semi-sensed movement, then clapped his lower hands as one of the humans surreptitiously hefted her own bead rifle and cracked off a single, irreplaceable round.

The hypervelocity bead was impossible to see, and the sound of the single shot was buried under the ongoing blasts from Erkum's cannon. The effect, however, was easy to discern as the barrel shattered into a thousand pieces.

"Hah!" Erkum grunted as he threw the gun over his back once more in satisfaction. "And they say I can't shoot."

He snorted magnificently, picked up the expended magazine, and slid it into one of the holders on his harness.

Fain shook his head in a gesture copied from the humans, and clapped his lower hands.

"No question," he agreed. "You're getting better."

"Me and my gun, we'll protect you, Krindi." Erkum rubbed a horn and shook his own head. "Did you see how it just exploded? I can't wait to get to use it for real."

Krindi looked to the stern of the ship and smiled as the human lifted her visor and gave a sardonic salute. And because the Mardukan was looking in that direction, he was one of the few to see the ocean open up behind the ship.

The opening was at least twenty meters across, a yawning cavern in the abruptly surfacing snout of a piscine easily as long as *Sea Skimmer* herself. The giant predator was an ambush hunter, like the terrestrial stone-fish, and the snap-opening of its tooth-filled maw created a low-level vacuum that literally stopped the ship in her tracks.

Then the schooner dropped.

There were screams, human and Mardukan, throughout the ship as it first stopped dead in the water, then dropped backwards to scrape its copper-sheathed hull across the beast's lower teeth. And there were more screams as the maw snapped shut. The jaws shattered the ship, cutting it nearly in half, and pulling the mainmast over backwards as they clamped down on the stays.

Krindi bit down his own scream as the schooner staggered backwards and he saw the human sergeant and Major Bes tumble off the stern of the ship and down the creature's gullet. There was nothing wrong with his reflexes, however, and his left true-hand lashed out and grasped a line just before the beast bit down.

Erkum bellowed in rage as the impact of the thing's jaws on the deck flipped them both into the air like toys. Instead of grabbing a rope, though, the big private was clawing at his cannon even as he roared his fury, and then everything came back down and the beast pulled back with a twist of its massive head that reduced the already shattered transom to splinters.

What remained of the truncated ship started to settle by the stern, the deck sloping precariously down to the water, masts shattered and over the side. Anyone who hadn't already grabbed a rope was left to scramble for lines as they slid towards the frothing green water, and Krindi cursed and grabbed his own flailing cable with a stronger false-hand. He heard screams and cries from below decks, and knew that any of his detachment he hadn't lost in the first tremendous bite were probably doomed. But for the moment, all he could think about was whether or not he, personally, would survive.

He snatched at Erkum as the still-cursing private slid past. Somehow, Pol had gotten his gun back off of his back, and now he was trying to fit a magazine into place. What he thought he was going to do with it was more than Fain could have said, but the captain wasn't about to let him die just because he was being an idiot.

Krindi glanced at the water and hissed in anger as he saw the shadow of the beast, surrounded by a pool of red, whip around and come back. Apparently, the first taste hadn't been good enough, and it wanted the rest of the ship.

Unfortunately, there wasn't much the Diasprans could do about that.

Roger had been leaning on the ship's rail, looking at nothing in particular, when the beast surfaced. It wasn't in his direct line of sight, but movement draws the human eye, and as the company had found out, a combination of natural genetics and engineering had left Roger with reactions that were preternaturally quick. Which let him get his head around in time to watch the giant fish eat half the ship and a good bit of one of his better battalions.

The thing submerged after half a moment, swirling off to the ship's port side, its massive gills opening and closing. The gills obviously doubled as strainers, and the water went crimson behind it as it pulsed out a trail of shattered wood and blood. It nosed around to the stern and picked off a few of the flailing Mardukans on the surface by sucking them under with comparatively delicate inhalations. Then it dove once more, apparently lining up for another run at the beleaguered ship.

The sight was enough to give anyone pause, but Roger and most of the surviving Marines were still alive because they'd proven they were the fastest, luckiest, and—above all—deadliest of an already elite group. Shock no longer noticeably slowed them.

The prince heard commands from behind him—crisp and clear over the company net from Pahner, slightly louder and more shrill from the surprised Mardukan officers. But that was for others. In his case, there was only one action that made sense. He reached over his shoulder for his own rifle.

That weapon went everywhere with him, even aboard
Hooker. It was an anachronism, a "smoke pole," as the
Marines had derided it when they first landed. They'd
thought he hadn't heard the sniggers and comments. The
antique weapon of a spoiled rich boy. A "big game
hunter" who'd never faced a real threat in his life.

Most of the bodyguards hadn't been with him for very
long at that point. Guarding the original, patented,
spoiled-rotten Prince Roger had been a rotating assignment for the Bronze Battalion's personnel. It had also
been the equivalent of Purgatory, and anyone who'd been
able to avoid it had done so . . . with alacrity. Which
meant that very few of his current crop of babysitters
had realized that he habitually shucked his bodyguards
whenever he hunted. Or that many of the *things* he had
hunted over the years would have made their blood run
cold. The four-meter-long, gold-threaded Arcturian hyper-
tiger in his trophy room was not a gift . . . and it had
been taken with that same "smoke pole."

The Marines used hypervelocity bead guns, which were
good weapons for killing people and overcoming conventional body armor. But the prince's rifle was for killing
animals, and big animals, at that. When they'd first
landed, the Marines had assumed the major threats would
be the hostile natives, and so it had turned out. But
they'd discovered that the wildlife was no picnic, either.
And that was where the prince, and his "pocking leetle
rifle," as Poertena had christened it, came in. There was
no question in anyone's mind that the casualties due to
wildlife, especially an ugly creature called the damnbeast,
had been at least halved by the prince and his pocking rifle.

And now, once again, he proved why.

The prince had the old-fashioned, dual-action rifle off
his shoulder, with a round chambered, and aimed faster
than most people could draw and fire a bead pistol. The
beast had submerged even more quickly, though. It was
no more than a green-gray shadow in the aquamarine
water, and he weighed his options as he watched it over
his sights. He could see it coming around for another

run, and he considered shooting through the waves. He'd made shallow-water shots often enough on the trek upcountry, and the relatively low velocity bullets of the rifle would penetrate where the hypervelocity beads shattered on the surface or skipped off. But the bullets also lost most of their energy in the first meter or so. Unless the creature was right at the surface, and basically raising a water-foot, shooting it submerged would be pointless.

Even as he considered that, another part of his brain was pondering shot placement. The fish was huge, with a body nearly as long as one of the schooners and a head twice as wide. In fact, it looked somewhat like one of the fish that was a staple in K'Vaern's Cove, their port of embarkation. If it really was something like a giant *coll*, then shot placement was going to be a bitch.

Coll were traditionally served whole, since there was a "pearl" that formed at the rear of the skull and collecting it was part of the ritual of the meal. Because of that, and because he'd been to more dinners in K'Vaern's Cove then he cared to count, he had a fair idea of the fish's anatomy. The opalescent jewel was of varying quality, but it rested directly above the spot where the fish's spinal cord connected to its skull. Given the angle from which Roger would be firing, if he tried for a spinal shot—not impossible for him, even from the moving deck—the round would probably bounce off the ersatz armoring of the pearl. If he tried for a heart shot, however, even he was likely to miss. That organ was deep in the body, and the round would have to travel through several meters of flesh to reach it. But any other body shot would be useless.

The rear of the head would be the best shot, then. The head was wide, and it was bone, but it was also filled with cavities. Rather than being primarily for armoring the brain, it was based upon the mechanics of the huge jaws. If he put the shot right at the rear of the skull, it should penetrate to the brain and "pith" the fish. Given the disparity in size between the bullets and the target, it was the best chance he'd have.

The entire train of thought flashed through his mind in a moment, and he took a breath and timed the roll of the ship as the fish started to surface for another tremendous bite.

Fain suddenly realized that although Erkum sounded incoherent, his actions made perfect sense. The private was not an intellectual, by any means, but he was—in that wonderfully ambiguous human term—"good with his hands." Fain had been in far too many fights for his few years, and he'd long since discovered that Erkum was a good person to have by your side, be it with hands, pipes, or guns. He might not be able to hit the broad side of a temple at any sort of range, but he instinctively acted in ways that kept him alive when it all fell into the pot. He left the thinking to Fain, but when it came to up close and personal mayhem, Erkum was as good as it got.

And he was about to lay down some mayhem. Fain had grabbed one of the feet of the furiously cursing private, preventing him from falling into the water, but Erkum could have cared less. He'd finally gotten a magazine of solid shot lined up, and he was waiting for his turn at the big fish. Fain suspected that the private had known he would be grabbed, trusted his boss to do the right thing, just as Fain trusted him, and now Erkum waited for the thing to surface.

Fain risked a look around and saw that Pol was not the only one planning a probably hopeless defense. A few of the remaining riflemen, those who'd had the presence of mind to grab a line or rail, instead of slipping down the rapidly tilting deck, were already pointing their rifles at the water. But several others were simply holding on for dear life. Couldn't have that.

"Company! Prepare to volley fire!" he called, trying to fumble out his own pistol with the fourth hand that wasn't occupied holding onto ropes or Erkum.

They were only going to get one shot.

CHAPTER THREE

"Move it! We're only going to get one shot!"

Kosutic turned from the harpoon gun crew to watch the Marines fanning out along the starboard rail. The ships hadn't come about, and the shattered schooner, which had been in the lead position, was slowly falling astern. If the harpoon gun didn't get into action quickly, it might not get a shot. Not unless they came around for one, and Pahner would never agree to that. He was trying to get the prince's ship away from that . . . that . . . *thing* as fast as he could.

At least the harpoon gear had been set up, ready, by the gun when all hell broke loose. It was against normal practice to pile charges for the ship's guns on deck. Partly that was because black powder was too dangerous. Sparks or open flame weren't the only things that could set it off; even the friction of grinding a few loose or spilled grains underfoot could do that, under the wrong conditions. But mostly it was because it would have been too easy for the powder to become wet and useless. But this particular weapon had been designed for just this contingency, and the need to get it into action as quickly as possible had dictated ready availability of ammunition. The humans had empty stores containers, plasteel boxes that maintained temperature and humidity, and one of

37

those had been pressed into duty as a standby magazine.

Now the Mardukan gun crew threw back the lid and snatched out the first cartridge. The charge bag was small, only half a kilo or so of powder. But it would throw the harpoon far enough, and without shattering the hardwood shaft.

As the gunner shoved the charge into the muzzle, the assistant gunner assembled the harpoon. Fitting the steel head to the shaft took only a moment, then the coiled line was attached with a human-designed clip. Last, the plug-based shaft was shoved down the barrel of the cannon, acting as its own ramrod.

But drilled and quick as the gun crew was, all of that took time. Time *Sea Skimmer* didn't have.

Krindi Fain had often wondered if he was going to die. He'd wondered the time a stone wall fell on the crew he was working with. That time, he'd been sheltered by a few sticks of scaffolding, and he'd survived. He'd wondered again, as a private in his first pike battle, by the canals of Diaspra. And he'd wondered repeatedly while fighting the Boman inside and outside of Sindi. But he hadn't *known* he was going to die.

Until now.

The beast opened up its maw, and he grunted in anger as he saw it surging up behind the sinking ship once again. He could see bits of wood and cloth, and red flesh, sticking to the thousands of teeth lining the inside of the fish's mouth. But he still didn't scream. He was frightened. God of Water knew he was! But he was going to go to his God as a soldier and a leader, not a coward.

And so, instead of screaming, he paused for a moment. That brief pause, so necessary for everyone to get fully lined up. And then, he yelled *"Fire!"*

Five of his men were still more or less on their feet, with their wits sufficiently about them to obey his command, but they were almost incidental. The two things that drove the fish off were Erkum and the prince.

The five rifle bullets all impacted on various places in and around the mouth. Two of them even penetrated up into the skull of the fish, but none of them did any vital damage, nor did they particularly "hurt."

Erkum's round, on the other hand, hurt like hell.

The sixty-five-millimeter bullet penetrated the roof of the mouth and traveled upward, blowing a massive tube through the skull of the sea monster. By coincidence—it could have been nothing else, given the quality of the marksman—the huge slug severed the right optical nerve, blinding the fish on that side, and blew out the top of its skull in a welter of gore.

At almost the same moment, the prince's round entered the *back* of the beast's head.

It wasn't the pith shot Roger had been trying for, but the round was much higher velocity than anything the Mardukans had, and it generated a significant "hydrostatic shock" cavity—the region in a body that was damaged by the shock wave of a bullet. In this case, the prince had missed his shot down and slightly to the right, but the region that the shot passed through was directly beneath the spinal cord, and the shock wave slapped against that vital nerve.

The combined result was that instead of slurping down the rest of the *Sea Skimmer*, the fish thrashed away to port and dove. But it did so wildly, uncontrolled. It was half-blind, there was damage to its spinal cord, and half its muscles weren't responding properly.

This food had spines.

"*Pentzikis*, come about to port and engage. *Sea Foam*, come to starboard and engage. *Tor Coll*, prepare depth charges."

Pahner glanced at the prince, who was still tracking the thrashing shadow. He didn't know if Roger had gotten off another impossible shot, or if it was the flurry of blasts from the sinking ship. But whichever it had been, it had at least momentarily dissuaded the fish. Now to put it down.

"Grenadiers to the rigging. Set for delay—I want some

penetration on this thing, people," Pahner continued, cutting off a fresh slice of *bisti* root and slipping it into his mouth. The general outline of this fight had been worked out in advance—as well as it could be, at least, when no one had ever actually seen whatever it was that ate ships in this stretch of ocean. Well, never seen it and lived to report it, at any rate. But, as usual, the enemy wasn't playing by the plans. It had been assumed that they'd at least get a glimpse of the beast before it struck, which should have given them at least some chance of driving it off first. Now, all they could do was fight for the remaining six ships and hope to rescue a few of the survivors.

Sea Skimmer was sinking fast by the stern, but she was going down without a list. If they could finish the fish off in a few shots and send in boats, they might save most of those on her deck. The ones below deck were doomed, unless they could fight their way to the main hatch or swim out. It was still a hell of a way to lose a quarter of a battalion, its commander, and probably a damned fine junior officer with them. But there hadn't been many *good* places to die on this damned trek.

He glanced at Roger again, and shook his head. The prince had headed for the shrouds and was trying to get a better vantage point. Give him credit for trying, but Pahner doubted the prince's rifle was going to win this round.

As he thought that, the first harpoon gun boomed.

"I doubt that even *you* can do anything with a pistol, cousin," Honal said with a handclap of grim humor. His cousin, the former crown prince of Therdan, had drawn all four pistols at the first cry and had them trained over the side before the warning's echoes had faded.

"True," Rastar said now, and reholstered three of the percussion revolvers. "But if it comes after us, I'll at least let it know I'm here."

"Best stand clear, whatever else you do," Honal said

dryly. "Our fine sailor friends are about to see if a harpoon is better than a pistol!"

"Well, that depends on the harpoon and the pistol," Rastar grunted in laughter. "After all, it's not what you use; it's how you use it!"

"And I intend to use it well!" the chief of the gun crew called. "But if you're in the way of the line as it flies, you'll be a red smear! Clear!"

The gun was fitted with a percussion cap hammer lock. Now the gun captain gave Honal and Rastar a heartbeat to duck to the side, then took a deep breath and yanked the firing lanyard.

The bang wasn't really all that loud, but the smoke cloud covered the entire foredeck, and there was a *whippity-thwhip!* as the coil of hawser at the base of the pintle reeled out. Then there was a cry from the rigging.

"Target!"

"Rig the line!" the gun captain bellowed, and the crew warped the five-centimeter hawser around a bollard as the rope began to scream and smoke.

"Prepare to come about on the port tack!" *Pentzikis'* captain shouted.

"Rig the line into the clamps!" the gun crew chief called. "The damn thing is going to go right under the keel! If the captain's not careful, it'll take us right over on our side!"

"Let that line run!" the ship's captain barked. "Come onto it when we're on tack!"

"Haul away!" the gunner cried. "We're getting slack!"

"Hold on!" Rastar shouted. "The *Tor Coll* is about to run across the rope!"

"Contact!" Sergeant Angell called over the company net from *Tor Coll's* afterdeck. "Sir, we have solid contact."

"Right," Pahner acknowledged, glancing at the formation. "Have your captain keep falling off to port. I want you to take a heading of nearly due south and try to drag this thing off *Sea Skimmer*. *Sea Foam*, take another shot. All units, engage with care. Try to get some rounds on it, but don't hit the other ships."

Hooker's own harpoon gun boomed behind him as the schooner came around to starboard. It wasn't, strictly speaking, proper. The ship with the prince on it should be sailing out of harm's way, not into it. But with the fish pinned, it was probably safe enough.

Tor Coll passed above the thrashing shadow, and a huge white and green waterspout appeared behind the schooner. The depth charges used a combination of a grenade detonator and local blasting powder. Pahner hadn't been sure they would function as intended, but it turned out that they worked just fine. Bilali's very first drop scored a direct hit, and the monster fish flopped a few more times, then drifted gently to the surface, belly-up. Its underside was apparently covered in chromatospores, since it was flickering through a riot of colors when it broke the waves. It rippled a dozen shades of violet, then through the spectrum until it began flickering green, and finally stopped and slowly turned a cream color.

"Get that target longboat alongside *Sea Skimmer*. Launch all the ships' boats, and let's start recovering survivors. Warrant Officer Dobrescu!"

"Yes, Captain?" a calm tenor replied. Pahner glanced over his shoulder, and saw the speaker standing beside the mainmast while he gazed at the floating monster with an air of almost detached contemplation.

Chief Warrant Officer Dobrescu had been one of *DeGlopper*'s shuttle pilots. Flying a shuttle was a relatively safe job, although it hadn't quite worked out that way this time around. But in a previous life, he had been a Raider Commando medic, a person trained not only to stabilize a combat casualty, but to repair one if necessary. His accidental inclusion on the trip had been, literally, a lifesaver. A factor he was sometimes at pains to point out, not to mention complain about.

"I want you to prepare to receive casualties. If there are none, or if they're limited, I'll want your input on our little find here."

"Yes, Sir," the medic replied. "Of course, I'm a shuttle pilot, not a xenobiologist, but it looks like a *coll* fish to me. And that's my professional opinion."

✧   ✧   ✧

"It's a *coll* fish," Captain T'Sool said. *Ima Hooker*'s captain rubbed his horns, then clapped his hands. "It's impossible, but may the White Lady damn me if it isn't one."

One of the *Hooker*'s sailor's held up a dripping bag in both true-hands. The oil-filled sac was common to the *coll* fish, part of its buoyancy system. But in normal-sized ones, the sac was the size of the last joint of a human thumb and filled with what, to Mardukans, was a deadly poison. As it had turned out, that oil was possibly the only substance on the planet that the Marines' nanites packs could convert into the numerous lipid-based vitamins and amino acids the planet's food lacked.

"Well," Kosutic said. "At least we've got plenty of feed for the *civan*. And that's enough *coll* oil to keep us for quite a while," she added, gazing at an oil sac that was at least a meter across.

"It's still a net zero," Pahner growled. "We lost an entire ship getting it, along with half of its crew, damned near two full companies of infantry, and three more Marines. I don't like losing troops."

"Neither do I," Kosutic agreed. "And this trip says it all. His Putridness' hand has certainly been over us the whole time."

"What just happened?" Eleanora O'Casey asked, as she climbed up through the main hatch to the deck.

The prince's chief of staff was the only remaining "civilian" caught on the planet with him. Although none of the shuttle pilots had been as prepared for the conditions here as the Marines, they'd at least had some background in rough conditions survival and a basic military nanite pack. But prior to the crash landing of the shuttles on the backside of the planet, the chief of staff had never set foot outside a city, and her nanites— such as they were—were designed for a nice, safe, *civilized* environment.

The "adventure" had had some benefits for her. She was in the best shape she'd ever been in her life. But her stomach, never the most robust, had not taken the journey well, and it was taking the voyage aboard ship even worse. Now the short brunette turned her head from side to side, counting masts.

"Aren't we missing one ship?" she asked.

"Not quite yet," Pahner said dryly. "But it won't be long now." He pointed over the side, to where *Sea Skimmer*'s shattered hull was beginning its final plunge. "We've discovered what ate the other expeditions," he added.

O'Casey walked to the side of the gently rocking schooner, and her eyes widened.

"Ooooooh!" she gasped, and quickly ran to the far rail, where she wouldn't get anything on the Mardukans butchering the vast fish.

"Well, I guess she won't be coming to dinner," Kosutic observed with a shake of her head.

"I guess this stuff gets tougher as it gets older."

Julian bounced the tines of his fork off of the slab of *coll* fish on his plate to emphasize his point.

There'd been no more attacks on the ship, and soundings indicated that the area in which *Sea Skimmer* had been ambushed was a seamount. Dobrescu theorized that a line of such seamounts might be the haunt of the gigantic *coll* fish. If he was right, it might be possible to create an industry to harvest the species, once its habits were better understood. The profit would certainly be worth it, if it didn't involve losing a ship every time.

"It probably does," the medic agreed now. "Not that anyone in K'Vaern's Cove ever saw a *coll* fish this big to give us any sort of meter stick." He rolled the head-sized opalescent pearl back and forth on the table top, and the bright, omnipresent cloud-light of Marduk made it seem to float above the surface.

"On the other hand, this thing seems to be identical to the ones from the smaller fish," he went on, rapping the pearl with a knuckle. "It's a hell of a lot bigger, of course, and it has more layers. There's a bone directly under it that's layered as well, and I'd suspect from the markings that the layers indicate its age. And these things must grow fast as hell, too. If I've figured out how to calculate its age properly, this fish was less than five times as old as the ones we ate in K'Vaern's Cove."

"How can that be?" Roger asked while he sawed at the tough flesh. He wasn't particularly hungry, and the meat was both oily and unpleasantly fishy, unlike the normally dry and "white" *coll* fish. But he'd learned that you just ate. You never knew if there would be worse tomorrow. "This thing was at least a hundred times that size!"

"More like forty or fifty, Your Highness," Despreaux corrected. She and Julian were relatively junior, but both of them had become a regular part of the command conferences. Julian by dint of his background in intelligence, and Despreaux because she kept Roger calm. Of course, her background in communications and tactics helped.

"The layers indicate massive growth spurts," Dobrescu said with a shrug, "but the genetic material is identical. These things could interbreed with the K'Vaern's Cove variety; ergo they're the same species. I suspect that studying their life-history would be difficult. At a guess, they probably breed inshore, or even in freshwater. Then, as they grow, they begin jockeying for territories. If they get the territory of a larger version, they grow very fast to 'fill' the territory." He paused and rolled the pearl again. "I also suspect that if we went back through this area, we wouldn't run into another specimen this large. But there would still be some damned big *coll* fish around."

"And in a few years . . ." Pahner said with a nod. "By the way, Your Highness, nice shot."

"Excuse me?" Roger gave the fish another stab, then gave up. He wasn't the first to do so, by any means.

The heavyset red and black striped beast occupying the entire corner of the compartment knew its cue. Roger had picked the pet up quite by accident at the village of D'Nal Cord many months before. The lizardlike creatures fulfilled the role of dogs among Cord's people, although Roger had seen no sign of any similar species elsewhere on their travels.

Now Dogzard stood up and gave a vertebrae-popping stretch that extended her practically from one end of the compartment to the other. Being the only scavenger in a group that had blasted its way through endless carnivore-infested jungles had been good for the former "runt," and if she ever returned to her village, she would be double the size of any of the ones that had stayed behind.

Now she flipped out her tongue and regarded Roger's plate carefully as he held it towards her. After a brief moment verifying that, yes, this was food and, yes, she was permitted to have it, her head snapped forward in one of its lightning fast strikes, and the chunk of meat disappeared from the plate.

Satisfied that that was all for now, she returned to the corner to await the next meal. Or to fight. Whichever.

"There was a good solid crack on that vertebra," Dobrescu replied for Pahner in response to Roger's question. "One of the reasons, at least, that it didn't come back at that ship was your shot."

Dobrescu flicked his own lump of fish towards the prince's pet. The chunk of meat never came within a meter of the deck before it disappeared.

"There was also a fist-sized hole through the roof of its mouth," the warrant officer continued, and raised an eyebrow in question as he glanced at the junior Mardukan at the foot of the table.

Fain was desperately trying to figure out the tableware. He'd tried watching Honal, Rastar, Chim Pri, and Cord, but that wasn't much help. The Mardukan officers had never quite mastered the knife and fork, either, and Roger's *asi*—technically, a slave, although Fain rather doubted that anyone would ever make the mistake of treating D'Nal Cord as anyone's menial—refused to use them at all.

In Cord's case, at least, Fain suspected, the refusal was mostly a pose. The old Mardukan shaman took considerable pains to maintain his identity as a primitive tribesman, but it was obvious to the Diaspran that the *asi*'s knowledge—and brain—were more than a match for any

Water Priest he'd ever met. In the others' case, the captain was less certain. Honal had hacked off a chunk of the rubbery meat and was gnawing on it, while Rastar and Pri had lifted slightly larger chunks and were doing much the same. The human ability to hold the meat down with a fork and cut off small pieces was apparently beyond them.

Now, trapped by the medic's implied question, Krindi cleared his throat and nodded in a human gesture many of the mercenaries had picked up.

"That would be Erkum," he said. "At least one shot, perhaps more. It was very . . . confused on board, of course."

"Not so confused that you lost your head," Pahner noted, and took a sip of water. "You had everyone with a weapon fire a volley. I doubt most of the Marines would have kept control of their units that well."

"Thank you, Sir." Fain rubbed a horn. "But from what I've seen, I will politely disagree. Certainly, you and Prince Roger kept control of yours."

"No, I didn't," Roger said. He reached for the pitcher of water and poured himself another glass. "I should have been giving orders, not shooting myself. But I got angry. Those were good troops."

"Hmmm." Kosutic frowned. "I don't know, Your Highness. Let the cobbler stick to his last, as it were." The slight frown became a smile. "I have to admit that having you with a weapon in your hand never seems to be a *bad* idea."

Pahner smiled at the chuckles around the table, then nodded.

"Whether His Highness should've been shooting or ordering, we need to find a berth for Captain Fain. The infantry side was already short, so I'm just going to consolidate your personnel into a combined company. We lost Turkol Bes on the *Sea Skimmer* along with your boys, so we need a replacement for Captain Yair, who will be promoted to major and take Bes' place. Initially, I'm going to attach you to His Highness as a sort of aide-de-camp. The bulk of your company's survivors are

already aboard the *Hooker*. We'll work them into the rest
of her detachment, and giving you a little experience with
the 'staff' will give you a chance to see how things run.
Hopefully, we'll have you fully on board by the time we
land. Clear?"

"Yes, Sir." Fain kept his face placid, but seeing "his" company lose its identity was not pleasant, however necessary
its survivors' absorption might be. "One question . . ."

"Yes, you can hang onto Pol," Roger said with a very
Mardukan grunt of laughter.

"Please do," Captain—no, Major—Yair endorsed. "You're
the only one who can handle him."

"We don't know how many more of these things there
might be," Pahner continued in a "that's settled" tone
of voice, and gestured at the pearl Dobrescu was still
fondling. "Or any damned thing else about threats along
the way. But we've found out we can kill them, at least.
Any suggestions about how to keep them from doing this
again?"

"Mount a cannon at the rear. Maybe a couple," Fain
said without thinking, then stopped when everyone looked
at him.

"Go on," Roger said, nodding. "Although I think I
know where you're going."

"Keep them loaded," Fain continued. "Ready to fire,
with a crew to man them at all times. When it surfaces,
fire. You have about a second and a half from when they
appear to when you have to shoot."

"You'd have to have somebody being very vigilant on
a continuous basis." Julian shook his head. "Then you'd
have to make sure the powder didn't get wet and misfire.
I don't think we have the technical capability to do that
without modifications we'd need a shipyard to carry out."

"But a defense at the rear . . ." Roger rubbed a fingertip on the table, obviously intrigued by the notion.
Then a sudden, wicked grin lit his somber face like a
rising sun. "Who says it has to be a *local* cannon?" he
demanded.

"Ouch!" Kosutic laughed. "You've got an evil mind,
Your Highness."

"Of course!" Julian's eyes gleamed with enthusiasm. "Set up a plasma cannon on manjack mode. If something disturbs the sensor area: Blam!"

"Bead," Pahner corrected. Julian looked at him, and the captain waggled one hand palm-down above the table. "Those things get too close for a plasma cannon. We'd torch the ship."

"Yeah, you're right." Julian nodded. "I'll get it set up," he said, then wiped his mouth and looked unenthusiastically down at the chunk of meat still sitting on his plate. "You want me to break out some ration packs?" he asked in a decidedly hopeful voice.

"No." Pahner shook his head. "We need to eat what we've got. Until we know how long this journey is going to be, we still need to conserve our off-world supplies." He paused and took a breath. "And we also need to shut down the radios. We're getting close enough to the ports that we have to worry about radio bounce. They're low-intercept, but if the port has any notion that we're here, we're in the deep."

"So how do we communicate between the ships, Sir?" Despreaux asked. The sergeant had been particularly quiet all evening, but she was one of the two NCOs in charge of maintaining communications. With Julian setting up the weapons, it was her job to plan a jury-rigged replacement com net for the flotilla's units.

"Com lasers, flags, guns, flashing lights," Pahner said. "I don't care. But no radios."

"Yes, Sir," Despreaux said, making a note on her toot. "So we can use our tac-lights, for example?"

"Yes." Pahner paused again and slipped in a strip of *bisti* root while he thought. "In addition, the sailors in K'Vaern's Cove reported that piracy is not an unknown thing on Marduk. Now, why am I not surprised?"

Most of the group chuckled again. Practically every step of the journey had been contested by local warlords, barbarians, or bandits. It would have been a massive shock to their systems if it turned out these waters were any different.

"When we approach the far continent, we'll need to

keep a sharp lookout for encroaching ships," Pahner continued. "And for these fish. And for anything else that doesn't look right."

"And His Dark Majesty only knows what's going to come next," Kosutic agreed with a smile.

CHAPTER FOUR

"Land ho!"

The lookout's cry rang out only two days after the attack by the giant *coll*. No one was really surprised by it, though. The evidence of an approaching landfall had been there for at least a day—a thin gray smoke on the horizon, and a golden alpenglow before dawn.

Julian swarmed up the ratlines to *Hooker*'s fore top-mast crosstrees with an agility which might have seemed at odds with his determinedly antiseaman attitude. He took his glasses with him. They were considerably better than his helmet visor's built-in zoom function, and he spent several minutes beside the Mardukan seaman already perched there, studying the distant land. Then he zoomed the glasses back in and slid back down to the deck.

"Active volcano, sure enough," he reported to Pahner. "The island looks deserted, but there's another in the chain just coming over the horizon."

Pahner consulted his toot and nodded. "It doesn't appear on the map," he said, "but at this resolution, it wouldn't."

"But there *is* a line of mountains on the eastern verge of the continent," Roger pointed out, projecting a hologram from his pad. He pointed at the light-sculpture mountains for emphasis. "They could be volcanic in nature. Which would *probably* make this a southern extension of that chain."

"Hullo, the deck!" the lookout still at the crosstrees called. " 'Nother to the south! We're sailing between them."

None of the islands were visible from deck-level, yet, but Captain T'Sool, more accustomed to the shallow, relatively confined waters of the K'Vaernian Sea than the endless expanse of the open ocean, looked nervous.

"I'm not sure I like this," he said. "We could hit shoals anytime."

"Possibly," Roger conceded, with a glance at the azure water over the side. "It's more likely that we're still over a subduction trench or the deep water around one. Water tends to be deep right up to the edge of volcanic formations. I'm glad to see our first landfall be volcanoes, actually. You might want to slow the flotilla and get some depth lines working, though."

"What are these 'volcanoes' you keep speaking of?" T'Sool asked. Roger checked his toot and realized that it had used the Terran word because there was no local equivalent.

"Have you ever heard of smoking mountains?" he asked.

"No," the seaman said dubiously.

"Well, you're in for a treat."

"Why does smoke come from the mountain?" Fain asked in awe.

The flotilla had slowed as it approached the chain, and now it proceeded cautiously between two of the islands. The one to the south was wreathed in thick, leafy, emerald-green foliage that made it look like a verdant paradise. Of course, as the Marines had learned the hard way, it was more likely to be a verdant hell, Mardukan jungles being what they were.

The island to the north, however, was simply a black hunk of basalt, rising out of the blue waters. Its stark, uncompromising lines made it look bigger than it actually was, and the top—the only portion formed into anything resembling a traditional cone—trailed a gentle plume of ash and steam.

"I could tell you," Julian replied with a grimace. "But you'd have to believe me rather than your religion."

Fain thought about that. So far, he'd found nothing that directly contradicted the doctrines of the Lord of Water. On the other hand, the dozens of belief systems he and the other infantry had encountered since leaving Diaspra had already indicated to him that the gospel of the priests of Water was not, perhaps, fundamentally correct. While there was no question that the priests understood the science of hydraulics, it might be that their overall understanding of the world was less precise.

"Go ahead," he said with a handclap of resignation. Then he chuckled. "Do your worst!"

Julian smiled in response and gestured at the vast expanse of water stretched out around the flotilla.

"The first thing you have to accept is that the priests' description of the world as a rock floating in eternal, endless waters isn't correct."

"Since we're intending to sail to the far side, I'd already come to the conclusion that 'endless water' might not be exactly accurate," Fain admitted with another handclap.

"What the world really is, is a ball floating in noth-ingness," Julian said, and raised both hands as Fain started to protest. "I know. How is that possible? Well, you're going to have to trust me for now, and check it out later. But what matters right now is that the cen-ter of the ball—the world—is very, very hot. Hot enough to melt rock. And it stays that way."

"That I have a hard time with," Fain said, shaking his head. "Why is it hot? And if it is, when will it cool?"

"It's hot because there's . . . stuff in there that's some-thing like what makes our plasma cannon work," Julian said, waving his hands with a sort of vague frustration as he looked for an explanation capable of crossing the technological gulf yawning between his worldview and Fain's. "Like I said," he said finally. "You'll just have

to trust me on some of this. But it is—hot, I mean—
and somewhere under that mountain, there's a channel
that connects to that hot part. That's why it smokes.
Think of it as a really, really big chimney. As for when
the inside of the world will cool, that won't happen for
longer than I can explain. There will no longer be
humans—or Mardukans—when it starts to cool."

"This is too strange," Fain said. "And how do I explain
it to my soldiers? 'It's that way because Sergeant Julian
said so'?"

"I dunno," Julian replied. "Maybe the sergeant major
can help you out. On the other hand . . ."

Roger watched Bebi's team begin the entry. The team
had already worked on open area techniques. Now they
were working on closed . . . and they looked like total
dorks.

There was nowhere to create a real shooting environment on the flotilla's ships, so the troopers were using
the virtual reality software built into their helmet combat systems and their toots. The "shoot house" was
nothing more than the open deck of a schooner, but with
the advanced systems and the toots' ability to massage
sensory input, it would be as authentic to the partici-
pants as if there were real enemies.

But since their audience could see that they were standing on nothing more than an unobstructed stretch of deck
planks, the "entry team" looked like a group of warrior-
mimes.

The virtual reality software built into the troops' helmets would have been a potent training device all by
itself, and its ability to interface with the Marines' toots
was sufficient to make the illusion perfect. Now Macek
smoothed thin air as he emplaced a "breaching charge"
on the fictitious door he could both "see" and "feel" with
total fidelity, then stepped to the side and back. As far
as he could tell, he was squatting, nearly in contact with
a wall; to everyone else, he looked as if he were getting ready to go to the bathroom on the deck.

The sergeant major next to Roger snorted softly.

"You know, Your Highness, when you're doing this, one part of you knows how stupid you look. But if you don't ignore it, you're screwed. I think this is one of His Wickedness' little jokes on Marines."

Roger smoothed his ponytail and opened his mouth to say something, then closed it.

"Yes, Your Highness?" Kosutic said softly. "I take it there's something about that statement that bothers you?"

"Not about your observation," Roger said as Bebi triggered the notional charge and rushed through the resulting imaginary hole. The prince had set his helmet to project the "shoot house" in see-through mode, and the team seemed to be fighting phantoms in a ghost building as he watched. Combined with his question, the . . . otherworldly nature of their opponents sent something very much like a shiver down his spine.

"It was that last comment," he said. "I've been wondering. . . . Why is Satanism the primary religion of Armagh? I mean, a planet settled by Irish and other Roman Catholic groups. That seems a bit . . . strange," he finished, and the sergeant major let out a chuckle that turned into a liquid laugh Roger had never heard from her before.

"Oh, Satan, is that all? The reason is because the winners write the history books, Your Highness."

"That doesn't explain things," Roger protested, pulling at a strand of hair. "You're a High Priestess, right? That would be the equivalent of—an Episcopal bishop, I guess."

"Oh, not a *bishop*!" Kosutic laughed again. "Not one of those evil creatures! Angels of the Heavens, they are!" Roger felt his eyes trying to cross, and she smiled at his expression and took pity on him.

"Okay, if you insist, Your Highness, here's the deal.

"Armagh was a slow-boat colony, as you know. The original colonists were primarily from Ireland, on Old Earth, with a smattering from the Balkans. Now, Ireland had a bloody history long before Christianity, but the whole Protestant/Catholic thing eventually got out of hand."

"We studied the nuking of Belfast at the Academy as an example of internal terrorism taken to a specific high," Roger agreed.

"Yes, and what was so screwed up about those Constables was that they killed as many—or more—of their own supporters as they did Catholics." She shrugged. "Religious wars are . . . bad. But Armagh was arguably worse, even in comparison to the Belfast Bomb.

"The original colonists were Eire who wanted to escape the religious bickering that was still going on in Ireland but keep their religion. They didn't want freedom from *religion,* only freedom from *argument* about it. So they took only Catholics.

"Shortly after landing, though, there was an attempted religious schism. It was still, at that time, a purely Catholic colony, and the schismatic movement was more on the order of fundamentalism rather than any sort of outright heresy. The schismatics wanted the mass in Latin, that sort of thing. But that, of course, threatened to start the arguments all over. So, as a result, to prevent religious warfare from breaking out again, they instituted a local version of the Papal College for the express purpose of defining what was religiously acceptable."

"Oh, shit," Roger said quietly. "That's . . . a bad idea. Hadn't any of them studied history?"

"Yes," she said sadly, "they had. But they also thought they could do things 'right' this time. The Inquisition, the Great Jihad of the early twenty-first century, the Fellowship Extinction, and all the rest of the Jihads, Crusades, and Likuds were beside the point. The worst of it was that those who founded the Tellers were good people. Misguided, but good. The road to Heaven is paved with good intentions, after all. Like most ardent believers, they thought God would make sure *they* got it right. That their cause was just, and that the other people who'd screwed up exactly the same idea before them had suffered—unlike them—from some fundamental flaw in their vision or approach."

"Rather than from just being human." Roger shook his

head. "It's like the redistributionists that don't see the Ardane Deconstruction as being 'what will happen.' "

"The one thing you learn from history, Your Highness, is that we're doomed to repeat it. Anyway, where was I?"

"They set up an Inquisition."

"Well, that wasn't what they'd intended to set up, but, yes. That was what they got." Kosutic shrugged grimly. "It was bad. That sort of thing attracts . . . bad sorts. Not so much sociopaths—although it does attract them—but also people who are so sure of their own rectitude that they can't see that evil is evil."

"But you're a Satanist. You keep referring to 'His Wickedness,' so why does the concept of evil bother you?" Roger asked, his tone honestly perplexed, and Kosutic shrugged again.

"At first the organized opposition to the College was purely secular. The Resistance actually had a clause in its manifesto calling for an end to all religion, always. But the planet was too steeped in religious thought for that to work, and the Tellers, the Determiners of Truth, insisted on referring to anyone in the Resistance as 'minions of Satan.' "

"So instead of trying to fight the label, you embraced it for yourselves."

"And changed it," Kosutic agreed. "We won eventually, and part of the peace settlement was a freedom of religion clause in the Constitution. But by that time, the Satanists were the majority religion, and Christianity—or, at least, Armagh's version of it—had completely discredited itself. There's a really ancient saw that says that if Satan ever replaced God, he'd have to act the same. And to be a religion for the good of all, which was what we'd intended from the outset, we had to be good. The difference between Armaghan Satanism and Catholicism is a rejection of the supremacy of the Pope, a few bells and whistles we stole from Wicca, and referring to Satan instead of the Trinity. It really is Episcopalianism, for Satanists, which makes your bishop comparison even more humorous."

She'd been watching the training entry team as she

spoke, and now she grimaced as Bebi flinched. The exercise was simple, "baby steps" designed to get the Marines back into the close-combat mode of thinking. But despite that, the team hadn't taken the simple security precaution of checking all corners of the room for threats, and the "enemy" hiding behind a pillar had just taken out the team leader.

"It's the little things in life," she muttered.

"Yep," Roger agreed. "They don't seem to be doing all that well."

He watched as Macek "responded" to the threat by uncovering his own area. At which point another hidden enemy took advantage of the lack of security to take out Berent. Kosutic's nostrils flared, and Roger grinned mentally as he pictured the blistering critique of the exercise she was undoubtedly compiling. But the sergeant major was one of those people for whom multitasking came naturally, and she resumed her explanation even as she watched Berent become a casualty.

"One of the big differences between the Church of Rome and Armaghan Satanism is our emphasis on the Final Conflict and the preparations for it," she continued, her expression now deadly serious. "We believe that the Christians are dupes, that if God was really in charge, things would be better. It's our belief that Lucifer was cast out not by God, but by the other angels, and that they have silenced The One True God. It's our job, in the Final Conflict, to uphold the forces of good and win this time."

She turned to face the prince fully, and smiled at his widened eyes. It was not an especially winsome expression.

"We take that belief very seriously, Your Highness. There's a reason that Armagh, a low-population planet, supplies three percent of all the Imperial Marines, and somewhere around ten percent of all the elite forces. The Precepts of the Elders call for all good Satanists to be ready for the Final Conflict at all times. To uphold good in all their doings, and to be morally upright so that when the time comes to free God from the Chains of the Angels, we won't be found wanting."

She turned back to watch the training and shook her head.

"I mention this only to note that the Brotherhood of Baal would eat Bebi's team for lunch. The Brotherhood has used the Imperial freedom of religion clause to perform some tinkering on themselves that gives most of the rest of us Satanists cold chills. I doubt that any court would consider an abbott of Baal human if he or she didn't have documents to prove it. But you have to see them to believe it."

Roger watched as Bebi collected his "dead" and "wounded" and started the debrief.

"I imagine that Christians are . . . somewhat ambivalent about that approach."

"We don't preach," Kosutic said. "We don't proselytize. We certainly don't discuss our beliefs around the general public. And, frankly, we believe that as long as Christians and Jews and Muslims are being 'good,' they're violating the intent of their controllers. So we applaud them for it." She turned and gave him a truly evil smile. "It really confuses them."

Roger chuckled and shook his head as Despreaux began enumerating the team's faults. The plan had been good, but when they'd hit the door, they'd forgotten it and fought by the seat of their pants. They had, in fact, been fighting the way they would have fought Mardukans. But the next major conflict would probably put Bravo Company—what was left of it—up against humans. True, those humans would probably be pirate scum and garrison troopers, but standard colonial defenses called for space-intercept capable plasma cannon, monomolecular "twist" wire, and bunkers with interlocking fields of fire. And then they had to capture a ship.

It wasn't going to be a walk in the park.

"Well," Roger said with a sigh. "I just hope whoever the 'good guys' are, they're on our side."

Captain Pahner looked around the cramped cabin. The one fault of *Ima Hooker*'s design, which no one had considered in advance, was that the schooner had never been intended as a command ship. Poertena had recognized the necessity of designing around higher deckheads to allow more head room for the towering Mardukans of her crew. There was a limit to what he could do, but the final result—however claustrophobic the natives might still find it—was that even the tallest of the humans could stand upright without worrying about hitting his head on a deck beam. But however the ship might have been stretched vertically, there was only so much that could be done horizontally in a hull of *Hooker*'s length and beam. Despite the fact that Pahner, or Prince Roger, rather, had a minimal "staff," its members packed into the wardroom of the command schooner only with difficulty. Especially the Mardukans.

And that was before adding Roger's pet. Or his *asi* "bodyguard."

"All right," Pahner said with a grim smile. "We need to keep this meeting short, if for no other reason than so that Rastar can unbend his neck."

He looked over at Rastar Komas Ta'Norton, who stood hunched forward with his horns banging on the ceiling. The former prince of the Northern League wasn't large for a Mardukan, but he still towered over the humans.

"How're the *civan* doing?" the captain continued.

"As well as could be expected," the Northerner said with a shrug. The ostrichlike, omnivorous cavalry mounts were actually related to the vastly larger packbeasts, so they had leathery skin and were more capable of handling desiccation than the slime coated, amphibian-derived Mardukans. But they still weren't well-suited to a lengthy sea voyage. "They fit into these toys as well as we do, and they never had to deal with the pitching and rocking before. At least they have more head room aboard *Snarleyow* than we do here, and that outsized *coll* fish has stretched their feed supply nicely, but they aren't happy. We haven't lost any, yet, but we need to get to land soon."

"According to our map, we should," Julian commented. He tapped his pad, and an image of the large island or small continent they were approaching floated into view. "This is as detailed a zoom as I can get from the world map we had. It appears there's only one main river, and that it travels in a sort of semicircle through a good part of the continent. There should be a city on or near its mouth, and that *should* be less than three more days sailing from where we are right now— assuming this line of islands extends from the eastern chain."

"The spaceport is on the central plateau," O'Casey added, "and the continent is . . . extensively mountainous. In fact, it makes Nepal look flat—the province or the planet. Travel to the spaceport may take some time, and it could be arduous."

"Oh, no!" Roger chuckled. "Not an arduous march!"

Pahner grinned momentarily, but then shook his head.

"It's an important point, Your Highness. *Coll* oil or no, we're short on dietary supplements, and there won't be any more *coll* fish to get oil from once we head inland. That means we're short on time, too, so traveling through that region had better be fast."

"We have the additional problem of overhead coverage, Captain," Kosutic pointed out. "From here on out, we need to consider our emissions. If we're able to hear them, and we have been, then they can hear us, if they're listening. And they can also detect our heavy weapons. Plasma cannons especially."

"Also, Sir," Julian said diffidently, "it's likely that the people from the ships visit more than just the starport. There are always tourists, even on planets where the local critters can't wait to eat them. We need to keep that in mind."

"Noted and agree." Pahner nodded. "Anything else?"

"The Diasprans," Despreaux commented. "They're . . . not happy."

Pahner turned to Fain. The infantry captain was still settling in to command Yair's old company (and the transferred survivors of his own, original command), but he was continuing to demonstrate an impressive capacity for assuming additional responsibilities. He was also working out well as Roger's aide-de-camp, and he'd ended up being the regular liaison to the human command conferences, despite being junior to the other two Diaspran commanders.

"Comments, Captain?" Pahner invited, and Fain rubbed a horn gently.

"It's the water. And . . . the space, I suppose."

"It's the lack of a chaplain," Kosutic snorted.

"Perhaps." Fain shrugged. "We probably should have brought a priest. But they didn't like the God in such abundance. It was troubling for them. And now, it's becoming troubling to the men, as well."

"The Diasprans are having a spiritual crisis, Captain," Kosutic explained.

"Not all that surprisingly," O'Casey snorted. The prince's chief of staff was a historian's historian, with a specialization in anthropology (human and nonhuman) and political history and theory. Those interest areas had made her an ideal choice as a tutor for a member of the Imperial Family, the position from which she had segued into the then-unenviable assignment as Prince Roger the Fop's chief of staff. They'd also made her absolutely invaluable in the trek across Marduk.

For all that, though, she'd been frustrated on more than one occasion by the tyrannical time pressure which had prevented her from spending long enough with any one of the cultures they'd encountered to feel that she'd truly had time to study it on its own terms. Too much of the expertise and analyses she'd been called upon to deliver had been based on little more than hurried, off-the-cuff analogies. That was the way *she* saw it, at least, although every Bronze Barbarian—and Roger—recognized the fact that her "off-the-cuff analogies" had done at least as much as the plasma cannons to get them this far alive.

This voyage, however, had finally offered her an opportunity to sit down and do some of the detailed study she loved so dearly, and Roger knew that one of the primary sources she'd spent hours with was *The Book of the Water*, the oldest and most sacred of the Diasprans' religious texts.

"It's not at all surprising that the Diaspran religion worked out the way it did," she said now. It was apparent to Roger that she was choosing her words and tone carefully, no doubt out of consideration for Krindi Fain's beliefs. "After all, they have historical—and accurate—proof that the God of Water is the only reason Diaspra exists."

"It is?" Despreaux asked.

"Yes," O'Casey confirmed, and nodded at Dobrescu. "Despite the inadequacies of our database on Marduk, Mr. Dobrescu and I have managed to confirm Roger's original observation on the day we first met Cord. It may seem ridiculous, given the climate we've encountered here, but this planet actually experienced a fairly recent period of glaciation. It produced the rock formations Roger observed then . . . and must also have killed off a substantial proportion of the planet's total population."

"Hell, yes!" Roger snorted, remembering how dreadfully vulnerable Cord and his nephews had been to the mountainous climate they had encountered crossing from Marshad to the Valley of Ran Tai. What humans regarded as little more than a pleasantly cool morning had been well-nigh fatal to the cold-blooded Mardukans.

"As you know," O'Casey continued, "this planet has only a very slight axial tilt, which gives it a relatively narrow equatorial belt. As nearly as Chief Dobrescu and I have been able to figure out, just about everyone outside that narrow zone must have been killed by the climatic changes involved when the glaciation set in. Geologically speaking, it was extremely recent, as well, which probably explains why the planetary population is so low, despite a climate—now—which permits several crops a year.

"There were, however, some isolated enclaves of Mardukans who survived outside the equatorial zone. The only one of those on which we have any specific documentation, so far, was Diaspra."

"The lake!" Roger said, snapping his fingers suddenly, and O'Casey nodded.

"Exactly. Remember how incredibly ancient the buildings

around those volcanic springs looked?" She shrugged. "That's because the Diaspran priesthood is entirely correct about how old their city really is. There's been *a* city on that site since before the glaciers; it was the heat output of the volcanic springs that made it possible for that city's population to survive. No wonder they look upon water as the preserving miracle of all life!"

"That explains a lot," Kosutic said, tipping thoughtfully back in her chair. "Have you loaded *The Book of the Water* into your toot, Eleanor?" The chief of staff nodded. "Then can I get you to download a translation of it to mine after supper?"

"Of course," O'Casey agreed.

"Good! I'll be looking forward to reading it, because I'm pretty sure it will flesh out what I've already picked up from talking to people like Krindi here." She pointed at Fain with her chin. "In the meantime, though, I think I've already got enough of the handle on their theology to see where our current problem lies."

She turned her attention back to Roger and Pahner.

"Essentially, their cosmology calls for a piece of land floating in an eternal, endless body of water," she said. "It also calls for all water that hasn't been specifically contaminated to be 'good,' which means potable. So here we are, way out of sight of land, sailing over an apparently eternal body of . . . bad water."

"Water, water everywhere, and not a drop to drink," Pahner said with a slight grin, then looked serious again. "I can see where that would be a problem, Captain Fain. Do you have a suggestion for solving it?"

"As Sergeant Major Kosutic has just suggested, I've been discussing the problem with her, Sir," the Mardukan said diffidently. "I believe it would be useful for her to deal directly with the troops as a replacement for our usual priests. And, if possible, when the ships go back to K'Vaern's Cove, it would also be useful if, upon return, they brought a priest over with them."

Pahner gazed at him for a second, then shook his head in resignation.

"By the time they could get back here from K'Vaern's

Cove, hopefully, we'll be well on our way to the port. If we're not, we might as well not have made the trip." The Marine tapped his fingers together while he thought, then gave Kosutic another slight grin. "Okay, High Priestess, you're on. Just no converting."

"No sweat," the sergeant major said. "I'll just point out to them that there's no problem, within their cosmology, with there being more than one 'world.' We're traveling across what is, technically, infinite water—a sphere *is* infinite, looked at in a certain way. For that matter, their definition practically cries out for multiple worlds, or, in fact, continents. And from what I've gleaned, there's nothing saying that all water is potable. In fact, they deal with certain types of nonpotable waters all the time. Waters that have been soiled by wastes, for example. And the God of Waters loves them just as much as he loves potable waters, and rejoices whenever they are restored to potability. Gets us into the concept of sin and redemption."

"The Prophet Kosutic," Roger said with a chuckle, and the sergeant major smiled at him.

"I'd invite you to a service, but I don't think the Empire is ready for that just yet."

"Now that we hopefully have that crisis dealt with," Pahner said, "there's another one to consider. Taking the port isn't going to be a picnic, and I've been watching the squad close-tactics training. It's not going well. Comments?"

"Train, train, train," Julian said. "We're barely scratching the surface yet, Sir. The teams *are* improving. Just not very rapidly."

"Sergeant Major?"

"Well . . ." Kosutic frowned. "I gotta say I don't feel like they're there, Julian. They're not concentrating. They're just going through the motions. We need to put some steel in their asses."

"With all due respect, Sergeant Major," Despreaux interjected, "I don't think you can say any of us are lacking in 'steel.' I think our credentials on that are fairly clear."

"Maybe," Kosutic returned. "And maybe not. One thing about being in battle as long and as often as we have is that for just about everybody, after a while, the edge goes away. You can't be on Condition Red forever, and we've been on it for a helluva lot longer than is recommended. So I think that that steel, Sergeant, is starting to melt. And it couldn't come at a worse time. You do realize that after we take the port, we're going to have to take a *ship,* right?"

"Yes." Despreaux nodded, her eyes dark. "I do realize that."

"Obviously, we're not going to hit the port when we know there's a ship in orbit to watch us do it," Kosutic said. "But that means that whenever a ship *does* turn up, we're going to have to grab any shuttles it sends down the instant they hit dirt." She leaned forward and stabbed a rock-hard finger into the wooden table. "*And* prevent communication between them and their ship when we do it. Then, we'll have to send our own shuttles up, blow the hatches, and do a forced boarding. We'll have to blast our way through the whole ship without smashing *anything* that can't be fixed. And it's probably going to be a ship used to bad ports—to the idea of pirates trying to grab it. So its crew won't be sitting there with their guard down. Now how easy do you think that's going to be?"

"Sergeant Major," Roger said in mild reproof. "We're all aware that it's not going to be a walk in the park. But we'll get it done."

"Will we?" Kosutic asked. "It won't be Voitan or Sindi, Your Highness. We won't be in a fixed position waiting for the scummies to throw themselves onto our swords. It won't even be just a smash and grab, like Q'Nkok and Marshad. We'll have to move like lightning, in the boarding and taking the port. And we'll have to be precise, as well. And we're *not* moving like that right now."

"Can you take this ship without our help?" Rastar asked suddenly. "Isn't this what you brought us for? To fight by your side, your foes as ours?"

All the human heads in the cabin swiveled like turrets as their owners turned to look at him. Roger's mouth flapped for a moment before he could spit out a sentence. Then—

"It's . . . not that easy."

"This environment isn't one you want to fight in, Rastar," Eleanora said quietly. "You'll undoubtedly be involved in the taking of the port. But the ship will be another issue."

Roger nodded then leaned forward in the lamplight and placed his hand atop the Mardukan's.

"Rastar, there are very few people I would rather have by my side in a firefight. But you *don't* want to fight on shipboard. Onboard, if you press the wrong button, you can find yourself without any air to breathe, your breath stolen and your skin freezing until you die, quickly."

"There are . . . hazards, Rastar," Pahner agreed. "Hazards we would prefer not to subject your forces to. They aren't trained for that sort of environment. And despite the difficulty, a short platoon of Marines will be able to take most freighters. For that matter, since there will probably be functional armor at the spaceport, we can probably take a pirate down, as well. If, as the sergeant major has noted, we're trained to a fine edge."

He rubbed his cheek for a moment in thought.

"Who are the best at this sort of thing?" Roger asked. "I mean, of the troops we have."

"Probably myself and Despreaux, Your Highness," Julian answered.

"Don't count *me* out, boy," Kosutic said with a wink. "I was door-kicking when you were in swaddling clothes."

"Why don't we have a demonstration?" Roger asked, ignoring the byplay. "Set up a visible 'shoot-house' on the deck, made out of—I dunno, sails and stuff—and let the teams watch Despreaux and Julian do their thing. And the sergeant major, of course, if she's not too old and decrepit. Show them how it's done."

"Decrepit, huh?" The senior NCO snorted. "I'll show you *decrepit,* sonny!"

"That's 'Your Highness Sonny,'" Roger retorted with his nose in the air.

The comment elicited a general chuckle. Even Pahner smiled. Then he nodded more seriously.

"Good call, Roger. It will also give our allies a look at what we're doing. Since we're not going to be using live rounds, we can give them detectors and let them be the opposition. Let them see if they can stop the sergeant major's team."

"Surprise is the essence of an assault," Despreaux said quietly. "If they watch us prepare, they're not going to be too surprised."

"We'll train in the hold," Kosutic said, tugging at the skull earring dangling from her right ear. "Then duplicate the conditions on deck."

"That sounds good," Julian said, but his tone was a bit dubious. She cocked her head at him, and he shrugged. "You know how much of this is about muscle memory," he said. "Even with the helmet VR and our toots, we're still going to need at least some room to move in, if we're going to do it right. And, frankly, I don't think there's enough room in *Hooker*'s hold."

"He's got a point, Smaj," Roger said. The prince frowned for a moment, then shrugged. "On the other hand, there's a lot more room below decks on *Snarleyow*. I bet the *civan* have eaten enough of the forage to give us a lot more room in *Snarleyow*'s forward hold than we could find in any of the other ships."

"That's an excellent idea, Roger," Pahner approved. "Her between-deck spaces are even deeper than ours are, and she's got a lot more beam, as well."

"Still not as much room as I'd really like, but a lot better, " Kosutic agreed.

"And we'll be the 'opposition'?" Rastar asked.

"Yes," Pahner said with a nod. "We'll set up a facility above decks on one of the other schooners. It may still be a little cramped for troopers the size of yours, but it should work out. As far as the demonstration itself goes, you'll know they're coming, but not quite when. And you'll be armed with your standard weapons, but no ammunition. The computer will be able to tell which shots hit and which miss, and the system will tell you with a buzzer if you're hit or killed."

"Can I participate also?" Fain asked.

"Certainly," Pahner said, then chuckled. "A sergeant major and two sergeants going after a prince and his officers. It should be interesting."

"Could I participate, too, instead of being the objective?" Roger asked. "I'd like to see how I'd do on this tac team."

Julian started to open his mouth in automatic protest, then thought about it. Every single time he had doubted the prince's abilities in a firefight, he'd been wrong. And so, after a moment more of thought, he shut his mouth, instead.

Kosutic frowned contemplatively. Then she nodded.

"We'll . . . introduce you to it, at least. It's more than just being able to shoot straight. Some people who aren't much good at other fighting are very good at close-quarters work, and vice versa. If you do well in the preliminary training, you'll participate in the final demonstration. If not, not."

"Fine," Roger said with a nod. "How long to set this up?"

"Start in the morning," Pahner said. "Captain T'Sool and I will get with *Snarleyow*'s skipper and have *Hooker*'s main deck set up to duplicate the conditions in *Snarleyow*'s hold. You do your prep down there, then do the assault on the deck. That way we can all watch."

"And make rude comments, I'm sure," Kosutic snorted.

"So are we going to play shirts and skins?" Julian ogled Despreaux luridly. "If so, I say *we* take skins."

The sergeant major's palm-strike would have been a disabling or even killing blow if it had landed a few inches farther forward on the side of his head, or if she'd used the base of her palm instead of the side. As it was, it just hurt like hell.

"You're toast, buddy," she said, chuckling as he rubbed the side of his head.

"Man," he protested. "Nobody around here can take a joke!"

"And don't let this interfere with your discussions with the Mardukans," Pahner reminded the sergeant major, ignoring the byplay. "I'm not sure that either takes precedence over the other."

The captain was still unsure and unhappy about the relationship between his senior NCO and his intel sergeant. They were discreet, and there wasn't a hint of favoritism, but small unit command was about managing personalities, and sex was one of the biggest destabilizers around. There were strict rules against the type and degree of fraternization the two of them were engaged in, and they knew it just as well as he did. But, he reminded himself yet again, none of the rules had contemplated a unit being cut off from all outside contact for over six months.

"Got it," the sergeant major nodded, noting his dark expression.

"Should we load anything else onto the list?" Roger asked, deliberately trying to reclaim a less serious mood. "I don't think Sergeant Major Kosutic has enough on her plate, yet."

"Ah, you just wait, Your Highness," the NCO told him with an evil smile. "As of tomorrow, you're just 'Recruit MacClintock.' You just keep right on joking."

"What's the worst that can happen?" Roger said with a smile. "Going back to Voitan?"

CHAPTER FIVE

"ARE YOU GOING TO KEEP AN EYE ON YOUR OWN SECTOR NEXT TIME, RECRUIT?"

"One hundred and twenty-seven. YES, SERGEANT MAJOR!"

There were several axioms, handed down from generation to generation by the noncommissioned officers who were the true keepers of the tribal wisdom, in which Sergeant Major Eva Kosutic firmly believed. "No plan survives contact with reality." "In battle, His Wickedness always has a hole card." "If the enemy is in range, so are you." All of them were rules the military forgot at its own peril, but the one that was currently paramount in her own mind was "The more you sweat, the less you bleed."

And at the moment, some people obviously needed to do a little more sweating than others, she thought bitingly.

Roger MacClintock had several things going for him when it came to close combat. He had been gifted, both naturally and through long ago manipulation of the MacClintock genotype, with the reactions of a pit viper. He was a natural-born shot, with the hand-eye coordination of a master marksman, and he had spent many a lonely hour building on that platform to perfect his aim. And he had a good natural combat awareness; in a fight, he always knew "where" he was and had a good feel for where the enemies and friendlies were around him. That was an often underrated ability, but it was crucial in the sort of high-violence and sudden-death environment for which they were training.

But although he'd learned to be a "team player" in soccer, he'd never really had to perfect that in combat. Worse, perhaps, he tended to go his own way, as had been proven repeatedly on the long march from the shuttles' dry lakebed landing to K'Vaern's Cove. Roger was never one to integrate himself into a fire plan. Which made it a good thing that he always led from the front, since he also tended to kill anything that got in front of *him*.

"Your job, when we do an entry, is to watch my *back*! Not to watch where I am *going*! If I run into resistance, *I* will deal with it. But if I have to watch *your* sector at the same time, you are OFF THIS TEAM! Do I make myself perfectly clear?"

"CLEAR, SERGEANT MAJOR!" Roger hammered out his final push-up. "One fifty, Sergeant Major!"

"You just stay there in the front leaning rest position, Recruit MacClintock! I'll get to you when I'm ready."

"Yes, Sergeant Major!" the prince gasped.

The schooner *Snarleyow*'s forward hold was hotter than the hinges of hell and reeked of decaying filth in the bilges. But it was also the largest concealed open space aboard any vessel of the flotilla, which, from Eva Kosutic's perspective, made it the best possible place for training. It still didn't offer as much unobstructed area as she would have liked—not by a long chalk—but the cavalry's *civan* had already consumed the fodder which had originally been piled into it. And unlike the upper cargo deck, there were no *civan* in the hold itself.

Which was a very good thing. *Civan*, and especially the trained war-*civan* Prince Rastar and his men favored, were much more intelligent than most humans might have thought upon meeting them for the first time. But what they most definitely were *not* was cute or cuddly. In fact, any *civan* tended to have the temper of an Old Earth grizzly bear with a bad tooth. The temperament—and training—of those selected as cavalry mounts only exacerbated that natural tendency. Which was why the *civan* stalled along the sides of *Snarleyow*'s upper cargo deck were "tethered" (if that was the proper verb for it) not with halters or ropes, but with five-point chain tie-downs.

Even so, the Mardukans charged with their care and feeding were extremely careful about how close they got to the beasts' axlike jaws and razor-sharp, metal-shod fighting claws. For herself, Kosutic was delighted to have a training space, be it ever so hot, dank, and smelly, in which she didn't have to worry about losing a limb because she strayed too close to a *civan* in a worse mood than usual.

Of course, at the moment, *she* was in a worse mood than usual, and she shook her head, then gestured for the other two NCOs to follow her. She led them to the forwardmost end of the hold, then turned to face them.

"Options," she said quietly, and Julian wiped away a drop of sweat and shook his head.

"He's good, Smaj. Very good. But he won't stay focused on defense."

"He's too used to having us do that for him," Despreaux pointed out. "He's used to barreling through the opposition while we cover his back. Now *you're* barreling through the course, and he's supposed to cover *your* back." She shrugged ever so slightly. "He can't get used to it."

"Yeah, but a big part of it is that he's one aggressive son-of-a-bitch," Julian said with a quiet chuckle. "No offense intended to Her Majesty."

"There's that," Kosutic agreed, tugging at an earlobe. "I don't really want to switch him out for somebody else, either. He's got the moves to be better than just about anybody else in the company, if we can ever get them harnessed and coordinated, and only Macek might be able to equal him as it is. But I'm not going to get whacked because he's not covering his sector."

And that was exactly what had happened, three times so far.

When the helmet systems came on and their connection to the team's toots kicked in, the hold became a virtual shoot-house, and Kosutic had set the difficulty level very high. That meant that enemies weren't just in plain sight, on the route that the team took. Which, in turn, meant there had to be eyes turned in every direction . . . and Roger insisted on facing forward, along the line of assault. Not only did that permit the "enemies" he would otherwise have neutralized a clear shot at the team, but in one case he'd managed to "shoot" the sergeant major in the back.

Something had to be done, and Despreaux furrowed her brow as all three of them considered the problem.

"We could . . ." she said, then stopped.

"What?" the sergeant major asked.

"You won't like it," Despreaux replied.

"I've done a lot of stuff I don't like," Kosutic sighed. "What's one more thing, by His Evilness?"

"All right," Despreaux said with a shrug. "We could put Roger on point."

"Uh," Kosutic said.

"Hmmm." Julian rubbed his jaw. "She's got a point. I think he might do pretty well."

"But . . ." the sergeant major said. "But—"

" 'But that's *my* spot!' " Julian finished for her with a faint, humorous whine.

Kosutic looked daggers at him for a moment, then shook her head sharply.

"It's more than that, Adib. Do you really think the captain isn't going to use us? He put us together for more than just to show how it's done. My guess is that he's thinking of using us for something, as a team."

"What? His company's sergeant major, two of his squad leaders, and *the prince*?" Julian laughed. "You're joking, right?"

"No, I'm not," the sergeant major said seriously. "Just take it as a given that that might happen. Then think about putting Roger on point."

"Oh," Julian said.

"I can see your objection, Sergeant Major," Despreaux

said carefully. "But I'm not sure it matters. Perhaps we should get Macek or Stickles instead of the prince. But if we *are* going to use him, I still think he should be on point. Frankly, I think, with all due respect, that he might be . . . a touch better even than you."

Despreaux gazed calmly at the sergeant major, waiting for the explosion, and Kosutic opened her mouth again. Then she closed it with a clop, fingered her earlobe for a moment, and shrugged.

"You might be right."

"I think she is, Smaj," Julian said with equal care. "The pocker is fast."

"Is that any way to talk about the Heir Tertiary to the Throne of Man?" Kosutic demanded with a grin. "But you're right. The pocker *is* fast. And he can shoot, too. But I hate to seem to . . . reward him for screwing up."

"You think point is a *reward*?" Julian shook his head.

Roger stood with his right elbow just touching the wood of the bulkhead, his head and body hunched and turned to his left. The wood was real, but just to his right was a large doorway that had been cut into it only recently. In his helmet systems, the doorway was visible only as an outline sketched on the wall with explosives. And the wall wasn't wood; it was plascrete. And in just a moment, the "explosives" were going to go off and blow a new door through it. And they would be going off less than a half-meter from his arm.

It was going to be an unpleasant experience. Roger rather doubted that even the sergeant major appreciated the full capabilities of his own toot. All the Marines were accustomed to using their implanted computers as both combat enhancers and training devices, and their toots' abilities in those regards far exceeded those of the hardware available to most citizens of the Empire. But Roger's toot was at least as much more capable than theirs as theirs were than the average civilian model. Which meant that the training simulation was even more "real" for him than for anyone else in the team. He'd considered kicking in the filters in an effort to spare himself some of the sergeant major's simulation's . . . energetic programming tricks, but he'd decided against it. He'd come to embrace the wisdom of another of Kosutic's beloved axioms: "Train like you're going to fight."

He pushed that thought away and concentrated on the moment at hand. Other than the initial walk-through of the simulated rooms, this was his first time on point, and he suspected that the sergeant major was going to be making a statement. In fact, it would be just her style to make the course unsurvivable. That would fit her passion for making training harder than real life could possibly be, and he'd already discovered from painful personal experience that she had an undeniable talent for doing her passion justice. On the other hand, this was supposed to be training for *her*, too, so whatever was waiting for him was waiting for her, as well. Of course, to get to her, it probably had to go through him first, and he couldn't help wondering what the simulator AI was going to throw at them. He hadn't bothered even to attempt to wheedle any more information out of the sergeant major. She wouldn't have told him, of course. But even if she might have, she probably couldn't. The way she'd set things up when she punched the basic scenario parameters into her computer to generate the simulation, not even she should know exactly what was on the other side of the wall.

But it was bound to be bad.

Despreaux quietly laid in the last bit of the simulated breaching charge and stood back. The explosion should fill the room beyond with flying fragments, along with a world's worth of overpressure, smoke, and noise. The Marines' helmets and chameleon suits would serve to reduce that same concussion, so it should give them a moment of surprise and shock in which to overcome whoever might be defending the room. Assuming that the defenders weren't outfitted with equipment similar to that of the Marines.

Despreaux held up a thumb, indicating that she was ready to go, and watched the rest of the team. Julian held up a thumb as well and hunched away from the blast area, followed by Kosutic.

Roger held up his own thumb and gripped his bead rifle tightly. The weapon was the standard issue field rifle for the Marines, but its "bullpup" design made it equally handy at close quarters. He'd become familiar with the weapon in the course of the battle across the continent, and it was now as much an extension of his body as his pistol or his personal rifle. In addition, his toot's combat pack had come with a slot for bead rifle, and he'd used the training system assiduously, building up his ability and confidence day by day. He'd never had much call for automatic weapons' training before, but he instinctively tended to be light on the trigger, so his bursts were always short and clean. With most targets, he'd tended to put two or three rounds into the upper chest, neck, or head. But except for the few targets which had presented themselves to "ass end Charlie" in the run-throughs, that had been against stationary targets. Now it was time to see if he really had what it took.

Despreaux took one more look at the team, hunched away herself, and triggered the breaching charge.

The suit systems—and toots—did the best they could to simulate the conditions, and that "best" was very good indeed. The helmets simulated a vast overpressure on their ears as they clamped onto the team's heads, their toots gave their sense of balance a hard jolt, and their chameleon suits went momentarily rigid and squeezed hard in kinetic reaction to the "pressure wave." But even before the cloth had started to settle again, Roger was through the door.

The room beyond was fairly small, no more than four or five meters square. A table in the center occupied much of its volume, and there was another door in the far wall. The scenario had called for no reconnaissance on the room, so the numbers or locations of hostiles had been unknown. But, as it turned out, there was plenty for a young prince to work on.

As he plunged through the smoke, he identified a hostile on the far side of the room. But that hostile was only just drawing a bead pistol, and something made Roger look to his right.

There was a human in the corner with a bead rifle trained right on him. The person wore the shoulder patch of a Colonial Garrison Trooper, but otherwise his equipment and uniform were identical to the Marines'. And it was clear that he'd reacted immediately to the detonation and entry. But as fast as the sim was reacting, "he" had never dealt with Prince Roger MacClintock.

Roger flipped the bead rifle sideways and "double-tapped" the defender in the corner off-hand, then flipped back to the left to engage another defender in the other corner. Only then did he engage and neutralize the first threat . . . who was just starting to level her bead pistol. Beads caromed off the floor and past his legs as that threat flew back against the far wall in a splash of red.

But by then, Roger was already gone.

Kosutic followed the prince through the smoke and covered left. In this case, she *did* know the layout and position of defenders, and she was shocked to see all three of them already dead. The two "sneaks" in the corners were both headless corpses, and the primary threat against the far wall had one round through the forehead and two more in her chest. The sergeant major was even more shocked as Roger threw a flashbang through the far door and followed it before it could detonate.

"*Roger!* Satan damn it, *SLOW DOWN!*"

The prince vaguely heard the sergeant major, but his helmet visor's heads-up display showed that so far the team had taken no casualties. That was how he intended to keep it. He followed the disarmed flashbang through the door, and, as he'd expected, all the defenders on the far side had hunched away in anticipation of the flash that never came. This room was larger, with an open door along the right wall, and a closed-door in the left wall. There were also quite a few defenders—seven, to be precise. For some reason the words "target-rich environment" came to mind. And also "Eva Kosutic is a bitch."

He shot two that were arrayed beside the door to his right, then took cover behind a handy workbench. From under the bench, he began single-tapping knees and shins as the other five defenders dropped to the floor and thus into view.

A grenade from one of the "wounded" defenders flew over the workbench, and it appeared to be the just and proper time to abandon his position. However, that wasn't all to the bad. The grenade was a standard issue frag, and the explosion, while unpleasant, would only manage to lift him over the bench a little faster. The chameleon suit was proof against all but high-velocity beads, and the shrapnel from the grenade wouldn't penetrate it. He wasn't sure if the combat simulator was designed to simulate shocked amazement on the part of the "enemy," but real ones would have stopped in dazed wonder at the front-flip that he managed over the workbench, riding the wavefront of the explosion.

Kosutic caught a flicker out of the corner of her eye as she came through the door, but realized it was the prince. Just then, a notional "grenade" went off to her right and slapped her against the wall. That was okay, but it threw off her first shot, and by the time she'd reacquired the two remaining defenders, they were both down with head and throat shots.

"Roger!"

Apparently there *had* been a purpose for all those saddle exercises they'd put him through in boarding school. Either his maneuver had temporarily locked up the simulation processor, or else it *was* designed to allow for amazed shock, because both of the remaining targets just sat there, frozen, clutching their wounds while he terminated them. The sergeant major was yelling about something, but *he* hadn't set up this nightmare, and he damned sure wasn't stopping or even slowing down until all the targets were cleared. He thumbed a frag grenade, set it for two-second detonation, and pitched it through the open door. Then he followed.

"Roger!" Kosutic shouted in exasperation. She'd seen the grenade go through the door, and he was following it far too closely, antiballistic chameleon suit or no. Putting him on point might make some sense; *she* could barely keep up with him, so Satan only knew what it would be like for the opposition! But it was just as clear that with him in the lead, His Wickedness was running wild.

The system finally threw Roger a curve and graded his bead rifle as damaged by the grenade explosion. It also graded his right hand as damaged, and his toot obliged the AI by sending a stab of all-too-genuine pain through the hand. That reduced his options considerably, so as the three targets in the room tried to recover from the slap of the fragmentation grenade, he reached across and drew his pistol with his left.

He also made a mental note to figure out a better way to enter rooms. Maybe it would be better not to follow his grenade "door knocker" *quite* as closely next time.

Despreaux shook her head over the carnage in the room. It was pretty clear that the sergeant major had intended to stack the deck. But apparently she hadn't stacked it well enough.

Nimashet had nothing to do as "ass-end Charlie," so she backed along, covering Julian now, and keeping the single closed door in the edge of her vision. If they were counterattacked, it would probably come from there. But it didn't pay to concentrate on only one threat axis. It was better to be open and ready to engage in any of "her" directions, she reminded herself.

Which reminder was of no damned use at all when the ceiling fell in.

Roger's new room had only the three defenders, and they were all down with double-taps before they recovered from the grenade. Unfortunately, the left end of the room was a plasteel wall with an armored gun-port. The cannon in it had been unable to engage as long as there were live defenders in its way, but as the last hostile fell, it opened up.

Roger managed to duck under the stream of bead-cannon rounds and crouched along the wall, sheltered from its fire. Unfortunately, there was a certain amount of ricochet, and Kosutic wasn't able to follow him through the door. He could hear a firefight going on in the other room, so he knew he couldn't stay where he was for long. And it looked as if there was just enough room to get a hand through the firing slot past the bead cannon.

He slipped a grenade from his pouch, and as he did, the indicators for Despreaux and Julian went to yellow, then orange. Both were wounded and would die without support.

Eva crouched behind the workbench Roger had abandoned and cursed. Despreaux and Julian were both down, and she herself was pinned by fire from the ceiling and the three heavily armored commandos who'd dropped through the hole. The targets were advancing cautiously, but their heavier armor was shrugging off most of her shots, even after she'd switched to armor piercing. It wasn't powered armor, just very heavy reactive plate, but if something didn't come through soon, they were going to lose this one.

Roger set the grenade to one second, flipped it into the bead cannon bunker, and dove for the door. If the damned simulator's AI didn't have the people in the bunker at least trying to get the grenade back out of their position, it wasn't very well written.

He wasn't punctured by the heavy weapon, so it appeared to have worked. But the situation in the far room sounded bad, and he was tired of going blind. He thought about it for just a moment, then flipped on his helmet's vision systems.

As it turned out, the "dead"—or at least "seriously wounded"—Julian had his head turned to the side. Roger looked in the same direction through the camera on his helmet and saw three heavily armored targets closing on the workbench he had flipped across on his own way through. He slipped a fresh magazine into the pistol and contemplated his right hand. It was still graded as "yellow" (and that damnably efficient toot of his was still giving him direct neural stimulation that hurt like hell to back up its "damage"), and he wasn't sure how much use he could make of it. But there was only one way to find out, so he drew a throwing knife and approached the door in a crouch.

This was going to take timing. Lots of timing.

Timing is everything, and in this case it was on the side of the righteous. Kosutic's HUD showed her the icon of the prince approaching the door, and she smiled. As the prince's actual figure appeared in the opening, she concentrated on the shooter in the ceiling.

Time to get some of their own back.

Roger stepped through the door as Kosutic started tearing into the ceiling with long, concentrated bursts of blind fire. His own firepower was more limited, but unlike her, he could actually see the shooter. He flipped up the knife and threw it towards the hole in the ceiling even as he fired at the three crouched targets in the room.

He saw the backs of each of their necks go red, then grunted in anguish as his chameleon suit hardened and the toot threw some more neural stimulation at him. Pain echoed through his chest, and his helmet's HUD flashed a brief schematic of his body with his torso outlined in yellow. But by then he had directed the pistol towards the ceiling, and before the shooter could get off another round, he was credited as a kill. The hostile fell through the hole to the deck, and Roger noted the knife blade buried in the bad guy's left arm.

Roger rotated to the right along the wall, trying to disregard the flashes of pain his toot obediently sent along his nerves each time he moved. At least one rib broken, he estimated. It hurt like hell, but his nanny pack was already deadening the pain—or, at least, his toot was grudgingly acting as *if* the nanites were doing their job—so he made himself ignore it as he reloaded his pistol.

Then he picked up Julian's bead rifle in place of his own, attached it to his harness' friction strap, and reloaded it, as well. Then he sidled towards the remaining closed door, cradling the rifle in his undamaged left hand.

He looked across at the sergeant major and gestured to the door and the hole in the ceiling, then shrugged. She grimaced back at him and gestured at the ceiling. He nodded, thumbed himself, then jabbed the same thumb upward. She grimaced again, but she also nodded and crouched down, setting her rifle on the floor and interlacing her fingers.

Roger let the friction strap pull Julian's rifle up, drew his pistol again, and stepped over to the sergeant major. He put one boot into her hands, leapt upward into the hole—

—and slammed into the intact deck overhead.

The next thing he knew, he was on the floor, clutching his head and neck in pain (which was not at all simulated) as Kosutic, Julian, and Despreaux tried not to laugh.

"Clear VR," the sergeant major said, and the simulator's AI obeyed, although Roger was half-surprised it could understand the command through her laughter. She leaned over him, and shook her head in an odd mixture of amusement and contrition.

"Satan and Lucifer," she got out. "I'm sorry about that, Your Highness. Are you okay?"

Roger lay on the floor of the poorly lit hold, clutching his neck and stared up at her—and the completely solid deckhead above her.

"Good Christ," he groaned. "What in hell happened?"

"I got so into the scenario, I forgot it wasn't real," Kosutic admitted. "*Snarleyow*'s big enough that I could build two or three rooms into the hold, but there wasn't anything I could do about the *vertical* limits, and I got so involved I forgot that there couldn't really be a hole in the 'ceiling.' That's the upper cargo deck planking. There's not even a *hatch*."

"Where's the targets?" Roger moaned pitifully. "Where's the *bead-cannon*? Where's the *door*? We were doing so welll!"

Julian rolled over on his side, still laughing, while Despreaux climbed to her feet.

"Fortunately," she observed with a disdainful glance at the giggling armorer, "*I'm* not dead."

"Oh, my head," Roger said, ignoring her. "I *hate* VR! Sergeant Major, did you just *piledriver* me into the ceiling?"

"That's more or less what I just said, Your Highness," Kosutic said, still chuckling.

"Oooo," Roger groaned. "Can I just lie here for a while?"

CHAPTER SIX

BAM!

"Man, I want my bead rifle back!" Julian muttered as his round plunked into the water, well clear of the floating target.

He and Roger stood side by side at *Ima Hooker*'s rail, between two of her starboard carronades. They'd just watched Rastar's team run through its own training on the schooner's main deck, and the experience had been fairly . . . ominous. They were due to have their "close contact" contest with the Mardukans the next morning, and it didn't look like it was going to be a walkover, even with Roger on point. The Vashin cavalry and selected Diaspran infantry who were going to act as the notional "guards" on key defenses of the spaceport would be graded as having light body armor. And since all the Vashin carried at least three weapons, it was going to be interesting.

"You're just jealous," Roger retorted as the floating barrel Julian had missed shattered from his own shot. "And it pains your professional ego to be shooting a 'smoke pole,' " he added with a grin.

The new rifles had been produced just in time for the battles around Sindi, and with their availability, the Marines had, for all practical purposes, put away their bead rifles until they reached the starport. The weapons had been designed using Roger's eleven-millimeter magnum Parkins and Spencer as a model, but modified in light of available technology.

The Parkins and Spencer's dual bolt-action/semiautomatic system had been impossible to duplicate, but the base for the bolt form was a modification of the ancient Ruger action, and *that* worked just fine. With the addition of scavenged battery packs from downchecked plasma rifles and various items of gear dead Marines no longer required, the electronic firing system built into the Parkins' cartridge cases also worked just fine. And since the prince had doggedly insisted on policing up his shooting stands whenever possible and dragging along the empty cases, there was sufficient brass to provide over two hundred almost infinitely reloadable rounds for each of the surviving Marines.

The black powder which was the most advanced form of explosives available on Marduk had made for a few compromises. One was that the rifles' slower-velocity bullets simply could not match the flat trajectory of a hypervelocity bead, which meant that at any sort of range, the barrel had to be elevated far beyond what any of the Marines were comfortable with. Which also explained why so many of their rounds tended to fall short.

"You can throw a rock faster than these bullets go," Despreaux growled from Roger's other side. "I still say that guncotton I made would have worked—and given us a hell of a lot better velocity, too!"

"Overpressure," Roger commented with a shake of his head. "And it was unstable as hell."

"I was working on it!" she snapped.

"Sure you were . . . and you're lucky you're not regrowing a set of fingers," Julian told her with another chuckle as he fired again. This time the round was on range for the second barrel, but off to the left. "Damn."

"Windage," Roger said laconically as he shattered that barrel, as well.

"Sight!" Julian snapped.

"Care to trade?" the prince offered with a smile.

"No," the Marine replied promptly, and glowered at Despreaux when she snickered.

While a good bit of it was the sight, most of it—as Julian knew perfectly well—was the sighter.

"Seriously," Roger said, gesturing for Julian's rifle. "I'd like to try. I turn the sight off from time to time, but it's not the same. And what happens if I lose it?"

Julian shook his head and traded rifles.

"It's going to be a bit tough to zero," he warned.

"Not really." The prince looked the rifle over. He'd checked them out when the first of them came off the assembly line, even fired a few rounds through one of them. But that had been months ago, and he took the time to refamiliarize himself with the weapon. Especially with the differences between it and his own Parkins.

Dell Mir, the K'Vaernian inventor who'd designed the detailed modifications, had done a good job. The weapons were virtually identical, with the exception of removing the optional gas-blowback reloading system—which Roger had to disengage anyway, when he used black-powder rounds in the Parkins—and the actual materials from which it was constructed.

It was fortunate that while the Mardukans' materials science was still in the dark ages, their machining ability was fairly advanced, thanks to their planet's weather. Whereas industrial technology had been driven, to a great extent, by advances in weaponry on Earth—and Althar, for that matter—the development of machining on Marduk had been necessitated by something else entirely: water. It rained five to ten times a day on this planet, and the development of any sort of civilization with that much rain had required advanced pumping technology. It was a bit difficult to drain fields with simple waterwheel pumps in the face of four or five meters of rain a year.

Production of the best pumps, the fastest and most efficient ones—and the ones capable of lifting water the "highest"—required fine machine tolerances and resistant metals. Thus, the Mardukans had early on developed both the machine lathe and drill press, albeit animal driven, as well as machine steel and various alloys of bronze and brass that were far in advance of those found at similar general tech levels in most societies.

But because they'd never developed electricity, there was no stainless steel, and no electroplating, so the rifle was made out of a strong, medium-carbon steel that was anything but rust-proof. And the stock, instead of a light-weight, boron-carbon polymer like the Parkins and Spencer's, was of shaped wood.

The weapon's ammunition was slightly different, as well. The cases were the same ones Roger had started with—as long as his hand, and thicker than his thumb, necking downward about fifteen percent to a bullet that was only about as thick as his second finger. The major changes were in the propellant and the bullet.

Roger's rifle used an electronic firing system that acti-vated the center-point primer plug, and in the one oper-ation that had been handled almost entirely by the Marines, Julian and Poertena had installed firing systems in each of the rifles created from spare parts for their armor, downchecked plasma rifles, and odd items of personal gear that hadn't been used up on the trek. Each of the weapons had the same basic design, although each had a few different parts. Mostly, though, it used parts from the plasma rifles, including the faulty capacitors which had made the off-world weapons unsafe to use. There was no problem using them for this application, since the energy being temporarily stored was far below that necessary to cause the spectacular—and lethal—detonations that had forced the weapons' retirement.

Julian had recommended, effectively, scrapping *all* of the plasma rifles and using their stocks for the base of as many of the black-powder rifles as possible, but Captain Pahner had nixed the idea. There hadn't been enough of the plasma rifles to provide all the black-powder weapons the company was going to require, so the majority of them would still have had to be made from native materials. Besides, he was still debating whether or not Julian and Poertena might be able to come up with a "fix" good enough to use the energy weapons for just one more battle. Given the probable difficulty of taking the starport, the plasma rifles might be the difference between success and failure, and he'd been unwilling to completely foreclose the possibility of using them.

The propellant in Roger's original rounds had been an advanced smokeless powder. From the perspective of the Marines with their electromagnetic bead rifles, long-range grenade launchers, and plasma rifles, that propellant had been a laughable antique. Something dating back to the days when humans were still using steam to make electricity. But that same propellant was far, far out of reach of the Mardukans' tech base, so Dell Mir and the Marines had accepted that black powder was the only effective choice for a propellant.

Black powder, however, had its own peculiar quirks. One, which was painfully evident whenever someone squeezed a trigger, was the dense cloud of particularly foul-smelling smoke it emitted. Another was the truly amazing ability of black powder to foul a weapon with caked residue, and that residue's resistance to most of the Marines's cleaning solvents. Old-fashioned soap and water actually worked best, but the Bronze Barbarians' sensibilities were offended when they found themselves up to their elbows in hot, soapy water scrubbing away at their weapons with brushes and plenty of elbow grease.

But the biggest functional difference between black powder-loaded rounds and the ones Roger had brought out from Old Earth with him was that black powder exploded. More modern propellants *burned*—very rapidly, to be sure, but in what was a much more gradual process, relatively speaking, than black powder's . . . enthusiastic detonation. While nitro powders might well produce a higher absolute breech pressure, they did it over a longer period of time. For the *same* breech pressure, black powder "spiked" much more abruptly, which imposed a resultant strain on the breech and barrel of the weapon.

Not to mention a particularly nasty and heavy recoil.

Fortunately, the old axiom about getting what you paid for still held true, and the Parkins and Spencer was a very expensive weapon, indeed. Part of what Roger had gotten for its astronomical purchase price was a weapon which was virtually indestructible, which was a not insignificant consideration out in the bush where he tended to do most of his hunting. Another part, however, was the basic ammunition design itself. The Parkins' designers had assumed that situations might arise in which the owner of one of their weapons would find himself cut off from his normal sources of supply and be forced to adopt field expedients (if not quite so primitive as those which had been enforced upon the Marines here on Marduk) to reload their ammo. So the cases themselves had been designed to contain pressures which would have blown the breech right out of most prespace human firearms. And they had sufficient internal capacity for black-powder loads of near shoulder-breaking power.

In fact, the power and muzzle velocity of the reloaded rounds, while still far short of what Roger's off-world ammunition would have produced with its initial propellant, had been sufficient to create yet another problem.

The rounds Roger had started out with had jacketed bullets—old-fashioned lead, covered in a thin metal "cladding" that intentionally left the slug's lead tip exposed. On impact, the soft lead core mushroomed to more than half-again its original size and the cladding stripped back into a six-pronged, expanding slug. The main reason the cladding was necessary, however, was because the velocity of the round would have "melted" a plain lead bullet on its way up the barrel, coating the barrel and rifling in lead. Modern chemical-powered small arms ammunition was manufactured using techniques which were a direct linear descendent of technology which had been available since time immemorial: copper or some other alloy was added to the outside of lead bullets by a form of electroplating. But Mardukans didn't *have* electroplating, and it was a technology there'd been no time to "reinvent," so the humans had been forced to make do.

There'd been three potential ways to solve the problem.

The first had been to reduce the velocity of the rounds to a point where they wouldn't lead the barrel, but that would have resulted in a reduction in both range and accuracy. The second choice had been to try to develop a stronger alloy to replace the lead, but since that wasn't something the Mardukans had ever experimented with, it would once again have required "reinventing" a technology. Finally, they'd settled on the third option: casting thin copper jackets for the rounds and then compressing the lead into them. There was an issue with contraction of the copper, but the compression injection—another technique garnered from pump technology—took care of that.

So the rounds were copper jacketed—"full-metal jacketed," as it was called. They weren't quite as "perfect" as Roger's original ammunition, of course. Every so often one of the bullets was unbalanced, and would go drifting off on its own course after departing the muzzle. But however imperfect they might have been by Imperial standards, they were orders of magnitude better than anything the Mardukans had ever had.

Now Roger cycled the bolt and popped up the ladder sight. The sight—a simple, flip-up frame supporting an elevating aperture rear sight and graduated for "click" range adjustment using a thumbwheel—was necessary for any accurate really long-range work. Elevating the rear sight forced the marksman to elevate the front sight, as well, in order to line them up, thus compensating for the projectile drop. It was another contraption the humans and Mardukans had sweated over, but once the design was perfected (and matched to the rounds' actual ballistic performance), the Mardukans had had no problem producing it.

But the sights weren't exactly a one-size-fits-all proposition, because everyone shot slightly differently, if only because everyone was at least slightly different in size, and thus "fitted" their weapons differently. As a result, the sights of any given rifle were "zeroed" for the individual to whom it belonged, which meant this rifle was zeroed for Julian, not Roger. Given that the range was about two hundred meters, the bullet could actually miss by up to a meter even if Roger's aim was perfect according to Julian's sight. But there was only one way to find out how bad it really was, so Roger calculated the wind, let out a breath, and squeezed the trigger.

The recoil was enough to make even him grunt, but he'd expected that, and he gazed intently downrange. Although the rounds were comparatively slow, they weren't so slow that he could actually watch them in flight. But the surface of the ocean swell was sufficiently smooth for the brief splash—to the left, and over by about half a meter—to be clearly visible.

"Told you it was the sight," Julian said with a slight snicker.

"Bet you a *civan* he makes the next one," Despreaux countered.

"As long as you're referring to the coin and not the animal, you're on," Julian replied. "Crosswind, rolling ship, bobbing barrel, and an unzeroed rifle. Two hundred meters. No damned way."

"You make a habit of underestimating the prince," Cord observed. Roger's *asi* had been standing behind Roger, leaning on his huge, lethal spear while he silently watched the children play with their newfangled toys. "You don't tend to underestimate enemies twice, I've noticed," the shaman continued, "which is good. But why is it that you persist in doing so where 'friendlies' are concerned?"

Julian glanced up at the towering native—the representative of what was little better than a hunter-gatherer society, who was undoubtedly the best-read and probably best educated Mardukan in the entire expedition. As always, his *facial* expression was almost nonexistent, but his amusement showed clearly in his body language, and Julian stuck out his tongue at him.

"That was my zero shot," Roger announced, ignoring the exchange between the Marine armorer and his *asi*. Then he put the rifle back to shoulder and punched out another round.

This time, the barrel was smashed.

Julian gazed at the bobbing wreckage for a moment, then reached into his pocket and pulled out a thin sheet of brass, which he handed over to Despreaux.

"I give."

Despreaux smiled and pocketed the brass, a K'Vaernian coin equal to a week's pay for a rifleman.

"It was a sucker bet, Adib. Have you *ever* won a shooting contest with Roger?"

"No," Julian admitted as Roger hefted the rifle once again. There were four more barrels scattered across the surface of the ocean, each floating amid its own cluster of white splashes as the Marines lining the schooner's side potted at them.

Roger lined up a shot at the most distant barrel, then shook his head when the round plunked into the sea well short.

"I'll admit that the scope does help," he confessed as he chambered another round. He brought the rifle back into firing position, but before he could squeeze the trigger, a shot rang out from the foredeck. Three more followed in rapid succession, and each bullet struck and shattered a barrel in turn.

Roger lowered Julian's rifle and looked forward as Captain Pahner lowered his own rifle and blew the gunsmoke out of the breech.

"I guess the captain wanted me to be sure who was king," the prince said with a smile.

"Well, Your Highness," Julian told him with a shrug, "when you've been doing this for fifty more years, you *might* be at the captain's level."

"Agreed, Julian," Roger said, leaning on the bronze carronade beside him. "I wonder if we'd have survived to this point with any old Bronze Battalion commander along. Captain Grades seemed—I don't know, 'okay.' But not at Pahner's level. Or am I wrong?"

"You're not," Despreaux said. "Pahner was a shoo-in for Gold Battalion. Hanging out at each level on the way there was just a formality."

"I thought he was going back to Fleet." Roger frowned.

"So did he," the sergeant replied. "I doubt it would've

happened, though. Somebody was going to tell him to go on to Steel, and then to Silver. Most of the officers in those battalions didn't 'choose' to be there, you know."

"This is weird." Roger shook his head. "I thought the Regiment was voluntary."

"Oh, it is," Despreaux told him with a wink. " 'Captain Pahner, you just volunteered to take Alpha Steel. Congratulations on your new command.' "

"So does *Pahner* know this?"

"Probably not," Julian said. "Or, if he does, he's trying to ignore it. Even with rejuv, he's getting a bit long in the tooth to be a line commander. And he doesn't want to go higher. So he wants one last Fleet command before he retires. For him, Steel or even Gold would be a consolation prize."

Roger nodded with an understanding he could never have attained before marching halfway around the circumference of Hell with Pahner at his side. Then he chuckled softly.

"You know, when we get back Mother is going to owe me one huge favor. I'd thought about asking for a planetary dukedom as an alternative to hanging out at Imperial City, but maybe there's something else I should throw into the pot with it. Seems to me that if the captain wants a Fleet command, a 'friend at court' couldn't hurt his chances!"

"I'd guess not," Julian agreed with a grin, then cocked his head at the prince. "I'm glad to hear you're thinking beyond the end of the journey, Your Highness. But why a dukedom?"

"Because I want to be something more than the black sheep," Roger said with a much thinner smile. "Of course, you haven't asked me which planet I want."

"Oh, no!" Despreaux shook her head. "You've got to be joking!"

"Marduk has all of the requirements for a successful and productive Imperial Membership planet," Roger replied. "The fact that it's held directly in the Family's name would make it a lot simpler for Mother to designate it as such, and the Mardukans are fine people.

They *deserve* a better life than that of medieval peons. And if one Roger Ramius Sergei Alexander Chiang MacClintock shepherds them from barbarism to civilization over five or ten decades, then that prince is going to be remembered for something more than being an unfortunate by-blow of the Empress."

"But . . ." Despreaux stopped and looked around at the ocean. "You want to raise *kids* on this planet? *Our* children?"

"Right, well, I'll just be going," Julian said as he stepped back. "Remember, no hitting, Nimashet. And no removing any limbs or vital organs."

"Oh, shut up, Adib," the sergeant said sharply. "And you don't have to leave. It's not like Roger's plans are any huge secret."

"Our plans," the prince corrected mildly. "And, yes, I think this would make a fine dukedom. Among other things, it would get you away from Imperial City's biddies—male and female, alike. I don't think they'll be able to handle having me marry one of my bodyguards as opposed to, say, one of their own well-trained, highly-qualified, and exquisitely-bred daughters. None of whom would have lasted ten minutes on Marduk. Princess of the Empire or not, some of those dragons will make your life Hell, given half a chance, and to be perfectly honest, neither you nor I really have the skills to respond in an appropriate—and nonlethal—fashion." He flashed her a wicked smile.

"And if you think I'm going to set up shop at K'Vaern's Cove or Q'Nkok, you're crazy," he went on. "I was thinking of the Ran Tai valley, frankly."

"Hmmm." Despreaux's expression was suddenly much more thoughtful. The valley was four thousand meters above the steamy Mardukan lowlands, and actually got chilly at night. It wasn't subject to the continuous rain of the jungles, either. All in all, it was a rather idyllic spot for humans. Which meant it was hell for Mardukans, of course.

" 'Hmmm,' indeed," Julian said. "But you're assuming the Empress doesn't have some other task perfectly suited to you. She probably has a half dozen things she would've liked to throw your way if she'd trusted you before we left. Frankly, letting you 'languish in a backwater' is probably going to be at the bottom of her list."

"I may not give Mother the choice," Roger said darkly. "Frankly, I don't give a damn about Mother's needs at this point. My days of caring what Mother thinks ended in Marshad."

"She's your Empress, just as she is mine, Roger," Despreaux said. "And it's your Empire, just as it is mine. And our children's."

"One of these days, I will stop having to say this . . ." Cord began with a gesture that was the Mardukan equivalent of a resigned sigh.

"I know, I know," Roger answered. " 'I was born to duty.' I got it the first time."

"And it's a big cruel universe out there, Your Highness," Julian said with unwonted seriousness. "If you think the Boman and Kranolta were bad, you need to pay a little more attention to the Saints. There's not much worse than a 'civilized' society that considers human beings expendable. 'One death is a tragedy, a million is a statistic.' They *live* that philosophy. Also, 'The only problem with biospheres is that they occasionally develop sophonts.' I mean, these people aren't just into human extinction; they want to get rid of the Phaenurs and the Mardukans and the Althari, too. *All* sophonts. Except, of course, the best of the 'enlightened' Saint leadership, who—unlike any other enviro-destructive tool-using species—are capable of 'handling' the management of planets. Amazing how they think our pissant population growth rate is so bad when their Archon has six kids and nearly fifty grandkids."

"Okay, okay," Roger said. "I get the point. If Mother has something worthwhile she wants me to do, I'll do it. Okay?"

"Okay," Despreaux agreed. "Of course, that assumes we live to get off this mudball. But so far nothing's been able to stop our Rog," she added with a smile.

"Sail ho!" the Mardukan at the fore topmast crosstrees

called suddenly. "Sail on the starboard bow, fine!" After a moment he leaned down and shouted again. "Looks like some more behind it!"

"And where there are sails, there are cities and trade," Julian observed.

"And where there's trade, there are pirates," Despreaux added. "And multiple sails means either a convoy, or . . ."

"Pirates," Roger said. The platform at the foremast crosstrees was crowded with four humans, D'Nal Cord, and Captain T'Sool. Fortunately, the Mardukan lookout had remained at his post at the fore topmast crosstrees, twelve meters above them. His greater height above sea level gave him a marginally better view, but the humans could see the oncoming sails themselves, and everyone who could had climbed the ratlines for a better look.

"Why pirates?" Pahner asked.

"The ship in the lead is carrying too much canvas for conditions," the prince replied. "They're running with the wind, but the breeze has been steadily increasing all afternoon. Between seeing another ship coming towards them— and I assume they've spotted us—and the increasing breeze, not to mention the way it's clouding up for a storm, she should have reduced sail by now. And she hasn't. So whatever she's sailing away from is more dangerous than risking a cracked mast or even capsizing."

The Marine glanced speculatively at the prince. Roger was still gazing out at the approaching ships, but he seemed to feel the weight of Pahner's eyes, and turned to meet them.

"So what's our call?" he asked the captain.

Pahner returned his own attention to the unknown ships and dialed the magnification back up on his helmet systems as he pondered that. The safe bet was simply to avoid the entire situation. There was no upside to an engagement . . . except that they had almost no information about the continent towards which they were traveling.

If Roger's analysis was correct, and if they were able to make contact with the ship being pursued, it might be to their benefit. There appeared to be six of the—probable—pirate ships. Each was similar to an ancient cog, but with a pair of masts, not just one. Each mast carried only a single square sail, however, and their deep, rounded, high-sided hulls had clumsy-looking, castlelike foredeck citadels which undoubtedly mounted some of Marduk's massive, unwieldy bombards. They were scarcely the sleekest ships he'd ever seen, and he wondered why pirates, if that was what they were, didn't have ships a tad faster.

"What's an alternative to pirates?" he asked.

"Is this a trick question, Captain?" Kosutic inquired.

"I don't think so," Roger said. "I think his point is that if they *are* pirates, all well and good. If we blow the crap out of them, we establish our bona fides with the local powers that be. But if they're not pirates, announcing our intentions with a broadside might be a Very Bad Idea. We have to make peaceful and, hopefully, smooth contact with the local government. So what if they're harmless merchant ships which are supposed to be sailing in company, and the lead ship just has a lousy captain who's gotten too far ahead of the rest? In that case, blowing them away without a warning would *not* be a good way to make 'smooth' contact."

"Exactly," Pahner said. "So what are the other possibilities?"

"The boat in the lead could be a smuggler," Kosutic suggested. "Or something along those lines. And the ones behind could be revenue cutters. Well, revenue boats. Revenue tubs."

"And it could be even more complex than that," Roger pointed out. "They could be operating under letters of marque or some equivalent. So the ones in back could be both pirates *and* representatives of a government we need to contact. And if that's the case, asking the lead ship won't tell us so."

"All right," Pahner said with a nod. "We'll tack to intercept the group. We will not fire until fired upon. Get a helmet system for Ms. O'Casey so she can use the amplifiers for communication. We'll move alongside or send off a boarding party to make contact. If we take fire from either group, we'll respond with a single broadside. That should make the situation clear. If they continue to press it, we sink 'em."

"And if they *are* 'official' pirates?" Roger asked.

"We'll deal with that as we have to," Pahner answered. "We need intel on this continent . . . but we also need to live to use it."

CHAPTER SEVEN

ʼ Tob Kerr, master of the merchant vessel *Rain Daughter*, closed the glass and cursed. He wasn't sure where the strange ships had come from—there wasn't anything on that bearing but the Surom Shoals, and nobody actually lived in these demon-infested waters—but they were headed right for him. And sailing at least forty degrees closer to the wind than any tack he could take. He not only didn't recognize the origin of the ships, he couldn't even begin to identify their design, or imagine how sails like that could work.

However they did it, though, they obviously did a better job than his own ship could manage, and he wondered where they could possibly have sprung from.

The Lemmar Raiders behind him, on the other hand, were all too well known a quantity. With luck, they would only take his cargo. More likely, though, they would sell him and the crew into slavery, and sell his ship for a prize. Either way, he was ruined. So the best bet was to continue on course and hope for a gift from the Sar, because this was clearly a case of worse the devil you knew than the devil you didn't.

He looked back at the oncoming strangers. The more he studied them, the odder they looked. They were low, rakish, and almost unbelievably fast, and they carried an

enormous sail area—one far larger than anything Kerr had
ever seen before. It was amazing that they could sail the
deep ocean at all; with so little freeboard, he had to
wonder why the water didn't wash right over their decks.
But it didn't. In fact, they rode the swells like *embera*,
green foam casting up from their bows and their strange,
triangular sails hard as boards as they sliced impossibly
into the oncoming wind.

He grabbed a line and slid to the deck. The calluses
of decades at sea made nothing of the friction, and his
mate, Pelu Mupp walked over to him and flipped his
false-hands in an expression of worry.

"Should we change course?" he asked.

It was a damnably reasonable question, Kerr thought
grimly. The Lemmar Raiders had been in a fairly unfavor-
able position at the start. Well, as far as *Rain Daughter* was
concerned. Certain other ships had been less fortunate, but
Kerr had taken full advantage of the slim opportunity for
escape the pirates' preoccupation with the convoy's other
members had offered him. By the time they'd been free to
turn their full attention to *Rain Daughter*, Kerr had managed
to put enough distance between them to give him and his
crew a better than even chance. A stern chase was always
a long one, and under those conditions, victory could go
to either side. The pirate ships were a bit faster than the
merchantman, but the *Daughter* had a good lead, and any
number of circumstances could have resulted in the Kirstian
ship's escaping, especially if Kerr could only have kept clear
of the Lemmar until darkness fell. But now, with the
unknowns closing from almost dead to leeward, the trap
seemed to have closed.

"No," Kerr said. "We'll hold our course. They *might*
be friendly. And how much worse than the Raiders could
they be?"

If the crew went into slavery, they would probably end
up back in Kirsti, but as "guests" of the Fire Priests.
And if that was the alternative, he preferred to throw
himself over the side now.

"We'll hold our course, Mupp. And let the Lady of the
Waters decide."

✧   ✧   ✧

Roger pulled on a strand of hair and sighed.

"Captain, much as I hate making suggestions—" he began, only to stop dead as Pahner let loose an uncharacteristic bark of laughter that momentarily made him jump. Then the captain snorted.

"Yes, Your Highness?"

"Well, I *don't*," Roger retorted.

"I know you don't, Your Highness," Pahner said with a smile. "You tend to do something by yourself, and then ask me if it was okay later. That's different from making suggestions, I'll admit. So let's have it—what's the suggestion?

"I was thinking about wind position," Roger continued, after deciding that it wasn't a good time for a discussion of whether one Prince Roger MacClintock had been making too many stupid mistakes lately. Most of the watchers had returned to the deck once the general outline of the approaching ships and their formation had been established. A Marine private was now perched at the fore topmast crosstrees beside the Mardukan lookout, using her helmet systems to refine the data. But at this point it was a matter of waiting nearly two hours as the ships slowly closed the intervening gap.

"They're coming in on our starboard bow, straight out of the wind, but the formation of six ships is spread to our west, and it takes a few minutes for us to wear around. If we stay on this course, when the pursuers come up to us, the most westerly ship will be in a position that would make it hard for us to completely avoid her."

"I'm . . . not quite getting this," Pahner admitted.

Roger thought for a moment, then did a quick sketch on his toot, detailing the human/K'Vaernian flotilla, the lead unknown, and the trailers.

"I'm sliding over a graphic," he said, flipping the sketch from his toot to the Marine's. "From the point of view of avoiding contact, we can break off from the lead ship easily. But if we decided to avoid the trailers, we'd have three choices. One would be to tack to starboard when

we come up to them. That would put us in a position
to take full advantage of the schooners' weatherliness to
run past them into the wind and avoid contact handily. But it takes a bit of time to tack, and there's a small
risk of getting caught in irons."

Pahner nodded at that. A couple of times, especially
early in the voyage, when the native Mardukan captains
were still getting accustomed to the new rig, one or more
of the ships had been caught "in irons" while tacking,
and ended up facing directly into the wind, effectively
unable to move or maneuver until they could fall off
enough to regather way. It was not a situation he wanted
to be in with potential hostiles around.

"We don't want that to happen," he observed. "Go
on."

"Our second choice would be to fall off to the west,"
Roger said, "opening out our sails and either sailing
across the wind, or coming around to let it fill our sails
from behind while we run almost away from it. That's
a 'reach' or a 'broad reach.' The problem is, on either
tack, the westernmost ship would have at least some
opportunity to intercept us. We could probably show them
our heels—I'd back any of ours, even *Snarleyow*, to
outrun anything they've got. But there's a risk of inter-
ception."

"In which case, we blow away whatever unfortunate
soul intercepts us," Pahner noted as he brought up the
sketch on his implant and studied it.

"Yes, Captain, we can do that," Roger agreed, licking
a salty drop of sweat off his upper lip. "But I submit
that it would be better to be in a position where we
can avoid contact altogether, if that's what we decide to
do. Or control the maneuver menu if we decide to
engage."

"Can we?" the captain asked. "And should we be discussing this with Poertena or the Skipper?"

"Maybe," Roger said. "Probably. But I was thinking.
If we tack to starboard and put them on our port side,
we've got all that maneuver room to starboard. It's a
better wind position. Also, if we decide to jump in, we

can get to windward for maneuvering better from that position. But we need to wait a bit, until we're a little closer."

"I'll talk it over with T'Sool," Pahner agreed. "But unless I'm much mistaken, that's a very good idea."

"They're wearing around," Pelu said.

"I can see that," Kerr answered. He rubbed his horns as he considered the small fleet's maneuvers. Its units were changing to an easterly heading on the port tack, and the maneuver was a thing of beauty for any seaman to watch. The sails seemed to float into position naturally, and in a remarkably short period of time, all five ships were hove over and flying before the wind.

"They're in a better position to drop on us from windward," Pelu worried. "Could they be some new ship type out of Lemmar?"

"If Lemmar could build ships like that," the captain snorted, "we'd already be in chains in Kirsti! And if they're in a better position to drop on us, they're also in a better position to *avoid* all of us. They can leave us in their wake any time they want to now, but before, they could have been cut off by the western Reavers. Actually, I think what they're doing now is a better sign."

"I wish we knew who they were," Pelu fretted.

"I wonder if they're wishing the same thing?"

"Ready for some more unsolicited input?" Roger asked with a grin.

"Certainly, Your Highness," Pahner replied with a slight smile. "Every fiber of my being lives to serve the Empire."

"Somehow, I think I detected just a tad of sarcasm attached to that answer," Roger said with an answering grin. "But I digress. What I was going to say is that we need to make contact with these folks."

"Agreed. And you have a suggestion?"

"Well, for first contact, we'll need someone who's well versed with the translator program and whose toot has enough capacity to run it. And that means either Ms.

O'Casey or myself. And since it's a potentially dangerous situation . . ."

"You think it makes more sense to send the person
I'm supposed to be guarding," Pahner finished. Then he
shook his head. Firmly. "No."

"So you're going to send Eleanora?" Roger asked
sweetly.

"Quit smiling at me!" Pahner snapped. "Damn it. I'm
the commander of your bodyguard, Your Highness. I'm
not supposed to be sending you into situations because
they're too *dangerous* to send somebody else!"

"Uh-huh," Roger said. "So, you're sending Eleanora?"

"There is no way you're going over to that ship,"
Pahner said. "No. Way."

"I see. So . . . ?"

"Ah, freedom!"

Roger leaned back in the sailing harness, suspended
from a very thin bit of rope less than an arm length
above the emerald sea as the catamaran cut through the
water at nearly sixteen knots. D'Nal Cord shifted and
tried to get into something that felt like a stable
position—difficult for someone his size on the deck of
the flimsy craft—and rubbed a horn in exasperation.

"You have an unusual concept of freedom, Roger."

Most of the small boats of the flotilla were traditional
"v" hulls, but both Roger and Poertena had insisted on
at least one small "cat" for fast movement. Building it
had required nearly as much human-provided engineering knowledge as the much larger schooners—light, fast
catamarans require precise flexion in their crossbraces—
but the result was a small craft that in any sort of decent
weather was even faster than the schooners.

And it was *fun* to sail.

"I have to admit that this is sort of fun," Despreaux
said, fanning her uniform top. "And the breeze is
refreshing."

"Back on Earth, catting and skiing were as close as
I ever got to being free," Roger pointed out, bounding
forward in the harness to see if it improved the point

of sail. "You guys would actually let me get away for a little bit."

"Don't complain," Kosutic replied. "Your lady mother's spent most of her life wrapped in cotton. As your grandfather's only child, there was no way the Regiment was willing to risk her at all. She rarely even got to leave the palace grounds."

"Frankly, I could care less about Mother's problems," Roger said coldly, swinging back in his harness as Poertena altered the cat's course slightly.

"Maybe not," the sergeant major replied. "But you've had more experience with 'real people' in the last six months than she has in her whole life. The closest she ever got to dealing with anyone but Imperial functionaries and politicians was the Academy. And even there, she spent the whole time still wrapped in cotton. They wouldn't even *consider* having her do live zero-G drills— not out of atmosphere, at least. It all had to be in simulators, where there was *no* possibility of exposing her to death pressure. And if they never let her do that, you can just imagine how much less likely they were to let her do things like, oh—just as an example that comes from the top of my head, you understand—leading a charge into a barbarian horde. And no cut-ups like Julian were allowed within a kilometer of her."

"And your point is?" Roger asked. He leaned further outward and dangled his hand into the water as a slightly stronger puff of wind hit the sail. "Speaking of risks, you do realize that if there are any of those giant *coll* around, we're toast?"

"That sort of *is* the point," Kosutic said soberly. "Imperial City is filled with professional politicians and noble flunkies, most of whom have never had to scramble for money to supply a unit in the field. Who've never been exposed to 'lower class' conditions. Who have never slept on the ground, never gone to bed hungry. In some cases, that means people who not only don't understand the majority of the population of the Empire, but who also don't like them or care about them. And in other cases—which I happen to think are worse—they don't understand them, but they *idealize* them. They think there's a special dignity to poverty. Or a special quality to being born into misery and dying in it."

"Saint Symps," Despreaux said.

"And various soclibs," Kosutic agreed. "Especially the older style pro-Ardane redistributionists."

"There's at least an argument there," Roger said. "I mean, too much concentration of power, and you're not much better off than under the Dagger Lords." He paused and grinned. "On the other hand, I *know* you're all a bunch of low-lifes!"

"And if you live entirely by what you think is 'the will of the people,' you get the Solar Union," Kosutic continued, pointedly ignoring the prince's last comment.

"Pockers," Poertena growled, and spat over the side.

"Yeah, Armagh mostly sat that one out," the sergeant major admitted. "But Pinopa got it bad."

"What really burned some of the early members of the Family was that the ISU used Roger MacClintock's policies as their 'model' for that idiocy," Roger said. "Prez Roger, that is. Roger the Unifier. But without accepting the societal sacrifices that were necessary. And then, when it all came apart, they tried to blame *us!*"

"I could kind of understand getting involved in planetary reconstruction," Despreaux commented. "Some of those planets were even worse off than Armagh. But leaving your main base completely uncovered was just idiotic."

"And why did they do that?" Kosutic asked, and proceeded to answer her own question. "They had to. They were already so wrapped up with social welfare programs that they couldn't build the sort of fleet and garrison force they needed and still be redistributionist. So they depended on bluff, sent the entire damned fleet off to try to do some planet-building, and the Daggers nipped in and ate the Solar System's lunch."

"The Daggers were very good at killing the golden goose," Roger said. "But we—the MacClintocks, that is—learned that lesson pretty well."

"Did we?" Kosutic asked. "Did we really?"

"Oh, no," Roger moaned. "This isn't another one of those 'let's not tell Roger,' things, is it?"

"No." The sergeant major laughed, but her eyes were on the native ship they'd come to meet, and her gaze was wary as Poertena wore around its stern, preparing to come alongside to port. "But take a good look at your grandfather's career," she continued, "and then tell me we've learned. Another person who'd never worked a day in his life and thought the lower classes were somehow magical. And, therefore, that they should be coddled, paid, and overprotected . . . at the expense of the Fleet and the Saint borders."

"Well, that's one mistake *I* would never make as Emperor," Roger joked as Poertena completed his maneuver. "I know you're all a bunch of lying, lazy pockers."

"Be about time to hail," Poertena said. The ship and the catamaran were about a hundred meters apart now, on near parallel headings, with the cat slightly to the rear of the much larger merchant ship. Since that put the wind at their stern, Poertena had brought the sail in until it was luffing and dangerously close to jibing, or falling over to the other side of the boat. It might make them a little anxious about collisons between things like heads and booms, but it also slowed them down enough that they wouldn't pass the slower Mardukan ship.

"Get us a little closer," Roger ordered as he unclipped the harness and secured it to the mast. "I need to be able to hear their reply. And I don't see any guns."

"Odd, that," Kosutic said. "I agree we need to get closer, but if those are pirates, or even letters of marque, chasing them, you'd think they would have defenses. And I don't even see a swivel gun."

"Something else to ask about," Roger said as Poertena fell off to starboard. The change quickly filled the sail, set as it was for a reach, and the cat began skipping across the rolling swell.

"Shit!" Despreaux flattened herself and tried to figure out where to move as it suddenly seemed obvious that the cat was about to go clear over on its side.

"*Hooowah!*" the prince said with a laugh, throwing his weight back outboard again to offset the heel. "Don't dunk us, for God's sake, Poertena! We're trying to show our good side."

"And *I* cannot swim," Cord added.

"Lifejackets!" Roger laughed. "I knew we forgot something!"

"T'is close enough?" Poertena asked as he brought the boat back to port with a degree more caution. They had closed to within sixty meters or so, and the Mardukan ship's crew was clearly evident, lining the side, many of them with weapons in their hands.

"Close enough," Roger agreed, then stood back up and grasped a line to stay steady. "Try not to flop us around too much."

"What? And have you get all wet and sloppy?" Despreaux said.

"Hea'en forbid!" Poertena laughed. "I try. Never know, though."

"You'd better," Kosutic growled. "Straight and steady."

"Just keep us on this heading," Kerr said to the helmsman. "They don't seem to be threatening us. And I don't see what they'd be able to do with that dinky little boat, anyway."

"Who are they?" Pelu asked.

"How the hell do I know?" Kerr shot back in exasperation. "They look like giant *vern*, but that's crazy."

"What do we do if they want to come aboard?"

"We let them," Kerr answered after a moment. "Their ships can run rings around us, and I think those ports showing on the sides are for bombards. If they are, there's not much we can do but heave to and do whatever they say."

"It's not like you just to give up," Pelu protested.

"They're not Lemmar, and they're not Fire Priests," Kerr pointed out. "Given the choice of them, or the Lemmar and the priests, I'll always take the unknown."

✧   ✧   ✧

"Here goes nothing," Roger said.

"What language are you going to use?" Despreaux asked.

"The kernel that came with the program. It's probably taken from the tribes around the starport, and we're finally getting close to that continent. Hopefully it will at least be familiar to them for a change." He cleared his throat.

"Hullo the ship!"

"Oh, Cran," Pelu said.

"High Krath," Kerr muttered. "Why did it have to be High Krath?"

"Are they Fire Priests?" the helmsman asked nervously. "It can't be Fire Priests clear out here, can it?"

"It could be," Kerr admitted heavily. "Those could be Guard vessels."

"I never heard of the Guard having ships like that any more than the Lemmar," Pelu said. "Anyway, they would've used Krath, not High Krath. Most Guard *officers* can't speak High Krath."

"But they're not priests!" Kerr snarled, rubbing his horns furiously. "So where did they learn High Krath?"

"No response," Despreaux said. The unnecessary comment made it evident just how nervous the veteran NCO was.

"They're talking it over, though," Roger said. "I think the two by the helmsman are the leaders."

"Concur," the sergeant major agreed. "But they aren't acting real happy to see us."

"Oh, well," Roger sighed. "Time to up the ante. *Permission to come aboard?*"

"Well, at least they're asking," Pelu observed. "That's something."

"That's odd, is what it is," Kerr answered. He stepped to the rail and took a glance at the more distant ships. They had crossed his course almost a glass before, and then swung back to the west. At this point, they were still to his east and the range from them to *Rain Daughter* would have been opening as she ran past them on her southeasterly heading . . . except for how close they were to the wind. As it was, their nearest approach was still to come. But it didn't seem that they intended any harm. Either that, or they were jockeying for a good wind position.

"What do we do?"

"Let them board," Kerr said. His curiosity was getting the better of his good sense, and he knew it. But he didn't suppose, realistically speaking, that he had very many options, anyway. "One, I want to know who they are. Two, if we've got part of their crew on board, they're less likely to attack us."

He walked over to the rail and waved both true-hands. *"Come aboard!"*

Roger caught the dangling line and swarmed up it. Technically, he should have let either Kosutic or Despreaux go first, and he could hear the sergeant major's curses even through the sound of rigging and water. But of the three of them, he was the most familiar with small boats, and he felt that even if it was a deliberate trap, he could probably shoot his way clear of the four-person welcoming party.

The scummies waiting for him were subtly different from those on the far continent. They were definitely shorter than the Vashin Northerners who made up the bulk of the cavalry, closer to the Diasprans in height. Their horns were also significantly different, with less of a curve and with less prominent age ridges. Part of that might have been cosmetic, though, because at least one of them had horns which had clearly been dyed. They were also wearing clothes, which, except for armor, had been a catch-as-catch-can item on the far continent. The "clothing" was a sort of leather kilt, evidently with a loincloth underneath. Otherwise (unless they were *very* unlike any of the other Mardukans the humans had met), certain "parts" would be showing under the kilt. The two leaders also wore baldrics which supported not only swords, but also a few other tools, and even what were apparently writing implements.

The leader of the foursome, the one who had waved for them to board, stepped forward. His horns were undyed and long, indicating a fairly good age for a Mardukan. He wasn't as old as Cord, though, or if he was, he was in better condition, because his skin was firm and well coated in slime, without the occasional dry spots that indicated advanced age in the locals.

Roger raised both hands in a gesture of peace. It wasn't taking much of a chance; he could still draw and fire before any of the four raised a weapon.

"I am pleased to meet you," he said, speaking slowly and distinctly and using the words available on the kernel that was the only Mardukan language the software had initially offered. "I am Prince Roger MacClintock. I greet you in the name of the Empire of Man."

"*Sadar* Tob Kerr . . . greet," the officer responded.

Roger nodded gravely while he considered what the toot was telling him. The language the local was using was similar to the kernel, but it contained words which were additional to the kernel's five-hundred-word vocabulary, combined with some that were clearly from another language entirely. It appeared that the leader was attempting to use the kernel language, but that it was a second language for him, not primary. The toot was flagging some of the words as probably being totally bogus. The captain—this Tob Kerr—clearly wasn't a linguist.

"Use your own language, rather than the one I'm using," Roger invited as Kosutic followed him over the side. If the others were on plan, Cord would be the next up, then Despreaux. Poertena would remain in the cat. "I will be able to learn it quickly," he continued. "But I must ask questions, if I may. What is the nature of your position, and who are the ships that pursue you?"

"We are a . . . from the Krath to the . . . base at Strem. Our . . . was . . . by Lemmar Raiders. The Guard ships were destroyed, and we are the only ship who has made it this far. But the Lemmar are . . . I do not think we'll . . . Strem, even if we can . . ."

Great, Roger thought. *What the hell is Krath?* Then he realized that the answer was lodged in the back of his brain.

"Krath is the mainland ahead?" he asked. The toot automatically took the words it had already learned from the language the captain was using where it had them, and substituted kernel words where it didn't. The sentence was marginally understandable.

"Yes," the officer replied. "The Krath are the . . . of the Valley. Strem is a recent acquisition. The . . . is attempting to subdue the Lemmar Raiders, but taking Strem means they have to supply it. We were carrying supplies and ritual . . . for the garrison. But the Lemmar came upon us in force and took our escorts. Since then, these six have been running down the survivors. I believe we are the last."

"Oh bloody hell," Roger muttered. "Are the rest between us and the mainland?"

"Yes," the local told him. "If you're making for Kirsti, then they are on your path. They're just below the horizon from the mast."

"Great. Just . . . great," Roger muttered again, then shook himself. "Tob Kerr, meet Sergeant Major Eva Kosutic, my senior noncommissioned officer." Cord dropped to the deck, and Roger rested his left hand lightly on the shaman's lower shoulder. "And this is D'Nal Cord, my *asi*." He had to hope that the translation software could explain what an *asi* was.

"I greet you, as well," Kerr said, then returned his attention to Roger and spoke earnestly. "Your ships can wear around and make sail for Strem. It's less than a day's sail from here, and you would surely make it. Those fine craft of yours are the fastest I've ever seen. But I cannot guarantee the garrison's greeting when you arrive there—this convoy was important to them."

"Are you getting this, Sergeant Major?" Roger asked, shutting off the translation circuit and slipping into Imperial.

"Yes, Your Highness," the NCO replied. Roger's toot had automatically updated her onboard software with its translations of the local language. As soon as he got back into proximity with the rest of the party, the updates would be transferred to them, as well, skipping from system to system. The Marine toots were well insulated against electronic attack, and while the greater capacity and power of Roger's toot made him the logical person to do the initial translation, his much more paranoid design required a manual transfer, rather than the automatic network of the Marines.

"I'm still not sure of *what* the Lemmar are," the prince continued. "But if this fellow is telling the truth, they're enemies of the continental forces. And there are apparently a stack of prize ships, with some crew to fight, between us and the continent. Again, if this guy is telling the truth."

"Pardon me," Kerr interrupted, "but I'd like to ask a question of my own, if I may. Who *are* you, and where did you come from?"

"We came across the Eastern Ocean." Roger trotted out the set response. "We are the first group we know of to actually make it, although others have tried. Our intent is to travel to the larger continent to the north—to Krath—and establish trade routes. But you say there are pirates between here and there?"

"Yes, both the six you see, and the prizes, some of whom are armed," Kerr said. "And as far as I know, you are indeed the first group to make the crossing. A few from our side have also attempted the crossing, including one large group of ships. It was assumed that there were very hostile people on the far side of the ocean. I take it that was wrong?"

"Oh, yeah," Kosutic broke in. "Your problem was very hostile and very large fish *between* here and there. *Coll* fish the size of a ship. We lost one of our vessels to one of them."

"We must make decisions and communicate with the other ships," Cord pointed out. Without a toot, the shaman was unable to understand anything Kerr had said, but, as always, he maintained his pragmatic focus on the matter in hand.

"You're right," Roger agreed. He nodded to his *asi,* then turned back to the merchantman's captain. "Tob Kerr, we must cross back to our own ships and advise them as to the situation. Then we will decide whether to turn for Strem or to go on."

"You cannot go on," Pelu broke in excitedly. "There are six of them—plus the armed prizes!"

Roger snorted, and Cord, standing at his back, sighed at the sound. Not so, the sergeant major.

"And your point is?" Eva Kosutic asked with a snort of her own.

"The Lemmar are an island nation," Roger said, pointing to the chart they had extracted from Tob Kerr. "They live in this volcanic archipelago that stretches down from the continent to this large island to the southeast. South from *that,* there's open ocean which is apparently also infested with killer *coll* fish. Nobody's ever come back to say 'aye or nay,' at any rate. But there's another archipelago to the southwest of it that stretches to the southern continent, and they're in contact with that continent on a fairly tenuous basis. This 'Strem Island' is apparently the crossroads of the trade between them, which makes it a rather rich prize. But while it can produce sufficient food, it also requires additional supply from the mainland. And it was a supply convoy that got hit. They were taking down weapons, new soldiers, and 'temple servitors,' and they would have brought back the goods—mostly spices—that have been stored at Strem awaiting safe transport.

"But the Lemmar changed their plans," Pahner said.

"Yes, Sir," the sergeant major answered. "The Lemmar are pirates, and there have been plenty of times in human history when pirates banded together into fairly large groups. But from what Tob Kerr says, having six of their 'large' ships pounce on the convoy simultaneously was a fairly bad surprise. And the Krath apparently aren't particularly good sailors—or, at least, their Navy is no great shakes. The Lemmar took out the three galleys that were supposed to guard the convoy without any ship losses of their own, then tore into the merchantmen like dire wolves on a flock of sheep. As far as Kerr knows, his ship's the only survivor."

"We have an opportunity here," Roger noted carefully.

"I'm aware of that, Your Highness," Pahner said. "Remember that little talk about going out on a limb, though? This is the classic Chinese sign for chaos: danger and opportunity mixed. Of course there's an opportunity . . . but my job is to pay attention to the danger, as well."

"If we take out the pirates," Roger pointed out, "and recapture most of the ships, the authorities on the continent should automatically treat us as the good guys."

"*Should*," Eleanora O'Casey interjected. "But that depends on the society, and there's no societal data at all in the database where these people are concerned. In fact, there's no societal data for *any* of the locals on this continent. Which, even allowing for the general paucity of data on this godforsaken planet, is a remarkable oversight.

"Without any information at all, it's impossible to say how they might actually react to our intervention. They could resent our showing our military prowess. They could be worried by it. They could even have an honor system under which saving their people would put *us* in *their* debt. There are a thousand possibilities that you haven't explored which could arise from recapturing those ships. And that assumes that, militarily, we can."

"Oh, I think we can," Pahner noted. He knew he was a landlubber, but it would take someone without eyes to miss the clear difference in capabilities between the ships. The pirate vessels were somewhat sleeker than the merchantman, and obviously had much larger crews—a common sign of pirates. But they mounted only a few clumsy swivel guns for broadside armament to back up the single large bombard fixed and pointed forward in their heavy bow "castles." *Sinking* them wouldn't be difficult, not with the flotilla's advantage in artillery. Reducing the crews, and then taking them by a boarding action, wouldn't even have been too costly in casualties, given all the bored Diasprans and Vashin they had on board. But there would be *some* casualties, and the end result had better be worth every one of them.

"Militarily, we can take these six fairly easily," the captain continued. "But we *will* take casualties, especially if we try to take them intact."

"How much are these ships worth?" Fain asked, with a slight clap of his hands that indicated mild humor. "I'm sorry to interrupt, but from the point of view of the people taking the casualties, there are only two things they're going to worry about. Will it prevent us from taking the starport—which is our big mission—and how much money will we get for those ships?"

"Mercenary," Roger said with a smile. "In most societies, ships cost a good bit. I'd say that if we can get them to port, and if the authorities permit us to sell them as a matter of standard prize rules, then there'll be a fair amount to spread around. Even if we take only one. And we may be able to claim most or all of the ships the pirates have already taken as legitimate prizes of war, assuming we manage to retake them, as well. If we can, it would be enough for an officer to retire on."

"Well, I already have that," Fain said. "But not all of the troops were in on the sack of Sindi. As one of the potential casualties, and if we can determine that we can sell them as prizes, my choice is to take the ships."

"T'ey going to slow us down sailing upwind to Krat'," Poertena pointed out. "We migh' be able to rig some jib sails, but t'ey still ain't gonna be as fast as us. Not enough keel, for one t'ing."

"That's something to think about quite a bit down the line," Pahner noted. "Taking these six warships is the significant issue. After that, we contact Kerr again and get his reaction. If it's favorable, we'll determine where to get sufficient prize crews, then sail on our way. If we encounter the rest of the prizes, we'll engage as seems most favorable at the time."

"In other words, we're going to play it by ear," Roger said with a grin. "Where in hell have I heard that operations order before?"

CHAPTER EIGHT

Cred Cies fingered his sword as five of the six ships changed course to windward. The biggest of the strangers held its initial course, heading to intercept—or protect— the fat merchantship *Rage of Lemmar* had pursued so long.

"They're going to engage us," Cra Vunet said. The mate spat over the side. "Six to five. The odds favor us."

Cies looked at the skies and frowned.

"Yes, they do. But no doubt they can count as well as we can, and they've obviously chosen to leave their biggest ship behind. I'm not sure I like the looks of that. Besides, it will be pouring by the time they get here. Only the bombard is sure to fire under those circumstances, and they seem to have nearly as many men aboard as we do. It will be a tough fight."

"And after it, we'll sail back to Lomsvupe with five ships of a new and superior design—six, after we scoop up the one that's hanging back!" the mate said with a true-hand flick of humor. "That will pay for a thousand nights of pleasure! Better than a single stinking landsman tub."

"On the other hand, they clearly think they can take *us*," Cies pointed out, still the pessimist. "And we'll have to wear around to engage, while they'll have the favor of the wind. If I'd been sure they were going to attack before, I would have changed course to attack *them* from upwind, and with our bombard bearing. But I didn't. So, like I say, the fight will be a tough one. Tough."

"We're the Lemmar," Vunet said with another gesture of humor. "A fight is only worth bragging about if it's a tough one!"

"We'll see," Cies replied. "Wear ship to port; let's see if we can't get to windward of them after all before we engage."

"There they go," Roger said, leaning on the anti-*coll* bead cannon mounted on *Ima Hooker*'s afterdeck. "Wearing to port, just like I predicted."

"I don't get it," Pahner admitted. "Even if they manage to get to windward of us, it still leaves them in a position where we can rake their sterns."

"They don't think that way, Captain," Roger said. "They fight with fixed frontal guns, which means they don't have a concept of a broadside. They're expecting us to do what *they'd* do: turn to starboard just before we come opposite them, and try to sail straight into their sides. By that time, if they have the respective speeds figured right, they'll be slightly upwind and in a position to swing down on our flank. The worst that could happen is that we end up with both of us going at each other front-to-front and both broad-on to the wind, which isn't a bad point of sailing for one of those tubs.

"Now, the question is whether or not there's some way we can tap dance around out of range of those bombards while we get into a position to hammer them broadside-to-broadside."

"I thought the idea was to cross the enemy's 'T,'" Julian interjected as he watched the "tubs" wearing around. It was evident that the pirate vessels had extremely large crews for two reasons—both as fighters and because the squaresail ships just plain required more live bodies on the sheets and braces. "That's what they're always talking about in historical romances."

Roger turned towards him and lifted first his helmet visor and then an eyebrow.

"Historical *romances?*" he repeated, and Julian shrugged with a slightly sheepish expression.

"What can I say? I'm a man of many parts."

"I wouldn't have expected romance novels to be one of them," Roger commented, dropping the visor back as he returned his attention to observing the enemy. "But to answer your question, crossing the 'T' is an ideal tactic against an enemy who uses broadsides. But except for some swivel guns to discourage boarders, these guys don't have any broadside fire at all to speak of. Which isn't quite the case where those big, pocking bombards in the bows are concerned. So we're going to try very, very hard *not* to cross their 'T.' "

Pahner was uncomfortable. For the first time since hitting Marduk, it was clear that Roger's expertise, his knowledge, far exceeded the captain's own. On one level, Pahner was delighted that *someone* knew his ass from his elbow where the theory of combat under sail was involved. But "Colonel MacClintock" was still, for all practical purposes, a very junior officer. A surprisingly competent one, since he'd gotten over the normal "lieutenant" idiocy, but still very junior. And junior officers tended to overlook important details in combat operations. Often with disastrous consequences.

"So what plan do you recommend, Your Highness?" the captain asked after a moment.

Roger turned to look at him. The mottled plastic turned the prince's face into an unreadable set of shadows, but it was clear that his mind was running hard.

"I guess you're serious," Roger said quietly. He turned back to gaze at the distant ships and thought about it for perhaps thirty seconds. "Are you saying I should take command?" he asked finally, his voice even quieter than before.

"You're already in command," Pahner pointed out. "I'll be frank, Your Highness. I don't have a clue about how to fight a sea battle. Since you obviously do, you should run this one. If I see anything I think you've overlooked, I'll point it out. But I think this one is . . . up to you."

"Captain," Kosutic asked over the dedicated private command circuit, "are you sure about this?"

"Hold on a moment, Your Highness," Pahner said, turning slightly away from the prince. "Gotta let 'em out of the nest eventually, Sergeant Major," he replied over the same channel.

"Okay. If you're sure," the noncom said dubiously. "But remember Ran Tai."

"I will," Pahner assured her. "I do."

He turned back to the prince, who was pacing back and forth with his hands clasped behind him, looking at the sky.

"I'm sorry, Your Highness. You were saying?"

"Actually, I wasn't." Roger stopped pacing, pulled out a strand of hair, and played with it as he continued to look at the sky. "I was thinking. And I'm about done."

"Are you going to take full command, Colonel?" the captain asked formally.

"Yes, I am," Roger replied with matching formality, his expression settling into lines of unwonted seriousness as the weight of responsibility settled on his shoulders. "The first thing we have to do is reef the sails before the squall sinks us more surely than the Lemmar."

"They're reducing sail," Cra Vunet said. The five other raider ships had completed their own turns before the wind from the storm hit and were following the *Rage* in line ahead.

"Yes," Cies said thoughtfully. "Those edge-on sails probably tend to push them over in a high wind. I imagine we'll be able to sail with it quite handily, compared to them."

"We'll lose sight of them soon!" Vunet yelled through the sudden tumult as the leading edge of the squall raced across the last few hundred meters of sea towards the *Rage*. "Here it comes!"

The squall was of the sort common to any tropical zone—a brief, murderous "gullywasher" that would drop multiple centimeters of rain in less than an hour. The blast of wind in front of the rain—the "gust front"—was usually the strongest of the entire storm, and as it swept down upon them, the placid waves to windward started to tighten up into an angry "chop" crested with white curls of foam.

The wind hit like a hurricane, and the ships heeled over sharply, even with their square sails taken up to the second reef. But the Lemmar sailors took it with aplomb; such storms hit at least once per day.

"Well, they're gone!" Cies shouted back as the strange ships disappeared into a wall of wind, rain, and spray. "We'll stay on this course. Whether they fall off to windward or hold their own course, we'll be able to take them from the front. One shot from each ship, then we go alongside."

"What if they alter course?" Vunet shouted back.

"They're going to find it hard to wear around in this," Cies replied. "And if they try it, they'll still be settling onto course when we come on them. And the storm will probably be gone by then!"

"Come to course three-zero-five!" Roger shouted.

"I'm having a hard time punching a laser through to *Sea Foam*!" Julian yelled back over the roaring fury of the sea. "The signal's getting real attenuated by all this damned water!"

"Well, make sure you get a confirmation!" Pahner shouted, almost in the NCO's ear. "And we need a string confirmation on it!"

"Will do!"

Roger looked around the heeling ship and nodded his head. The Mardukan seamen were handling the lines well, and the situation, so far, was well in hand. The human-designed schooners had come well up into the wind, steering west-by-northwest, close-hauled on the starboard tack, in a course change which would have been literally impossible for the clumsy Mardukan pirates' rigs to duplicate. In many ways, the current conditions weren't that different from other storms they'd sailed through along the way, but they hadn't tried to maneuver in those. They'd simply held their course and hoped for the best. In this case, however, his entire plan depended upon their ability to maneuver *in* the storm.

It wouldn't be disastrous if they were unable to effect the maneuver he had in mind. It wouldn't be pleasant, but he was fairly certain that the schooners could take at least one or two shots from the pirates' bombards, assuming the simplistic weapons could even be fired under these conditions. But if they managed to pull off what he had in mind, they should suffer virtually no casualties. If he had to take losses, he would, but he'd become more and more determined to hold them to the absolute minimum as the trek went on.

The rain seemed to last forever, but finally he sensed the first signs of slackening in its pounding fury. That usually meant one more hard deluge, then the storm would clear with remarkable speed. Which meant it was almost time to start the next maneuver.

"Julian! Do you have commo?"

"Yes, Sir!" the sergeant responded instantly. "I got confirmations of course change from all ships."

"Then tell them to prepare to come to course two-seven-zero or thereabouts. And warn the gun crews to prepare for action to port, with a small possibility that it could be to starboard, instead. Tell the captains I want them to close up in line, one hundred meters of separation, as soon as the rain clears. I want them to follow us like beads on a string. Clear?"

"Clear and sent, Your Highness. And confirmed by all ships."

"Do you really have any idea where they are?" Pahner asked Roger over the helmet commo systems.

"Unless I'm much mistaken, they're over there," Roger said, gesturing off the port bow and into the blinding deluge.

"And what do we do when the other ships follow us 'like beads on a string'?" the captain asked curiously.

"Ah," Roger said, then glanced back at the commo sergeant. "To all ships, Julian. As soon as we clear the rain, send the sharpshooters to the tops."

The ship heeled hard to port as a fresh blast of wind from the north caught it, and Roger casually grabbed a stay.

"It's clearing," he observed. "Now to see where our other ships are."

"The *Foam* is right behind us," Julian said. "But they say some of the others are scattered."

The rain stopped as suddenly as it had begun, without even the slightest tapering off, and the rest of the K'Vaernian "fleet" was suddenly visible. The *Sea Foam* was some two hundred meters behind the *Hooker*, but the rest were scattered to the north and south—mostly south—of the primary course.

Roger looked the formation over and shrugged.

"Not bad. Not good, but not bad."

Pahner had to turn away to hide his smile. That simple "not bad" was a miracle. It was clear that getting the flotilla back together would take quite a few minutes, and any hope of simply turning and engaging the enemy whenever they appeared, was out of the airlock as a result. But the prince had simply shrugged and accepted that the plan would need revising. That was what a half a year of almost constant battle on Marduk had taught the hopeless young fop who'd first arrived here . . . and that, by itself, was almost worth the bodies scattered along the trail.

"Captain T'Sool," Roger said, "come to course two-seven-zero and take in the mainsail. We need to reduce speed until the rest of the fleet can catch up."

"Yes, Sir," the Mardukan acknowledged, and began shouting orders of his own.

"Julian," Roger turned back to the sergeant while T'Sool carried out his instructions. "To all ships: make all sail conformable with weather and close up in order. Get back in line; we have pirates to kill."

"Kral shit," Vunet said. Then, "Unbelievable!"

The rain had finally cleared, and the enemy fleet was once more visible . . . well upwind of their position, jockeying itself back into line. Neither he nor anyone else aboard the raiders' ships had ever heard of vessels that could do that. They must have tacked almost directly into the wind instead of wearing around before it! But it was clear that however well the individual ships might sail, they weren't well-trained as a group, and they'd gotten badly scattered by the storm.

The Lemmar ships, by contrast, were still in a nearly perfect line, and Cred Cies wasn't about to let the enemy have all day to get his formation back into order.

"Make a signal for all ships to turn towards the enemy and engage!"

"We'll be sailing almost into the teeth of the wind," Vunet pointed out.

"I understand that, Cra," Cies said with rather more patience than he actually felt. They wouldn't really be sailing into the "teeth of the wind," of course—it wasn't as if they were galleys, after all! And it was painfully evident that the strangers could sail far closer to the wind than any of his ships could hope to come. But if he edged as close to it as he could without getting himself taken all aback . . .

"We can still catch them before they reassemble," he told his mate. "Maybe."

Pahner tried not to laugh again as Roger folded his hands behind his back and assumed a mien of calculated indifference. The expression and posture of composed *sang-froid* was obviously a close copy of Pahner's own, and he'd seen more than one junior officer try it on for size. Roger was wearing it better than most, but then the prince smiled suddenly and swung his hands to the front, slamming a closed fist into the palm of his other hand.

"*Yes,*" he hissed. "You're mine!"

Pahner watched as the pirate ships swung up into the wind. Or, rather, *towards* the wind. It was obvious that they could come nowhere near as close to it as the schooners could, and the way their square sails shivered indicated even to his landman's eye that they were very close to losing way. But for all that, it also brought those big, bow-mounted bombards around to line up on the *Ima Hooker.*

"Doesn't look so good to me," he opined.

"Oh, they're going to get some shots off at us," Roger admitted. "We may even take a few hits, although I doubt that their gunnery is going to be anything to write home about. But as soon as everyone is back in line, we're going to turn onto a reciprocal heading to put the wind behind us. We can put on more sail and really race down on them. They're going to get off one—at the most two—shots at us, and most of those are going to miss. If we lose a ship, I'll be astonished, and I don't even anticipate very many casualties. Then we'll be in among them, and we'll rip them up with both broadsides. They're about to get corncobbed."

"So this is a particularly good situation?" Pahner asked, looking back at the ships assembling behind the *Hooker*. The flagship was close-reaching on the starboard tack now, sailing about forty-five degrees off the wind. That was nowhere near as high as she had been pointing, but apparently it was still high enough for Roger's purposes, and Pahner could see that it gave the rest of the flotilla additional time to catch up. *Sea Foam* had reduced sail dramatically to conform to the flagship's speed, whereas *Prince John* had crammed on extra canvas now that the squall had passed and was driving hard to get into position. *Pentzikis* and *Tor Coll* were coming up astern of *Prince John,* and it looked like everyone would be back into formation within perhaps another fifteen minutes.

"Well, if they'd held to their original course and tried to continue past us, then work their way back up to windward behind us, it would have been a pain," Roger told the Marine. "They'd have played hell trying to pull it off, but to get this over within any short time frame, we have to sail in between them, where our artillery can hammer them without their bombards being able to shoot back, and their line was spaced a lot more tightly together than I liked. If they'd continued on their easterly heading, we'd have run the risk of getting someone rammed when we went through their line. By turning up towards us, they've effectively opened the intervals, because those ships are a lot longer than they are wide, and we're looking at them end-on now. In addition, at the moment we actually pass them, we'll be broadside-to-broadside. That means our guns will be able to pound them at minimum range, but that those big-assed bombards are going to be pointing at nothing but empty sea.

"The other choice would have been to sail around behind them, come up from astern, and pick them off one by one. That would keep us out of the play of their guns, too, but I don't want to still be fighting this thing come morning. Among other things, there're those other prize ships to chase down."

"We'll see," Pahner commented. "After this fight, and if Kerr's response is good. I don't want to do this sort of thing for nothing."

"What are they thinking?" Cies asked himself.

The lead enemy ship had waited patiently as the Lemmar ships put their helms down and headed up as close into the wind as they could. In fact, the entire enemy formation seemed to have deliberately slowed down, which didn't make any kind of sense Cies could see. It was painfully obvious to him that those sleek, low-slung vessels were far more weatherly than his own. He was edging as close into the wind as he could come, and by slowing down, the enemy was actually going to allow him to bring his artillery to bear on the last three or four ships in his line. He hadn't had to let Cies do that, and the raider captain was suspicious whenever an opponent provided opportunities so generously. His own ships would miss the lead enemy vessel by at least two hundred meters, but after they'd hammered the other ships and then boarded them, there would be plenty of time to deal with the leader. If it decided to run away, there wasn't much the Lemmar could do about it, given its obvious advantages in both speed and maneuverability. But if it tried to come back and do anything to succor its less fortunate consorts, it would have to reenter Cies' reach.

In which case there definitely *was* something he could do about it.

"Perhaps they're like the damned priests," Vunet said. Cies glanced across at him. He hadn't realized that he'd asked his rhetorical question aloud, but now his mate clapped his hands in a "who knows?" gesture. "Maybe they plan on sailing into our midst and trying to grapple us all together so they can board, like the priests would."

"If that's what they're thinking, they'll take a pounding," the captain replied. "We'll get off several shots as they close, then sweep their decks with the swivel guns as they come alongside."

"Julian, do we have hard communications in place?" Roger asked.

"Yes, Sir," the intel NCO answered. "Good fix on the *Foam* and the *Prince John*. We're all linked, and we're not emitting worth a damn."

"Okay, put me on."

Roger waited a moment, until each of the ship icons on his helmet's HUD flashed green, then spoke across the tight web of communications lasers to the senior Marine aboard each schooner.

"This needs to be relayed to all the ships' captains. On my mark, I want them to put their helms up, and we'll bear away ninety degrees to port. That will let us run directly downwind. Once we're on course, put on all sail conformable with the weather. I'm designating the enemy vessels one through six, starting from the most westerly. *Hooker* will pass between one and two; *Pentzikis* will pass between two and three; *Sea Foam* will pass between three and four; the *Johnny* will pass between four and five; and *Tor Coll* will pass down the starboard side of number six. If the enemy holds his course, we'll wear to port after we pass, and rake them from astern. Prepare to bear away on my mark. Flash when ready to execute."

He raised one arm as he stood beside Captain T'Sool and waited until all the HUD icons flashed green. It only took a moment, and then his arm came slashing down.

"All ships: execute!"

✧   ✧   ✧

"They're actually doing it," Cies said in disbelief.

"I don't even see a forecastle," Vunet said in puzzlement. "Where the hell are their bombards?"

"How the hell do I know?" Cies growled back. "Maybe all they've got are those overgrown swivels on the sides!" He rubbed his horns, pleased that the enemy was being so stupid but anxious that it still might turn out that it wasn't stupidity at all, just something the enemy knew . . . and Cies didn't.

"Get aloft and direct the swivel guns. I don't want anything unexpected to happen."

"Right," Vunet grumped. "Something like losing?"

Roger walked down *Hooker*'s port side, greeting an occasional Mardukan gunner on the way. Most of the flotilla's gunners had been seconded from the K'Vaernian Navy and had served in the artillery at the Battle of Sindi. Roger had been away from the city for much of the battle, having his own set-to with a barbarian force that had refused to be in a logical place. But he'd arrived towards the end, after successfully protecting the main army's flank and annihilating the threat to its line of retreat, and he'd spent quite a bit of time around the artillerymen since. Most of them were native K'Vaernians, like the seamen, and figured that kowtowing to princes was for other people. But, like members of republics and democracies throughout the galaxy, they also had a sneaking affection for nobility, and they'd really taken a shine to Roger.

"Kni Rampol, where did you come from?" the prince asked as he reached up to clap one of the gun captains on his back. "I thought you were on the *Prince John?*"

"Captain T'Sool asked me to shift places with Blo Fal because he couldn't get along with the mate." The gunner stood up from his piece and caught a backstay to steady himself. The ship was running with the wind coming from astern, and with all sail set, she was swooping up one side of each swell, then charging down the other.

"Well, it's good to see you," Roger said with a

modified Mardukan gesture of humor. "No playing poker during the battle, though!"

"I don't think so," the Mardukan agreed with a grunt of humor. "Before you know it, Poertena would find the game, and then I'd be out a month's pay!"

"Probably so, at that," Roger laughed. "In that case, better hang on to your money, keep the muzzle down, and keep firing until you're told to quit. This will be a solid battle to tell the children about."

"Good afternoon, Your Highness," Lieutenant Lod Tak said. The port battery commander was doing the same thing as Roger—walking the gun line, checking and encouraging his gun crews.

"Afternoon, Lod," Roger acknowledged. "You know the fire plan?"

"Load with grape and ball," Tak replied promptly. "Hold our fire until we bear, then a coordinated broadside at point blank, and go to individual fire. Grape if we're close enough; ball, if we're not. Sound good?"

"Sounds fine," Roger answered. "I don't think they'll know what hit them. The game plan is for us to wear round to the port tack after we pass side to side. That will bring us across their sterns, and we'll get a chance to give them a good, solid rake at close range that should take most of the fight out of them before we board. Grape shot should do the job just fine . . . and leave the damned ships in one piece as prizes, too!"

"That sounds good to me, Your Highness," the Mardukan agreed with cheerful bloodthirstiness. K'Vaern's Cove had always paid excellent prize money for enemy ships captured intact, and every member of *Hooker*'s crew knew exactly how this game was played.

Roger nodded to the lieutenant and continued forward, to where Despreaux stood beside the pivot gun. The bronze carronades along *Hooker*'s side threw eight-kilo shot, and their stubby tubes looked almost ridiculously small beside the towering Mardukans. But the pivot gun was a long gun—with a barrel as long as one of the three-meter natives was tall—and it threw a fifteen-kilo solid shot. Or a fifteen-*centimeter* explosive shell.

Despreaux and Gol Shara, *Hooker*'s chief gunner, had just finished fussing over loading the gun, and Shara's body language expressed an unmistakable aura of frustration.

"What's his problem?" Roger asked Despreaux, jabbing his chin at the gunner.

"He wanted to try the shells," she replied, never taking her eyes from the approaching enemy vessels.

"He did, did he?" Roger gave Shara a quick grin, which the Mardukan returned with complete impassivity, then turned back to admire Despreaux's aquiline profile. He decided that she would definitely *not* like to be told that she looked like a ship's warrior maiden figurehead. "The object is to take them as close to intact as we can get them," he pointed out mildly, instead.

"Oh, he *understands*; he just doesn't like it," Despreaux said, but still she never looked away from the Lemmar, and Roger frowned.

"You don't look happy," he said more quietly. He also thought that he would like to wrap her in foam and put her in the hold, where she wouldn't be exposed to enemy fire. But she was *his* guard, not the other way around, and any suggestion of coddling on his part would undoubtedly meet with a violent response.

"Do you ever wish it could just end, Roger?" she asked quietly. "That we could call over to them and say, 'Let's not fight today.' "

It took the prince a moment to think about that. It was a feeling that he'd had before his first major battle, at Voitan, where better than half the company had been lost, but he'd rarely experienced it since then. Rage, yes. Professional fear of failure, yes. But as he considered her question, he realized that the normal and ordinary fear of dying had somehow fallen behind. Even worse, in some ways, the fear of having to kill was doing the same thing.

"No," he said after the better part of a minute. "Not really. Not since Voitan."

"I do," she said still very quietly. "I do every single time." She turned to look at him at last. "I love you, and I knew even when I was falling in love with you, that you don't feel that way. But sometimes it worries me that you don't."

She looked deep into his eyes for moment, then touched him on the arm, and started back towards the stern.

Roger watched her go, then turned back to watch the oncoming enemy. She had a point, he thought. On Marduk, the only way to survive had been to attack and keep on attacking, but sooner or later, they would make it back to Earth. When they did, he would once again become good old Prince Roger, Number Three Child, and in those conditions, jumping down the throat of the *flar-ke* to kick your way out its ass was not an effective tactic. Nor would Mother appreciate it if he blew some idiotic noble's brains all over the throne room's walls, he supposed. Sooner or later, he'd have to learn subtlety.

At that moment, the lead Lemmar ship opened up with its bombard, followed rapidly by all five of its consorts.

Yes, she had a point. He had to admit it. One that bore thinking about. But for now, it *was* time to kick some ass.

CHAPTER NINE

"Prepare to run out!" Roger called, gauging the speed of the oncoming ships. The two formations sliced towards one another, the schooners moving much faster through the water than the clumsier raider vessels, and he frowned slightly. They were going to pass one another on opposite tacks, all right, but considerably more quickly than he had anticipated.

"I want to reduce sail as we pass through them, so we can get in more than one broadside."

"Agreed," Captain T'Sool said. *Hooker*'s Mardukan captain stood beside the prince, eyes narrow as he, too, calculated the combined approach speed. "I think taking in the middle and topmast staysails should be enough. If it isn't, we can always drop the mainsail and the inner jib, as well."

Despite the tension, Roger smiled faintly. There'd been no terms for those types of sails in any Mardukan language before Poertena had introduced them, so the diminutive armorer had been forced to use the human ones. It had worked—at least it precluded any possibility of confusing Mardukan words—but it was more than a bit humorous to hear a Mardukan make a hash of pronouncing "topmast staysail" . . . especially with a Pinopan accent. But T'Sool was almost certainly correct. What he'd

137

suggested would reduce sail area significantly, and with it, *Hooker*'s speed, but the foresail was the real work-horse of the topsail schooner rig. Even if they did have to drop the mainsail, as well, her agility and handling would be unimpaired.

"I think just the staysails should be enough," he responded. "Julian, send that to the other ships along with the word that we'll be engaging shortly."

"Yes, Sir." The NCO grinned. "I think we can all figure out that last part on our own, though!"

Another boom echoed from the oncoming ships, and the ball from the nearest bombard was clearly visible as it flew well above the *Hooker*. It was audible, as well, even over the sounds of wind and sea. Roger was almost too intent to notice, but several people flinched as the whimpering ball sliced away several lines overhead. The two sides were little more than two hundred meters apart, with Roger's vessels swooping down upon the Lemmar.

"I think we're in range," Roger observed dryly.

"Indeed?" D'Nal Cord's tone was even drier. He stood directly behind Roger, leaning on his huge spear while guarding the prince's back, as any proper *asi* should when battle loomed. "And as Sergeant Julian is so fond of saying, you think this because . . . ?"

Roger turned to smile fiercely up at his *asi,* but other people on *Hooker*'s afterdeck had more pressing details to worry about.

"Srem Kol!" T'Sool shouted, and pointed upward when a Mardukan petty officer looked towards him. "Get a work party aloft and get those lines replaced! Tlar Frum! Stand by to reduce sail!"

Even as shouted acknowledgments came back to him, there was more thunder from the Lemmar line, and Roger heard a rending crash.

"*Prince John* just took a hit," Pahner said, and Roger looked over to see that the captain's gift for understate-ment hadn't deserted him. The third schooner in his own line had lost her foremast. It had plunged into the water on her starboard side, and the weight of the broken spars and sodden canvas was like an anchor. The ship swung wildly around to the right, exposing her broadside to the oncoming Mardukan raiders.

"Not much we can do about it now," Roger observed with a mildness which fooled neither Pahner nor himself. "Nothing except smash the shit out of the scummies, anyway. And at least anybody who wants her is going to have to come close enough for her carronades to do a little smashing of their own. Still—" He looked at the Marine standing beside Cord. "Julian, tell the *Johnny* to concentrate on Number Four's rigging. *Sea Foam* and *Tor Coll* will have to hammer Number Three and Number Five to keep them off her."

"Got it," Julian acknowledged. The NCO had switched to a battle schematic on his pad and sent the updated plan to all five ships. "I've got a response from everyone except *Prince John*," he reported after a moment.

"I can see some damage aft." Pahner had the zoom dialed up on his helmet visor. "It looks like Number Four and Number Five were concentrating fire on her. She looks pretty beat up."

"I don't doubt it," Roger grunted. "Those are dammed big cannonballs." He shrugged. "But we'll settle their hash in a few minutes now. It's about time to open the ball. All ships—run out!"

"What do they think they're doing now?" Vunet demanded as *Rage of Lemmar*'s bombard thudded again.

"Just at a guess, I'd say they're finally getting ready to shoot back at us," Cred Cies said bitingly as the smooth sides of the strange, low-slung ships were suddenly barbed with what certainly looked like stubby bombard muzzles.

"With those tiny things?" the mate made a derisive gesture of contempt.

"With those tiny things," Cies confirmed.

"My son could hurt us worse with a toy sword," Vunet scoffed.

Given its angle of approach, the K'Vaernian flotilla could have opened fire with its forward pivot guns even before the Lemmar did. Roger, however, had chosen not to do so. Powerful as the pivot guns were, it was unlikely that they could have incapacitated any of the raider vessels by themselves without using the explosive shells, which would probably have destroyed their targets completely. Wooden ships waterproofed with pitch and covered with tarred rigging were tinderboxes, just waiting for any explosive shell to set them ablaze. And even if that hadn't been the case, Roger had had no interest in alerting the Mardukan pirates to the power of his vessels' weapons. The K'Vaernian Navy had been unimpressed by the carronades when they first saw them . . . and with considerably less excuse, since the K'Vaernians had already seen human-designed artillery in action at Sindi. The longer these scummies remained in ignorance about their capabilities, the better.

But the time for ignorance was about over. Especially for *Prince John*. Roger could see axes flashing on her forward deck as her crew frantically chopped away at the rigging holding the wreckage of the foremast against her side. If things worked out the way he planned, the raiders would be too busy to bother with the *Johnny* anytime soon, but if things *didn't* work out, it was going to be a case of God helping those who helped themselves.

In the meantime . . .

"Fire as you bear!"

Ima Hooker and her consorts each carried a broadside of twelve guns. Once upon a time, on a planet called Earth, those guns would have been described as eighteen-pounder carronades—short, stubby weapons with a maximum effective range of perhaps three hundred meters. Beside someone the size of a Mardukan, they looked even shorter and stubbier, and perhaps the pirate captains could be excused for failing to grasp the menace they represented. Certainly Roger had done everything he could to keep the Lemmaran crews from doing so . . . until now.

Despite the threat bearing down upon her, the *Prince John* did not fire first. Her guns, like those of every unit

of the flotilla, had been loaded for a basically antiper-
sonnel engagement, with a charge of grapeshot atop a
single round shot. That was a marvelous combination
for smashing hulls and slaughtering personnel at close
range, but it left a bit to be desired in terms of long-
range gunnery. The other schooners, continuing their race
towards the enemy, were going to reach that sort of
range far more quickly than any clumsy Lemmaran tub
was going to claw far enough up to windward for her
to reach. So the *Johnny* held her fire, waiting to see
what—if anything—got by her sisters and into her effective range.

Of course, even with their superior weapons, four
schooners might find themselves just a bit hard-pressed
to stop *six* raiders from getting past them.

Or perhaps not.

Cred Cies watched in disbelief as the side of the nearest enemy vessel disappeared behind a billowing cloud
of dirty-white smoke. Those short, silly-looking bombards
obviously threw far heavier shot than he had believed
possible. The quantity of smoke alone would have made
that obvious, but the hurricane of iron slamming into his
vessel made it even more obvious. *Painfully* obvious, one
might almost have said.

Those low-slung, infernally fast ships slashed down into
the Lemmaran formation, and as they did, they showed
him exactly why they'd adopted the approach they had.
The raiders' bombards might have gotten off three or four
unanswered shots each as the strangers drove in across
their effective range, but the accuracy of those shots had
left much to be desired. One of the enemy vessels had
been crippled, and had clearly taken casualties, as well,
but the others were unscathed.

Now they swept into the intervals in his own formation, and his teeth ground together in frustration as he
realized that even as they did, they were actually reducing
sail. They were slowing down, sacrificing their impossible
speed advantage, and the shriek and crash of shot—the
dreadful, splintering smash as round shot slammed into

and through his own ship's timbers—was like a hammer blow squarely between the horns as he realized why.

"*All right!*" someone shrieked, and it took Roger a moment to realize that it had been him. Not that he was alone in his jubilation.

The endless hours of drill inflicted upon the K'Vaernian gunners had been worth it. The range to target was little more than fifty meters, and at that range, every shot went home. Jagged holes magically appeared in the stout planking of the raider ships. Grapeshot and splinters of their own hulls went through the massed troops, drawn up on the pirates' decks in obvious anticipation of a boarding action, like scythes. Bodies and pieces of bodies flew in grisly profusion, and the agonized shrieks of the wounded cut through even the thunder of the guns.

Roger wanted to leap to the rail to help serve one of the guns personally. The strength of the fierce, sudden temptation took him by surprise. It was as if the screams of his enemies, the sudden spray pattern of blood splashed across the lower edges of the square sails as wooden "splinters" two meters and more in length went smashing through the raider crews like ungainly buzz saws, closed some circuit deep inside him. It wasn't hunger . . . not precisely. But it was a *need*. It was something all too much like a compulsion, and deep inside him a silent, observing corner of his brain realized that Nimashet had been right to worry about him.

But there was no time for such thoughts, and it wasn't fear of his own inner demons which kept him standing by *Hooker*'s wheel as the artillery thundered and the enemy shrieked. It was responsibility. The awareness that he had accepted command for the duration of this battle and that he could no more abandon or evade that responsibility than Armand Pahner could have. And so he stayed where he was, with Julian poised at one shoulder and D'Nal Cord at the other, while someone else did the killing.

Hooker's carronades bellowed again and again. Not in the single, senses-shattering blast of the perfectly synchronized opening broadside but in ones and twos as the faster crews got off their follow-up shots. There was more thunder from overhead as sharpshooters— Marines with their big bolt-action rifles, and Mardukans, with their even bigger breech-loaders—claimed their own toll from the enemy.

The main "broadside" armament of the Lemmaran ships was composed of "swivel guns," which weren't much more than built-up arquebuses. They were about fifty millimeters in caliber, and they had the range to carry to the K'Vaernian schooners slicing through the Lemmaran formation, but without rifling, they were grossly inaccurate. On the other hand, the already short range was going to fall to zero when the flotilla finally closed to board the raider ships, and the swivels could still wreak havoc among the infantry who would be doing the boarding. So the sharpshooters were tasked with taking out the gun crews, as well as any obvious officers they could spot.

Even with the much more accurate rifles, the shots weren't easy to make. The ships were tossing in the long swells of the Mardukan ocean and simultaneously moving on reciprocal headings, so the targets were moving in three dimensions. Since the sharpshooters were perched on the fighting tops at the topmast crosstrees or lashed into the ratlines with safety harnesses, they were not only moving in three dimensions, they were moving *very broadly* in three dimensions, swaying back and forth, up and down, in a manner which, had they not become inured to it already, would have guaranteed seasickness. There were enough Mardukans on the raiders' decks to give each rifle shot an excellent chance of hitting someone, but despite all of their endless hours of practice, the odds against that someone being the target they'd *aimed* at were much higher. The sharpshooters claimed their own share of victims, but their best efforts were only a sideshow compared to the carnage wreaked by the carronades.

Each of the four undamaged schooners was engaged on both sides as they drove down between the Lemmaran vessels. The thundering guns pounded viciously at the stunned and disbelieving raiders, and Roger shook his head grimly as the first Lemmaran foremast went crashing over the side. A moment later, the hapless ship's mainmast followed.

"That's done for that one, Captain," he observed to Pahner, and the Marine nodded.

"What about supporting *Prince John?*" the captain asked, and Roger glanced at him. The Marine's tone made it clear that his question was just that—a question, and not a veiled suggestion. But it was a reasonable one, the prince thought, as he looked astern at the cloud of powder smoke rising above the crippled schooner. From the sound of her guns, though, the *Johnny* was firing with steady deliberation, not with the sort of desperation which might have indicated a close action.

"We've got time to settle these bastards first," Roger said, nodding at the incipient melee, and Pahner nodded again.

"You're in command," he agreed, and Roger took time to give him a quick, savage smile before he turned his attention back to T'Sool.

"Put your helm alee, Captain!" he ordered, and T'Sool waved two arms at his helmsman.

"Hands to sheets!" the Mardukan captain bellowed through the bedlam. "Off sheets!" Seamen who had learned their duties the hard way during the voyage scampered through the smoke and fury to obey his orders even as the gunners continued to fire, and T'Sool watched as the line-handlers raced to their stations, then waved at the helmsman again.

"Helm alee! Let go the sheets—handsomely there!" he thundered, and the helmsman spun the wheel.

Hooker turned on her heel like the lady she was, coming around to port in a thunder of canvas, with a speed and precision none of the raiders would have believed possible.

"Haul in and make fast!" T'Sool shouted, and the schooner settled onto her new heading, with the wind once more broad on her port beam. The sail-handlers made the sheets fast on the big fore-and-aft foresail, and her broadside spat fresh thunder as she charged back across her enemies' sterns.

There were *no* guns—bombards or swivels—to protect the raiders' sterns, and the carnage aboard the Lemmaran ships redoubled as the lethal grapeshot went crashing the entire length of the vessels. A single one of the iron spheres might kill or maim as many as a dozen—or even two dozen—of the raiders, and then the anti-*coll* bead cannon mounted on *Hooker*'s after rail opened fire, as well.

For the first time since the Marines landed on Marduk, their high-tech weapons were almost superfluous. The ten-millimeter, hypervelocity beads were incredibly lethal, but the storm of grapeshot and the flying splinters of the ships themselves spread a stormfront of destruction broader than anything the bead cannon could have produced. The beads were simply icing on the cake.

"Bring us back up close-hauled on the port tack, Captain T'Sool!" Roger snapped, and *Hooker* swung even further to port, riding back along a reciprocal of her original course that took her back up between the battered raider ships towards *Prince John*'s position. Both broadsides' carronades continued to belch flame with deadly efficiency, and Roger could clearly see the thick ropes of blood oozing from the Mardukan ships' scuppers.

The flotilla flagship broke back through the enemy's shattered formation with smoke streaming from her gun ports in a thick fog bank shot through with flame and fury. Another raider's masts went crashing over the side, and Roger sucked in a deep, relieved breath of lung-searing smoke, despite his earlier confident words to Pahner, as he saw *Prince John*.

The broken foremast had been cut entirely away; he could see it bobbing astern of her as she got back underway under her mainsail and gaff main topsail alone. It was scarcely an efficient sail combination, but it was enough under the circumstances. Or it should be, anyway. She wasn't moving very quickly yet, and her rigging damage had cost her her headsails, which meant the best she could do was limp along on the wind. But her speed was increasing, and at least she was under command and moving. Which was a good thing, since raider Number Four had somehow managed to claw her way through the melee.

The *Johnny* had seen her coming, and her carronades were already pounding at her opponent. The bigger, more heavily built raider vessel's topsides were badly shattered, and her sails seemed to have almost more holes in them than they had intact canvas, but she was still underway, still closing on the damaged schooner, and the big, slow-firing bombard protected by the massive timber "armor" of her forecastle was still in action. Even as Roger watched, it slammed another massive round shot into the much more lightly built schooner, and he swore viciously as splintered planking flew.

"It *would* be the *Johnny*," he heard Pahner say almost philosophically. He looked at the Marine, and the captain shrugged. "Never seems to fail, Your Highness. The place you least want to get hit, is the one you can count on the enemy finding." He shook his head. "She's got quite a few of the Carnan aboard, and they already took a hammering when we lost *Sea Skimmer*."

"Don't count your money when it's still sitting on the table," Roger replied, then turned to Julian. "All ships," he said. "Close with the pirates to leeward and board. We'll go to *Johnny*'s assistance ourselves."

"Your Highness," Pahner began, "considering that our entire mission is to get you home alive, don't you think that perhaps it might be a bit wiser to let someone else go—"

Roger had just turned back to the Marine to argue the point when Pahner's helmet visor automatically darkened to protect the captain's vision. Roger didn't know whether or not *Prince John*'s Marine detachment had originally set up a plasma cannon for their anti-*coll* defense system. If they had, he thought with a strange detachment, they were probably going to hear about it—at length—from Pahner and the sergeant major. But it was also possible that they'd switched out the bead cannon at the last minute while the rest of the crew worked on repairs to the schooner's crippled rigging. Not that it mattered. Raider Number Four had managed to get around behind *Johnny*'s stern, where her deadly carronade broadside wouldn't bear. And in achieving that position of advantage, the pirate vessel had put itself exactly where the schooner's crew wanted it.

The Marines' plasma cannons could take out modern main battle tanks, and if *Hooker*'s bead cannon hadn't seemed to add much to her carronades' carnage, no one would ever say that about *Prince John*'s after armament. The round ripped straight down the center of the target ship, just above main deck level. It sliced away masts, rigging, bulwarks, and the majority of the pirates who had assembled on deck in anticipation of boarding. What was worse, in a way, was the thermal bloom that preceded the round. The searing heat touched the entire surface of the ship to flame in a tiny slice of a second, and the roaring furnace became an instant sliver of Hell, an inferno afloat on an endless sea that offered no succor to its victims. Those unfortunate souls below decks, "shielded" from the instant incineration of the boarding party, had a few, eternal minutes longer to shriek before the bombard's powder magazine exploded and sent the shattered, flaming wreck mercifully into the obliterating depths.

"I thought we wanted to capture the ships intact," Roger said almost mildly.

"What would you have done, Your Highness?" Pahner asked. "Yeah, we want to capture the ships, and recapture the convoy, if we can. But *Prince John*, obviously, would prefer to avoid being boarded herself."

"And apparently the Lemmar agree with that preference," D'Nal Cord observed. "Look at that."

He raised an upper arm and pointed. One of the six raider vessels drifted helplessly, completely dismasted while the blood oozing down her side dyed the water around her. Her deck was piled and heaped with the bodies of her crew, and it was obvious that no more than a handful of them could still be alive. Three more raiders each had one of the flotilla's other schooners alongside, and now that *Hooker*'s carronades were no longer bellowing, Roger could hear the crackle of small arms fire as the K'Vaernian boarders stormed up and over them. *Prince John*'s plasma cannon had accounted for a fifth raider, but the sixth and final pirate vessel had somehow managed to come through the brutal melee with its rigging more or less intact, and it was making off downwind just as fast as its shredded canvas would allow.

"Do we let them go, or close with them?" the prince asked.

"Close," Pahner said. "We want to capture the ships, and I'm not a great believer in giving a fleeing enemy an even break. They either surrender, or they die."

"They're not letting us go," Vunet said.

"Would you?" Cies shot back with a grunt of bitter laughter as he looked around the deck.

The crew was hastily trying to repair some of the damage, but it was a futile task. There was just too much of it. Those damned bombards of theirs were hellishly accurate. Unbelievably accurate. They'd smashed *Rage of Lemmar* from stem to stern and cut away over half her running rigging, in the process. Coupled with the way they'd shredded the sails themselves, the damage to the ship's lines—and line-handlers—had slowed their escape to a crawl.

The bombards had done nearly as much damage to the crew, as well. The quarterdeck was awash in blood and bodies, and the crew had put a gang of slaves to work pitching the offal over the side. The enemy's round shot had been bad enough, but the splinters it had ripped from the hull had been even worse. Some of them had been almost two-thirds as long as Cies himself, and one of them had gutted his original helmsman like a filleted fish. Nor was that the only crewman who'd been shredded by bits and pieces of his own ship. Some of that always happened when the bombards got a clear shot, but Cies had never imagined anything like *this*. Normal bombard balls were much slower than the Hell-forged missiles that had savaged his vessel. Worse, he'd never seen any ship that could pour out fire like water from a pump, and the combination of high-velocity shot and its sheer volume had been devastating beyond his worst nightmares of carnage.

Now the *Rage* was trying to limp to the south and away from the vengeful demons behind her. He'd hoped that with one of their own crippled (by what, for all intents and purposes, had been a single lucky shot) the other four might have let his own ship go. But it appeared they had other plans.

"We could . . ." Vunet said, then paused.

"You were about to suggest that we surrender," Cies said harshly. "Never! No Lemmar ship has ever surrendered to anyone other than Lemmar. Ever. They may take our ship, but not one crewman, not one slave, will be theirs."

"They're not heaving to," Roger said with a grunt. "Captain Pahner?"

"Yes, Your Highness?" the Marine replied formally.

"If we really want that ship intact, this is about to become a boarding action. I think it's about time to let the ground commander take over."

"You intend to take them on one-on-one?"

"I think we have to, if we don't want them to get away," Roger replied. Pahner gazed at him, and the prince shrugged. "*Pentzikis*, *Tor Coll*, and *Sea Foam* already have their hands full. *Prince John* can probably take the fourth pirate—I doubt there's more than a couple dozen of these Lemmar still alive aboard her, and she sure as hell can't get away with no masts at all. But this guy in front of us isn't just lucky. He's smart . . . and good. If he weren't, he'd be drifting around back there with his buddies. So if you want him caught, we're the only one with a real shot at him."

"I see. And when we catch up with him, you'll be where, precisely, Your Highness?" Pahner asked politely.

"Like I say, Sir," Roger said, "it's time to let the ground commander take over."

"I see." Pahner gazed at him speculatively for several

moments, considering what the prince *hadn't* said, then nodded with an unseen smile.

"Very well, Your Highness. Since boarding actions are *my* job, I'll just go and get the parties for this one assembled."

CHAPTER TEN

"Come off the guns and rig the mortars!" Despreaux ordered, pulling gunners off the carronades as she trotted down the line of the starboard battery. "We're going to be boarding from port!"

The *Ima Hooker* was slicing through the water once more, rapidly overhauling the fleeing pirate vessel. It would have been difficult to guess, looking at the sergeant's expression, just how unhappy about that she was. Not that she was any more eager than Captain Pahner to see the raiders escape, if not for exactly the same reasons. Nimashet Despreaux had a serious attitude problem where pirates—any pirates—were concerned, but she would have been much happier if at least one of the other schooners had been in position to support *Hooker*. There were still an awful lot of scummies aboard that ship, however badly shaken they must be from the effects of the carronades. And as good as the K'Vaernians and their Diaspran veterans were, hand-to-hand combat on a heaving deck was what the Lemmar did for a living. There were going to be casualties—probably quite a lot of them—if the raiders ever got within arms' reach, and a Mardukan's arms were very, very long.

And Despreaux was particularly concerned about one possible casualty which wouldn't have been a problem if any of the other schooners had been in *Hooker*'s place.

But at least if they had to do it, it looked as if Roger intended to do it as smartly as possible. He was steering almost directly along the Lemmaran ship's wake, safely outside the threat zone of any weapon the raider mounted. Given *Hooker*'s superior speed and maneuverability, Despreaux never doubted that Roger would succeed in laying her right across the other ship's stern. Nor did she doubt that he would succeed in raking the pirate's deck from end to end with grapeshot with relative impunity as he closed. After which, *Hooker*'s crew and Krindi Fain's Diasprans would swarm up and over the shattered stern and swiftly subdue whatever survived from the Lemmaran crew.

Sure they would.

And Roger wouldn't be anywhere *near* the fighting.

And the tooth fairy would click her heels together three times and return all of them to Old Earth instantly.

She skidded to a halt beside another device that was new to Marduk. The boarding mortar, one of three carried in each of *Hooker*'s broadsides, was a small, heavy tube designed for a heavily modified grapnel, affixed to a winch and line, to fit neatly into its muzzle. Charged with gunpowder, it should be able to throw the grapnel farther and more accurately than any human or Mardukan. Of course, that assumed it worked at all. The system had been tested before leaving K'Vaern's Cove, but that was different from trying to use it in combat for the very first time.

Despreaux pulled open the locker beside the mortar, dragged out the grapnel, and affixed the line to the snaphook on its head as one of the gun boys ran down to the magazine for the propelling charge. He was back in less than a minute with a bag of powder, and Despreaux watched one of the Mardukan gunners from the starboard battery slide the charge into the heavy iron tube. A wad of waxed felt followed, and then Despreaux personally inserted the grapnel shaft and used it as its own ramrod to shove the charge home. When she was certain it was fully seated, she stepped back. A hollow quill, made from the Mardukan equivalent of a feather and filled with fulminating powder, went into the touchhole, the firing hammer was cocked, and the mortar was ready.

All three of the portside weapons had been simultaneously loaded, and Despreaux spent a few seconds inspecting the other two, then activated her communicator.

"Portside mortars are up."

"Good," Roger replied. "We're coming up on our final turn."

Despreaux grabbed a stay and leaned outboard, careful to stay out of the carronade gunners' way as she peered ahead beyond the sails and the tapering bowsprit. *Hooker* was coming up astern of the Lemmaran ship rapidly, and she heard the rapidfire volley of orders as seamen scampered to the lines. One of the portside gunners rapped her "accidentally" on the knee with a handspike, and she looked up quickly. Mardukan faces might not be anywhere near as expressive as human ones, but she'd learned to read scummy body language in the past, endless months, and she recognized the equivalent of a broad grin in the way his false-hands held the handspike.

She gave him the human version of the same expression and got the hell out of his way as the gun captain squatted behind the carronade and peered along the stubby barrel. Then he cocked the firing hammer.

"Back all sails!"

Now that the battle had resolved itself into a series of ship-to-ship actions, Roger found himself an admiral with no commands to give. It was all up to the individual ship captains now, like T'Sool, and Roger decided that the best thing he could do was get out from underfoot.

And he was planning on sitting out the boarding, as well. Everyone's comments on the stupidity of his putting himself out on a limb were finally starting to hit home. If he took point, the Marines aboard *Ima Hooker* wouldn't be able to pay attention to taking the ship, or to keeping themselves alive, because they would be trying too hard to protect him. So he'd taken a position in the ratlines, where he could observe the fighting without participating.

Getting a good look required that elevated position, because the ships could hardly have been more unlike one another. The Lemmaran was a high-sided caravellike vessel, fairly round in relation to its length, whereas the schooner was long, low, and lean. The result was a difference of nearly three meters from the top of the schooner's bulwarks to the top of her opponent's.

The boarders from *Hooker* would be led by some of the Diaspran veterans, under the command of Krindi Fain, with the human Marines—led by Gunny Jin—as emergency backup. The Diasprans weren't exactly experienced at this sort of combat, but the K'Vaernian seamen had explained the rudiments of shipboard combat to them before they ever set sail, and they'd practiced for it almost as much as they'd practiced their marksmanship. Given the disparity in the height of the two ships' bulwarks, even the Mardukans were going to find it an awkward scramble to get across the raider's high stern, but at least the savage battering the carronades' grapeshot had delivered upon arrival gave them an opening to make the crossing.

On the other hand, not even the Mardukans had been able to actually see across to the other ship from deck level. That was one reason Cord had joined Roger, perching precariously in the ratlines, along with his nephew Denat. The other reason was to get them close enough to Roger to let them throw up their outsized shields in the event that the Lemmar decided to hurl their throwing axes at him.

Roger watched the Marines forming up behind the Mardukan boarders and was just as glad that Despreaux was in charge of the grapnel mortars. For better or worse, he worried more about her than about the other Marines. Managing the grapnels, and the fast winches they were attached to, she would be in no position to participate. Whether that was simply a happy coincidence

or something Pahner and Kosutic had considered with
malice aforethought when they detailed her to the job,
he didn't know. Nor did he particularly care. Not as long
as it kept her out of the firing line.

The final broadside roared, and Roger nodded in grim
approval as the hurricane of grapeshot swept most of the
pirate ship's afterdeck clear. It also did a splendid job
of cutting away rigging and what was left of the ship's
canvas. It looked like the spars themselves were still more
or less intact, though. Rerigging this prize would be an
all-day task, but one that would be nowhere near as
difficult as repairing the ships that had lost entire masts.

He watched as Despreaux ordered the mortars to fire
and the lines flicked out across the enemy ship. The
grapnels flew straight and true, arcing over the Lemmar
ship's stern rail, and the Mardukan sailors on the fast
winches started reeling them back in. The mortars
appeared to have been a successful experiment, he
observed, and allowed himself a certain smugness as the
author of the idea. Trying to do the same thing with
hand-thrown grapnels would have been a chancy process,
at best.

Pedi Karuse refused to give in to despair. The worst
had happened the moment the Krath raiding party hit
the village. From there, it was only a matter of how long
it took her to die.

In a way, her capture by the Lemmar had actually
stretched out her existence. They were probably going to
sell her back to the Fire Priests, eventually. Or she might
end up as a bond slave, or in the saltpeter mines. But
at least she wasn't on a one-way ticket to Strem. Or
already a Handmaiden of the God.

So she'd been prepared to look upon her current situation with a certain degree of detachment, biding her time
and husbanding her strength against the vanishingly slim
chance that she might actually find an opportunity to
escape. That attitude had undergone a marked change in
the past few hours, however.

The problem, of course, was the peculiarly Lemmaran

method of dealing with boarding actions. The Lemmar had a simple answer to the possibility of capture: don't allow it. In part, their attitude stemmed from their dealings with Fire Priests; unlike the Shin, they flatly refused to let themselves be captured to face the Fire Priests' . . . religious practices. But an even larger part of their attitude was the terror factor; no Lemmar would ever surrender under any circumstances, and they made certain all of their enemies knew it.

Generally, that meant that the Fire Priest's guards didn't bother trying to capture Lemmaran ships. They might sink them, but fighting a suicidal enemy hand-to-hand was a casualty-heavy proposition which offered minimal profit even if it was successful. Nor did the Fire Priests raid the Lemmar islands. They might have taken Strem away from the Confederation, but the island itself was all they'd gotten. And if they wanted to keep it, they'd have to completely repopulate it, since the Lemmar had killed even their women and children, rather than have them captured.

What that meant for Pedi Karuse, and the half-dozen other captives chained on the deck of the *Rage of Lemmar,* was that having avoided the Fire Priests on Krath, having avoided being shipped to Strem, and having lived through the splinter-filled hell of the broadsides, they were about to be slaughtered by their captors.

Some days it just didn't pay to do your horns in the morning.

She flattened herself as close to the deck as her chains allowed, even though her brain recognized the futility of her instinctive reaction, as another enemy salvo hit. Most of this one was aimed high, something that whistled through the air with an evil sound and shredded the ship's rigging like a *greg* eating a *vern*. But some of it flew by lower, and a splinter the size of her horn took one of the other Shin slaves in the stomach. It was really a rather small splinter, compared to some of the others that had gone howling across the deck, but the slave seemed to explode under the impact, and his guts splashed across the red-stained deck . . . and Pedi.

Even over the screams and the thunder of the enemy

guns, she could hear the prayers of the captured Guard next to her, and the sound finally pushed her over the brink as her fellow clansman's blood sprayed over her.

"Shut up!" she shouted. "I hope you burn in the Fires for the rest of eternity! It was your stupid Guard that got me into this!"

There wasn't much she could do, with her arms chained behind her and coupled to the rest of the slaves, but she did her best—which was to lean sideways and snap-kick the stupid Krath in the head. It wasn't her best kick ever, but it was enough to send him bouncing away from her, and she grunted in delighted satisfaction as the other side of his skull hit a deck stanchion . . . hard.

"Shin blasphemer!" He spat in her direction. "The Fire will purify your soul soon enough!"

"It will purify you both," one of the pirates said as he drew his sword. "Time to show these *vern* why you don't board the Lemmar."

"Piss on you, sailor!" the Shin female snarled. "Your mother was a *vern* and your father was a *kren*—with bad eyesight!"

"Piss on *you*, Shin witch," the Lemmar retorted, and raised his sword. "Time to meet your Fire."

"That's what you think," Pedi said. She flipped her legs forward and both feet slammed home as she snap-kicked the pirate in the crotch. He bent explosively forward in sudden agony, and she wrenched herself as far upward as the chains allowed. It was just far enough. Their horns locked, and then, in a maneuver she knew would have left her bruised and sore for a week if she'd been going to live that long, she let herself fall backward and hurled the much larger male over her head and onto his back. Another wrench unlocked her horns just before he crashed down on the planking, and she flipped herself upward onto the back of her head, spun in place on the pivot of her manacles, and drove both heels down onto the winded pirate's throat.

The entire attack was over in a single heartbeat, along with the pirate's life, and she bounced back up into a kneeling position on the deck to survey the remaining pirates, clustered to repel borders.

"Next?" she spat.

Several of the Lemmar swore, and two of them started towards her to complete the imperative task of killing their captives. But before they could take more than a single stride, a grapnel came flying through the air. It was only one of three, but this particular grapnel landed two meters in front of Pedi, with the line running between her and the Krath guards.

"Oh, Fire Priest shit," she whispered as the four-pronged hook began skittering rapidly back along the deck. It was headed for the after rail, gouging splinters out of the planking as it went . . . and aiming directly for the chain binding all the slaves together.

It caught the chain and barely even slowed as it ripped away the forward of the two heavy iron rings that had anchored it—and the slaves—to the deck.

"This is gonna *hurt!*"

Pedi leaned forward and tightened her muscles against what was coming, but it was still incredibly painful when all four of her chained-together arms were wrenched backwards. Only one of the rings had come out of the planking, which made it even worse. Instead of dragging them all straight aft, the rampaging grapnel cracked the chain like a whip. Sparks flew as the grapnel's tines raked furiously down the heavy links, and someone's scream ended in a hideous, gurgling groan as the grapnel disemboweled him. She could hear the other slaves screaming as the whole group was snatched along the deck until the grapnel finally yanked entirely free of the chain. But not before it had slammed all of them bru-tally into the ship's starboard bulwark.

She felt as if her arms had been pulled out of their sockets, and when she looked sideways, she saw that that had literally happened to one of the other Shin. But she refused to let that stop her as she rolled over on her head again and slipped her legs between her arms.

That contortion would have been difficult enough for a human; most Mardukans would have found it virtually impossible, but the same training which had saved Pedi's life against the first pirate came to the fore once more. She folded practically in half and slipped first one, then the other leg out until she could lie with her arms bound in front of her. Of course, they were now flipped around, false-hands above true-hands, but her wrists slid in the manacles to let her relieve the pressure on her elbows and shoulders, and even with false-hands high, she was happier this way. Besides, it was also an insulting hand gesture, which suited her frame of mind perfectly.

Roger had been paying strict attention to the preparations for the attack. Despite his concentration on other things, he'd been vaguely aware of the low-voiced conversation between D'Nal Cord and Denat, but he hadn't paid it very much attention. Not until Cord suddenly snapped an angry retort at his nephew. The deep, sharp-edged sentence was short, pungent, and spectacularly obscene.

"What?" Roger's head whipped around at the highly atypical outburst from his *asi*.

"They appear to be trying to kill their prisoners," Denat said with a gesture towards the other ship.

Roger followed the waving true-hand and saw half a dozen Mardukans chained to the deck near the center line. One of them was only too obviously dead, clearly a victim of *Hooker*'s broadsides. A chain, stretched between two raised iron rings, joined them all together, running up through a complex four-point restraint behind each Mardukan to hold his arms behind him. As Roger watched, one of the grapnels caught the chain, and he winced in sympathetic pain as it ripped one of the chain's anchoring rings out of the planking and yanked the prisoners across the deck. It also killed another of them, and then the rest of the captives were slammed into the ship's bulwarks with more than enough force to kill anyone who hit awkwardly. Indeed, it looked to Roger as if all but one of them had been injured, possibly severely. But that didn't prevent several more of the Lemmar from advancing on them with swords ready just

as *Hooker*'s boarders started over the side of their own
ship.

Pedi Karuse rose on her knees once more, examined
her situation, and allowed herself one vicious curse. The
grapnel had only managed to rip out one ring; the other
one remained firmly fixed to the deck, still holding her
prisoner. Worse, the other slaves chained to her had fared
far worse than she had as they were hurled against the
side of the ship and lay about like so many more inert
anchors. Aside from having her arms in front of her
again, she was as helplessly chained as before, and she
looked aft, where the first of the boarders were coming
over the stern. At first, she thought they might be Shin,
for they wore bright blue harnesses, like those common
to the Fardar clan. But in the next instant, she realized
that it couldn't be her people. The boarders were using
weapons she had never seen before, and their tactics were
unlike any Shin.

The first wave over the transom formed a shield wall, more
like the sort of thing Krath heavy infantry would do, which
held off the pirates while reinforcements swarmed aboard
behind them. The second rank bore something like long-
barreled arquebuses. Unlike any arquebus Pedi had ever
heard of, however, these had no problem with water or
weather—as they demonstrated with the very first volley.
At least some of that many normal arquebus would have
had their priming soaked during the crossing, but *all* of these
weapons fired successfully into the mass of pirates hammering at the shield wall.

The long-barreled arquebuses also had knives on the
ends, and after the first volley the entire group charged
forward. They wielded the guns more like spears than
firearms, but they did so with a discipline and purpose
that was decidedly un-Shin-like. They strode forward in
step and struck in unison, while the shield bearers
stabbed forward with short spears, sliding the thrusts
upward from below their shields.

Unfortunately, she didn't have long to contemplate this
new mode of warfare before some of the pirates recalled

their duty as Lemmar and decided that killing bound captives was a better use of their time than fighting the boarders. She finally knew despair as four of the pirates approached, one of them slicing down to kill the mostly unconscious Guardsman while two more approached her warily.

"Lemmar slime! I'll eat your tongues for my breakfast!" she shouted, bouncing up to spin a kick into the nearest one's belly. He flew backwards, but so did she, and as she slammed down on her back, the one she hadn't kicked sprang forward, sword upraised.

Roger lost track of the prisoners as he watched the boarding party foam across onto the other ship's deck's under Krindi Fain's direction. Once again, the young Mardukan was proving his stuff, first sending over a small team of assegai-and-shield troops, then following it up with a double line of rifles. A command rang out, the assegai troops squatted instantly and simultaneously, with their shields angled, and the riflemen fired a double volley over their heads. The massive bullets smashed into the tight-packed Lemmar, and the Diasprans followed up immediately with a bayonet charge that was a beautiful thing to see. The combination scattered the remaining Lemmar defenders on the pirate ship's afterdeck, and the boarders stormed ahead towards the surviving clumps of raiders further forward.

"*Yes!*"

Even as Roger yelled in triumph, he felt rather than saw Cord leave his side. His head snapped around, and his eyes widened in a moment of pure shock as the shaman bounded down the ratlines. The huge Mardukan moved with unbelievable speed and agility, and then he flung himself through the air, onto the enemy deck.

He landed, absolutely unsupported, half-way up the ship from *Hooker*'s boarders. And as if that hadn't been enough, he'd thrown himself in front of what must have been the largest single remaining group of Lemmar still on their feet—a cluster of about twelve, with four in the lead and six or eight more following.

Roger couldn't believe it. In every battle, from the day he had first saved Cord's life, his *asi* had always been at his side, guarding his back. The only time he hadn't been, it was because he'd been too seriously wounded in the *previous* battle to stay on his feet. It was an unheard of violation of his *asi*'s responsibilities for him to desert his "master" at such a time!

The prince didn't even curse. Cord had backed him too often for him to waste precious seconds swearing. He just checked to ensure that his revolvers were secure in their holsters and his sword was sheathed across his back.

Then he leapt outward in Cord's wake.

The Lemmar with the sword snarled at Pedi and brought his weapon flashing down . . . only to be flung violently backwards by the enormous, leaf-bladed spear which suddenly split his chest.

Pedi didn't know where the fellow, frankly dangling, above her came from, but he was the best sight she'd ever seen in her life. Even from this angle.

The guy was old and naked as a *slith*, without even a harness, much less a bardouche, but he wielded his huge spear with a deft touch that reminded her of her father's personal armsman back home. That old armsman had seen more battles than she'd seen breakfasts, and could whip any three young bucks while simultaneously drinking a cup of wine. And it looked like this fellow was cut from the same cloth.

Nor was he by himself, although she'd never seen anything weirder than the creature beside him. It looked like a two-*sren*-tall *vern*. It had only two arms, long yellowish head tendrils, similar in color to her own horns, dangling down its back and gathered together with a leather band, and a most peculiar pistol in either hand. Right behind the two of them came another odd creature that looked like a cross between a *sorn* and an *atul*. It was longer than she was tall, about knee-high on the old guy with the spear, equipped with a *most* impressive set of fangs, and striped in red and black. The . . . striped thing hit the deck, took one look around, and charged into the pirates with a keening snarl.

Definitely the oddest threesome she'd ever seen, she thought with an oddly detached calm.

The older fellow took out two more of the pirates with his spear—another thrust to the chest, and the second with a really economical throat slash that was a pleasure to watch—and the striped creature dragged another down with jaws that took the pirate's head neatly off. But the rest of the Lemmar had formed up to charge, and they'd attracted at least another dozen of their fellows to assist them. The fresh cluster of assailants caught the attention of the red-and-black whatever-it-was, and the creature looked up from its initial victim to lunge forward in a counter-charge . . . just as the maybe-*vern* cocked his pistols.

Pedi considered pointing out that there was no way two pistols, especially pistols as puny as those, were going to stop two dozen pirates. Fortunately, he opened fire before she could. Her father had told her often enough to observe before she opened her mouth, and he turned out to have been right once more as the pistols spat shot after shot. They were accurate, too, as was the shooter. Each round hit one of the pirates just below the armoring horn prominence in a thundering cascade of explosions. After a few moments, all that was left was a drifting pall of gunsmoke and dead pirates with shattered, brain-leaking skulls.

Beauty.

Captain Pahner nodded in approval as the Diaspran infantry swept across to the enemy ship. Fain was no officer to let the enemy get the upper hand, and the young captain had thrown his assegai troops across the instant the vessels touched, even before Pahner could pass the order, then followed up with his rifles in an evolution so smooth it was like silk. Effective subordinates were a treasure, and Krindi Fain was as good as any the Marine had met since Bistem Kar.

Everything rikky-tik, he thought.

In days to come, Armand Pahner would reflect upon the premature nature of that thought. He would ponder it, as a sinner pondered the inexplicable actions of an irritated deity. He would wonder if perhaps, by allowing himself to think it, he had angered the God of Perversity, and Murphy, who is His Prophet. It was the only offense he could think of that might have explained what happened next.

Even as he allowed himself to enjoy Fain's success, something flickered at the corner of his eye, and he turned his head just in time to see Roger take a flying leap off of the ratlines, catch the hanging end of a severed Lemmar shroud, and go swinging through the air like some golden-haired ape to land square-footed on the enemy deck.

Pahner just . . . looked for a moment. He was that shocked. The prince, with Dogzard right on his heels, had landed next to his *asi* . . . in exactly the right spot to draw the last remaining formed group of pirates like a magnet. There was no way in hell for Pahner to support them, either. Even if he told the sharpshooters to cover the noble *idiot,* the Lemmar would be on the pair before the snipers could understand the order and redirect their fire.

Cord took down one of the group, which appeared to be intent on slaughtering the captives who'd been chained to the deck. Dogzard dragged down a second pirate, and the shaman dispatched another pair with ruthless efficiency as Roger drew both pistols, and then the prince opened fire. The revolvers—considerably smaller than the monsters Rastar favored, but still firing a twelve-millimeter round with a recoil sufficient to dislocate many humans' wrists—were double-action. Roger's rate of fire was far slower than he could have managed with his off-world bead pistol, but it was impressive, nonetheless. Especially to pirates from a culture that had never been exposed to the concept of repeating firearms at all. The deck of the Lemmar ship was already heavily obscured by the gunsmoke from the Diaspran rifles and *Hooker*'s final broadside, but visibility abruptly deteriorated still further under the clouds of smoke pouring from His Highness's pistols.

It was fortunate that, once again, good subordinates were coming to Pahner's rescue, as at least two of the sharpshooters began engaging the group attacking the prince on their own. The captain could hardly see what was going on aboard the other ship, but it was also obvious that Fain had spotted the action and ordered his assegai troops to advance. The Diasprans were going to have to be somewhat cautious, though, since they were advancing more or less directly into Roger's fire.

The deck of the Lemmar ship had been cleared, but there seemed to still be plenty of the pirates below decks. Some of them were attempting to fight their way up through the hatches, while others were defending still other hatches Diasprans were trying to fight their way *down* through. With, of course, Roger squarely in the middle of it all.

Whatever had happened to the now fully obscured prince, Pahner somehow doubted that Roger was dead. Whatever severely overworked deity had dedicated his full time and effort to keeping the young blockhead alive would undoubtedly have seen to that. On the other hand, what might happen to Roger when one Armand Pahner got his hands on him was a different matter.

He'd *promised* he wasn't going to do this sort of . . . shit anymore.

A sudden, ringing silence filled Pedi's ears, and she realized she was on a deck clear of (living) pirates, still chained, lying on her back, and looking up at this old fellow . . . dangling . . . above her. And while the sight had been welcome, in one way, the angle could have been better. Not to mention the fact that her neck and shoulders hurt like hell.

"Ahem," she said as sweetly as she possibly could under the circumstances. "I don't suppose you could be convinced to take these chains off me?"

CHAPTER ELEVEN

"*Rooogger!*"

The prince closed one reloaded revolver cylinder and turned around as Despreaux came clambering over the side of the ship.

"God *dammit,* Roger! When are you going to *learn?*"

"Your Highness," Captain Fain said, striding across the deck. "That was most thoughtless of you. We were well on our way to clearing the ship, and you jumped directly into our line of fire."

"I know, Captain Fain," Roger said, switching his toot to Diaspran. "But—"

"*ROOOGGGER!*" Armand Pahner strode out of the clearing gunsmoke. "What in the hell was *that,* Your Highness? We had the damned battle well in hand!"

A babble of Mardukan broke out behind Roger as he turned towards the Marine captain with a harassed expression. Denat had made his own, slower way to the deck and was engaged in a full throated harangue of his uncle. From the tone of the shaman's attempted responses—not to mention the irate set of his lower arms—Cord was about to start hollering back like a howler monkey.

Which was remarkably similar to the way *he* felt, the

prince thought. Then he drew a deep breath and keyed the amplifier on his helmet.

"Everyone shut the hell up!"

The sudden silence was as abrupt as it was total, and Roger snorted in satisfaction. Then he turned the amplifier off and continued in a more normal tone.

"I will answer everyone's questions as soon as I have *mine* answered."

He turned to Cord and fixed the old shaman with a baleful look.

"Cord, what in the hell were you thinking?"

"They were killing the prisoners," the shaman answered in his best Imperial. His accent did . . . interesting things to it, but he'd spent many a long evening during the endless journey working on mastering the Empire of Man's universal tongue. He'd needed to, so that he could debate the way the Empire *ought* to be organized in long, evening discussions with Eleanora O'Casey. As a result, his basic grasp of the language was actually very good, despite his accent, considering that he lacked the advantage the humans' toots conferred upon them. It was also *much* better than his Diaspran, and Cord knew Fain would be able to follow at least some of the conversation if they all used that language.

"That's it? The whole explanation?" Roger asked, propping his hands on his hips. "We were clearing the whole ship, Cord. Most of those pirates were going to be overrun by Krindi's troops in no more than a few minutes. The usual pattern is, first, kill the enemy; *then* save the prisoners. Not the other way around!"

"They were killing them at that time, Your Highness," the *asi* pointed out in a tone of massive restraint. "The deaths would have been accomplished before even Captain Fain's soldiers could have stopped it. I could not, in good conscience, permit that to happen."

Pahner drew a deep breath and turned to stare up at the towering Mardukan.

"Hold on. You mean, *you* went first?"

"Yes, he did," Roger said with immense, overstrained patience. "I just followed him. And that's another thing," he continued, turning back to Cord. "What about me? Huh? You're supposed to cover my back. I *depend* on you to cover my back, for God's sake!"

"You were safe on the other ship," Cord said. "How was I to know you would follow me?"

"Of *course* I was going to follow you, you old idiot!" Roger shouted. "Cord— *Arrrgh!*"

"They were killing the prisoners," Cord repeated, gesturing at the one chained at his feet. "I. Could. Not. Let. That. Happen. As I am bonded to you for saving my life, so I am bound to save others. It is the only honorable thing to do."

"So, you were following Cord?" Despreaux asked. "I want to be clear about this."

"Yes," Roger said distinctly. "I was following Cord. It was not Prince Roger being a suicidal idiot. Or, rather, it was not Prince Roger *on his own* being a suicidal idiot."

"I was not being suicidal," Cord interjected. "As you yourself just pointed out, Captain Fain's group would have soon cleared the deck. All I needed to do was to hold off the pirates for a short time."

Roger grabbed his ponytail and yanked at it in frustration.

"Captain Pahner, do *you* want to handle this?"

"Shaman Cord," the captain said, very formally, "this was not a good decision on your part. It's not our job to endanger Roger unnecessarily."

"Captain Pahner," the shaman replied, just as formally, "I am Prince Roger's *asi*. He is not mine. It is not his duty to preserve my life, and he was in no danger of direct attack when I left his side. Moreover, the fact that I am *asi* does not absolve me from the responsibilities of every Warrior of the Way. Indeed, as one who is *asi*— whose own life was saved by one under no obligation to do so—I am bound by the Way to extend that same generosity to others. Symmetry demands it . . . which means that it was clearly my responsibility to prevent the slaughter of innocents. But it was *not* Prince Roger's responsibility to join me when I acted."

Pahner opened his mouth. Then he closed it again while he thought about it for a moment and, finally, shrugged.

"You know, Your Highness, he's got a point. Several of them, in fact." He thought about it a bit longer, and as he did, a faintly evil smile creased his face.

"What?" Roger asked angrily.

"Ah, well, Your Highness," the captain sounded suspiciously like a man who was trying not to chuckle, "I was just wondering how you feel with the shoe on the other foot for once."

Roger began a hot retort, then stopped abruptly. He glowered at the captain, then looked around as Despreaux began to laugh. Finally, he smiled.

"Ahhh, pock you all," he said with a chuckle of his own. "Yeah, okay. I get the point." He shook his head, then took a look around the deck. "So, now that that's out of the way, does anyone know what the situation is?"

"It appears to be mostly under control," Captain Fain said . . . just as two Mardukans—a Diaspran infantry private and one of the pirates—burst upward out of one of the hatches. They fell to the deck, rolling over and over, with the Lemmar using all four arms to push a knife at the private's neck while the private tried to push it back with his true-hands and flailed at the heavier pirate with both false-hands.

Roger and his companions watched the two of them roll across the deck, too surprised by their sudden eruption to do anything else. But Erkum Pol, as always following Fain like an oversized shadow, reacted with all of his wonted efficiency. He reached down with two enormously long arms, jerked the pirate up by his horns, head-butted him, and then let him go.

The pirate dropped like a rock, and the private waved a hand at Pol in thanks.

"As I was saying," Fain continued. "More or less under control. The Lemmar are fighting . . . very hard. None have surrendered, although a few—" he gestured behind him at Pol's victim "—have been rendered unconscious."

"I'm not sure that one's going to survive," Roger observed. "Maybe Erkum should have used a plank."

"Be that as it may," Fain said. "We have the ship."

"And these three surviving prisoners," Roger mused. He hooked one thumb into his gunbelt and drummed on the leather with his fingers while his free hand gestured at the female at Cord's feet. "Watch this one. She's a tough little thing."

Then he pulled out his clasp knife and stepped closer to her.

"So," he said, switching his toot to the local dialect. "What's your story?"

These new maybe-*vern* were very noisy, and the one with the pistols had a really incredible voice. It was so loud Pedi's ears were still ringing. More importantly at the moment however, and whatever language they were using, it was clear there was some disagreement, and she just hoped it wasn't over whether or not to throw everyone over the side, or burn the ships with them still on board. Finally, the one she'd tentatively pegged as the leader—although everyone seemed at first to be angry with him—turned to her.

"What you bard's tale?" he asked in a hash of Krath and High Krath.

Pedi knew enough Krath to figure out what he'd said, but the question didn't make very much sense. And she had to wonder what would happen if she told the truth. They knew Krath, so they were in contact with the Fire Priests. That meant that they would know what a Server of God was. But if she tried to tell them she and her fellow captives weren't Prepareds and they found out, it would only make things worse. Lie, or not lie? Some of them were dressed like Shin, though, and the old one had fought to save them from the Lemmar. Maybe they were allied to the Shin, and she'd just never heard of them?

Not lie.

"I am Pedi Karuse, daughter of the King of Mudh Hemh. I was captured by a raiding party to be a Slave of God. We were being sent to Strem, to be Servants there, but we were taken by the Lemmar in turn, and now by you. Who are you, anyway?"

One of the other Shin prisoners had recovered from the dragging and now looked over at her with wide eyes.

"What happened that the Vale of Mudh Hemh could be raided?" she asked Pedi in Shin.

"I guess the Shadem found a way through the Fire Lands," Pedi said, flicking her false-hands in the most expressive shrug her manacles allowed. "With the Battle Lands so picked over, they must have decided to strike deep. In our sloth and false security, we allowed them to come upon us unaware, but I was outside the walls and raised the cry. And was taken anyway, if not unawares," she snorted.

"What is the language you are using?" the leader asked. Or, she thought that was what he'd asked, anyway. It was difficult to be certain, given the mishmash of Krath and Shin he was speaking.

"It is called Shin," she told him, and decided to be diplomatic about his . . . accent. "How do you know it?"

"I know it from you," the leader said. Then he leaned over her, and a knife blade suddenly appeared on the . . . thing in his hand.

The one nearest him, another *vern,* caught her snap-kick in midair.

"Whoa, there," the *vern* said, with an even thicker accent. "He's just cutting the chain."

The leader had jerked back so quickly, despite being off center, that she probably would have missed anyway. She filed his—probably "his," although all of the *vern* wore coverings which made it hard to tell—extraordinary reflexes away for future consideration. But he seemed remarkably unbothered by her effort to separate his head from his shoulders and gestured at the chain with the knife.

"Do you want that cut off, or would you rather keep it on?"

"Sorry," Pedi said, holding out of her arms. "Off."

Now that she could see it clearly, the knife looked

remarkably like a simple clasp knife, albeit made of unfamiliar materials. But whatever it might *look* like, its blade cut through the heavy chain—and her manacles—effortlessly. The *vern* seemed to exert no strength at all, but her bonds parted with a metallic twang, as easily as if they had been made of cloth, not steel.

"That's a nice knife," she said. "I don't suppose I could convince you to part with it?"

"No," the leader said. "Not that I don't appreciate your chutzpah." The last word was in an unknown language, but the context made it plain, and her false-hands shrugged again.

"I am a Mudh Hemh Shin. It is our way."

"Pleased to meet you," the leader said. His face moved in a weird muscle twitch which showed small, white teeth. "I am Prince Roger Ramius Sergei Alexander Chiang McClintock, Heir Tertiary to the Empire of Man, and currently in charge of this band of cutthroats." His face twitched again. "I saw you kick that one guard to death; you look like you'll fit right in."

Only three of the six captives were still alive. One, the Fire Guard, had been killed by the Lemmar, and the other two by the weapons of the boarders or when the chain wrenched them across the deck.

Although both of those casualties had been Shin, Pedi didn't hold them against the newcomers, these . . . "humans" or their guard. War was a way of life to the Shin; from the lowliest serf to the highest of kings. To die in battle was considered a high honor, and many a serf, as the other captives had been, had won his or her freedom by heroic defense against the Krath raiding columns.

Pedi wondered what to do next. Although the serfs came from other clans, it was clearly her responsibility to take charge of them and insure their welfare until they could be returned to their fiefdoms. Should return prove impossible, she would be required to maintain them to the best of her own ability. And at the moment, that ability was rather low.

The female serf who had spoken so abruptly came forward, her arms crossed, and knelt on the deck, head bowed in ritual obeisance.

"Light of the Mudh Hemh, do you see me?"

"You must be from Sran Vale," Pedi said with a gesture of humorous acceptance.

"I am, Your Light," the serf said in obvious surprise. "How did you know?"

"If my armsman saw someone from Mudh Hemh bobbing and scraping like that to me, he would die of laughter," Pedi said. "Get up. Who are you?"

"I am Slee, serf to the Vassal Trom Sucisp, Your Light."

"And you?" Pedi asked the other serf.

"I am also of the lands of Vassal Trom Sucisp, Your Light," he said, kneeling beside Slee. "Long may you shine. Pin is my name."

"Well, in Mudh Hemh, we don't put much stock in all this bowing and scraping," Pedi said sharply. "Stand up and act like you know what your horns are for. We're better off than we were, but we're not home yet."

"Yes, Your Light," Slee said. "But, begging your pardon, are we to return to our lands?"

"If I can arrange it," she said. "It is our duty."

"Your Light, I agree that it is *our* duty," Slee said in a tone of slight regret. "But surely it is the duty of a *benan* to follow her master?"

Pedi felt her slime go dry as she replayed the memory of that tremendous leap on the part of the old man. She would surely have died without his intervention—the intervention of a stranger, with no obligation to aid her.

"Oh, Krim," she whispered. "Oh, Krim."

"You had not realized, Your Light?" Slee asked. Pedi just looked at her, and the serf inhaled sharply. "Oh, Krim."

"By the Fire, the Smoke, and the Ash!" Pedi cursed. "I had not *thought*. My father will kill me!"

"Your Light," Pin said, "anyone can find themselves *benan*. It . . . happens."

"Not for that," Pedi said, cursing even more vilely. "For *forgetting*."

✧   ✧   ✧

Roger watched the freed prisoners as the discussion of how to crew the vessels wrangled on. Usually, when a ship was captured, a small prize crew was put aboard by the victors. Its purpose was more to ensure that the survivors of the original crew took the captured vessel to the capturing ship's home port than to actually "crew" the prize itself.

But the Lemmar, almost to a Mardukan, had fought to the death. The reason for that ferocious, last-man defense had yet to be determined, but so far, the reaction to the pirates' efforts on the part of the Bronze Barbarians and their auxiliaries was fairly negative. The Lemmar had fought viciously and without quarter, but not particularly *well*. In the opinion of The *Basik*'s Own, that changed them from heroic defenders to suicidal idiots.

Whatever the Lemmar's reasons, there were too few left to man this ship, and much the same story was coming from all of the others. Coupled with the anticipated recapture of the convoy's merchantships to the north, it meant that most of the flotilla's present and prospective prizes would be severely undermanned by the time they reached their destination.

It was with that consideration in mind that Roger was examining the freed captives. Depending on their background, it might or might not be possible to press them into service as sailors. Thus far, though, they were looking fairly . . . odd.

For one thing, it was clear that the female Cord had "rescued" (to the extent that she'd needed rescuing) was in charge. That was strange enough, since there'd been only two places in their entire journey where women were considered anything but chattels. Even in those two places, a woman would not automatically be assumed to be the boss, but in this case, she most definitely was.

There was also the question of her age. Her horns were rather short and very light in color. That smooth, honey-yellow look was generally only found in very young Mardukans, but there was a darker, rougher rim at the base, so it was possible that their coloration and condition were manufactured rather than natural. The other female captive, who had been doing most of the talking thus far, also had horns that were smoother and somewhat lighter than normal. He wondered if the coloration and smoothness was a societal symbol? If that were the case, perhaps the warrior-female's companions were deferring to her because the condition of her horns marked her as belonging to a higher caste.

Whatever they'd been talking about seemed to have been wrapped up, though, because the leader—Pedi Karuse, if he recalled correctly—was striding over to the command group with a very determined set to her four shoulders.

"Your girlfriend's on her way over, Cord," Roger said.

"She is not my 'girlfriend.'" D'Nal Cord looked down at the prince and made an eloquent, four-armed gesture of combined resignation and disgust. "I do not play with children."

"Just save 'em, huh?" Roger joked. "Besides, I don't think she's all *that* young."

"It was my duty," the shaman answered loftily. "And, no, she is not 'that young'; she is simply *too* young."

"Then I don't see what the problem is," Roger continued. "Unless you're just feeling picky, of course."

He was enjoying the shaman's discomfiture. After all the months of having Cord follow him around, dropping proverbs and aphorisms at every turn (not to mention thumping him on the head to emphasize the points of his moral homilies on a ruler's responsibilities), it was good to see him off balance for once. And for all of his rejection of the local female as "just a child," it was clear that the shaman was . . . attracted to her.

Cord glowered at him, and Roger decided to let his mentor off the hook. Instead, he turned his attention to the Mardukan female as she arrived.

"Pedi Karuse? What can we help you with?"

Pedi was unsure how to broach the subject, so she fell back upon ceremony.

"I must speak to you of the Way of Honor, of the Way of the Warrior."

Roger recognized the formal phrasing as distinctly ceremonial, and his toot confirmed that the terms were in a separate dialect, probably archaic.

"I will be pleased to speak to you of the Way. However, most ways of the warrior recognize the primacy of current needs, and we are currently in a crisis. Could this discussion not wait?"

"I grieve that it cannot," the Mardukan female answered definitively. "Yet the full discussion should be short. I have failed in honor, through my failure to acknowledge a debt. The debt and other points of honor are, perhaps, somewhat in conflict, yet the debt itself remains, and I must address it."

"Captain," Roger called to Pahner. "I need Eleanora over here, please!" He turned back to the Mardukan and raised a hand. "I need one of my advisers in on this. I suspect it's going to involve societal differences, and we're going to need better translation and analysis than I can provide."

Although the *vern*'s accent was getting steadily and almost unbelievably quickly better, a great deal of what he had just said remained so much gibberish to Pedi. And whatever *he'd* just said couldn't change her obligations. Nor could the arrival of this "adviser" he mentioned.

"This cannot, on my honor, wait," she said, and turned to D'Nal Cord.

"I am Pedi Dorson Acos Lefan Karuse, daughter of Pedi Agol Ropar Sheta Gastan, King of the Mudh Hemh Vale, Lord of the Mudh Hemh. I bring to this place only my self, my training, my life, and my honor. I formally recognize the *benan* bond under the Way, and I thus pledge my service in all things, from here until we reach the end of the Way, through the Fire and through the Ash. Long may we travel."

"Oh, shit," Roger muttered in Imperial. He glanced at Cord, whose incomprehension of Pedi's language was only too apparent, and hastily consulted the cultural influence database of his toot. Then he consulted it again, cross indexing her words against the original language kernel and every other cultural matrix they'd passed through on their long trek. Unfortunately, it came out the same way both times.

"What?" Cord snapped. "What did she say?"

"Oh, man," Roger said, and shook his head bemusedly. "And you guys don't even have a language in common!"

"What?" Pahner asked, stepping over to the three of them.

"Hey, Cord," Roger said with an evil smile. "You remember all those times I warned you to think before you leap?"

"What did she say?" the shaman repeated dangerously. "And, no, that was usually myself or Captain Pahner speaking to *you.*"

"Well, maybe you should have listened to yourself," Roger told him, beginning to chuckle. He waved a sweeping gesture of his arm and Pedi. "She says she's *asi.*"

"Oh . . . drat," Pahner said. He gazed at Pedi for a moment, then swiveled his eyes to Cord. "Oh . . . pock."

"But . . . But only my people recognize the bond of *asi,*" Cord protested. "I have had long discussions with Eleanora about the culture of the People and the cultures of others we have met on our travels. And only the People recognize the bond of *asi!*"

Roger shook his head, trying—although not very hard— to keep his chuckle from turning into full-throated laughter. The attempt became even more difficult when he looked back at Pedi and recognized her frustration at finding herself just as incapable of understanding Cord as he was of understanding her. Their complete inability to communicate struck the prince as Murphy's perfect revenge upon the cosmopolitan shaman who had appointed himself Roger's "slave," mentor, moral preceptor, and relentless taskmaster. Especially since it looked very much to him as if Pedi was going to be at least as stubborn about this *benan* bond as Cord had been about the bond of *asi.*

"Well," he observed with a seraphic smile, "at least you guys will have *that* much in common."

CHAPTER TWELVE

"Oh, they have more than that in common," Eleanora O'Casey told the people gathered in *Hooker*'s once again crowded wardroom just over three hours later. *"Much more, in fact."*

The problem of prize crews had been partially solved. The five surviving pirate ships had been provided with skeleton crews drawn from all six of the flotilla's schooners, along with a few of the K'Vaernian infantry who knew the difference between a bow and a stern. Then *Hooker, Pentzikis, Sea Foam,* and *Tor Coll* had headed northwest, closehauled and throwing up foam, while *Snarleyow* and *Prince John* (busy stepping a new foremast) kept company with Tob Kerr's *Rain Daughter* and the captured Lemmaran vessels. It was fortunate that the flotilla had brought along replacement spars as deck cargo aboard *Snarleyow*. Replacing *Prince John*'s mast wouldn't be a problem, but Roger wasn't at all sure that they'd be able to replace the rigging of both dismasted pirates, as well. Whether repairs could be made or not, however, he felt confident leaving *Snarleyow* and *Prince John* to look after things while the rest of the flotilla tried to run down the rest of the convoy the pirates had captured.

The current meeting had been called to try to resolve

some of the problems that they would face taking or "recapturing" the remaining ships. In addition, Roger and Pahner were in agreement that it was also time to consider what problems might be anticipated following landfall. As part of that second objective, the meeting would also serve to bring most of the core of the command staff up to date—as far as possible, at least—with the mainland political situation.

"Go ahead," Pahner said now, pulling out a *bisti* root and cutting off a slice. "I've gotten bits and pieces of what we're sailing into, but you might as well tell everybody else."

"Of course." Roger's chief of staff pulled out her pad and keyed it on line. "First—"

"A moment, please," Cord interrupted. "While all of us—" a waving true-hand indicated the humans, Diasprans, and Northerners crowding the compartment "—will understand you well enough, my . . . *benan* will not. She must be aware of this as well."

"Oh, that's okay, Cord." O'Casey smiled with more than a hint of mischief. "We girls already hashed all this out. She's up to date."

"Ah," Cord replied stoically. "Good."

O'Casey waited a moment to see if she could get any more of a rise out of the shaman, but he only sat impassively. After several seconds, she smiled again—a bit more broadly—and continued.

"The pirates in the area, as Captain Kerr already informed us, are called the 'Lemmar.' Actually, I suspect that the term as he uses it isn't exactly accurate. Or perhaps it would be better to say that it isn't completely accurate. He seems to be using it as a generic ethnic term, but as nearly as I can tell, 'The Lemmar' appears to be a political unit, as well—similar to the Barbary Sultanate on Earth or the Shotokan Confederacy. It's based on raiding, high-seas piracy, and forced tribute. As for our particular lot of Lemmar, we captured charts and logs from two of their ships, and we've got a good fix on our position, the position of the raid, and the probable route the prize ships will be taking on their way home.

So we should be able to find most of them and chase them down. The little local fillip is that, as I'm sure everyone noticed, the Lemmar don't care to be taken prisoner."

A fairly harsh chuckle ran through the compartment at her last sentence. The fighters in the wardroom had been through too much—Diaspran, Vashin, and human, alike—in the last year to really care if someone wanted to be suicidal. If that was their society's choice, so be it; the group that had taken to referring to itself as The *Basik*'s Own would be happy to oblige local custom.

Which didn't mean that they were blind to the tactical implications of the situation, of course.

"That's going to cause some problems retaking the ships," Kosutic pointed out after a moment, "considering the fact that they apparently don't care to allow any of their prisoners to be liberated, either. Should we even try to retake the prizes if the Lemmar are going to slaughter any captured crewmen before we get aboard? Will the mainland culture prefer to have their ships and no crews? Can we navigate them to the mainland with no crews? And is there any political payoff to retaking the ships if we get all of their crews killed in the process?"

"From what I've gleaned from Pedi, there should be both a political and financial payoff," O'Casey assured her. "The ships are, technically, the property of the Temple, but if they're taken on the high seas, fairly 'universal' salvage rules apply. If we return them, we'll be in for at worst a percentage of their value. And the supplies they have on board were apparently very important to establishing the Temple's presence on one of the formerly Lemmaran islands. The local priestdom has put a lot of political capital into that project, so helping save it from utter disaster should be viewed well, unless there's some odd secondary reaction."

"So retaking the ships would be a politically positive action?" Pahner said. "I want to be clear on that."

"Yes, Captain," O'Casey said. "I won't go so far as to say it would be 'vital.' But failure to act could be construed as being less friendly—and certainly less 'brave'—than taking action would be. In my professional opinion, barring clear military negative factors, it should be considered highly useful in making *positive* first contact with the mainland culture."

"Okay," Pahner said. "We'll discuss means later. But getting most of the ships and getting them intact may be hard."

"They'll have scattered," Roger mused aloud. "We'll have to *find* them first. Then figure out how to take them without getting all of the original crews killed."

"What about the Lemmar?" O'Casey asked.

"What *about* the Lemmar?" Roger asked in return. His response evoked another general chuckle, and the chief of staff nodded and turned to the next item on her list.

"In that case, I'd like to talk about what we'll call 'The People of the Vales'—the Shin, that is—versus the valley culture, or the Krath. I'll also offer some specu- lation as to where the cultures come from. Julian will discuss the purely military aspects later.

"The Shin are a fairly typical upland barbarian culture. They're centered around small, fertile valleys—the Vales— each of which has a clan chief, or 'king.' All of them are nominally independent, with a few of them allied to each other—or involved in blood feuds—at all times. There's a 'great king' or war leader, in theory, at least, but his authority is strictly limited.

"We do have a contact with the Shin," the chief of staff pointed out, nodding at the female Mardukan who'd taken a position beside Cord. The Shin would have sat behind the shaman, but with him already sitting behind Roger, there simply wasn't room. It had occasioned a certain amount of negotiation when they first entered the cabin.

"And the straight-line distance from the valley entrance to the spaceport is shorter through the vales," the chief of staff continued. "On the other hand, given the infor- mation thus far developed, we're more likely to encounter difficulties passing through the vales than if we stay in the valley."

"Those blood feuds," Pahner said.

"Precisely." O'Casey nodded. "The clans are constantly feuding. We would—could—presumably make contact with and get help and passage from the Mudh Hemh clan, but if we did, we'd automatically find ourselves at war with the Sey Dor clan. There's also a 'cross-valley' dichotomy that Julian will discuss. But it shouldn't affect us."

"Great," Roger said. "What about the valley? And what about the similarities between these . . . Shin and Cord's people?"

"The similarities can be inferred from the linguistic and cultural matrix," O'Casey replied. "The Shin language is *remarkably* similar to the language of The People. Same basic grammatical rules, similar phonemic structure, even the same words in many cases, and only mildly modified in others. There's no question that they come from the same root society, and that the separation is historically recent."

"Which, presumably, explains the cultural similarity between the *benan* and the *asi* bonds," Roger murmured, then cocked an eyebrow at his ex-tutor. "Any idea what's going on there?"

"Best guess is that the Shin are an aboriginal race of this continent which, like the Diasprans, survived the ice age by centering their culture on volcanic secondary features. That is, they stayed around hot springs and naturally warmed caves that should be fairly common on this continent. If I were to hazard a guess, I'd say that some of them then somehow moved over to Cord's continent, on the eastern verge. That would be a heck of a sailing journey, but it's possible that there's a shallow zone between here and there that was partially or mostly exposed by the ice age. We'd have to do a lot of surveying and research to confirm that, though."

"So the divergence is relatively recent, and you think the ancestral group is from this continent?"

"Yes, and a good example is language divergence," O'Casey pointed out. "*Benan* is clearly derived from '*banan*,' which is the Krath word for 'bride.' But compare that to The People's '*benahn*,' which is their word for 'marriage.'" She shrugged. "Obviously, all three words are descended from a common ancestor."

"Obviously," Roger agreed, then grinned, leaned over, and punched Cord on the arm. "Feeling married yet, buddy?"

"Oh, shut up," Cord grumped. "It was for my honor."

"I know," Roger said, somewhat repentantly. "It was for mine, too. Sometimes, honor is a curse."

"Often," Pedi said, suddenly. "I . . . assure what . . . Light O'Casey understand. Word make sense. Some." She twitched one false-hand in a grimace of frustration. "Almost."

"Sort of," Roger agreed, switching to Shin. "But even if the languages are related, that was a real hash of a sentence."

"Yes, but I can learn People," Pedi said.

"No. I learn Shin," Cord said. "Here Shin. People not here."

"Good, it sounds like we can get over the language divide," Pahner interjected, then cocked his head at O'Casey and pulled the conversation back on track. "What about the Krath?"

"Looking at the map, the Shin vales probably make up the majority of the continent, which is mostly volcanic 'badlands,'" O'Casey said. "But the continent's bisected by a larger valley that curls like a tadpole, or a paisley mark, from the south in a big bend north and to the west. And that valley is where the majority of the population and real power of the continent lives.

"The valley of the Krath has a contiguous river that stretches, through some falls, all the way from a large upland vale to the sea. And, from Pedi's description, it's very heavily populated. The valley is one more or less continuous political unit, as well. I say 'more or less' because from the description of the scheming that goes on, the emperor, who is also the Highest of the High Priests and who rules from a capital near the spaceport, has only limited control over the lower valley.

"The society is a highly regimented theocracy, with the chief political officers of each region also being the high priests. And, unlike Diaspra, it is *not* a benevolent one. The society is similar to the latter medieval society of the Adanthi or the Chinese Manchu Dynasty. And it's also heavily slavery-based, as Julian will now discuss."

The NCO nodded at his cue and stood.

"We've got a bit of a problem. One of the reasons the Krath and the Shin don't get along is that the Krath see the Shin as a ready source of slaves for their theocracy— what are called 'The Slaves of God.' In addition, the base barbarian society is bisected by the valley. On the generally western and northern side are the Shin, but on the eastern and southern sides, the vales belong to the Shadem. And the Shin and the Shadem don't get along at all. In fact, the Krath use the Shadem for advance scouts for their raiding parties against the Shin. As a consequence, the Shin *really* hate the Shadem.

"As for the raiding parties themselves, they seem to be carried out by one of the three branches of the Krath military complex. In fact, the Krath military appears to be divided into these raiders, which are closely controlled by the Temple, and into an inner security military/police apparatus that maintains control of the civilian population, and a field army."

"The reason for having an 'army' in the first place is complex," O'Casey interjected. "With all due respect for Pedi's people, the Shin are at best a minor nuisance for the Krath. In fact, the valley has no effective external enemy, so there should be no need for a significant field army. But the satraps apparently engage in a certain amount of somewhat ritualistic warfare to settle disputes. The raiders and the internal security forces are controlled by the priesthood, but the priests in charge of them are almost a separate sect. The field army, in contrast, is closely controlled by the high priests, some of whom have even been officers. It's as if the internal security apparatus and these slave raiders are a 'subclass' of the military hierarchy. A necessary evil, but not particularly well regarded by the 'regulars.' "

"Just how big and how 'good' is this army of theirs?" Pahner asked. "We may need to use it against the spaceport."

"I'd guess they're pretty good in a set-piece battle, Sir," Julian replied. "All of our intel, presently, is from a single, biased source. Even allowing for that, though, my feeling is that they're not terribly flexible. I'm sure we could use them in a charge, or in a fixed defensive position, but I'm not sure how useful they'd actually be in taking the spaceport. Much as I despise the concept behind them, their slave raiders might actually be better."

"Justification?" Pahner asked. "And how numerous are they?"

"I don't have any firm estimates on their numbers at this time," Julian admitted. "From the fact that they appear to be the most . . . heavily utilized branch of the military, though, my guess is that they represent an at least potentially worthwhile auxiliary force. As for why they'd probably be more useful to us than the Krath field army, the raiders are the ones who regularly go in against the Shin, and the Shin are clearly no slouches on their own ground. The raiders have to be fast and nimble to handle them, and fast and nimble will probably be the way to go with the spaceport. So as . . . repugnant as they are, it would probably behoove us to try to . . ."

"Insinuate ourselves with them?" O'Casey asked. "Grand."

"I still don't get the whole thing with the slave raiders," Roger said. "They should have a surplus of labor in the valley, based on what Eleanor's just told us. So why go slave raiding?"

"Apparently, their slaves don't . . . have much of a lifespan, Your Highness," Julian said in a carefully uninflected voice. "That creates a constant need for fresh supplies of them. So the Krath raid the Shin lands for these 'servants.' Such as our own most recent recruits."

"Uh-oh." Roger grimaced. "Cord always wants to be at my back. And now Pedi has to follow him around—"

"And it will be evident that she's Shin, yes, Your Highness."

"That's going to cause problems in negotiations," O'Casey pointed out. "But we have another problem in that regard, as well. The Krath consider themselves the

center of the universe, with all other polities subject to
them. And their obeisance rituals are extensive."

"So they consider the Empress, as one more 'foreign
barbarian,' to be their subject," Roger said. "That's . . . not
an uncommon attitude in first-contact situations. Especially not with stagnant, satisfied planet-bound civilizations."

"Not for *first*-contact situations, no," Despreaux put in
just a bit grimly.

"I understand where you're going, Nimashet," O'Casey
said after moment. "And you're right. The Empire's policy
is to refuse to recognize the insistence of such govern-
ments on their primacy, especially over the Empress herself. But usually an ambassador has a drop battalion
available to *pointedly* refuse to make obeisance on the
Empress' part."

"And the person doing the refusing is usually just
that—an ambassador," Pahner pointed out. "Not a member of the Imperial family itself. So what do we do?"

"Well, I'll take point in the negotiations," O'Casey
replied. "The first officials we encounter probably won't
require a formal obeisance, so I'll politely tap dance for
as long as I can, pointing out that while the Son of the
Fire is, undoubtedly, a great sort, having our leaders do
a full prostration is simply out of the question. We'll
probably be able to avoid it by showing our personal
might and only dealing with lower-level functionaries."

"What about the possibility of their informing the port?"
Pahner asked.

"We may actually be in luck there," the chief of staff
said cautiously. "Although the Son of the Fire is undoubtedly a god, it appears that some of his ministers are very
secular in their desires. In addition, the valley is broken into five satrapies which are fairly independent of
the central government. The local satrap may or may not
contact the imperial capital at all, and even if he does,
it wouldn't necessarily get noticed by the imperial bureaucracy. Or sent on to the spaceport even if it was. I get
the feeling that the port authorities are avoiding contact
with the natives to a great degree."

"Basis?" Pahner asked sharply.

"Pedi had never heard of anyone like us," Julian replied for O'Casey. "But she's otherwise very knowledgeable about local customs and politics. That suggests the humans are keeping a fairly low-profile. For that matter, she'd never even heard of 'ships that fly.' If there were any sort of regular aerial traffic between the port and the Krath, one would expect rumors about it to be fairly widespread, but neither she nor any of the Shin ever heard a thing about it. On the other hand, she knows what was served at the emperor's latest feast."

"Okay, that brings me to the second point that's throwing me," Roger said. "In just about every other culture we've dealt with, females were considered less than nothing. What's with the Shin?"

"Pedi?" O'Casey asked, switching her toot to Shin. "Why are you a warrior? We humans have no problem with that; some of our best warriors are women." She waved at Kosutic and Despreaux. "But we find it strange on your world. Unusual. We have seen nothing like it elsewhere in our travels since coming here. Explain this to us, please. In Shin or Krath, as you prefer."

"I am not a warrior," the female answered in Shin. "I am a *begai*—a war-child. My father is a warrior, a King of Warriors, and I am expected to mate with warriors. That our union may be stronger, I am trained in the small arts—the arts of Hand, Foot, and Horn, and also in the small arts of the Spear and Sword. If you want to see someone who is truly good at the arts, you must see my father."

"Do the Krath treat their women as equals?" Roger asked. "Or, at least, near equals, as you've described?"

"No, they do not," the Shin practically spat. "Their women are *vern,* no offense."

"None taken," Roger told her with a grin. "I've heard it before—although they prefer '*basik*' on the other continent. But if the Krath don't, what about the Shadem?"

"The Shadem women are even worse—slaves, nothing else. They go around swathed in *sumei,* heavy robes that keep even their countenances covered. The same with the

Lemmar, the beasts!" She paused suddenly, cocking her head speculatively, as if something about Roger's tone had suddenly toggled some inner suspicion.

"Why?" she asked.

"Well," Roger said with another grin, "I think we've just found our disguise for the Shin."

"No, we have not!" Pedi said angrily. "I am no Shadem or Lemmar *vern* to go around covered in their stinking *sumei*!"

"Would you rather be a Servant of God?" Cord asked tonelessly in his native tongue. The shaman had clearly been following the conversation, in general terms, at least, and he turned a gaze as expressionless as his voice upon his new *benan*. "Or forsworn in your duty? The path of duty is not a matter of 'I will not.' Choose."

Roger doubted that Pedi understood Cord's words completely, either, but it was obvious that the gist had come through. Her mouth worked for a moment, then she hissed a one-word reply to him.

"*Robes*."

"There, all settled," the prince said brightly. "But what *kind* of robes? And where do we get them?"

"The *sumei* weighs at least five *latha*—that's 'what kind of robes,'" Pedi said bitterly. "And we can get them at Kirsti. That's one of the main weaving centers for all of Krath." After a moment she brightened up. "On the other hand, it's also one of the main producers of cosmetics." She made a complicated gesture of annoyance. "And on that subject, Light O'Casey has something else she needs to say."

"I'm not sure what we'll do about that, Pedi," the chief of staff said, with an odd, sidelong glance at Cord.

"What's the problem?" Pahner asked.

"Well," Julian began, heroically grasping the dilemma's horns for O'Casey, "you'll notice that most of the Mardukans we've run into on this side of the pond are clothed."

"Not Pedi," Roger objected, gesturing at the *benan* with his chin.

"Ah, yes, but she was a *slave*," O'Casey replied

carefully. "It turns out that the Krath and the Shin—even the Shadem—have strong body modesty taboos."

"Oh, dear," Kosutic said. "I think maybe we should get the young lady some clothes then, eh?"

"That would be good," Julian agreed. "Cord feels perfectly normal the way he is. He's just . . . undressed. Pedi, on the other hand—"

"Feels nekkid," the sergeant major finished. "Gotcha. We'll deal with that in just a moment. But how does it affect the rest of us?"

"Well, the Vashin are generally in their armor," Julian pointed out. "Same with the Diasprans and K'Vaernians. If we just explain that the local custom is to wear clothing, and staying in armor is the easy way to do that, they'll stay in armor most of the time."

"We need to get them some clothes, anyway," Pahner observed. "Armor all the time is bad hygiene."

"Yes, Sir," Julian acknowledged. "But they're *used* to the concept. Cord and Denat, on the other hand . . ."

"What about us?" Cord asked.

"If we go wandering around with naked 'savages' we'll be violating various local taboos," O'Casey explained delicately. "It might have a certain 'kick' to it politically, but it would be much more likely to be destabilizing."

"Since the local custom is to wear clothes like humans do, Cord," Roger translated, "we'll all have to do the same thing or these snooty locals will think we're uncivilized."

"What? Cover myself in cloth?" Cord sounded incredulous. "Ridiculous! What reasonable person would do such a thing?!"

"*Pedi* would," Roger reminded him with unwonted delicacy. "The Lemmar didn't take her clothes away to be *nice* when they captured her, Cord."

"You mean . . . Oh." The shaman made a complex gesture of frustration. "I'm too old to have an *asi—benan*! Especially one I can't even understand!"

"Hey, don't blame that on the *language*, buddy!" Roger retorted. "*Nobody* understands women!"

"You'll pay for that, Your Highness," Despreaux warned

him with a smile. Roger nodded in acknowledgment of her threat, but his expression had suddenly taken on an abstracted air. He tugged at a strand of hair for a second, then looked around the table.

"People wear clothes around here," he observed, and his eyes moved to Cord's new *benan*. "How many did the Lemmar assign to each of their prize crews when they took the convoy, Pedi?"

"It looked like five to ten—possibly as many as fifteen for the larger vessels. Why?"

"Rastar?"

The Vashin former prince looked up when Roger called his name. He'd been silent through most of the discussion, since it was related to seagoing matters, where he'd had little to add. Now he cocked his head, alerted by Roger's tone.

"You called, O Light of the East?"

Roger chuckled and shook his head.

"How many of these Lemmar do you think you can take. Seriously?"

"By surprise, I take it?" the Vashin asked. He let one hand rest on each of his revolvers' butts. "At least six, I believe. More if the range is great enough for additional shots before they can close. It all depends."

"And there, I think, is the answer to the question of how we capture the other ships," Roger said with a nod.

"And just who, if I may ask, backs him up?" Pahner asked darkly.

"Well," Roger replied with a smile of total innocence, "I suppose that depends on who—after Rastar, of course—is fastest with a pistol."

CHAPTER THIRTEEN

Tras Sofu had no intention of becoming a Servant of God.

Again.

He had escaped from the slave pens of the High Temple once. Only a handful of Servants could make that claim, and even fewer of those who had escaped had evaded recapture. That was a point which had been forcibly borne in upon Sofu when he realized that Agents of Justice were everywhere in Kirsti. That was also when he'd decided that the sailor's life was for him. Trade among the Lemmar Islands was dangerous—there were not only the pirates to consider, but many shoals and other hazards to navigation. But given the choice between sailing the shoals and risking the Agents, he'd take shipwreck any day.

Now, though, his bet had backfired, and he was probably headed right back to the pens. It was rumored, however, that the Lemmar would sometimes keep particularly good workers around. There were always plenty of Lemmar who wanted to work their ships—the greatest problem with the Islands was a lack of shipping, not lack of labor for the boats—but a good crewman, as Tras was, might be better than an untrained landsman. So whenever there was any little thing that needed doing, it was always Tras Sofu who was right on it. Any line that needed coiling was coiled immediately, and when the crew went aloft, it was always Tras Sofu in the lead.

His Lemmar captors—and his fellow crewmen, for that matter—knew what he was doing. Whether the Lemmar approved or were just sizing him up for the ax was another matter, though. He knew that the pirates could give slime whether any Krath lived or died. The way they'd casually chopped the heads off of the captain and the mate had made that point crystal clear. And, truth to tell, he wasn't all that much fonder of the pirates than he was of the Fire Priests themselves. But while a part of him hated acting as an accomplice in his own enslavement, being indispensable to his new masters was the only way he knew to avoid his old ones . . . and the pens.

None of the other crewmen seemed to share his attitude. They were sunk into apathy, never taking initiative at anything. The Lemmar literally had to whip them into position, and they acted as if they were already Servants, beyond redemption. Certainly none of them seemed to have any interest in emulating Tras's ingratiating eagerness.

Which was why it was Tras, always head-up and looking out for any change he might turn to advantage, who first spotted the strange, triangular sails on the horizon. The single ship closing fast on an impossible tack, practically straight into the wind, was the most outlandish thing Tras had ever seen—and he paused for a moment, staring at the sleek, low-slung craft as the slower Krath merchantman dipped into a swell. He wondered briefly what worm had devoured the brains of anyone stupid enough to sail *towards* a Lemmaran ship. Of course, the merchant ship didn't look very much like a raiding vessel, so perhaps these lunatics didn't realize what they were dealing with. If that were the case, was it his responsibility to try to warn them off before they sailed into such danger?

He considered the proposition from all angles for

several breaths, then decided that other people's sanity wasn't his problem. Staying alive was, so he cupped his true-hands into a trumpet and turned towards the prize crew's captain.

"Sail *ho!*"

Roger refused to look across at Kosutic.

He knew that whatever emotion the sergeant major might be feeling wasn't going to be evident. Which didn't mean what she was feeling was happy.

The prince's blistering argument with Pahner had been as private as possible on a ship as small as the *Hooker*. But the fact that the argument had taken place—and that the captain hadn't won—was obvious to the entire command. It was one of the very few times since their first arrival on this planet that Roger and the commander of his bodyguard, the man who had kept him alive through the entire nightmare trek, had had a clear and cold difference of opinion. And it was the very first time since landing on Marduk that Roger had pushed it to the wall.

He was aware that that sort of rift was a serious problem in any command, but he also felt that there'd been two positive aspects to it. The first was that even Pahner had been forced to concede that he really *was* the best close quarters fighter in their entire force, better even than Kosutic or Pahner himself. Both of those senior warriors had started the trip with far more experience than the prince. But this odyssey had involved more combat than any Marine usually saw in three lifetimes, and along the way Roger had proven that there was *no one* in the company as fast or as dangerous in a close encounter as the prince the company was supposed to protect. That meant that, argument or no argument, from any tactical viewpoint, he was the right person to have exactly where he was.

And the second positive aspect was that what he and Pahner had had was an *argument*. For all its ferocity, there had been no shouting, no screaming. The disagreement had been deep and fundamental, and in the end, Roger knew that his rank as a member of the Imperial family had played a major role in Pahner's concession of his point. But he also knew that Armand Pahner would never have conceded it anyway, whatever the potential future consequences for himself or his career might have been, if he hadn't learned to respect Roger's judgment. He might not share it, and at the moment the captain might not be particularly aware that he "respected," it either. But Roger knew. The spoiled prince it was Captain Armand Pahner's task to protect would never have won an argument with the Bronze Barbarians' company commander. The Colonel Roger MacClintock, the official commander of Pahner's regiment, who had emerged from the crucible of Marduk, could win one . . . if he argued long enough.

On the other hand, nothing Roger could say or do could change the fact that, from Pahner's perspective, this entire operation was completely insane. However great the political advantages of recapturing the Temple's merchant ships might be, the loss of Roger's life would make everything all too many of Pahner's Marines had died to accomplish on this planet totally meaningless. Roger knew it, and he knew Pahner did, too. Just as he knew that the commander of his bodyguard was capable of applying ruthless logic to the command decisions that faced him. Which left Roger just a bit puzzled. He supposed that some officers in Pahner's position might have looked at the shifting structure of interwoven loyalties and military discipline in The *Basik*'s Own and decided that it was time to apply that age-old aphorism, "Never give an order you *know* won't be obeyed." Especially not when the Marines' erstwhile object of contempt had metamorphosed into their warrior leader . . . and into *the* primary authority figure in the eyes of the "native levies" supporting them.

But that wasn't Pahner's style. If the captain had sensed that he was losing control—and, with it, the ability to discharge his sworn responsibilities—to a very junior officer (whatever that junior officer's birth-rank might happen to be), he would have taken steps to prevent it from happening. And Roger had come to know

Pahner well enough to be certain that any steps the captain took would have been effective ones.

So there had to be another factor in the equation, one Roger hadn't quite identified yet. Something which had caused Armand Pahner to be willing to allow the prince he was oath bound to keep alive, even at the cost of pouring out the blood of every one of his own men and women like water, to risk his neck on what was essentially an operation of secondary importance.

Not knowing what that factor was . . . bothered Roger. It seemed to underscore some deep, fundamental change in his relationship with the man who had become even more of a father figure for him than Kostas had been. And though he would never have admitted it to Pahner in so many words, that relationship had become one of the most precious relationships in his entire life.

But at least things had gone smoothly enough so far to suggest that Colonel MacClintock's plan was an effective one. This was the fifth ship they'd approached, and each of the others had fallen like clockwork. The Lemmar couldn't seem to conceive of the possibility that two people could be so dangerous. Kosutic and Honal were the only ones with obvious weapons, so they tended to focus the pirates' attention upon themselves . . . and away from Rastar and Roger himself. Which was unfortunate for the Lemmar.

Rastar wore a robe, similar to a djellabah, open on both sides, that concealed the four pistols he had holstered across the front of his body without slowing him down when he reached for them. The ancient Terran fable about the wolf in sheep's clothing came forcibly to mind every time Roger glanced at the big Northern cavalryman. Not that he was any less dangerous himself. Pahner might have lost the argument about just who was going on this little expedition, but he'd flatly refused to let Roger take the human-sized revolvers he'd been carrying ever since they left K'Vaern's Cove. Conserving irreplaceable ammunition for the Marines' bead pistols was all very well, but as he'd rather icily pointed out, there was no point saving ammunition if the person they were all responsible for protecting managed to get his idiotic self killed. Which was why Roger wore a cloak of Marshadan *dianda* to help conceal the pair of bead pistols holstered under his uniform tunic.

Now, as the sailing dinghy came alongside its fifth target, Roger stood behind Rastar, looking as innocuous as possible, while Honal and Kosutic handled their own weapons with a certain deliberate ostentation designed to make *certain* all eyes were on them.

"Hullo the deck!" Rastar bellowed in a voice trained to cut through the bedlam and carnage of a cavalry battle.

"Stand clear!" one of the pirates bellowed back almost as loudly. The caller was amidships, on the starboard side, shading his eyes to pick out the small craft. Most of the rest of his fellow pirates seemed to be concentrating on the *Hooker,* which had taken up station a tactful three hundred meters off the prize ship's starboard quarter. On the other hand, Captain T'Sool had his gun ports open and the carronades run out. These Lemmar wouldn't have any more clue about the deadliness of those weapons than the first pirates the flotilla had encountered, but they'd recognize them as a deliberate warning that their visitors had teeth of their own.

"We want none of you!" the pirate spokesman added harshly. "Stand clear, I say!"

"We're just here to buy!" Roger shouted up at him, taking over with the toot-given fluency in the local languages Rastar couldn't hope to match. "We've crossed the eastern ocean, and it was a longer voyage than we expected! We're short on supplies—especially food!"

He gazed upward, watching the Mardukans silhouetted against the gray-clouded sky, and glad that both Pedi Karuse and Tob Kerr had been able to confirm that it was fairly common practice to barter with chance-met ships when one's own supplies ran short. Of course, one normally avoided dealing with people like Lemmar raiders in the process, but there was—as far as these raiders knew—no way for the people in the small boat sailing up beside them to realize they weren't honest merchant traders.

"We'll send two people aboard—no more!" Roger added, his tone as wheedling as he could manage. "And we'll transfer anything we buy to small boats, like this one. Don't worry! We're not pirates—and our ship will stay will clear of you! We're willing to pay in gold or trade goods!"

There was a short consultation among the members of the prize crew, but in the end, as all of their fellows had done, they finally acquiesced.

"Keep your hands out from your sides—even you, *vern*-looking fellow! And only two! The leaders, not their guards."

"Agreed!" Roger called back. "But be warned! Our ship is faster than yours, and more heavily armed. And we aren't 'leaders'—just pursers and good swimmers! Try to take us prisoner, and we'll be over the side so fast your head swims. After which our crew will swarm over you like *greg,* and we'll take what we need and feed you to the fish!"

"Fair enough!" the Lemmar captain shouted back with an undergrunt of half-genuine laughter. He wasn't entirely happy about the situation, of course. After all, he'd seen how rapidly *Hooker* had overhauled his own lumbering command, so he knew perfectly well that he could never hope to outrun her. And however undersized those bombards looked, the strange ship obviously mounted a lot of them, whereas his captured merchantship mounted no more than four pathetic swivels. Nor was he unaware of the ancient law of the sea: big fish ate little fish, and at the moment this clumsy tub of a merchant ship might turn out to be a very small fish indeed if it came to that. So if he could get through this encounter by simply selling some of the cargo—especially for a good price—so much the better. After all, *he* hadn't paid for any of it!

And if the negotiations went badly, these two peculiar 'pursers' could become Servants, for all he cared.

Roger caught the thrown line and went up the side of the ship hand-over-hand. Like the other merchantmen they'd taken, this one was nearly as round as it was long. The design made for plenty of cargo space, and with enough ballast, it was seaworthy—after a fashion, at least. But the ships were *slow,* terribly slow. If this thing could break six knots in a hurricane, he would be surprised.

It was also the largest they had so far encountered, which probably meant the prize crew was going to be larger, as well.

He reached the top and nodded at the staring Lemmar who'd thrown the rope, keeping his hands well away from his sides and the one knife he openly carried on his belt as he swung over the rail. Two of the pirates greeting him held arquebuses lightly in their true-hands, not pointed exactly at him, but close. There was a third pirate by the helmsman, and another directing a work party up forward. There'd been five pirates aboard three of the four ships they'd already taken, and seven aboard the fourth, so there was at least one still unaccounted for here. Given the size of the ship, though, Roger's guess was that there were at least three more somewhere below-decks. Possibly as many as five or six.

Rastar climbed over the side behind him and made a complex, multi-armed gesture of greeting.

"I greet you in the name of K'Vaern's Cove," he said in the language of the Vashin. "I am Rastar Komas, formerly Prince of Therdan. We are, as we said, in need of provisions. We need ten thousand sedant of grain, at least fourteen hundred sedant of fruit, four thousand sedant of salted meat, and at least seven hogsheads of fresh water."

Roger nodded solemnly to Rastar and turned to the obviously totally uncomprehending pirates.

"This is Rastar Komas, formerly Prince of Therdan," he announced through his toot. "I am his interpreter. Prince Rastar is now the supply officer for our trading party. He has listed our needs, but to translate them properly, I require better knowledge of your weights and measures, which must obviously be different from our own."

He paused. The prize crews of the other four ships had all reacted in one of two ways at this point in his little spiel, and he and Rastar had a small side bet as to which of those responses this group would select.

"You said something about gold?" the larger of the arquebus-armed pirates asked.

Ah, a type two. Rastar owes me money.

"Yes. We can pay in gold by balance measure, or we have trade goods, such as the cloth from which this cloak is made."

Roger spread the drape of the silken cape to the sides, then spun on his toes to show how well it flowed. When he turned back around, his hands were full of bead pistols.

The inquisitive pirate never had time to realize what had happened. He and his companion were already flying backwards, heads messily removed by the hypervelocity beads, before he even had time to wonder what the strange objects in the outsized *vern*'s hands were.

"By the Gods of Thunder, Roger!" Rastar complained as he took two shots to drop the Lemmar by the helmsman. "Leave some for the rest of us!"

"Whatever," the prince snapped. A third shot dispatched the pirate who had been supervising the work party up forward, and he kicked the arquebus out of the hands of a twitching body at his feet. Then he turned to examine the hatches as Kosutic swarmed over the side. The work party forward had taken cover behind the body of their erstwhile supervisor and showed no inclination to move out from behind it, so he couldn't form any idea of where the other pirates might be hiding.

"Take the stern. We'll start from the bow," he said, stepping forward. "Be careful."

"As always," Honal answered for his cousin. The Vashin noble jerked the slide on his new shotgun, which had a six-gauge bore and brass-based, paper cartridges. Then he tossed off a salute. "And this time, watch your head," he added. "No ramming it into the undersides of decks!"

"Speaking of which," Kosutic said, clapping the prince's helmet onto his head. "Now be a good boy and flip down the visor, Your Highness."

"Yes, Mother," Roger said, still looking at the forward-most hatch. It was lashed securely down from the out-side, but it could just as well be secured from the inside, as well. He flipped down the helmet visor and sent out a pulse of ultrasound, but the region under the deck seemed to be a cargo hold, filled with indecipherable shapes.

"What do you think?" he asked the sergeant major.

"Well, I hate going through where they expect, but I don't want the damned thing to flood, either." Kosutic replied.

"At least they didn't have any bombards before they were captured," Roger pointed out. "Which means there's no powder magazine, either."

"Point taken," Kosutic acknowledged. "Swimming beats the hell out of being blown up, I suppose. But that wasn't exactly what I meant."

"I know it wasn't," Roger replied, and took the breach-ing charge the sergeant major had extracted from her rucksack. He laid out the coil of explosive on the foredeck and stood back from the circle.

"Shouldn't be any flooding problem coming down from above," he pointed out. "And I'm sure we can convince the original crew to fix any little holes in the deck for us later."

A deep "boom" sounded from the after portion of the ship as Honal broke in his new shotgun, and Roger reached for the detonator.

"Fire in the hole!"

Honal once again acknowledged how much the humans had taught the Vashin. The human techniques of "close combat," for example, were a novel approach. The tra-ditional Vashin technique for fighting inside a city, for example was simply to throw groups at the problem and let them work it out. But the humans had raised the art of fighting inside buildings, or in this case ships, to a high art.

He jacked another of the paper-and-brass cartridges into the reloading chute and nodded at his prince. Rastar had finally finished reloading one of his revolvers and nodded back. They were more than halfway through the ship, and so far they'd encountered four more of the Lemmar. None of the pirates had survived the meeting, and given that only one of the Krath seamen had been killed along the way, the "breakage," as the humans termed it, had been minimal.

Rastar closed the cylinder and eased cautiously forward towards the bulkhead door in front of them, then paused as he heard the distinctive *"Crack!"* of one of Roger's bead pistols. Then both Vashin heard a second shot. And a third.

"Careful," Rastar said. "We're getting close. One more compartment, maybe."

"Agreed," Honal replied, barely above a whisper, as he lined up on the latch of the door. "Ready."

"Go!"

Honal triggered a round into the latch and kicked the door wide, then stood to the side as Rastar went through it. The space beyond was apparently the ship's galley, and the only occupant was one of the Krath seaman— the cook, or a cook's mate, presumably—crouching in the corner with a cleaver in his hand. There were, however, two more doors: one in the far bulkhead, and one to starboard.

The sound of Roger's fire had come more from starboard, so Rastar kept one eye on that door in case the prince came barreling through it.

"Clear," Rastar called . . . just as the far door opened.

The Lemmar who came through it (a senior commander, from the quality of his armor and weapons) was tall as a mountain, and clearly infuriated. He'd turned to his left, towards the starboard door, as he entered, so he'd probably intended to intercept Roger and Kosutic on their way aft. Unfortunately, he'd run into the Prince of Therdan first.

Rastar's first shot took him high on the left side. It wasn't in a vital spot, which made it a poor shot indeed for Rastar, so he was able to raise his short sword and charge forward. Worse, two more Lemmar came through the door right behind him, both with arquebuses.

Rastar fired a second double-action shot at the leader from his upper left revolver, then followed up with his upper right true-hand. Both rounds hit his target's chest, barely a handspan apart, and the pirate officer's charge came to an abrupt end.

Rastar's lower left pistol was out of bullets, and only a single round remained in the lower right, but he used that one to hit the starboard arquebusman as he stepped around his now-falling commander. But that still left the *port* arquebusman, and Rastar's normally lightning reactions had never seemed so slow. His pistol hands seemed to be in slow motion as they swung towards the Lemmar, and his brain noted every detail as the Lemmar carefully raised his weapon, sighted, and lowered its burning slow match towards the touchhole—

Only to fly back in a welter of gore as Honal leaned around his cousin and triggered a single round.

"*Told* you to get a shotgun," Honal said as he stepped past the former prince.

"Oh, sure," Rastar grumped. "Just because they made you *real* cartridges, and I still have these flashplant things!"

The starboard door swung open, and Kosutic's head came slowly into view. She looked around the galley and shook her head.

"You're a fine one to talk about 'leave some for the rest of us,' "she observed dryly.

Roger watched the galley easing alongside *Ima Hooker* and shook his head.

"Why do I have this worm crawling up my spine? he asked softly.

"Because we're about to lose a measure of our control," Pahner replied calmly. "Uncomfortable feeling, isn't it? Especially since it's pretty clear that if we upset these people, they can squash us like bugs."

Kirsti was huge. The harbor was a collapsed caldera, at least twenty kilometers across, that was cut by a

massive river. The entire caldera, from the waterline to
its highest ridge, was covered in a mixture of terrace
cultivation and buildings. Most of the buildings were one-
and two-story structures of wood frame, with whitewashed
adobe filling the voids, and they were packed in cheek
by jowl.

Nearer water level, the majority of the buildings were
finer and larger. According to Pedi, they were residences
for the hierarchy of the city, and they were constructed
of well-fitted basalt blocks. On each of the caldera's land-
ward flanks, where it was bisected by the river, there
was also a vast temple complex. The westerly complex
was larger and ran from the base of the slope up the
massive ridge to the very crest.

Northwest of that temple were three obviously active
volcanoes whose faintly smoking crests rose even over
the massive caldera walls. And beyond the caldera a large
valley—presumably the famous Valley of the Krath—faded
into blue mystery.

The river was at least three kilometers across where
it entered the harbor. The flooded portion of the caldera
was close to twelve kilometers across, and the outer
break was at least six kilometers wide, so the harbor
enjoyed two massive natural breakwaters to either side
of the entrance. Strangely, given the quality of the har-
borage, most of the boats in sight were local craft—small
fishing caiques and dories, many of them pulled up on
the basalt and tufa of the shore. There were a few larger
merchant ships, like *Rain Daughter* and the other members of her ill-fated convoy, but most of the boatyards
looked to be capable only of building smaller vessels.

The majority of the merchant and fishing vessels were
in the eastern harbor, while the majority of the military
vessels—a collection of galleys and small sailing vessels—
were on the western side, close to the larger temple.
Massive forts with gigantic hooped bombards flanked the
outer opening, and a pile of wood and rusting chains
on the western shore indicated that the harbor could be
closed with a chain boom at need, despite the immen-
sity of its entrance.

The river's current was strong where it entered the caldera, and the harbor's outflow had been evident for the last two days of the flotilla's approach to the city. With that sort of current, and the river's obvious silt load, any normal harbor would have filled up and become a delta in very short order. In Kirsti's case, though, all the silt seemed to be washing on out to sea, which Roger thought probably said some interesting things about the subsurface topography. On a more immediate level, the effects from the river's current must make things even more "interesting" for the local navy.

The flotilla had acquired its escort very early the day before, when two Krath galleys had appeared over the horizon and headed rapidly towards them. They'd slowed down quite a bit when they realized just how large— and peculiar-looking—the flotilla actually was. But the minor priest in command of them had also quickly recognized the recaptured merchantmen for what they were and continued onward to make contact. After looking the situation over and taking testimony from Tob Kerr and some of the other crewmen aboard the retaken ships, he had determined that any decision making needed to be done at a higher level.

The convoy had been ordered to proceed to Kirsti, accompanied by the junior galley, while the CO took his own ship ahead. The schooners had continued to laze along behind the slower Krath ships until they finally reached port, still accompanied by the junior galley, which was obviously trying to decide whether it was an honor guard or a captor.

Now the other ship had returned, and a group of clearly senior functionaries was prominently visible on its afterdeck. Actual first contact was about to be made with a group that was also in contact with the spaceport.

No wonder it was an . . . uncomfortable moment, Roger thought. They'd come a long way to reach this point, and it had felt at times that, given all they'd already overcome, nothing could possibly stop them now. But the reality, as demonstrated by this massive city, was that the hardest part of the journey was yet to come.

"There's no good way to do this part, Your Highness," Pahner continued. "We don't even know if this end of the valley is aware of the Imperial presence, and we have no feel for what the upper valley's attitude might be. If Kirsti's rulers *are* aware of the Imperial presence, and happy with it, then we can't exactly come right out and say we're going to evict the current residents. If they're *not* aware of the Imperial presence, then trying to explain our purpose would require a lot more explaining than any of us want to get into. So we'll just tell them we're shipwrecked traders, traveling with other traders and envoys from 'lands beyond the sea' to their capital to establish commercial and diplomatic relations with their High Priest. Trying to talk our little army past them should be interesting, though."

Roger looked over at the captain, then back at the galley. The fact that Pahner had said that much, at this point, didn't strike him as a good sign. It was as clear an indication of nervousness as he had ever seen out of the normally sanguine Marine.

"We're not going to be stopped at this point, Captain," the prince said. "We're going to the port. We're going to take the port, commandeer the first tramp freighter to come along, and go home to Mother. And that's all there is to it."

Pahner shook his head and chuckled.

"Yes, Sir, Your Highness," he said. "As you command."

Roger took a deep breath as the first of the local guards swarmed up the boarding ladder, then nodded sharply to his bodyguard's commander. They *were* going home, he thought . . . or his name wasn't Roger Ramius Sergei Alexander Chiang MacClintock.

Sor Teb tried to simultaneously control his shock and wriggle gracefully out of the silly rope and wood contraption that had lifted him aboard. The returning galley commander's description had taken nearly a day to filter up the chain of priests and high priests until it hit someone who knew of the human presence on the Plateau. When it did, of course, everyone had panicked.

Given the political and personal friction between Gimoz Kushu and the Mouth of Fire, it had been immediately assumed that the humans had come as messengers from the Plateau, and that was the basis upon which Teb had been sent to greet them.

But one look at these visitors told him all of the hierarchy's elaborate calculations had been wrong. These people were clearly different from the ones on the Plateau.

First of all, there weren't very many of the humans. In fact, he saw no more than seven or eight of them currently in sight, which was a severe shock to the system. He'd never seen a senior human with so few guards! But apparently *these* senior humans had different priorities. Indeed, they actually seemed to be using the Mardukans in their group as *personal* guards, whereas none of the Plateau humans would have dreamed of trusting locals that deeply.

Second, although these humans' travel-worn uniforms were similar to the equipment of the guards of the Imperial port on the Plateau, their weapons were not. Those weapons weren't arquebuses, either, though. They fell into some middle ground, with that undeniable look of lethality which seemed to characterize all human weapons, but also with the look of something that had been manufactured locally, not brought in aboard one of their marvelous vessels from beyond the clouds. But what was most astonishing of all was that their native guards and attendants carried what were clearly versions of the same weapons which had been modified for their greater size. No human from the Plateau would *ever* have considered something like that!

At least one of the humans wore a holstered pistol of obvious Imperial manufacture, but Sor Teb saw none of the fire weapons—the "plasma guns"—that the Plateau guards carried. He didn't even see any of the "bead guns." There might be some on board this remarkable vessel, but if there were, why weren't any of the humans carrying them?

He wondered for a moment what their story was. And

he also wondered what they would say. And, last, he wondered how he would determine the difference between the two.

It would be interesting.

Eleanora O'Casey nodded and smiled, her mouth closed, then backed away from the cluster of priests.

"Curiouser and curiouser," she said as she turned to Roger and Pahner.

"Pretty cagey, aren't they?" Roger replied. "I'm not getting anything."

"They're in contact with the port," O'Casey said. "No question about that. And at least two of them have met humans. Notice how they don't seem as goggle-eyed as the others?"

"Yep," Pahner said. "But they're not being real forthcoming, are they?"

"No, they're not. I think there are two things going on. This satrap isn't in contact with the port, but one of the 'minor' members of the party, that Sor Teb, has been to the capital and had dealings with humans recently. That's probably why he's part of this whole party. I'm guessing that he's the closest they've got to a 'human specialist,' so he's here as something like an ambassador from the court."

"Or a spy," Pahner pointed out.

"Or a spy," O'Casey agreed. "I also think he's really the one in control of the entire group, too. Nothing that they've done, but whenever he says something, the entire conversation shifts."

"Can we land?" the Marine asked, getting back to the point of the conversation.

"Yes, although they're obviously not real happy about having a small army come right through their city."

"We have to have the guards," the captain said firmly.

"It's more a matter of how many," the chief of staff replied. "They're not willing to permit more than three hundred at a time off the ships. And all of them have to carry their edged weapons peace bonded and their firearms unloaded, though they can carry ammunition with them. Everyone's going to be issued 'identification' showing what they're permitted to carry and where. All very civilized, frankly. Oh! And officers can carry loaded pistols."

"Well, that's the first company of attackers," Roger laughed. "Between Rastar and me."

"Okay," Pahner said unhappily. "I don't see any option but to accept their terms. But we've got gear to get to wherever we're barracking. And that's another thing—we have to be located together in a defensible spot."

"I covered that," O'Casey assured him. "I pointed out that Roger was a high noble of the human empire, although I called him Baron Chang. It wasn't even a lie, since it's one of his minor titles. But as a human baron, he's required to be secure at all times. And I also told them that we have quite a lot of bags and baggage. They're okay with that."

"And they don't have a problem with the official reason for our visit?" Pahner asked.

"Not yet, at any rate," O'Casey said. "I explained that 'Baron Chang' was shipwrecked on the other continent, and that the locals there aided him and his party. As a reward, and to discharge his honor obligations to those who helped him, the baron has guided representatives of the local merchants and princes to this continent to establish relations with the Krath, as well as to accompany him as guards to his 'friends' at the spaceport. They seem to accept all of that as reasonable enough, but they want us to barrack down here in the port area. I don't think they've dealt with large contingents from other civilizations before, but they're reacting a bit like Meiji Japan did. They're establishing an acceptable zone for the foreigners and making the rest of the city off limits to general movement.

"You'll need to approve the quarters when we get there, but they should be adequate. Also, we won't be able to just let the troops roam at will. They're going to get upset if there's a noticeable presence of foreigners wandering around, so our people will need to stay mainly in quarters,"

"Remember Marshad," Roger said quietly.

"Oh, yes," Pahner agreed with a frown. "We'll deep sweep the walls this time."

He looked back at O'Casey.

"What about the *civan*? And how do we resupply? People will have to go to the markets. And I'm not sure about keeping all the troops cooped up until they decide what to do with us."

"These people aren't used to foreigners," O'Casey said with a shrug. "The leadership is going to try to quarantine us as much as possible, and the populace is probably going to be a bit hostile, so keeping the troops close would probably be a good idea, anyway. And whatever else happens, the *civan* will have to stay down here with us by the docks. The Temple doesn't seem to have any stables. For that matter, there don't seem to be any *civan* on this continent at all, although they do have *turom*. Anyway, there's no proper stabling to be had further up in the city, but there are stock holding areas down here by the docks which should work for them, and we can get fodder and forage from the local merchants."

"Can we trade directly with the merchants?" Roger asked. "Or do we have to trade through the Temple?"

"We have to turn over a portion of the trade goods to the Temple as a tax. Actually, the toots translate that as a 'tithe.' Other than that, we can deal direct with the local merchants."

"I'm sure T'Sool will get right to work setting up contacts for Wes Til," Roger said, laughing.

"There are some additional restrictions," O'Casey went on, her expression thoughtful as she accessed her toot. "Lots of them. We'll each be issued plaques that define where we can go and under what circumstances. None of us can enter a temple, cross to the eastern city, or enter any private residence without specific, official permission. Officers and specified guards—no more than five—may enter Temple offices which are more or less secular property. And there's a pretty strict curfew: no being out of our compound after dark or during religious observances. I've got a list of ceremonies for the next couple of weeks, so we should be able to schedule around them without too much trouble."

"Jeez," Roger said. "Real friendly folks. Now I wish we'd let their damned ships go!"

"Arguably, their response could have been worse," O'Casey pointed out. "The problem is that this is an *'alles verboten'* society. If it's not specifically permitted, it's forbidden. They also tax everything but breathing, apparently. And I'd bet they're working on that!"

"Well, if you're in agreement, Captain, I'd still say let's do it," Roger said with a frown. "We'll take a company of the Carnan Battalion, with Fain in command, and leave the rest on the ships. They can land to stretch their legs, and we'll rotate the units. Same with the cavalry, but we'll take Rastar and Honal with us and leave the ship side with Chim."

Pahner looked around the massive city, then nodded his head slowly.

"Concur, Your Highness. But we'd better keep our heads down and be really patient. Any alternative to getting along with these people just doesn't bear thinking on."

CHAPTER FOURTEEN

"Whoooeee, now *this* is what I call civilization!" Julian laughed as the column of troops wound its way inland from the docks. The area where they were to be sequestered was about halfway between the wharves proper and the beginning of the temple zone.

The local population had been systematically evacuated from their path, but it was clear that the roads normally swarmed with buyers and sellers. Both sides of the route were lined with temporary stalls and carts which had been hastily abandoned, probably at the behest of the staff-wielding guards who "escorted" the humans. This area seemed to be primarily a fishmarket, but the slope gave a fair view of other boulevards, and all of them were packed with crowds.

"Still sheep to be fleece'," Poertena grunted as he shifted his pack for a better fit.

That pack was something of a legend. Its base was a standard Marine field ruck, but it had been "expanded" by a specially formatted multi-tool into about four times its normal volume. No one was quite sure what all it contained. They knew that it did *not* have a table-top tester for plasma rifles, although it now contained a field expedient replacement for one. And it did *not* have a sink; several of the Marines had asked. Other than that,

it seemed to contain anything and everything normally
found in a first-class armory, including—but not limited
to—plasma welders, micrometers, parts, field lathes, and
even a "tool about town" christened the "pick pocking
wrench" that was stuffed sideways through the top flap.
The "pick pocking wrench" was Poertena's tool of last
resort—a meter-long Stilson adjustable. If a recalcitrant
weapon failed to function to specification, or, God forbid, a suit of armor locked up, it was exposed to the
"pick pocking wrench." Usually the piece of equipment
shaped up immediately. If not, its exposure was increased
until it shaped up or shipped out.

"We gonna teach 'em acey-deucy?" Denat asked. Cord's
nephew had followed the company across half the world,
more out of curiosity than for any other reason. Along
the way, he'd proven invaluable as a natural born "intelligence agent"—only impolite people called him a spy.
And he'd proven equally valuable, of course, as Poertena's
right hand man when it came to introducing people to
the new concept of "cards."

"Nah." The Pinopan spat. "For t'ese pockers? We teach
them canasta."

"Oooooooo,"Julian laughed. "That's nasty!"

"Canasta what I teach people I don' like," Poertena
said. "Next to bridge, t'ere's nothin' worse. An' even
t'ese bastards don' deserve to have bridge inflic' on
t'em. I don't t'ink I like t'em much, but bridge be too
nasty."

"I don't like this, Krindi." Erkum Pol turned the
embossed plaque hung around his neck upside down and
tried to read it. "I feel like a *civan* in the market."

"Get used to it," Fain replied, watching the line of
Diaspran infantry being issued the amuletlike identification badges. "If we don't have them, we'll get arrested
by the local guards for carrying illegal weapons."

"That's another thing—I don't like all these pocking
guards." Pol peered suspiciously at the ranks of local
Mardukans. The issuing ceremony was taking place in
a large warehouse by the waterfront, part of a complex

of four, and two walls of the warehouse were lined with Krath guardsmen.

Once everyone had been issued credentials and the area was considered secured, this warehouse and the other three would be turned over to the humans and their allies for their quarters and storage. The facility had very little going for it, but at least it was a roof, and it wasn't rocking. There was a public latrine just outside, and the locals assured them that it was capable of handling all the waste from the K'Vaernian contingent. Other than that, it would be not much better than camping out. All and all, it was in keeping with the unfriendly nature of their reception so far.

Krindi contemplated the ranks of guards for a moment, then made a gesture of negation.

"They're not anything to worry about," he grunted. Among other things, the guards were armed only with long clubs. It was obvious that they spent most of their "fighting" time dealing with robbers and rioters. His Diaspran infantry, by contrast, were armed with their breechloaders and still carried their bayonets. The guns were unloaded, and the bayonets were tied into their sheaths with cords, but that would take only a moment to fix.

Yet weaponry was only a part of it—and not the largest one. The veterans of The *Basik*'s Own were survivors of the titanic clashes around Sindi, where thirty thousand Diaspran, K'Vaernian, and Vashin soldiers had smashed over three times their own number of Boman warriors. Individually, caught in a bar fight by these Krath guards, their experience might not be of any particular consequence. But in a unit, under discipline, it was questionable whether there was another fighting force on all of Marduk that was their equal.

And if there *were* one, these pocking Krath pussies sure weren't it.

"Not a problem," Fain said with a quiet chuckle. "*Basik* to the *atul*."

"This isn't going well," O'Casey said as she slipped down onto one of the pillows and stretched out. Julian followed her into the room, and the intel NCO looked as if he'd bitten a lemon.

"More runaround?" Roger quirked an eyebrow.

"More runaround," O'Casey confirmed.

The meeting was small, composed of just the central command group: O'Casey, Roger, Kosutic, and Pahner, along with Julian for his intel information and Poertena to discuss supply. Even Cord and Pedi Karuse had wandered off somewhere. The difficulties O'Casey had already encountered suggested that they would have to meet again, with a larger group, if they were going to work out plans to deal with those same difficulties. But for now, it seemed wiser to discuss the bad news only with the commanders.

The bottom line was that they needed the Krath. On the K'Vaernian continent, there'd always been "handles" they could use—differing factions they could ally with or manipulate, or alternate routes they could use to go around obstacles. Here, though, the only way to get to their objective was through the Krath, and the Krath were turning out to be not only insular and hostile, but also remarkably lacking in handles.

"There are several things going on on the surface," she said with a sigh, "and who knows how many in the background! Sor Teb, our low-rank greeter, is actually the head of the slave-raiding forces. Technically, that's all he is, but the reality seems to be that he's something between a grand vizier and head of the external intelligence service. He's very much playing his own game, and my guess is that he's angling to succeed the local high priest. Everyone else in the local power structure seems to think he is, as well, and there seem to me to be two camps: one against him, and one neutral."

"No allies at all?" Roger's eyebrow quirked. "And what does this have to do with us?"

"No obvious allies, anyway," O'Casey replied with a headshake. "And what it has to do with us is that he not only has some of the best forces, but he's also the most probable danger to our plans. There's also the fact that, in general, nobody else on the council is willing to make a decision unless he's present, so it might be that what's actually happening is that his plotting is so far along everybody else is just staying out of his way."

"Guards like his troopers would probably make decent assassins," Julian pointed out. "And they are very feared—the Scourge, that is. Far more than the Flail."

"What's the Scourge? Or, for that matter, the Flail?" Pahner asked. "Those are new terms to me."

"We just picked up on them,"Julian admitted. "The names of the three paramilitary groups associated with the Temple are the Sere, the Scourge, and the Flail. The Scourge is Sor Teb's group of slave-catchers, but the Sere is the external guard force, while the Flail is the internal police force. Together, that triumvirate's COs make up a military high council."

"I would surmise that the high priests use these groups to counterbalance each other," O'Casey interrupted. She looked out the window at the trio of volcanoes looming over the city and shrugged. "There is resistance to Sor Teb, mostly from the Sere, the conventional forces whose function is to skirmish with the other satraps. The Sere's leader is Lorak Tral. Of all the High Council, Tral acts the most like a true believer, so he's well liked by the general population, and his appears to be the next most powerful faction. The local satrap, however, is beginning to fail. The jockeying for his position is coming to a boil, and it looks like it may be happening a bit too soon for Tral's plans or prospects. The fact that the last two high priests have been from the Sere is fanning the fire under the pot, too. Apparently, the other interest groups think it would be a Bad Idea to let the Sere build up any more of a 'dynasty' by putting its third CO in a row into the satrap's throne, which is making it very difficult for Tral to rally much support amongst his fellow councilors. It looks like, whatever the general public thinks about it, the Scourge's leader is going to be the next high priest."

"Can't be a popular pick," Roger observed. He scratched Dogzard's spine and shook his head. "A slave trader as a high priest?"

"It's not popular, Your Highness," Julian agreed immediately. "People don't say it outright, but he's not well liked at all. He's feared, but it's not even a respectful fear. Just . . . fear."

"So what does this succession struggle have to do with us?" Roger asked again, then stiffened as the floor shuddered slightly under them. "Uh-oh!"

The shuddering continued for a moment or two, then stopped, and Julian shook his head.

"You know, Your Highness, if you're going to turn on that earthquake-generator whenever you speak . . ."

"Damn," Kosutic said. "At least it was light. I hope it wasn't a pre-shock, though."

"Without a good sensor net, it's impossible to know," Roger said, leaning over and patting the hissing beast on her legs. "But I don't think Dogzard likes them."

"She's not the only one, Your Highness," Pahner said. "It would be a hell of a thing to get you this far and lose you to an earthquake!"

"Likewise, Captain." Roger smiled. "But where were we? Ah, yes. This Sor Teb and why he's important to our plans."

"It's starting to look like we're not going anywhere without his okay," O'Casey pointed out. "We haven't even gotten a solid yes or no on permission to leave the city, much less to head into the other satraps. The official position is that the local authorities have to get the permission of the other satraps in advance before letting us enter their territories, but that doesn't hold water."

"No, it doesn't," Julian agreed. "Denat's been talking with Pedi Karuse. It's funny, in a way. Cord is probably the best scholar we have, after Eleanora, of course, but Denat has a much better ear for languages."

Actually, Roger thought, Julian was considerably understating the case. He'd never met anyone, Mardukan or human, who had an ear for language that matched Denat's. Cord's nephew's natural affinity for languages was almost scary. The only native Mardukan who came close to matching it was Rastar, and even he had a much more pronounced accent, however good his grasp of grammar and syntax might be.

"He's picked up enough of the local dialect from her for a decent start," Julian continued, "and he went out doing his 'dumb barb' routine.

"According to what he's managed to overhear, a fairly large portion of the valley to the immediate north is controlled by Kirsti. The next satrap to the north is Wio, and Wio isn't well regarded by the locals. All of the satraps upriver from here—starting with Wio—charge extortionate tolls for goods to move through them, and Kirsti resents hell out of the way that subsidizes the other satrapies' merchant classes. In Wio's case, for example, the Kirsti merchants can either deal exclusively with Wio's . . . or lose half their value to Wio's tolls before they even get to another market on its other side."

"And, of course, trade can't pass through the tribal vales at all," O'Casey pointed out. "There's not much point trying to pass through the Shadem. Even if they wouldn't raid the caravans blind, they're on the 'outside' of the curve of the river, so there's nobody on their other side to trade with, anyway. And trying to pass through the Shin lands would be . . . really a bad idea."

"But there's a fair distance between Kirsti and the Wio border," Julian said. "They divide the satraps into districts called 'watches,' and it looks as if each watch is about fifty kilometers across. There are four of them between here and Wio, so we're looking at about two hundred kilometers of travel. And there's another entire major city between here and Wio, as well. They seem to have a pretty good internal transportation system. In fact, it looks to be far and away the best of any we've encountered so far. So there's no real physical bar to our making the trip. They just want to keep us in place."

"How far to the Imperial capital itself?" Roger asked. "And to the spaceport."

"Twenty marches," Julian promptly replied. "And three more satrapies."

"Could they have already sent a message?" the prince

asked. "To the capital, or even the port? I know they're independent of the capital, but 'what if'? For that matter, 'what if' the entire reason they're keeping us from leaving Kirsti is to keep us penned up here until a message comes back down the chain to tell them what to do with us?"

"Well," Pahner said. He leaned back, gazed thoughtfully up at the ceiling, pulled out a *bisti* root, and carefully cut off a sliver. Then he slowly and deliberately inserted the sliver into his mouth. So far as they'd been able to discover, the root was unknown on this continent, and his supply was dwindling fast.

"We've been here for ten days," he said finally. "If it's twenty marches to the capital, that means another ten days for any messenger to get there, or to the port. If a message got to the capital, I'd think that there'd be some discussion before it was sent on to the port. So, figure another twelve days or so before it gets to the governor . . . or whoever is running the port."

"And we could see an assault shuttle here within a day or two afterwards," Roger said with a grimace.

"Yes, Your Highness," the captain agreed evenly. "We could."

"And what do we do about that?"

"One thing is to try to get a better feel for the intentions of this Sor fellow," Pahner replied. "If he's ambitious enough to want to head up the local satrap, he'd probably be even more interested in knocking off the entire valley."

"Try to recruit him?" O'Casey asked dubiously, and grimaced. "He's a slippery little snake, Armand. Reminds me of Grath Chain in Diaspra . . . only competent."

"I don't like him either," Pahner said. "But he's the most likely to be willing to take a chance. If we back his coup, we use our better position and his raiding forces to move up through the other satraps and take the port."

"And if he balks?" Roger asked.

"Well, if Eleanora's negotiations aren't completed by the end of the week, I suggest we come up with a Plan B and implement it," Pahner said. "At that point, we can assume that the port is aware of our presence."

"And what do we do about *that*?" Roger asked again.

Pahner let a flash of annoyance cross his face, but the question wasn't really off-point. In fact, it was bang on-point.

"Then we cut our way out of the city, head for the hills, and hope like hell we can disappear in the Shin mountains before the port localizes us."

"I thought you said there was no alternative to being patient," Roger said with a smile, and almost despite himself, Pahner smiled back, ever so slightly.

"And the Shin?" the prince continued after a moment.

"We'll cross that bridge when we come to it," Pahner said, his smile fading into a frown. "Getting out of town will be hard enough," he went on, and turned to the intelligence NCO.

"Julian, we need to work up a full order of battle on the local forces. In addition, I want routes from here to the gates, alternate routes, and alternate gates. I want to know where all the guard houses are, what the forces at each guardhouse consist of, probable reaction times, and how they're equipped. I want to know as much as you can find out about the forces *outside* the city, as well. And we need a better feel for the relative capabilities of the three different forces here in Kirsti. Last, I want to know where the main units of this slaving force are. It's beginning to look like they're both the most effective force, and the one with the most effective commander. I want to know, if we make a move to break out of town, where the majority of them are, and when we can expect their reaction."

"Tall order, Captain," Julian said as he marked up his pad. "But I'll try. We've still got some of our remotes left. I'll get them deployed and then get Poertena and Denat to spread around a little silver, see what sort of HumInt they can shake free."

"Shanghai Despreaux and anyone else you need," the captain said. "You know what to do."

"Yes, Sir," Julian replied. "That I do."

"Poertena," Pahner continued. "Supplies."

"Bad, Cap'n," the Pinopan growled. "T'e price of grain is ou'rageous—worse t'an anyt'ing since Ran Tai! An' t'ese pockers gots no barbarian armies to drive t'em up, either. Food has to be nearly half an annual income. Jus' feeding t'e *civan* is gettin' expensive. I been laying in supplies for t'e trip, but t'ey low, Sir. Low."

"Julian, figure out what's stored in the area around us. Get with Poertena on that. Make up a list of targets."

"These guys really have you exercised, Captain," Roger said carefully. "You don't normally think in terms of looting."

"They have me nervous, Your Highness," the Marine replied. "Their invariable response has been at least passively hostile. They're very closed, in ways I don't care for, and we're looking at the possibility that they may be in contact with the port. All of those things tend to trip my professional paranoia circuit."

"Mine, too," Kosutic said. "And that's not the only thing making me nervous. Or, rather, one of the ways they're 'closed' . . . bothers me. I've been trying to keep from stepping on any toes by avoiding the subject of religion, and it's been remarkably easy."

"I can tell from your tone that that does a lot more than just 'bother' you, Smaj," Roger said. "But why does it?"

"You've been to a theocracy, Your Highness," the sergeant major replied. "Think about Diaspra. Or about the Diaspran infantry. They're constantly discussing religion; it's their main topic of conversation. But these people don't talk about their religion *at all*. That isn't normal by any theocracy's viewpoint. In fact, it's frankly weird. They say that in Armagh, if you ask the price of a loaf of bread, the baker will tell you that His Wickedness proceeds from God. But if you ask the butcher for a steak, *he'll* tell you that God proceeds from His Wickedness. The best I can determine, these guys worship a fire god. That's *it*, Sir. The whole enchilada. The sum total of all I've been able to learn about a theocracy's doctrine and dogma, and I got most of that from discussions with Pedi."

She shook her head.

"I don't trust theocrats who won't discuss theology, Your Highness. I have to wonder what they're hiding."

"We'd still be better off with their support," Pahner said. "But in the event that it drops in the pot, that they inform the port of our presence and we have to deal with that, we should have plans in place for how to exit the town and how to obtain the supplies we need. Fortunately, we have a week or two to figure all of that out."

"There's just one thing," O'Casey said, her expression pensive. Pahner looked at her, and she shrugged. "What if they're quicker than that? Quicker than twenty days up?"

"What do you mean?" Roger asked uncomfortably. "They don't have *civan*, so I don't see how they can move much faster than a *turom* caravan."

"I'm thinking about the Incas," his chief of staff said with an unhappy grimace. "They used to use teams of runners. You'd be surprised how much distance you can cover when each person is running, oh, twenty kilometers as fast as he can go. Or, rather, how much distance a *message* can cover in how little time if each relay is by someone who has to run *only* twenty kilometers as quickly as he can."

"No, I wouldn't be surprised at all," Pahner said with an even unhappier grimace. "That's a lovely thought."

"Yep," Julian agreed. "On that note, I guess I'd better get started on that order of battle," he added. Then he laughed.

"What?" Pahner asked.

"Well, what's the worst case, Sir?" Julian asked with a decidedly manic grin. "I mean, that's what we've got to think about, right?"

"Yes, it is, Sergeant," Pahner agreed tightly. He cut the NCO a certain amount of slack, because pressure brought out two things in Julian: brilliance, and humor. "The worst case? The worst case would be that the starport is fully under the control of the Saints, and that they're able to determine that the humans reported to them are being led by His Highness."

"Yes, Sir. That *is* the worst case from our perspective," Julian agreed. "But now think about their *reaction* to the news."

It was the worst tradecraft that Temu Jin had seen in all the thirty-plus years since he'd first left Pinopa.

The small gap in the security wall at the back side of the spaceport required the governor's "secret contact" to cross the entire compound just to meet the native runner. And since the hike required the receiver to break his normal routine—usually with no advance warning to let him build a believable reason for him to be here— anyone investigating the governor's (many) illegal activities would have found it ludicrously easy to identify, analyze, and break the communications chain. All they'd have had to do would be to watch for the idiot marching back and forth at the most ridiculous time of day for the least logical reason.

Short of wearing an illuminated holo-placard saying "Secret Courier!" in meter-high letters, Jin couldn't think of anything else he might have done to make the hypothetical analyst's job any easier.

There were only two saving graces to the incredibly stupid set up. The first was that it had been set up by a previous communications technician, so Jin didn't have to take responsibility for it. The other was that the person on the base responsible for trying to *find* the link was Jin.

It was also a "hard contact." That was, the people at both ends knew if there was a message to be exchanged. By way of comparison, his own tenuous communications with his control had been a soft-connect, and almost entirely "one-way." His outbound communications method—message chips passed via a dead-drop to well-paid tramp freighter pursers— had been cut out when all three of his contacts became victims of "piracy" in the sector.

Inbound, it was easier. The local garrison received a variety of e-zines and carefully crafted personal ads passed all the information he needed to receive. He occasionally wondered, as he perused them, how many of the other messages were code. He especially did that after the last missive—the message for "Irene" that told her it was over. That she should go on with her life.

The one that told him he was out in the cold.

It had been interesting, from a professional perspective, that there'd been at least twice as many personals as normal in that particular month's e-zines. The memory still brought a certain grim chuckle, and he wondered how many other people there'd been on how many other planets, looking at those messages and going "What the . . . ?"

The code had been the ultimate disaster message, telling him that "the World" was gone, and he was to sever all contacts, trust no one, respond to nothing but personal contacts. For him, it had simply been one more nail in the coffin. Heck, bad news on Marduk was as expected as rain, right?

He took the leather satchel from the Mardukan and walked back into the bushes at the edge of the field. The entire set-up was just *too* asinine. So imbecilic. So *amateurish* he was embarrassed every time he went through the charade. The Mardukan, some unknown "agent" of the Kirsti satrap, would now go back through a cleared passage in the minefields, through a portion of the mono-wire that had been changed out in favor of less lethal materials, and through an area where the sensors had been bypassed. The governor, whose life and limb, in the event of attack, *depended* on all those defenses, had ordered the changes so that these "secret communiques" could slip through. *Ordered* it!

Jin shook his head and cracked the seal on the pouch. The governor could not, of course, read Krath, despite having been here for over fifteen years, and despite the fact that "learning" it would require only an upload to his toot and a few minutes of his time. No, the governor had better things to do than learn enough of the language so that the minor messages—like, oh, *secret communiques,* for an example that just *popped* to mind—

could be read by someone other than his *communications technicians.* Such as the *governor.*

Jin shook his head again. Could it be possible that the Empire was truly so short on functional genetic material that they'd had no choice but to send this . . . this . . . *idiot* out to be governor?

No. No, he told himself. The Empire couldn't possibly be that hard up for talent. No, this was a brilliant ploy of the Imperial bureaucracy. They'd found themselves stuck with someone so stupid, so dazzlingly incompetent, that the only possible defense had been to send him someplace so utterly unimportant that even *he* could do no damage there.

Jin took a deep breath, clearing his mind of the governor and the asininity of whoever had assigned him to Marduk. It actually helped, and he felt marginally more cheerful as he unfolded the message. Then he read the first few words . . . and closed his eyes.

For just a moment, a remembered whiff of corruption seemed to fill his nostrils and he almost fell out of character. He knew—*knew*—that if anyone saw him in that moment, his life wouldn't be worth a Mardukan raindrop. He knew he had to get his composure together, that far more than just his life depended upon it, but for a moment it was all he could do not to cry. He *wanted* to cry. To scream. He wanted to shout for joy and terror. To announce the arrival of the moment he'd spent hours dreaming of as he stared up at the bunk above his. Although, he admitted, his dreamy imagination had never included the possibility that he'd want to throw up when the moment came.

He had a real problem, though. Not one that he hadn't planned for, but a problem nonetheless. Since returning from the aborted "rescue mission," he'd slowly and carefully worked himself into a position where he picked up most of these communications. It was generally shoved off on the low man on the totem pole—not only was it a long way across the port in the heat, but the messages rarely had any significance for the humans. They were generally about the shifting politics of the inter-satrap "wars," and how much was that going to affect the port? Other satraps sent messages to other locations, and he picked up most of those, as well. But this was the one communique that it was absolutely essential the governor never see . . . and the one he had set up the entire system to ensure that he *did* see.

Or would have, if Temu Jin had had any intention of ever allowing him to.

Unfortunately, the guv wasn't a *complete* idiot. He always had at least two people translate any missive from his local contacts, and he would be aware that Jin had gone out to collect this one. Which meant that Jin couldn't simply make this one disappear. There had to be a different one.

He reached into his tunic and pulled out a small package, then flipped through the various messages contained in it until he got to one that he liked. He read over it once more, and smiled thinly. It appeared that the Shin barbarians were contemplating allying with the Wio in return for the Wio's halting their raids. This was, in fact, bullshit. But since it was "unconfirmed" information from the Im Enensu satrap, when it turned out to be incorrect, it would simply be assumed that the Im Enensu satrap, or his intel chief, couldn't find his ass with all four hands.

Somebody might notice that the pickup signal had been the one for Kirsti, not Im Enensu, but that was unlikely. Temu had been the one to receive that as well . . . exactly as planned.

He heard a voice in his head, as if it were yesterday: *"Plan! Prior Planning Prevents Piss Poor Performance! Plan for every contingency. And be ready when your plans fail!"*

Come to think of it, he really wished someone had told his control that.

He put the new message into the satchel, closed it, and pocketed the original. He could analyze it later. It would be interesting reading.

He looked up at the eternal Mardukan clouds, flared his nostrils wide, and smiled into the first drops of rain.

"What a beautiful pocking day!"

CHAPTER FIFTEEN

Denat picked up the poorly baked clay cup and hunched his shoulders. A fine rain had started, and the denizens of the port bazaar had mostly sought the shelter of awnings. Personally, Denat was rather enjoying the gentle drizzle, and sitting out in the middle of it should make him look even more like an ignorant barbarian, too stupid to come in out of the rain. Certainly not the sort of eavesdropper a civilized city dweller would concern himself over—after all, the ignorant lout wouldn't be able to understand a *civilized* dialect, anyway!

But Denat understood enough to get along, and even from his place in the open, he could hear various conversations under the awnings. He grimaced as he sipped the thin, sour wine—just the sort of stuff any city barkeep would offer a dumb barbarian—and subconsciously sorted the discussions around him.

Denat's natural flair for espionage, like his gift for languages, had never been noticeable among the People as the nephew of the village shaman. His skill and expertise as a hunter, one who actually preferred to hunt the far more dangerous night than during the day, had been well-known. And even before the arrival of the Marines, he'd had an affinity for picking up information in Q'Nkok, which was one of the reasons Cord had asked him to accompany the humans as they made their way to that first city. But no one had ever seriously considered him for the role of a spy.

It had originally been assumed that he and the other village warriors would return after Cord and his *asi*'s companions had passed through Q'Nkok to begin their monumental, probably suicidal, trek halfway around the planet. Instead, he and a few others had stuck around, as much to play cards with Poertena as anything else, and the journey which had so noticeably changed the prince, had changed Denat almost as greatly.

He'd discovered his natural ability for languages, and a flair for the dramatic that permitted him to either blend into societies or to put on an excellent "dumb barbarian" routine. And he'd also discovered how much he enjoyed putting those talents to work.

It was in the dumb barb role that he had been wandering the city for the last few days, and the impressions he was picking up made him uneasy. He still had only a rudimentary grasp of Krath, and an even more rudimentary one of the society which spoke it, but nothing he had learned so far seemed to add up.

This city was filled with temples. In fact, it seemed that there was one on every third street corner, and they were all more or less identical, barring size. They had a square front that connected to a conical back. The cone was clearly meant to represent a volcano, and on the one holy day which had been observed since their arrival, smoke had issued from all the temples. And the smoke had been filled with the bitter-sweet scent of burning meat, which had to have been immensely expensive. Denat knew how much forage for the *civan* was costing Poertena, so he also knew that the cost of feeding meat animals had to be extremely high. So if the worshipers were prepared to tithe sufficient donations for the priesthood to fatten up sufficient sacrificial animals to scent that much smoke, then they must be *really* devout.

The *quantity* of smoke was explained readily enough. It had come from the endless loads of coal and wood that had been brought in through the previous few days by the many slaves of the Temple. What didn't add up was that there were no holding pens around the temples. The Diasprans hadn't practiced animal sacrifice, but other religions on Denat's home continent had, and behind all of those temples had been pens for the sacrificial animals. But there hadn't been so much as a single *turom* penned up around *these* temples.

In addition, as Sergeant Major Kosutic had pointed out, nobody *argued* religion. This city was clearly a theocracy, even more totally under the control of the local priesthood than Diaspra had been. But whereas, in Diaspra, everyone discussed the nature of Water, here no one discussed the nature of their god at all. It wasn't even clear what the god was, although Denat had been told it was a god of Fire.

The conversations around him were of no use. They were all complaining about the lack of trade, which was a pretty constant theme. Something had dried it up, and fairly recently, apparently. The immediate consequences were readily apparent, particularly in the dock areas, where many of the wharves were unused. Exactly what had happened to it was unclear, to say the least, though. The almost total lack of a long-range merchant fleet seemed to have had something to do with it, but the reason for the shipping shortage itself was, again, unclear.

Kirsti was turning out to be a mystery wrapped in a conundrum. And that was making him irritated.

Cord pushed his way through the bustling streets with his lower arms set in an expression of disapproval.

"A fine city, indeed," he growled, "but this covering of the body is barbarous." He pulled at the kiltlike affair, then snarled as one of the locals ran into him. "And the manners are atrocious."

"Krath, what to say?" Pedi looked around nervously. She was trying to simulate a Shadem accent while speaking in Imperial. Since she was far from eloquent in Shadem and even further from fluent in Imperial, it was tough. But the alternative was to let her Shin accent be noticeable, and she was trying very hard to avoid that.

She also knew that there were habits to maintaining and managing a *sumei* which she simply didn't have. Hopefully, the fact that so few of the Krath's Shadem allies made it as far as Kirsti would mean that no one was familiar enough with the proper way to wear a *sumei* to recognize her own lapses. She told herself that as long as she didn't have to remove the robes, she should be fine.

In fact, she told herself that at least once every four or five of the humans' "minutes."

So far, this combined shopping trip and intelligence mission had gone well enough to indicate that she was probably right. On the other hand, one item she intended to purchase before returning to the quarters the city council had assigned to them might be looked at askance. She wasn't sure if Shadem females knew its use or not. Some Krath did, but it was not looked upon with wide favor. So be it. She wasn't going another day without some *wasen*.

Cord paused at the mouth of an alley and consulted a map Poertena had drawn. The sawed-off Marine had already "scoped out" much of the shopping in the western city, and his chart indicated that this would be one of the better places to look for the items Pedi had listed. Now that they were here, though, the opening was a dark cavern, a set of steps downward into a brick-lined tunnel which Cord found particularly unappealing.

"Go," Pedi whispered. "People look."

"I hate cities," Cord muttered, and stepped into the darkness.

From the bottom of the short set of steps, it was apparent that the tunnel was lit, after a fashion, by high skylights which threw occasional, bright circles on its floor at irregular intervals down its length. It continued with a faint, mildly organic curve to the right, then turned sharply left about fifty meters in. There were doorways to either side, many of them low, and in front of each doorway were groups of Mardukans, most of them sitting on cloth covers. In several of the doorways, one or more of the locals were working on some item—here a metalworker was hammering designs on a pot, there a knife-maker was riveting grips to a tang, and about halfway down the aisle a jeweler under one of the skylights was meticulously setting a teardrop of Fire into a horn bangle.

The atmosphere was thick with a mixture of smoke from coal fires, drifting like wisps of fog through the light from the skylights, and the heady scent of spices. Several of the doorways sheltered Krath, some of them female, cooking over small grills. Most of the food being prepared was seafood, ranging from boiling seaweed to grilled *coll* fish, along with small pots of the ubiquitous barleyrice.

Cord strode forward, ignoring the looks his outlandish dress and peace-bonded spear drew, until he reached an alcove on the left, decorated with a variety of dried items and bottles of mysterious liquids.

The Krath who ran the apothecary's shop was short, even by local standards. He peered up at the towering shaman suspiciously and babbled a quick, liquid sentence in the local trade patois.

Cord caught only a bit of the meaning, but the question was fairly clear. He settled into a squat as Pedi obediently settled in behind him.

"I need to buy," he said. "Need stuff for me. Stuff for wife. Need *wasen.*"

The merchant made a gesture and grunted another fast sentence. Hand signs were closer to universal on Marduk, where so much was expressed by body language and gesture, than on many other planets. So while Cord had never seen this particular one, he'd seen one very much like it in K'Vaern's Cove.

His motioning true-hand stopped Pedi even as he felt her start to move forward. He waited for a breath or two to be certain she stayed stopped, then leaned forward until his ancient, dry face was centimeters from the merchant's.

"Don't think leather on spear save your life. Keep comments to self, or eat horn through asshole."

The shaman was beginning to distinctly regret this trip.

He wasn't sure what *wasen* was, but he'd already decided it wasn't worth the trouble.

Pedi was beginning to wonder if it had been worth-while herself. It might have made more sense just to forget about the *wasen*. It wasn't as if she were really going to need it anytime soon, after all. Or, failing that, it might have made more sense to come by herself, or in the company of one of the female Marines. Despreaux perhaps. But it was not permitted for a *benan* to leave her master, even for a moment.

Not when there was the possibility of danger . . . which happened to be the case anywhere in this Ashes-damned city.

She wondered suddenly if Cord lived under those stric-tures, as well. And, if he did, how he reconciled being away from Prince Roger. Or had her own insistence finally driven him to bend his honor? And, if it had, to what extent was her own honor tarnished by the action into which she had manipulated him?

Wasen was beginning to look less and less like a good idea.

She leaned forward and, keeping her hands draped in the *sumei,* gestured at one of the dried items. It was a type of sea creature that clung to rocks in the surf zone. Fairly rare on the continent, *wasen* was one of the major trade goods of the Lemmar Alliance, and one of the reasons for the recent successful effort to take Strem away from the Lemmar. Besides the use for which she intended it, it was employed in various industries, including textiles.

In a place like this, however, it would be bought only for less acceptable uses. Less acceptable, at least, to the Krath.

Cord looked at the dried bit of what looked like meat and pointed in turn.

"How much?"

He had learned as a boy traveling to far Voitan that along with "Where water?" and "Where food?" that was one of the three most important phrases any venturer could learn in the local dialect.

The merchant held up fingers indicating a number that certainly sounded outlandish to the shaman. But that was what bargaining was all about, and he automatically quoted a return price one-third the suggested one.

The merchant screamed like a stuck *atul* and grabbed his horns. The offer must have been just about right.

As Cord, with obvious reluctance, pulled out a pouch and started measuring silver against the merchant's weights, Pedi leaned forward and picked up the hand-sized mass of *wasen*. She noticed immediately that it was unusually hard, and after she brought it under her robes and broke it, she wanted to scream in anger. Instead, she leaned forward and pulled urgently at Cord's arm.

"Not good," she hissed in the little People she knew. "Bad quality. Old. Not good."

Cord turned around and fixed her with a glare.

"You use?" he asked.

"Too much," she insisted furiously. "Bad quality. Too old."

Cord turned back to the merchant.

"She say stuff too old," he snarled. "No can use."

"First quality *wasen*," the apothecary spat back. The rest of the sentence was too fast for the shaman to catch, but one word sounded particularly bad.

The apothecary didn't speak too rapidly for Pedi, though. She managed not to break into Shin, but after a moment's spluttering, she launched over the seated Cord and grabbed the merchant by the horns.

"Kick your ass, modderpocker!" she screamed, using the only Imperial curses she knew—so far. *"Kick your ass!"*

"Barbarian whore!" the merchant shouted back. "Let go of me, you bitch!"

Cord grabbed one of his erstwhile bodyguard's arms and disengaged it from the merchant, then pushed the Krath to the ground.

"Here's your silver," he said with a growl. "I'll keep the copper as a charge for calling my wife a whore."

"Barbarian *sathrek*," the merchant snarled.

Cord looked around at the other merchants. Some of them had started to come to the apothecary's aid, and he pulled the still cursing Pedi down the way until they were out of sight of the scene of the confrontation.

"Listen to me," he grated in a mixture of Imperial and People. "Do you want to kill us all? You want to kill your *asi*?" He could tell from the drape of her *sumei* that she had crossed all four arms under the muffling folds.

"Bad quality," she hissed. "Too much. And . . ." She stopped and stamped a foot. "Modderpocker," she muttered.

"What did he say?" Cord asked. "That was what really set you off, wasn't it?"

"He say . . . he say . . ." She stopped. "Don't know Imperial. Don't know People. Don't want say, anyway. Bad."

"What was it?" Cord asked. "I've been called some pretty bad things and survived."

"Was . . . was having season with slimer. With baby."

Cord thought about what she meant for a second, then fingered the peacebonds on his spear while he did a *dinshon* exercise to control anger.

"The Imperial term is pedophile," he said after a moment, once he was certain of his own composure. "And 'modderpocker' means having season with your own birther. If you should happen to be interested."

Pedi thought about that for a moment, then grunted a faint laugh.

"Wish pocking merchant speak Imperial," she said much more cheerfully, and Cord shook his head and sighed.

"Pedi Karuse, you are a lot of trouble."

Poertena flipped over the hole card and scooped in the pot.

"That was a a lot of trouble for a measly few

coppers," Denat growled, as he scooped up the cards to begin shuffling.

"Wha'ever it take," the Pinopan replied, leaning back with a shrug. "You not out looking por trouble?"

"You don't have to look with this lot," the barbarian said. "Most obnoxious group I've ever dealt with."

"You sure it's just one way?" Julian asked carefully. He usually sat out Poertena's card games—the Pinopan was deadly with a deck—but the waiting was getting on his nerves. And, apparently, on Denat's. "You've been pretty . . . touchy lately."

"What do you mean?" Denat shot back sharply. "I'm fine."

"Okay, you fine," Poertena agreed. "But you have to admit, you been pretty short temper lately."

"I am *not* short tempered," he insisted hotly. "What in nine hells are you talking about? When have *I* been short tempered?"

"Ummm . . . now?" the Pinopan replied easily. "And you nearly kill t'at Diaspran yesterday."

"He shouldn't have snuck up behind me! It's not my fault people go *creeping* around all the time!" Denat threw the cards down on their crate-card table and jerked to his feet. "I don't have to put up with this. You can just find somebody else to insult!"

"So," Julian asked as the Mardukan stalked away. "Did we start that, or were we right?"

"I t'ink you right," Poertena replied uneasily. "He didn' even insult me when he lef'. I t'ink we gots a problem."

"Should we talk to Cord about it?"

"Maybe." The Pinopan rubbed his head. "Cord pretty wrap up wit' his girlfrien', though. Maybe I ask Denat later. He might cool down, decide to talk. It could work."

"Better not let Cord hear you call her his 'girlfriend,' or Denat will be the least of your worries."

They had managed to secure better clothing at a small textile shop without even a single additional disaster. And at an herbalist, they had found some mysterious emollients. Not far from the herbalist's, Pedi had surreptitiously directed Cord's attention to two small swords, which he'd also purchased. These transactions had been relatively simple, although the locals were notably hostile towards both of them.

With those minimal supplies collected, Cord had unilaterally headed back to their assigned quarters, forcing Pedi to follow. The Shin clearly would have liked to have spent more time in the massive, dusky market, but the shaman was sure that something else would set her off if he allowed her to. She was the most difficult female it had ever been his misfortune to encounter. Smart, yes, but very headstrong, and unable or unwilling to rein in her temper. She'd shown some capacity to back up that temper, on the Lemmar ship, and the swords—which she had indicated she had some knowledge of—were to test whether or not she was all talk.

Back at their quarters, she snatched the packages—including the dual swords and the mysterious *wasen*—and disappeared into her private room. They had been scheduled to test their martial skills against one another after their shopping trip, but Cord found himself cooling his heels for some time while the sun glow moved across the clouds. In fact, the bright, pewter-gray light had swept low in the west before Pedi reemerged.

Her appearance had . . . changed.

The rough, dark rims at the bases of her horns were gone, and the overall color of the horns had faded slightly, to an even yellower honey with just a touch of rust. The mystery of the emollients' purpose was also revealed, for her skin had developed an even finer coating of slime. The clothing turned out to be a set of baggy pants and a vest that draped to her midsection, connecting at the base, but leaving all four arms free. The overall color was a light scarlet, with yellow embroidery along the edges of the vest and at the cuffs and waistline of the pantaloons.

"Do you like it?" Pedi stepped through the door and twirled lightly on one foot.

Cord looked at her for a moment and thought about saying what he thought. But only for a moment.

Instead, he controlled his initial reaction and cleared his throat.

"You are my *asi,* my *benan,* not my bond-mate. Your appearance matters only in that it does not bring disfavor upon me or my clan. Your skill with those puny swords matters far more."

Pedi stopped in mid-pirouette with her back turned to him. A moment passed, then she leaned through the door and picked up her "puny swords." She turned back to Cord and took a guard position.

"Are you ready?" she asked with a certain, dangerous levelness of tone.

"Would you care to warm up or stretch first?" Cord asked, still leaning on his spear.

"You don't get a chance before a battle," Pedi replied, and, without another word, charged him with one's sword held in a port guard, and the other stretched out before.

Cord had been expecting it, but he'd forgotten how fast she was, so his first reaction was to put the spearhead in position to spit her. It would have been a formidable obstacle, even with its leather binding. But after a bare hesitation, he checked that and brought the base of the spear around in a tripping blow, instead.

Her reaction made him wonder if she'd been actively courting the spitting maneuver. As the spear shaft swung around, she leapt lightly into the air, brought the left sword down to barely make contact with the spear. The right-hand sword licked around to meet it, and then she twisted through a midair course correction that left her with both sword hafts locked onto the spear.

A wrist twisted, a foot kicked lightly, and the spear was very nearly wrenched out of his hands. But the shaman had experienced a similar technique, albeit years before, and twisted his body through the disengage. He felt every lengthy year of his age as creaky muscles responded unwillingly to the move, but it seemed that Pedi had never dealt with the disengage before.

The spear shaft snaked through three dimensions, one of which pressed painfully on her wrists and nearly forced her to drop one of the swords. At the end of the maneuver, she was left leaning sideways and badly off balance, while Cord flipped his spear around and went back to peacefully resting on it.

Looking as if he had never moved at all.

"That was interesting," he said brightly, trying very hard not to let his earlier momentary lack of composure show. "Why don't we try the next one a little slower, so we can see where we went wrong?"

Pedi rubbed her wrist and looked at the shaman very thoughtfully.

"I'm not sure who needs the *benan* more," she said after a moment, with a gesture of rueful astonishment.

"I have been studying weapons since long before you were born," Cord pointed out serenely. "When I was your age, before the fall of Voitan, I was sent to the finest schools in the land, and I have studied and sought new ways ever since. The way of the sword—or the spear— is one of constant study. It is rich every day in new insights. Learn that, and you will be dangerous. Forget it, and we'll both be dead."

"Aargh!" Pedi groaned. "It wasn't pleasant to be caught by the Fire Priests. It wasn't pleasant to be shipped off to Strem as a Servant. It wasn't even pleasant to be captured by the Lemmar on my way there. But at least, at my darkest moment, I was able to console myself with the thought that I was finally rid of armsmasters!"

Cord wheeled around and stared out the window towards the mountains. It was a rather silly and dramatic pose, and he knew it, but he didn't want her to see his amusement. Or the fact that . . . parts of him had just surged.

Not the Season, he thought. *Please, not that. That would be . . . bad.*

"Whatever your life and destiny before," he said finally, solemnly, careful to keep any humor—or anything else— out of his voice, "your life and destiny now are to *become* an armsmaster."

So, as Julian would say, put that in your pipe and smoke it.

"I know that," Pedi said, with a gesture of resignation. "But that doesn't mean I have to like it."

"Perhaps you don't, but . . ." Cord began, only to
pause, looking more intently out of the window.

"But what?" she asked.

"But I have a question for you."

"Yes?" She looked down at her outfit. "Is something
wrong?"

"I'd rather hoped you could tell *me* that," Cord said,
gesturing out the window. "You are from here, after all.
So tell me, do the mountains often smoke?"

It was nearly noon, yet the only light in the room
came from oil lamps as the human and Mardukan staff
and senior commanders trickled into the room. Pahner
looked towards the window, listening to the slow, atonal
chanting that echoed through the darkened streets, and
shook his head.

"I have the funny feeling that this is not a good
thing," he muttered.

"They must have these eruptions on a fairly regular
basis," O'Casey pointed out as she flopped onto one of
the pillows. She pulled a strand of hair away from her
face and grimaced at the gritty ash that covered it. "At
least we know now why they wear clothing here. Getting this stuff out of a Mardukan's mucous must be an
almost impossible task."

Roger pulled up his own cushion without even glancing
behind him as the various entities who had taken to
following him jockeyed for position. It usually ended up
with Cord to one side, Pedi stretched in the same general
direction, and Dogzard curled up on top of Pedi. But for
the fact that every one of them was, in his or her own
way, heavily armed, it would have been humorous.

"I wish we had a better handle on their religion," he
said seriously, listening to the same chant. "I can't figure
out if this is a celebration or a funeral."

"The Krath Fire Priests consider this a dark omen of
their gods," Pedi said. "Many Servants will be ingath-
ered."

"More slave raids, then," Pahner said.

"Yes. And a great gathering." The Shin made a gesture of absolute disgust. "The Fire-loving bastards."

"T'e merchants have clam up," Poertena said. "Even t'e stuff we already contract for not getting delivered."

"How are we fixed?" Kosutic asked. "Can we hang on until things clear up, or do we need to talk to the Powers That Be?"

"We got ten days or so supply," the Pinopan said without consulting any of his data devices. "And more on t'e ship. But if we have to cut out, we gots problem."

"We may be able to avoid that," O'Casey said. "I think that something's broken free in the council. Maybe it has something to do with the eruption—I don't know." She shrugged. "Whatever it is, we've received a message from the High Priest indicating that he's willing to meet with Roger under the conditions we prescribed. That is, that Roger will not have to recognize the High Priest's sovereignty."

"I thought the council was more or less in control," Pahner said. "If that's true, what's the point of meeting with the High priest?"

"The council *is* in day-to-day control," O'Casey admitted. "But if the High Priest pronounces that we're free to travel, the council will have to accede to that."

"When is this thing?" Fain asked. "And who's going to accompany Roger?"

"Me, for one, obviously," O'Casey said with a faint smile. "After that, the guest list will be up to Captain Pahner. Who, I trust, will pack it with suitably lethal individuals."

"Kosutic in charge," Pahner said. "Despreaux and a fire team from her squad. Turn in your smoke poles and draw bead rifles. We've got enough ammo left for almost a full unit of fire for your team, and some of these people may recognize Imperial weapons when they see them. If they do, I want them to know we cared enough to send the very best. Fain, one squad from your infantry and one squad of cavalry. You, Rastar, and Honal stay back, though."

"I'll send Chim Pri," Rastar said. "It will get him off the boats."

"Where is this going to take place, Eleanora?" Kosutic asked.

"At the High Temple. That's the one all the way up at the crest of the ridge."

"I wish we knew whether or not this is a good sign," Roger said.

"I think it's a good one," O'Casey told him. "If there hadn't been some movement on their front, it wouldn't make sense to arrange a meeting with the High Priest."

"We'll see," Pahner said. "It could also be because they have such bad news to give us that the High Priest is the only appropriate spokesman to break it to us, you know. Rastar, how are the *civan*?"

"They don't like the ash," the Prince of Therdan said. "Neither do I, for that matter, and their hides are a lot more resistant to it than my slime is! Other than that, they're fine. They've recovered from their sea voyage, at least, and we're getting them back into training."

"Okay." Pahner nodded. "I don't know how this meeting is going to work out, but we're getting to the end of the time we can afford to spend here. I want everyone to quietly and not too obviously get ready to move out on a moment's notice. We'll have an inspection and get everything packaged for that. Eleanora, when is this meeting?"

"Tomorrow, just after the dawn service."

"Right. We'll schedule the inspection for the same time."

"Does all this martial ardor indicate that you think I'm going to have problems at the meeting?" Roger asked, unconsciously tapping the butt of one of his pistols.

"I hope not," Pahner said. "I'll go further—if I thought you were going to, I wouldn't let you go. Period. We haven't gotten this far taking things for granted, but I don't expect this to be the sort of problem you'll need a pistol for. Nobody's going to call a visiting Imperial nobleman and his bodyguards together with the High

Priest of the entire *satrap* for a shooting match, at any rate."

"Nah," O'Casey agreed with a smile. "Heads of state are too valuable to use for targets or get caught in cross fires. That's what lower-level functionaries are for.

CHAPTER SIXTEEN

The large meeting room was near the highest point of the entire High Temple complex, with a single broad balcony at one end that looked down and out over the city. A marginal amount of illumination came from there, but not much. The city was still shrouded in the darkness and ash from the ongoing, low-level eruption. The room was long and low (by Mardukan standards), stretching back in a series of low arches into absolute blackness, punctuated by dim lamps that barely penetrated the gloom.

The prince had forgone his helmet in the interests of diplomacy, and his hair—unbound due to the formal nature of the meeting—spilled down his back in a golden wave. In deference to his image, and the fact that the meeting, however formal, had been arranged suddenly and with no specific agenda, he wore his bead pistol and had his sword slung over his back. Formal was all well and good, but on Marduk, paranoia was a survival trait.

Roger's eyes had benefitted from as much genetic tinkering as the rest of him and managed to compensate for the dimness of the illumination as he entered the meeting chamber. He could pick out the guards, arrayed in two groups along the walls, almost as well as his Marine bodyguards with their helmet low-light systems. And he could also see the High Priest, standing and waiting to greet him at the far end, shrouded in shadow and flanked by Sor Teb. It seemed a fitting situation: dark places, inhabited by dark souls.

Roger stopped a measured ten paces from the priest and bowed. It had been determined that a certain amount of kowtowing was permissible, but the dose had to be properly balanced. Yes, he was a prince of a star-spanning empire. But the High Priest—they hoped—knew him only as "Baron Chang." And there was also the minor fact that he was fundamentally lacking in heavy backup.

The prelate, an extremely elderly Mardukan, certainly looked frail enough to justify the rumors of his impending demise. He beckoned his visitors forward, and Roger took a few more steps, followed by his own guards.

Ever since Marshad, whose ruler had taken advantage of a relatively small guard force to take the prince "captive," the rule of thumb had been that Roger never went anywhere "threatening" with less than a dozen guards.

As the humans had become fewer and fewer in number, with more and more missions to perform, the native Mardukans had assumed a steadily growing degree of responsibility for guarding his safety. Thus, more than half the guard force detailed for this meeting consisted of Mardukan cavalry and infantry. The block of guards following the prince was a mixture of bead rifle-toting humans, breechloader-toting Diasprans, revolver-toting Vashin, the *sumei*-swathed Pedi, and the still mostly naked Cord and his immense spear. It made for a motley but dangerous crew.

Roger stopped and bowed again, making a two-armed gesture that corresponded more or less to the local one for respectful greeting.

"I am pleased to meet you, Your Voice. I am Seran Chang, Baron of Washinghome, of the Empire of Man, at your service."

"I greet you, Baron Chang," the priest responded in an age-quavery voice. "May the God favor you. I speak as His Voice. It is time to speak of many things that have been long avoided." The Mardukan stepped backward, with Sor Teb supporting him, and settled onto a low stool. "Many things."

"Such matters are generally discussed at a lower level, first," Roger observed with a frown. "Unless you refer to our petition to travel upriver?"

"Travel is for others to discuss," the High Priest said with a cough. "I speak of the needs of the God. The God is angry. He sends His Darkness upon us. He has spoken, and must be answered. Too long have the humans avoided Service to the Fire Lord. It is of this we must speak. I speak as His Voice."

Roger tilted his head to the side and frowned again.

"Am I to understand that you are requiring a 'Servant of God' from among the humans of our party before we will be permitted to leave?"

"That is not *our* requirement," Sor Teb answered for the High Priest with what, in a human, would have been an oily smile. "It is the God's."

"Pardon me," Roger said, then turned to the side. "Huddle time, people."

His senior advisers closed in, and he looked at the cloth-swathed Pedi Karuse, who was practically jumping up and down.

"In a minute, Pedi. I know you don't think this is a good idea. Eleanora?"

"We don't know the parameters of being a Servant of God," she said simply. "I've tried to get some idea of the duties, but the locals are very reticent about it, and talking to Pedi has been circular. The duties are 'to Serve the God.' I don't know if that means as a glorified altar boy, as a drudge scrubbing stone floors, or what. You don't see any of the Servants in public at all, so I have no idea where they all *go,* much less what they all do."

"So you're saying that we might actually go for this?" Kosutic hissed. "I don't think that's a good idea. Not at all."

"Look," O'Casey said sharply, "if being a servant means participating in some harmless rituals, and the alternative is trying to fight our way out of the city, which would you rather do?"

Kosutic glanced over at Pedi and shook her head.

"People don't fight like wildcats to avoid some 'harmless rituals.' So far, she hasn't said anything about cleaning. And I don't like any religion that doesn't perform its rituals out in the open. Call me old-fashioned, but the only decent place for a ritual is the open air. Anything else smacks of—"

"—Christianity?" O'Casey asked with an arched eyebrow. "We can probably get some concessions on the nature of their duties. Then, after we retake the spaceport, we'll come back and negotiate some more. With some real firepower behind us."

Despite the tension of the moment, Roger almost smiled. His chief of staff might not have become quite as bloodthirsty as Despreaux thought *he* was becoming, but she certainly had become a convert to the notion of peace through superior firepower.

"You're saying that whether or not we should agree depends on the duties, then?" he asked her after a moment, and cocked an eyebrow of his own at Kosutic.

"Okay, okay," the sergeant major said. "If they're treated well, we could leave a volunteer behind. Somebody will be willing."

"I will," Despreaux said. "If it's ringing some bells and pouring some water versus fighting our way out of the city, well, just hand me the goddamned bells!"

"You're not under consideration," Roger said crisply.

"Why not?" Despreaux asked angrily. "Because I'm a *guuuurl*?"

"No." Roger's tone was curt. "Because you're my fiancée. And because everybody knows you are, and that puts you in a special category. Get over it."

"He's right," Kosutic said before Despreaux could swell with outrage. "And you *do* need to get over it, Sergeant Despreaux. Technically, we should be guarding *you*. If we were back on Earth, you'd have a ring around you twenty-four/seven. Since we don't have the manpower, you don't. But you are *not* 'just another troop' anymore." The sergeant major shook her head. "Probably me or Gunny Lai would be the best choice—both 'guuuurls,' you might note."

Roger chuckled at Despreaux's expression, then again, harder, as he looked at the group around him. Of the humans, better than half of his guards and advisers were females.

"I hadn't noticed until just now, but this does seem to be an episode of *Warrior Amazons of Marduk*."

"Smile when you say that, Your Highness," Despreaux said. But at least *she* smiled when she said it.

"I *am* smiling," Roger replied, making a face. "Okay, if the duties aren't too onerous—and *we'll* determine what 'onerous' means—we'll agree on the condition that the rest of us are given free passage to the spaceport."

"Agreed," Eleanora said, and Roger looked over at Pedi, who was still making surreptitious negative gestures under her *sumei*.

"Okay, why not?"

"Not Servant," she whispered in broken Imperial. "Bad, bad. Not Servants."

"And what if duties okay?" Roger asked in Krath.

"Duty of Servant is to *Serve*," the Shin whispered back. "*Is* no other duty."

"And what's so bad about that?" Roger asked quietly.

"*What?!*" The Shin's voice came out in a squeak as she tried not to scream the question. "Duty is to be of Service! How much worse could it be? To be of Service and to Serve! What you want, to Serve *twice*?"

Roger glanced over at O'Casey and Kosutic, both of whom looked suddenly very thoughtful.

"We're missing something," he said.

"Agreed," Kosutic said. "I mean, she's sliming, and this is a 'guuuurl' who killed two armed guards with her bare hands. While chained to the deck." She shook her head. "Could the translation be bad?"

"This is the only language group for which we actually had a comprehensive kernel when we landed," O'Casey said thoughtfully. "It's *possible* that the kernel has a bias built in. I'm not sure what to do about that, though."

Roger considered the translation program for a moment. Throughout the trip, the burden of translation of new dialects had fallen upon him and Eleanora due to their superior implants. To aid in that, he'd read most of the manual for the software, but that had been a long time ago. There was a section on poor translations related to initial impressions and inaccurate kernels, but at the moment he couldn't find it on the help menu.

"The only thing I can think of to do is to dump the kernel," Roger said. "Dump the whole translation scheme, and start fresh."

"We need time to do that," O'Casey objected.

"Agreed," the prince replied, and turned back to the local leaders. They were showing signs of impatience, and he smiled much more calmly than he felt.

"We need to discuss this with the other members of our party, and we seem to be having a problem with our translation system. Could we perhaps call a recess, and resume the discussion tomorrow?"

"It is with regret that I must decline that suggestion," Sor Teb replied. "The God speaks to us now. He sends His darkness upon His people now. Now is when we must gather our Servant, and you are the leader, the decision maker, of your people. If you would prefer that the Servant come from one of your lesser minions at your headquarters rather than from those here with you, we can send a runner. But the decision must be made now."

"Pardon me for a moment longer, then," Roger said slowly, and turned back to the others.

"Oh, shit," Despreaux said quietly.

"Did he just say what I think he said?" Cord asked.

"So much for 'minor functionaries,'" Kosutic said with a snort. "Marshad time."

"Stop talking," Roger said, pointing a finger directly at Pedi. As soon as she froze, he sent a command to his toot, "dumping" the entire Krath language and everything they had determined of Shin. Then he locked out the "kernel" that had come with the system, as well. It was now as if he had never heard of Shin or Krath, and any biases would be erased, as long as he concentrated on ignoring them. He also locked out the low-level interplay between the systems, so that his own would

not be corrupted by the Marines' and O'Casey's. Taking
a guess, based upon O'Casey's idea of a migratory connection between the Shin and Cord's people, he loaded
the language of "the People" as a potential kernel.

"Okay," he said, crooking the petrifiying finger. "*Now*
talk."

At first, what the *benan* was saying was only a low,
unintelligible gabble. But after a moment, bits and pieces
began to join together.

" . . . temple . . . priests . . . death . . . serve . . . sacrifice . . . serve
the worshipers . . . feast."

"Oh, shit."

Roger pulled up the two translations, and the difference was immediately apparent. In the kernel, the word
"*sadak,*" when used in the context of the priests, was
translated as "Servant." When the kernel was dumped,
though, it translated as "sacrifice." In fact, there was an
entire series of synonym and thematic biases built into
the system, but changing a few words around and
removing a syntactic bias made everything clear.

Including why the Lemmar refused to be captured.

He punched the changes into his toot with the flashing
speed of direct neural interfacing, then reloaded the
corrected kernel and turned slowly back to the Scourge
and the High Priest.

"We have determined the problem with our translator.
What you want is a human sacrifice. Which will then
be shared as a feast among your worshipers. The body
and blood, so to speak."

"Oh, shit," Kosutic whispered, and grimaced as she
took another look at the guards. "I *knew* I didn't like
these guys. They're Papists! Man, I *hate* fanatics!"

"We recognize that certain lesser peoples refuse to
accept this rite," Sor Teb replied, with a gesture of
contempt at Cord and the swathed Pedi. "But humans
are, after all, civilized."

"Civilized," Despreaux whispered. She was too well-
trained to actually check a weapon, and she could *feel*
the stillness that had descended over the troopers behind
her. Each of them was very carefully not reaching for

a weapon. They were carefully *not* counting their rounds, or ensuring that their bayonets were loose in the sheaths. Not, at least, on the outside.

Roger reached slowly into a pouch and extracted a thin leather band. Then he tossed his hair behind him and bound it slowly into a ponytail.

"And if we politely decline this invitation?" he asked, pulling his locks into place one by one as he smoothed the hair on the top of his head. Behind him, O'Casey drew a surreptitious breath and made sure her weight was balanced on her toes.

Sor Teb glanced at the High Priest, now apparently asleep on his stool, then back at the humans.

"My guards in this room outnumber you, and I have over a hundred in the corridors. At a word, you are all Servants. And then I will take all of the rest of you at the docks, and the people will know that it was the Scourge which brought humans to the God at last."

His false-hands moved in a complicated shrug which signified total confidence.

"Or," he continued, "you may surrender a single sacrifice of your choice. That will suffice for my purposes . . . and the God's, of course. But either way, I will have the Servant I require, and the people will know it. Those are your only alternatives."

"Really?" Roger said quietly, calmly, as he tugged one last time on his ponytail to tighten it down. "Hmmm. A binary solution set. Just one problem with your plans."

"What?" Teb's eyes narrowed, and Roger smiled gently.

"You've never seen me move."

The prince and his bodyguards had blasted their way through half a dozen city-states on their bloody march across Marduk. Roger knew he could depend upon them to do their job and back him up. So as his hands descended to the pistols holstered at his side, he concentrated solely on what was in his own field of view.

The local arquebuses weren't particularly accurate, and the Marines' uniforms were designed to protect against high-velocity projectiles by hardening to spread the impact over a wide area. Neither Roger nor O'Casey, however, were wearing helmets, so an unlucky hit from one of the arquebuses would be fatal. And Cord and Pedi were completely unarmored.

The first target, therefore, was the arquebusier to the left of the throne. The High Priest was no threat, and hitting the target to the left would permit Roger to track right and take Sor Teb with the next shot.

But by the time Roger had shifted targets, before the headless body had even had time to start to fall, Sor Teb had just *moved*. Roger had heard the Marines comment on his own speed, often in hushed tones. Now he understood why. When you see someone who is *preternaturally* fast—Rastar was one such—it is awe-inspiring. and Sor Teb, it turned out, was preternaturally fast at surviving. The councilor was behind the throne and out a side door before anyone besides the prince could target him.

But that didn't mean people were sitting on their hands.

Kosutic dropped the muzzle of her bead rifle and took down the arquebusier to the right of the throne even as the Scourge guards along the walls flung themselves forward. Their primary weapon seemed to be double sticks. The long rods were nearly as thick as a human's forearm, and the guards wielded them with precision. One of them descended towards the sergeant major's forearm, obviously intending to disarm her, but it was abruptly blocked by a short sword.

"*Mudh Hemh!*" Pedi screamed like a damnbeast and spun in place, flinging off her *sumei* as both swords appeared. She chopped down, to take all of the fingers off one of the guard's hands, then swept upward to gut him like a fish.

"*The vales!!*"

The astonished guards recoiled at the sight of the blades and frosted horns. Humans were unknown bogeymen from beyond even the farthest reaches of the valley, but the Shin were *always* there. And *never* underestimated. Even the females.

"*Shin!!!*"

The Mardukan female spun again, blocking another blow directed at her from behind and back-kicking the guard in the groin. She turned towards the throne, where the majority of the surviving guards had clustered in defense of the High Priest, and spat.

"TIME TO MEET THE FIRE, BOYS!"

"Boots and saddles!"

Pahner shot to his feet, rubbing an ear as the shout over his helmet commo systems rocketed him upright.

"Your Highness?" he called, heading for the door of his office while the sudden icy calm of a man who's seen too many emergencies—and has just heard the unmistakable sound of rifle volleys in the background of a truncated radio call—flooded through him.

"To all units, Bravo Company relay! Terminate all Krath guards in view with extreme prejudice. Do this NOW!"

Pahner heard screams from the warehouse, and firing broke out as he hit the door. Two Krath guards were attacking one of the Diaspran infantry by the main doors, but two shots took them down before the captain could even draw his sidearm. All the others in sight had already been dealt with.

"Prince Roger, this is Captain Pahner," he said calmly as he strode towards the piles of gear that were half ready for loading. "What's happening?"

"Servants are human sacrifices," Kosutic cut in on the command circuit, panting. In the background, Pahner heard a knife-hitting-a-melon sound with which the entire company had become all too familiar. "We're trying to fight our way out of the Temple. For some reason, they're just a bit ticked with us."

"That might be because Pedi Karuse cut her way through to the High Priest on our way out of the room," Roger said with a grunt against the background of a fading scream. "Fortunately, all the guards have been unarmored so far. We're conserving ammo by quite literally *cutting* our way out. But Sor Teb got away, dammit! He set us up."

"We're on our way," Pahner said, gesturing for the

teams to drop what they were doing. The most vital equipment had already been packed for a run, most of it loaded into large, hard-sided leather trunks with multiple carrying rings, so that they could be easily on-loaded and off-loaded from pack animals. The remainder was food and other similar nonvital items that could be seized on the way. It was cold, but if you had bullets, you could always get beans.

"Negative!" Roger snapped. "We're heading for the city's main gate. You know the drill—Vashin to take the gate, flying columns to secure the intersections and block response, tell the ships to head for K'Vaern's Cove, and the rest all run like hell for the gates. We're going to join up in that vicinity. If you try to cut your way into the Temple, we'll never make it. Follow the plan, Captain. That's an order."

"Tell me you can fight your way out, Your Highness," the captain grated. "Tell me that."

"Hold one," Roger responded. Behind his voice, someone else bellowed in rage. The bellow grew louder, as if the throat from whence it sprang was charging towards Roger, but then the sound was cut abruptly short, and Pahner heard a thump, and a spraying sound.

"Pthah! Just make sure you bring a pocking towel."

CHAPTER SEVENTEEN

Temu Jin strode up to the last few meters of path and nodded to the Mardukan waiting for him. The Shin chieftain was middle-aged for one of the locals, calm and closed faced. He propped himself on the long ax which was his symbol of office—the symbol which had permitted him to pass more or less unmolested through the intervening tribes.

Now the chieftain leaned forward and fixed the human with a glare.

"I have traveled two weeks from my home for you, Temu Jin," he growled. "I have done this while my people are in jeopardy, when the young warriors are questioning my utility. I have done this because you indicated that it was vital that we meet. All I can say is that it had better be important."

"Decide for yourself," Jin said. "Humans have landed in Kirsti."

"*That* is not important!" the chieftain snapped. "*Everything* passes through Kirsti sooner or later, as I know all too well."

"Ah, but what humans?" Jim replied. "These humans did not travel to Kirsti from our base here. They arrived aboard ships—ships built here on Marduk, which crossed the sea to reach this continent."

257

"And what of that?" the chieftain demanded. "Why should the fact that they floated across the water rather than flew through the air excite me?"

"As I've told you, the Empire is not going to look kindly upon the Krath when I finally get word to my superiors. But I don't know when that will be. These humans could help in getting the word out."

"Why? Why *these* humans and not the waifs you have already dumped upon us?"

"These humans are . . . important," Jin temporized. "But they'll need some support."

"Of course. Don't they always?" the chief grumped. "What now?"

"I'll send you some packages. Ammunition and some essential spare parts they could probably use. Also some modern weapons. If you can make contact with them, it will greatly benefit us. It would be even better if you could woo them away from the Krath and into the Shin lands."

"What? No blankets? No 'sleeping bags'? No insect repellent?" the chief gave a Mardukan snort. "I hope that your superiors come to your aid soon—all these visitors are becoming tiring. As to 'wooing them away from the Krath,' I can send out the word to the clan-Chiefs, but it will be up to them individually. And they don't think much of humans. Only if they come directly to my lands will it be possible for me to ensure their safety."

"I think you'll find these folk a bit different," Jin said grimly. "And I doubt they'll need much looking after. Among other things, at least some of them are Marines."

"Marines?" the chief scoffed. "These are your space warriors, yes? Warriors we have aplenty."

"You don't have Imperial Marines," Jin cautioned. "And if they're the Marines I think they are, you don't have anything close."

The chieftain regarded him balefully for moment, then rubbed his horns in thought.

"Anybody have any idea where we are?" Roger asked. His stripped-down command group stood at the intersection of five dome-roofed corridors. A single oil lamp gave miserly illumination, and the prince idly wiped blood from his sword blade as he looked about himself.

They had lost their pursuers, mostly by leaving field expedient booby traps behind. After the first few explosions, the Scourge guards had become remarkably circumspect in their chasing. But that didn't help the fugitives find their way out of the palace. Or to the gates. Their helmet systems could tell them where they were in reference to their starting point and the gates their bug-out plans specified as their way out of the city, as well as which direction they were headed, but that was of strictly limited utility. The temple had backed onto the outer wall of the city, so there was probably a connection between where they stood and the walls' defenses—like the gates they needed. But they couldn't tell which of the myriad corridors would get them there.

"We're about a hundred meters below the gates," Kosutic pointed out, looking at the various corridors with him. "And still to the south. I think we need to head northeast and up."

"Uh-huh. Unfortunately," Roger noted, "that still leaves two."

"Eenie-meenie-miney-moe," the sergeant major said. "Chim, take the left corridor."

"Yes, Sergeant Major," the Vashin replied. "It smells like the kitchens are ahead."

"It does," Roger agreed uneasily. "A bit." Chim was right, a distinct odor of cooking came down the passageway to them, but it was overlaid by a fetid, iron smell that was unpleasantly familiar.

The corridor was a five-meter high arch, leading into darkness. Unlike the intersection, it lacked even the dimness of an oil lamp. The Marines' helmet vision systems let them see clearly even under those conditions, but did nothing for the Mardukans in the party—or for Roger or O'Casey, neither of them had brought helmets to what was supposed to be a diplomatic conference—so the Marines turned on the lights mounted on their rifles. The lights' white spots seemed to reveal and conceal in equal measure, for the walls were of basalt blocks, which seemed to swallow the light. The complex interplay of lights and dark lent an additional air of unreality to their flight, but at least the natives (and Roger) could see something.

After perhaps a dozen meters, the corridor terminated in a heavy wooden door. Fortunately, it was bolted on their side, and Chim waved one of the Diasprans forward to pull the bolt. As soon as the door opened, the Vashin nobleman darted through the opening, his pistol held in a two-handed grip. The rest of the Vashin poured through behind him, and Roger heard the blast of arquebuses, answered by pistol cracks and a bellow of rage.

The prince followed before the echoes of the pistol shots could fade, and as he stepped through the door, the reason for the bellow was obvious. The large room beyond was filled with bone pits. He could see a group of Krath Servants escaping through the far door, leaving the baskets of ash and bone they'd been carrying spilled across the floor.

Chim was down as well, caught in a death grip with one of the four guards. The smell in the room was much stronger than it had been in the corridor—a mixture of rotting meat and charred bone that caused Roger to flash back to Voitan. He swallowed his gorge and checked to make sure everyone else was okay. When he glanced sideways at Pedi, she seemed strangely unaffected. She simply glanced at the charnel pits, then looked away.

"You don't seem too broken up," Roger said. "This is . . . foul."

"Sometimes you get the priests," Pedi replied. "Sometimes they get you. We don't eat them, but we don't let any we capture live, either."

Cord's *benan* headed for the far door, but Roger put a hand on her shoulder.

"Let the professionals go through first. Any idea what's on the other side?"

"Not many come out of the Fire," Pedi pointed out. "But with the pits here, the kitchens should be to the right, and the sanctuary up and to the left."

"Sergeant Major," Roger said, gesturing at the door. "Head for the sanctuary. It's got to have public access, and that means a primary point of entry . . . and exit. That makes it our best chance to find a way out of this damned maze quickly."

"Yes, Sir," Kosutic said. She put her hand on the closed door's bar and glanced at the other grim-faced warriors crowding around the prince. "Let's dance."

The corridors beyond were more of the same black basalt, drinking the light from the Marines' lights. A few more meters brought them to a narrow staircase up and to the right. Kosutic flashed a light up it, then climbed its treads with quick, silent steps. At the top, she found another heavy wooden door, this one with red light coming under it, and she cocked her head as she listened to the loud, atonal chanting coming from above.

"Lord, I hate Papists," she muttered, checking her ammunition pouches and fixing her bayonet. Then she drew a belt knife as Roger arrived beside her. "We really should have brought shotguns for this, Your Highness."

"Needs must," Roger replied. He left his bead pistol holstered, conserving its ammunition against a more critical need, and balanced a black powder revolver in his left hand. "Do it."

The sergeant major slid her knife into the crevice where the bar should be, and moved it upwards. The monomolecular blade sliced effortlessly through the locking device, the door sprang loose on its hinges, and she pushed forward into Hell.

The nave of the temple was packed with worshipers, females on one side, males on the other. Worship in the High Temple was clearly only for the well-to-do of Kirsti's society—most of the worshipers were not only clad in elaborate gowns and robes, but wore heavy jewelry, as well.

A double line of "Servants" ran down the centerline of the temple, surrounded by guards. The line led up to the sacrificial area, where three teams of priests were involved in mass slaughter. The priests wore elaborate gowns, rich with gold thread, and caps of gold and black opal that simulated volcanoes, and the decorations of the temple were of the finest. The walls were shot through with semi-precious gems and gold foil, adorned again and again with the repeating motif of the sacred Fire. All in all, it was a barbaric and terrible sight, made all the worse by the heavy leather aprons that the priests *also* wore. Of course, if they hadn't worn them, the gore from their butchery would have ruined the pretty gold thread.

Like a machine—or like what it really was: an abattoir—each bound captive would be placed upon an altar, then quickly dispatched and butchered, the parts separated into manageable chunks. The offal was hurled by teams of lower priests into the maw of the furnaces at the rear, while others bore the edible materials away even as another "Servant" was brought forward. The worshipers' deep, rhythmic chanting was a bizarre counterpart for the frantic screams as the captives were dragged forward . . . until the screams were abruptly cut off by the priests' knives.

If anything was worse than the hideous efficiency of the sacrifices, with its clear implication of frequent and lengthy experience, it was the well-dressed worshipers, swaying back and forth in hysterical reaction to the slaughter and chanting their ecstatic counterpoint to the prayers of the priests.

When Kosutic opened the door, the priests' prayers stopped abruptly, and the chanting shuddered to a halt in broken chunks of sound. Roger looked out over the suddenly silent tableau and shook his head.

"I'm just not having this," he said in an almost conversational tone.

"We're low on ammo, Sir!" Kosutic pointed out. "We can retreat. The door will hold them for a bit."

"Hell with that." Roger reached over his shoulder with his right hand. "The best, shortest way out is through the temple, Sergeant Major. And I don't think they're going to just let us walk through, do you?"

"No, Your Highness," the Satanist replied.

"Well, there you are," Roger said reasonably. "And I suppose if we're low on ammo, it'll just have to be cold steel, won't it?"

Steel whispered in the near-total silence as he drew his sword once more, and Dogzard lashed her tail back and forth. The smell of blood had hit her, and her spikes were shivering.

"*Roger!*" Despreaux yelled from the press around the door, then—"Ow! Dammit, Dogzard—watch the tail!"

"You hang back, Nimashet," Roger snarled. "Let me and the Vashin handle this."

"Allow me to note that this is not a wise endeavor," Cord observed as he hefted his spear. "That being said, clear the door, Your Highness!"

"Let me at them!" Pedi called, waving both blood-stained swords over her head. "I'll give them 'lesser races'!"

"Oh, the hell with that!" Despreaux said, stepping forward as the ceremonial guards in the temple below raised their staves. "You're not going any place without me!"

"No," Kosutic interjected, never taking her eyes from the waiting guards. "Cover the back door. We don't want to get hit from behind."

"But . . ."

"That wasn't a request, *Sergeant!*" The sergeant major snapped. "Cover our damned *backs!*"

"Vashin!" Roger called. "One volley, and draw! Cold steel!"

"Cold steel!"

"*The People!*"

"*SHIN!*"

"Two of the main intersections are secure," Rastar called as his *civan* trotted down the broad boulevard past Pahner. "We took the main Flail headquarters for the sector on the way. They tried to fight, but these guard pukes are no use at all."

"*Basik* to the *atul,*" Fain agreed as another volley crashed out. The Diaspran had tucked his company tight around the retreating wagons, letting the Vashin clear the way ahead. "They just fight dumb. Almost as dumb as barbs. No style, no tactics—simple personal attacks, and they just advance into our fire. Dumb."

"Not dumb, just . . . stagnant," Pahner corrected. "They're so used to fighting one way they don't know any other. And they haven't figured out how to change. I suspect that they're as good as it gets against other satrap forces or when it comes to suppressing riots in the city. But they've never dealt with rifle volleys or snipers."

The latter—mostly Marines, but a few of the Diasprans as well—had been picking off any leaders who showed real imagination.

"Any word on Roger?" Rastar asked.

"Nothing since they called from the Temple," the captain said.

"They'll make it, Sir," Fain said. "It's Roger, isn't it?"

"Yeah, that's what they tell me." Pahner shook his head. "I almost wish he was still considered incompetent. Maybe then I'd have sent a decent sized force to look after him."

"You know," Roger parried a blow from a staff and slid his blade down the shaft to cut off the Mardukan wielder's fingers, "I could wish that Pahner didn't have so much confidence in me!"

"Why?" Kosutic punched her bayonet through the roof of the staff wielder's screaming mouth. Unlike the Diaspran riflemen, the Marine's bayonets were made of monomolecular memory plastic, not locally produced steel blades. The impossibly sharp bayonet sliced up and outwards in an effortless spray of blood, and she kicked the falling body out of her path with a grunt.

"Well, if the captain hadn't been so sure we could handle anything, he would have sent more troops with us!" Roger yelled as Dogzard, unnoticed, landed on the back of a guard about to strike Cord. The Mardukan might have been able to support the one hundred and twenty kilos from a standing start, but when it hit him at forty kilometers per hour, he went over on his face in the red mash of the floor. And down on his face, with an enraged Dogzard on his back, there wasn't much he'd be doing but dying.

"But more troops would mean fewer guards for each of us!" Pedi protested as she slashed the throat out of one attacker and wheeled to chop another's true-arm just below the shoulder. A staff clanged off her horns in response, and she kicked out at the wielder, slashing at him with the edge of her horns and following up with the thrust to the chest. A handspan of bloody steel protruded out of the Krath's back, and she twisted her wrist. "Fewer Krath to kill and bodies to loot! What fun would that be?"

She withdrew her blade in a flood of crimson, and Roger paused to survey the blood-soaked sacristy. The area—fortunately or unfortunately—had been designed for adequate drainage, and a nasty sizzling sound and a horrible burned-steak smell rose from the furnaces at the rear, where the gutters terminated. The ground was littered with the bodies of priests and guards left in the Vashin's and Marines' wake. The few worshipers who had joined the guards to attempt to stop them had fared no better, and the Vashin had been particularly brutal. Many of the corpses showed more hacks than were strictly necessary.

"I suppose when you look at it that way," Roger said as one of the Vashin pried an emerald the size of his thumb out of a statue. Between the ornamentation and the clothing of the priests and worshipers, there was probably a month's pay per Vashin in this room alone. The prince leaned down and picked up a more or less clean cloth from the . . . debris and wiped his sword. There was hardly a sound in the entire Temple, except for the sizzle from the rear and an occasional groan from their only serious casualty. The Vashin had been particularly efficient in ensuring that there were no Krath wounded.

The sacrifices had scattered. Whether they would be able to survive and blend into the population, Roger didn't know. All he knew was that the way out was clear, and that there were no living threats in view. On Marduk, that was good enough.

"Three minutes to loot, and then it's time to go, people!" he called, waving his sword at the door. Even after a quick wipe, the blade left a trail of crimson through the air. "Let's find a way out of this place!"

"Third Squad has closed up, Captain, but we're getting quite a bit of pressure from the rear," Fain said. A rifle volley crashed out from someplace downslope, answered by high-pitched screaming. "Nothing we can't deal with. Yet."

"Still haven't heard from Roger," Pahner said with a nod. He looked around in the gloom and shook his head. One of the "civilized" aspects of Kirsti was that many of the major boulevards had gaslights. Now he knew *why* they had gaslights; it was so they could see during broad day.

"There's been the occasional explosion from his direction, so I take it he's on his way," the Marine continued. "Now, if we could just take the gate before he gets here."

"Sorry about that." Rastar shrugged. "It was closed when we arrived. They probably did it ahead of time."

"Why not use a plasma cannon, Sir?" Fain asked.

"Signature." Pahner pulled out a *bisti* root and cut off a sliver; it was covered with a thin layer of bitter ash by the time he got it into his mouth. "If they're going to be watching for advanced weapons anywhere, it will be on this continent. And plasma cannons aren't the weapon of a lost hunter. Much the same reason why, after his first message, we've been out of contact with His Highness. No, we're going to have to take this thing the old-fashioned way."

"That will be expensive," Fain said, looking at the gate defenses. The central gatehouse was flanked by two defensive towers, both of them loopholed to sweep the exterior of the gatehouse with arquebus and light artillery fire. The fortifications were obviously meant to be equally defensible from either side, so that if an enemy made it over the wall, he would still have a hard fight for the gate tower.

"Boiling oil will be the least of it," the Diaspran added.

"Well, I'm not planning on stacking bodies to climb up and over it," Pahner said, and pointed to a stairway. It ran up the inner face of the gatehouse to a heavily timbered door at the third-story level. "We go up there, blow the door with a satchel charge, and take the interior. Somewhere in there will be the controls."

The doorway in question was on the top of the wall, in full view of the western tower. Firing slits along that tower's eastern side had a clear shot at the stairs and the area in front of the door. Rastar surveyed the slits, which probably concealed heavy swivel guns. They would undoubtedly be loaded with canister, like giant shotguns. He'd seen the same sort of weapon in Sindi, used on the Boman barbarians, and knew exactly what the effect would be.

"We'll still take quite a few casualties."

"I know, Rastar," Pahner said sadly. "And it will fall mostly on the Diasprans and the Vashin. I can't afford to lose many more Marines. Hell, most of the ones I still have left are already busy, anyway."

"What's to be done, must be done," Rastar said philosophically, drawing his pistols. "We'll need the satchel charge prepared."

"I got t'at," Poertena said, pulling out his pack. "Two satchel charge. One or t'e other gonna work."

"Not your specialty, Sergeant," Pahner said. "Somebody will need to go into the gatehouse and find the gate controls. That won't be like working in an armory."

"I'm a po . . . a Marine, Sir," the Pinopan shot back. "Gots to die someplace."

Pahner gazed at him for perhaps one second, then shrugged.

"Very well. It appears that the Vashin will have the honor of taking the gate, supported by the unit armorer."

"What's next?" Julian asked with a smile. "Arming the pilots?"

"And the cooks, the clerks, and the sergeant major's band," Pahner told him. "Take it from here, Rastar."

"Right." Rastar had revolvers in all four hands now, checking to make sure the ash hadn't jammed the actions. "Honal?" he said to his cousin.

"Vashin!" Honal called in turn to the cavalry drawn up behind him. "Good news! We get to take the gates! Up the stairs, the shorty blows the door, and we're in!"

"Well, I suppose that's as close as they're getting to an operations order," Pahner murmured as he stepped back. He hoped they would at least dismount. The *civan* might possibly make it up the stairs—all the Vashin were superb riders, after all—but getting them through the doorway would be tough.

As Honal was waving the cavalry to the ground, the lower embrasure on the western tower suddenly gouted flame. A tremendous explosion rocked the fortification, smoke poured through the structure, and a racket of rifle fire sounded from the conflagration.

"I believe His Highness has made an appearance," Pahner observed. "Go! Get up there now, Rastar!"

"About bloody time, Roger!" the former Vashin prince yelled. Then he waved his pistols at the wall and looked at his own men.

"*Therdan!*"

"I think we may have overdone it there, Sergeant Major," Roger said with a cough as he scrabbled in his pouch for cartridges. He'd expended the last of his irreplaceable pistol beads on the way out of the Temple. Then he'd expended all of the rounds for his own, human-sized revolver on his way *into* the gate tower defensive complex. That was when he'd picked up the revolver and ammo pouch from a wounded Vashin. It was oversized, designed for Mardukan hands, and fit to fracture even Roger's wrists each time he fired. But the one thing he really hated about it was that he was flat out of ammo for it, too.

"Oh, I dunno, Your Highness." Kosutic shook her head to clear the ringing. "I think a keg of gunpowder was about right."

"The door is stuck!" St. John (J) announced. Through the smoke, Roger could just barely make out Kileti, levering at the door with a piece of bent iron. The prince smothered a curse and squinted, but even with his superb natural vision, details were impossible to make out. All morning, he'd regretted leaving his helmet behind at the barracks, since the entire trip had been from gloom to deeper gloom. And smoke-filled deeper gloom, at that.

"Well, we'd best get it unstuck," he said calmly as another volley echoed from behind him. "Don't you think?"

"And they would do that how, exactly, Your Highness?" Cord asked, then looked up suddenly. "*Down!*"

The spear had somehow flown past the blockade of Diasprans and Vashin holding the rear guard. How his *asi* had even seen it under such conditions was more than the prince could say. Unfortunately, just seeing it wasn't quite enough.

Cord's arm sweep knocked Roger to the side, but the short, broad blade of the spear took the shaman just below the right, lower shoulder.

"Bloody hell!" Roger rebounded painfully off the stone wall. Then he saw Cord. "Bloody *pocking* hell!"

The spear was embedded deep in the shaman's lower chest. Cord lay on his back, breathing shallowly and holding the spear still, but Roger knew the pain had to be enormous.

"Ah, man, Cord," he said, dropping to his knees. His hands fluttered over the surface of the shaman's mostly naked body, but he wasn't sure what to do. The spear was in the shaman's gut up to the haft. "I gotta get you to Doc Dobrescu, buddy!"

"Get out," Cord spat. "Get out now!"

"None of that," Roger said, and looked across at Pedi. The shaman's *benan* had both blood-covered swords crossed across her knees. "I guess we both missed that one, huh?"

"Will my shame never end?" she asked bitterly. "I turn my back only for a moment, and this—!" She shook her head. "We must take it out, or it will fester."

"And if we do that, we'll increase the bleeding," Roger disagreed sharply. "We need to get him to the doc."

"Whatever we do, Your Highness, we'd better do it quick," Kosutic said. "We've got the door clear, but the rear guard isn't going to last forever."

"Take the Marines. Clear the tower," Roger snapped as he pulled out his knife. Even with the monomolecular blade, the spear shaft twisted as he secured a firm grip on it, then sliced through it. The shaman took shallow breaths and slimed at every vibration, but the only sound he actually made came with the last jerk, as the shaft parted—a quiet whine, like Dogzard when she wanted a snack.

"We'll carry him out," Roger said as he threw the truncated shaft viciously across the stinking, smoke-choked stone chamber.

"We who?" Kosutic asked, shaking her head as she imagined trying to lift the two hundred-kilo shaman. Then she drew a deep breath. "Yes, Sir."

"Ammo! Anybody got any?" Birkendal called from the door. "Most of the lower room is clear, but we're taking fire from the second story."

"I do." Despreaux threw him her ammo pouch. "St. John, take your team and clear the upper stories," she continued. "I'll take an arm, Pedi takes an arm, Roger takes a leg, and we let the other one dangle."

"Chim Pri's down," Roger said as he grabbed a leg. "Who in hell is in charge of the Mardukans?"

"Sergeant Knever," Despreaux said. "Knever! We are *leaving*!"

She saw a thumbs-up sign come out of the force packed around the doorway and grabbed Cord's arm.

"Let's *go*!"

Poertena stepped over the remains of one of the Vashin cavalry. He placed the satchel charge against the door, pulled the friction tab to start the fuse, and looked around in the gloom for some cover. His helmet adjusted everything to a light level of sixty percent standard daylight, but the rendering washed out shadows, which had a negative effect on depth perception. Despite that, he could clearly tell that there wasn't much cover on the wall, but at least ducking around to the right of the door put a slight protuberance between his body and the two kilos of blasting powder.

He set his helmet to "Seal," folded his body into the smallest possible space, and pushed against the tower wall, but the overpressure wave still shook him like a terrier shaking a rat. The oversized pack was no help at all, as the blast wave caught it where it protruded from cover, spun him away from shelter, and hammered him down on the wall's stonework. He picked himself up and shook his head, trying to clear the cobwebs, and took a mental inventory of the situation. The downside was that he couldn't hear a thing; the upside was that there was now a hole where the door used to be.

Not that he had a whole long time to evaluate things.

Poertena had never been much of a hand with a rifle. He realized that no true Marine would ever admit to such an ignoble failing, yet there it was. And he was an even worse shot with the chemical-powered rifles the company had improvised in K'Vaern's Cove. Which was why he'd built himself a pump-action shotgun at the same time he designed Honal's.

It was smaller bore than the Vashin's portable canon, and shorter than normal, with a pistol grip carved from wood and a barrel barely thirty centimeters long. It held only five shells, and kicked like a mule, but it had one saving grace—as long as you held the trigger back, it would fire with each "pump."

Poertena demonstrated that capability to the Mardukans picking themselves up off of the floor in the room beyond the demolished door. There were clearly more of them than shells in the ammo tube, but he didn't let that stop him as he furiously pumped and pointed, filling the room with ricocheting balls of lead, smoke, and patterns of blood.

The hammer clicked on an empty breech, and he rolled out of the doorway and back into his original cover. He lay there, licking a slice on the back of his hand where one of the ricochets had come too close, then reloaded while the second wave of Vashin finally made it up the slippery stairs.

"I t'ink I leave it up to you line-dogs from here," he said to the Mardukan cavalrymen as the last round clicked into the magazine.

"What? You mean leave some for us?" Honal asked. He stopped by the hole and glanced in. "So, how many were there?"

"I dunno." Poertena glanced at the far tower as shots rang out from its top floor. "Not enough, apparen'ly."

He'd decided not to stare at the muzzle of the medium bombard pointed from the top of the other tower to sweep the wall. It had fired once—carrying away the entire first wave of Vashin who'd been supposed to cover his own approach with the demo charge—and he'd fully expected it to sweep him away, as well. But the bombard crew had apparently had more important things on their minds after firing that first shot. Now the gun shuddered for a moment, then rolled out of the way to reveal a human face.

"Birkendal, what t'e pock you doing up t'ere?" Poertena called. "Get you ass down here and do some real work!"

"Oh, sure!" the private called back. "Expecting gratitude from a Pinopan is like expecting exact change from a K'Vaernian!"

"What is t'is t'ing, 'exact change'?" Poertena asked with a shrug, and followed Honal through the hole.

Roger thrust the blade of his sword through the doorway, then moved forward. There was a hole in the base of the opposite tower, which was apparently the inner side of the main gatehouse, and he could hear shots from the upper stories. But the top of the wall was momentarily clear.

There was more fighting to the south, back into town. It looked like the Diasprans and Vashin were being used to hold off the Kirsti forces. From the looks of the locals, there were more of the city guards, armed only with staves, and a sprinkling of the formal "Army." They were distinguishable by their heavier armor and heavier spears. The weapons were something like the Roman *pilum,* and the soldiers wielded them well, holding a good shield wall and pressing hard against the human-trained infantry.

The Diasprans and Vashin had been pushed back by force of numbers, and now they were so compacted they could barely use their firearms. It was obvious, however, that neither group had forgotten its genesis as cold steel fighters, for the Diasprans had brought forward their assegai troops. That elite force had started as city guards, similar to the locals, and had since smashed two barbarian armies in its travels with humans. Side-by-side with the Vashin, who had drawn their long glittering swords, the Diasprans held the Kirsti forces at bay. More than that, they were probably killing at least three of the locals for each of their own who fell.

But the locals had the numbers to take that casualty rate, and Roger could see more moving up the roads to reinforce the attack. It was only a matter of time before the Vashin and the Diasprans were overwhelmed. Time to get the hell out of Dodge. Or Kirsti, or wherever this was.

"So many cities, so many skirmishes," he muttered as the remnants of his own party poured through the door behind him.

Sergeant Knever was the last through, and the Diaspran closed it behind him.

"We've sealed the doors on the other side and set a slow fuse on the gun powder store," the sergeant said with a salute. The nice thing about Mardukans was that they could salute and keep their weapons trained at the same time, and Knever was careful to cover his prince even while saluting. "Shaman Cord is being evacuated back to the company, and all live personnel are clear of the building. We had three more killed in action, and two wounded, besides Shaman Cord. Both of those have also been evacuated."

The sergeant paused for a moment, then coughed on the harsh, smoky air.

"What about the dead?" Roger asked.

"Per your instructions, we loaded them in the Marine disposal utilities and burned them, Sir," the sergeant replied.

"I'm really tired of this shit," Roger said, checking his toot. It was barely ten A.M., local time. In a day which lasted thirty-six hours, that made it barely two hours after sunrise. "Christ, this is going to be a long day. We need to didee, Sergeant."

"Yes, Sir," Knever agreed, and waved towards the far tower. "After you, Sir."

The sergeant took one more look to the north, into the mysterious darkness of the valley. As far as the eye could see, there were thousands, millions—billions—of scattered lights, lining the darkness of the valley floor. What created the lights was unclear, but it appeared that the city continued for kilometers and kilometers and kilometers. He gazed at the vista for a moment, then shook his head in a human gesture.

"This is not going to be good."

"Now, this is not good," Honal said sharply. The upper compartment of the tower was a mass of wheels, belts, and chains. "We need some Diasprans up here, or something."

"Nah, you gots me," Poertena panted as he made it up the last stairs. He grabbed the wall and his side. "Jesu Christo, I t'ink t'ose step kill me!"

"It wasn't the stairs; it was your pack," Honal said. "But now that you're here, we need to get the gate open. You have any idea what any of this stuff does?"

Poertena took a look around, then another. He frowned.

"I . . . t'ink t'at big wheel in front of you is t'e capstan."

"You think," Honal repeated. "And what is a capstan?"

"It what you turn to open t'e gate," Poertena replied. "Only one problem."

Honal looked at the wheel. It was, as far as he could tell, devoid of such minor things as handholds.

"Where do we grab?" he asked.

Poertena shoved himself off the wall and walked forward. There were embrasures on the northern side of the room, and he walked over and looked down through them. They were clearly for pouring stuff on attackers, but he felt quite certain that they functioned very well for disposing of unnecessary equipment, as well.

"Took you a little bit to get in here, huh?" he asked. He turned back to the great drumlike wheel.

"Yes, it did," the Vashin nobleman admitted.

"Looks like t'ey had time to strip out the actual capstan," the Pinopan said, gazing at the capstan thoughtfully. It was nearly four meters across, clearly impossible to turn without a massive lever. On the other hand, there was a very convenient nut right at the top. "I jus' need a lever. . . ."

"Big enough to move the world?" Roger asked, stepping through the door. "Time to get the gate up, Poertena. What are you waiting for? A metaphysical entity?"

"No, You Highness," the Pinopan said, stooping to pick up a long baulk of wood. "A physical notion."

The dowel was wide, nearly ten centimeters, and longer than Poertena—probably a replacement for an interrupting rod. The armorer contemplated it for a moment, then dropped his pack and dove in.

"Okay, first you get out the metaphysical entity extractor," Roger agreed, and glanced at Rastar's cousin. "Honal, is this room secure?"

"Well, we haven't been counterattacked," the cavalryman said. "Yet."

"Hell, on t'is pocking planet, t'at t'e *definition* of secure," Poertena said as he extracted a roll of tape from the pack. "And *of course* I wasn't going to get a metaphysical extractor!"

"Of course not," Roger said as he went down on one knee and picked up the dowel. "I should have known it would be space-tape. That, or drop cord. What else? And what, exactly, are we going to do with it?"

"Well," Poertena replied, reaching into the top of the pack. "You know when we first met."

Roger eyed the wrench warily, remembering a recalcitrant set of armor and the armorer who had gotten him out of it so quickly.

"You're *not* going to hit me with that, right?"

"Nope," Poertena said as he laid the haft of the wrench along the dowel and began to apply tape, "but we going to see if it can move t'e world!"

Doc Dobrescu shook his head as he ran the sterilizer over his hands. They had over two dozen wounded, but of the ones who might survive, Cord was by far the worst.

"All I wanted to be was a pilot," he muttered, kneeling down beside the shaman. He looked across at the local female, who had shed her enveloping disguise somewhere along the way. "I'm going to need six arms for this, so you're elected. Hold out your hands."

"What is this?" Pedi asked, holding out all four hands as the human ran a wand over them.

"It scares away the demons," Dobrescu snapped. "It will reduce the infection—the gut-fever, you'd call it. He's hit bad, so it won't stop it entirely. But it will stop us from increasing the infection."

"He'll die," Pedi said softly. "I can smell the gut. He will die. My *benan*. What can I say to my father?"

"Screw your father," Dobrescu snarled. He tapped the female, who seemed about to drift off into la-la land, on the forehead. "Hey! Blondie, look at me!"

Pedi snapped her head up to snarl at the medic, but froze at his expression.

"We are *not* going to lose him!" Dobrescu barked, and thumped her on the forehead again. Harder. "We. Are. Not. Going. To. Lose. Him. Get that into your head, and get ready to help. Understand?"

"What should I do?" Pedi asked.

"Exactly what I say," Dobrescu answered quietly. He looked at the mess in Cord's abdomen and shook his head. "I'm a goddammed medic, not a xeno-surgeon."

Cord was unconscious and breathing shallowly. Dobrescu had intubated the shaman and run in an oxygen line. He didn't have a decent anesthetic for the

Mardukans, or a gas-passer, for that matter. But he'd given the shaman an injection of "sleepy juice," an extract of one of the most noxious of Marduk's fauna, the killerpillar. If he had the dosage right, Cord wouldn't feel a thing. And he *might* even wake up after the "operation."

"Here we go," the warrant muttered, taking the spear by the shaft.

He started by using a laser scalpel to elongate the opening in the abdominal wall. The shaman's muscles had bound around the spearhead, and it was necessary to open the hole outward to extract the weapon. He applied two auto-extractors that slowly spread the opening, pulling away each of the incised layers in turn.

He finally had a good look at the damage, and it was pretty bad. The spear was lodged on the edge of the Mardukan equivalent of a liver, which was just about where humans kept one. There was a massive blood vessel just anterior of where the spear seemed to stop, and Dobrescu shook his head again at the shaman's luck. Another millimeter, a bad drop on the way back, and Cord would have bled out in a minute.

The spearhead had also perforated the shaman's large, small, and middle-zone intestine—the latter a Mardukan feature without a human analog—and ruptured a secondary stomach. But the damage to each was minor, and it looked like he wouldn't have to resect anything.

The worst problem was that a lesser blood vessel, a vein, *had* been punctured. If they didn't get it sewn up soon, the shaman would bleed to death anyway. The only reason he hadn't already was that the spear was holding the puncture partly closed.

"I'm going to pull this out," Dobrescu said, pointing to the spearhead. "When I do, he's going to bleed like mad." He handed the Mardukan female two temp-clamps. "I'm going to point to where I want those while I'm working. You need to get them on *fast,* understand?"

"Understand," Pedi said, seriously. "On my honor."

"Honor," the medic snorted. "I just wanted to fly shuttles. Was that too much to ask?"

CHAPTER EIGHTEEN

For the first time in a career that had seen the term used more times than he cared to remember, Armand Pahner had just discovered what "having your back to the wall" really felt like.

It was a much more powerful metaphor, under the circumstances, than he had previously believed. But that was because it was unpleasant to literally stand with his back to a closed gate while more and more enemies closed in on the humans and their allies. The *Basik*'s Own was being pushed back into a broad "C" around the gate, and he knew that unless they got the gate opened—somehow—they were all going to be killed.

And eaten.

That was more than enough to convince any CO that he was in for a bad day. In Pahner's case, however, it was only one minor, additional item. Armand Pahner was widely known as a man who got steadily calmer as the situation got worse. Which was undoubtedly the reason his voice was very, very calm when Sergeant Major Kosutic turned up to report in.

"And where," he asked her, "is Roger?"

The same circumstances which produced monumental calmness in the captain produced a sort of manic humor in the sergeant major, and Kosutic swept off her helmet and cocked her head at him.

"Feeling a bit tense, Captain?" she inquired, and Pahner gave her a thin smile.

"Sergeant Major," he replied quietly, "I have known you for some years. And we need every gun we can muster. So I will *not* kill you. If . . . you tell me where Prince Roger is. Right Now."

"Up there." Kosutic pointed upward as a sound of releasing locks echoed through the gate tower. "Opening the gates."

"Great," Pahner said with the grumpiness reserved for the moments when he found himself with no option but to depend upon his rambunctious charge's talent for surviving one near-suicidal bit of mayhem or another without him. "Now if we can just break contact, we'll be home free."

Poertena winced as the breaching charge blew in another heavy wooden door. The tower's internal defenses required double charges, and the overpressure slapping at the Marine caused his suit to go momentarily rigid yet again.

There probably wasn't much of a threat left on the other side of the portal, given the hail of splinters the charge should have blasted into the room. But Momma Poertena's boy hadn't made it this far on the basis of "probably," and he wasn't about to take chances when they were this close to home. So he thumbed the tab on a concussion grenade, tossed it into the room beyond, and waited until the weapon had gone off before following it through the shattered doorway.

The room was filled with a haze of propellant residue, but two Krath were still partially functional on the far side of the room. One was hopping up and down, clutching a piece of shrapnel in his leg, and the other was just climbing back to his feet after the dual explosions. Two shotgun rounds sufficed to deal with them, then Poertena took a closer look at the room and grunted in satisfaction as he spotted the large barrels stacked against the wall.

"About pocking time. CLEAR!"

"That what we came for?" Neteri asked as he entered behind the Pinopan and swept his rifle from side to side.

"Yeah," Poertena replied. "Get some of t'em Vashin up here; we gonna need some muscle." The armorer pulled the wrench he'd reclaimed once the gate was raised out of his pack and looked at the chocks holding the barrels in place. "I hope I don' bury myself doing t'is."

Pahner stepped through the second set of gates, looked around, and nodded. At least there wasn't an immediate threat on the far side of the walls.

The area beyond the gate was open for about a hundred meters—an obvious cleared defensive zone. Beyond that, however, a solid bank of buildings stretched as far as could be seen in the gloom. Obviously, the city continued well beyond the walls.

The heavy ash-fall seemed to be easing, and a little light was starting to peek through. Both of those changes were—probably—good signs. The ash was a misery for everyone, and some additional light on the battle would be helpful.

"Okay," the captain said to Kosutic. "We're through the gates. Now all we have to do is collect our charge and get him safely back under *our* protection, instead of the other way around. Oh, and somehow break contact with several thousand screaming religious fanatics. Any suggestions?"

"Well," a disembodied voice said from the darkness overhead, "I think using the plasma cannon is right out." Roger hit the release on his descender harness to flip out of his head-down position and dropped the last few meters to the ground. "Morning, Captain."

"And good morning to you, Your Highness," the Marine said tightly. "Having fun?"

"Not really," the prince replied. "I seem to have gotten my *asi* the next best thing to killed, I lost a Marine and four Vashin, and I seem to have really pissed off the Krath. Other than that, everything is peachy."

"Yeah, well," Pahner said, after a moment. "We'll talk about it later. I doubt from the brief bit Eleanora told me that you could've done much different."

"I'm of the same opinion," Roger admitted. "But that doesn't make me any happier about it. And the fact that I keep having to shoot my way out of these situations is becoming . . . annoying."

"I'd say that it was 'annoying' for your enemies as well, Your Highness," Kosutic observed with a bark of laughter. "Except that they don't usually survive long enough to *be* annoyed."

"Sor Teb did," Roger admitted. "That pocker is fast. I took out the arquebusier first, and by the time I'd shifted target, Teb was behind the throne and then *gone.*"

"It happens." Pahner shrugged. "The important point is that we've got you back, along with most of your party. We're into the gatehouse, and we've closed up our forces, too. Now all we have to do is break contact."

"Poertena's working on that," Roger said. "We need to get everyone to this side of the gate, though. And we need to do it fast."

Pahner looked at the traffic jam of *turom,* Mardukan mercenaries, porters, and hangers-on in the gateway and sighed.

"I don't know about 'fast,' Your Highness. But we'll get to work on it."

"As long as the gate is cleared by . . ." Roger consulted his toot, "fifteen minutes from now."

"Got it," Kosutic said. "I'll extricate some of the Vashin and get them out here as security, then get the noncombatants moving."

"Do it," Pahner agreed. "In the meantime, we need to start planning what disaster we're going to have next."

Poertena took another peek through the hole in the floor and shook his head.

"Come on, You' Highness," he muttered. "Time's a'wastin'."

"We've got company," Kileti said from the demolished doorway. "There are Krath in the gate control room."

"Good t'ing we smashed t'e control, t'en, huh? T'ese gates ain't closing until somebody get a whole new set built. T'ey can drop t'e portcullis, but even t'at won't be easy, not wit' t'e way we jam it!"

"Yeah, but if they get into the second defense room, we're cut off," the rifleman pointed out.

"Yes," one of the Vashin cavalrymen standing by the barrels of oil said. "And then we go kill some more of these Krath bastards."

"Timing on t'is is tricky," Poertena said, with another glance through the hole as the sound of axes biting into wood came from the far room. "I t'ink you Vashin better get in t'e other room and keep it clear, huh?"

"Right," the Vashin NCO said, and nodded to his fellows. "Let's go collect some horns, boys."

Poertena shook his head as the four cavalrymen left the room.

"I swear, t'ose guys *enjoy* t'is shit." There was movement below, and he saw the Diaspran infantry reforming and beginning a slow back march into the gut of the gate tunnel, all the while keeping up a steady crackle of rifle fire. "Almost time to start t'e ball."

"Back one step, and *fire!*" Fain barked. His throat was raw from the combination of gun smoke, ash, and shouting, but the company was maintaining a good fire, and at least half of their steadiness was because of their confidence in the voice behind them. He wasn't about to stop now. He did turn at the polite tap on a shoulder, though.

"Good morning, Captain Fain," Roger said. "I need to adjust your orders slightly, if you don't mind."

Fain looked at the prince, then shook his head. He could tell by now when Roger was being tricky.

"Of course, Your Highness. How can the Carnan Battalion—what's left of it—be of service?"

Roger winced at the qualification.

"Has it been bad?" he asked.

"Now that we have the Krath on a limited front, it's much better," Fain said, gesturing to the gate opening his men filled. "But the street fighting was quite bloody."

"I'm sorry to hear that," Roger said quietly. "I'm

getting tired of losing friends." He gazed into the smoke and ash for a heartbeat or two, then drew a sharp breath.

"We need to break contact sharpish," he said more briskly. "Sergeant Major Kosutic has gotten everyone out of the way behind you, with the exception of one rank of Vashin. I need you to coordinate a high-firepower retreat to the rear of the gate area. It's imperative that the city half of the gate tunnel be absolutely clear of all our people, including the wounded. Understood?"

Fain looked upward at the murderholes above him. He been half waiting for them to open up on his company at any moment, and he hadn't enjoyed the mental image of that eventuality which his imagination had conjured up. Now, however, the thought of descending slaughter was downright comforting.

"Understood, Your Highness," he replied, with a false-hand flick of grim amusement. "Will do."

Poertena waved in an ineffectual attempt to disperse the smoke drifting up through the hole as the Diasprans went to a higher rate of fire. That wall of lead couldn't be sustained for very long—individuals would quickly run out of ammunition, for one thing—but while it lasted, it permitted them to begin retreating, opening up the gap between them and the pressing Krath.

"I t'ink it's time to get to work," he said, as another volley of pistol shots sounded from the far room. He pulled out his wrench one last time and waited until the first Krath came into view through the hole.

"Say hello to my leetle priend!" he shouted, then swung over and down at the head of the barrel like a golfer.

Fain nodded as the first gush of fish oil fell through the holes. The Krath, who'd expected it to be hot or even boiling, were pleasantly surprised that it was nei-ther. The slippery substance made it even harder for them to move forward over the bodies piling up in the tun-nel, but as far as they were concerned, that was a more than equitable trade-off. Fain doubted they'd feel that way much longer.

"That's right," he whispered. "Just a little further. . . ."

Poertena rolled the third, massive barrel aside as the last of the oil gushed from it, then nodded at Neteri and pulled out a grenade.

"One, two, t'ree—"

He thumbed the tab on the grenade and dropped it through the hole. Neteri dropped his own grenade simultaneously through the hole beside it, then both of them moved on to the next pair of holes and repeated the process.

"Time to get t'e pock out of here," Poertena said, headed for the door and accelerating steadily. "T'is t'e next best t'ing to teaching t'em bridge!"

The incendiary grenades were ancient technology—a small bursting charge, surrounded by layers of white phosphorus. Simple, but effective.

The burning metal engulfed the interior of the gate, and some of it spread as far as the front rank of the Diaspran infantry. Despite the weight of their rifle fire, they had been unable to keep the fanatic Krath from staying closer to them than Roger had hoped. Unfortunately, in the words of that most ancient of inter-species military aphorisms, "Shit happens," and so a few of the humans' allies learned the hard way that the most terrible thing about white phosphorus is that there is no way to extinguish it. You have to get it off, or simply let it burn out. Water doesn't quench it; it only makes it burn hotter.

Yet what happened to the Diasprans was only very bad; what happened to the *Krath* was indescribable. The blazing phosphorus raised the temperature in the gate tunnel to over a thousand degrees Kelvin in a bare instant. The dozens of Mardukans who were covered in Poertena's fish oil never had a chance as it flashed into vapor and flame. The only mercy—if such a noun could possibly be applied to a moment of such transcendent horror— was that death came very swiftly, indeed.

It came less swiftly for the forces gathered around the interior side of the gate as the ravening flames licked outward. Some of those at least fifteen or twenty meters back actually survived.

The flame gouted up through the murderholes, as well, narrowly missing the last Vashin cavalryman as he scrambled down the scaling rope on the outer wall. The inside of the gate tower was like a chimney, channeling the explosion of heat and fury that set fire to all the woodwork and oil-drenched barrels in the tower's interior. Force fed from the conflagration underneath, which now included burning bodies, the flame and heat swept through the upper sections of the tower as if it were a blast furnace.

In seconds, the entire gatehouse was fully involved.

"Cut it out, you stupid beast!"

Roger jerked on the reins of his *civan* as it stamped nervously. He understood why the flames and the smell of burning flesh made all of the cavalry mounts uneasy, but understanding didn't make his own mount any easier to control, and he felt a sudden longing for Patty.

For virtually the entire march across the far continent, his primary mount had been a *flar-ta* pack beast—an elephant-sized monstrosity that resembled nothing so much as an omnivorous triceratops. His particular mount had had more than a touch of the much more dangerous wild strain that the Marines had taken to calling "capetoads." Patty had been five tons of ravening, unstoppable mean in a fight, and at times like this, when it looked like a hard slog all the way to the mountains and possible battles with barbarian tribes beyond, he missed her badly.

But there'd been No Way to fit a *flar-ta* onto a schooner, so for the time being, he'd just have to put up with these damned two-legged idiots, instead.

Pahner walked over and glanced up at the prince as Roger attempted to soothe the nervous *civan*.

"I think your plan worked, Your Highness."

"Better than I'd hoped, actually," Roger admitted, listening to the steady roar of the flames consuming the gate tower's interior. "They'll have to wait for it to cool before they can pursue us on this side of the river. Either that, or climb down the walls."

"But they'll have sent out runners on the far side," Pahner pointed out, gesturing across the barely glimpsed river. "You know there's a bridge upstream somewhere and garrisons are already being turned out."

"Then I suppose we should get headed out," Roger said, kneeing the beast around to face north, away from the inferno at the gate. He lowered his helmet visor and tightened his gauntlets.

"Time to show these religious gentlemen why you don't pock with House MacClintock."

CHAPTER NINETEEN

"You are an absolute *idiot,* Sor Teb," Lorak Tral snarled.

The general fingered his sword as he glared at the Scourge while smoke from the fires wafted even into the small interior meeting room. It hadn't taken long for the fire from the gate to spread throughout the upper temple district, especially with oil- and fire-covered soldiers running screaming in every direction. A brief, fortuitous deluge had helped control the worst of the flames, but the damage was extensive. And that didn't even count the damage to the gatehouse itself . . . or the loss of the High Priest. The jockeying for that position always led to social unrest, and in the wake of the chaos left by the retreating humans, the city balanced precariously on the brink of civil war.

"You may not speak to me that way, Lorak," the Scourge's reply made an insult of the naked name. "Whatever has happened, I am still the Scourge of God. I am the Chooser. Beware who you call an idiot."

"I'll call you anything I want, you idiot," the general told him in a voice of ice. "You may be the Scourge, but until this is settled, you are to refrain from *any* further action. Is that perfectly clear?"

"And who made you High Priest?" Teb snapped. He

refused to show it, but a tiny trickle of fear had crept into his heart. Lorak was normally a rather self-effacing type; there must have been notable changes in the last hour or so for him to take this high a hand.

"He is not the High Priest," Werd Ras said quietly. The Flail, the head of the internal police, had kept out of most of the maneuvering for the succession, but he had eyes and ears everywhere.

"However," Ras continued, "a quorum of the full council *has* determined that he will have plenipotentiary authority to deal with this situation. And he is specifically ordered to bring the humans to ground. The council was . . . not impressed by your actions, Sor Teb. Endangering the Voice was idiotic. Doing so with too few guards simply compounded your idiocy. And deserting him when it was clear your plan had failed was inexcusable."

"You're going to try to stop the humans with your *Sere vern*?" Teb said to Lorak scornfully. "All you know is how to make pretty formations. The humans are headed for the *Shin*. They had one with them, disguised as a Shadem female. You do know what that means, don't you?"

"You make too much of the Shin," the general replied with equal scorn. "It is high time to teach those barbarians a lesson."

Teb's eyes widened.

"You *are* joking, right?" He turned to Werd Ras. "Tell me he's joking."

"The fact that there was a Shin in the group that killed the Voice was reported to us. In fact, there are some indications that it was the Shin who actually did the deed. Be that as it may, if the Shin aid the humans, they will be pursued to destruction. Messages have been forwarded to Queicuf and Thirlot and will be passed to the Shin. If the Vales aid the humans, they will be put to the torch, and all of them will be taken as Servants."

"So now you're Choosing, as well," Sor Teb said with a gesture of humor. "I suppose the Shin are just going to take this lying down?"

"I don't care *how* they take it," Lorak said. "It is high time that those barbarians learned who their masters are."

" 'Masters,' " Sor Teb repeated thoughtfully. " 'Masters.' You know that the last three times Kirsti tried to mount punitive expeditions against the Shin, they were cut off and slaughtered."

"That's because none of them insured their line of supply," Lorak replied with a gesture of contempt. "We'll set up Thirlot and Queicuf as fortified supply depots and maintain heavily guarded convoys into the mountains. Like the Scourge, the only thing the Shin know is raid and ambush. They won't be able to cut that line of supply, because—like your precious Scourge—they don't even know what 'line of supply' means."

"Ah, yes, that's us," Teb said, tossing a false-hand in a gesture of mock agreement. "Not much more than barbarians ourselves. Just one last question; you say you informed Queicuf and Thirlot. Does that mean you're just going to let them scurry all the way to the hills before you go after them?"

"It's impossible to mount a prepared assault in the time it will take them to travel that far," Werd said. "And what's happened here today is sufficient proof that a prepared assault will be necessary to overcome the humans alone, far less crush the Shin, if they should be stupid enough to offer them aid. So, yes, we're going to let them 'scurry to the hills.' If the garrison in Thirlot or Queicuf is able to stop them, all the better. If not, we'll inform the Shin that they can turn the humans over to us or face the consequences."

Sor Teb fingered his horns for a moment. He hadn't come from within the social hierarchy like Werd or Lorak. He'd gotten his start as a junior Scourge raider, and he knew the true fire of the mountain tribes far better than this idiot, who'd only seen Shin after they had been "gentled" by the Scourge. The plan might even work, because the Sere had a point about the Shin's inability to organize a large action. But as for the tribes' simply rolling over and baring their bellies . . . that was about as likely as the mountains suddenly going flat.

"I see," was all he said. "It's apparent I don't have anything to do here. I'll go to my quarters and remain there until summoned."

"We'll need a few of your personnel for guides," Werd Ras said. "You'll be sent the list of requirements. With the exception of that group, you are to keep your forces in barracks. Any movement on their part will be considered hostile by the council, and will be met with all due force."

Teb considered that for a moment, then shrugged. "Very well. Am I free to go?"

"For now," Lorak replied. "For now."

Roger slid off the *civan* and slapped its muzzle as it turned to take a bite out of him.

"Cut that out, you son-of-a-bitch, or I'll shoot you for dinner!"

Pahner shook his head at the prince's mount while the rest of their caravan continued steadily past them.

"I never did like having to worry about whether or not my transport was going to try to take chunks out of me," he observed. "I think I'll just go on walking, thank you very much."

"No decent way to keep up on foot. You're pretty much stuck to one part of the caravan if all you have is your own feet," the prince opined. He glanced at the pack ambulances swaying by, and his face tightened. "Any word on Cord?"

"I don't know, but I do know that it's time to pick his *benan*'s brain," the Marine replied.

"Agreed." Roger strode over to his *asi*'s stretcher and shook his head. The contraption was swung between two *turom* and had to be incredibly uncomfortable, even for someone who was unwounded, he thought, just as Doc Dobrescu appeared out of the column as if summoned by magic.

"How are you doing, Your Highness?"

"Fine, I suppose. Taking my cod liver oil, and all that. How are the casualties?"

"Most of them are either gone, or out of the woods,

Your Highness," Dobrescu admitted. "St. John—Mark, that is—lost his *right* arm this time. An arquebus round, I think. He lost the left in Voitan, of course, just like the sergeant major. This one was low on the forearm, more lost his hand, really, and it should grow back fairly quickly. He'll be fully functional in a month or so. And we had one of the wounded Vashin expire—general systemic failure, I think."

"And Cord?" Roger asked, gesturing at the *asi*. Pedi was walking beside his stretcher, straight backed and stony faced. She looked the very dictionary image of the stoic tribesman, totally disinterested in asking quarter for herself or anyone else, yet she glanced occasionally at the shaman.

"Tough to tell," the medic admitted. "He took a solid hit, and the surgery was very rough and ready. Then there's the dosage on the anesthetic, and any secondary effects it might have, like increased bleeding. He's a tough old bird, but the emphasis on that could be on 'old.' If you know what I mean."

"Maybe, maybe not," Roger said with a sigh. "Do whatever you can, Doc."

"I won't ask if we could stop someplace, Sir," Dobrescu said to Pahner as the captain walked up. "I don't want to end up as somebody's lunch."

"You heard, I see," Pahner observed. "Yeah. Great guys, huh?"

"Gotta love civilization," Roger said, and gestured around. The ash had finally stopped falling, and the true expanse of the Valley of the Krath could be seen, opening out in a vast panorama before them.

The valley itself was at least a hundred kilometers wide, a broad U-shaped cut through the midst of rugged mountains, some of them rearing to well over five thousand meters. The Krath ran down its middle, a broad, silt-laden stream that fed and watered the valley via the repeated canals that ran up towards the flanking mountains.

The valley's floor and walls, though, were what caught the eye. As far as the eye could see, the valley was a patchwork of irrigation canals and tended fields. It was so intensively cultivated that not one square meter of land appeared to be unused. The majority of the houses, and all of the towns, were on the steep slopes of the mountains to leave every flat patch for cultivation, and each and every one was surrounded by growing greenery, most of it clearly edible.

The road itself followed the line where the flatter base of the valley started to climb up the mountain slopes. All of the towns they had passed had been evacuated before they arrived, leaving an eerie, unnatural feeling of ghost towns and mysterious disappearances. There was a sense of thousands, millions, of eyes watching from the distance, and there were actually a handful of visible Mardukans working in some of the more distant fields, plowing with *turom* or weeding rows of barleyrice and legumes.

Other than that, there wasn't a soul in sight.

The management of the valley—the regular roads, the neat villages, and the well tended canals—was arguably more frightening than the city of cannibals behind them, Roger thought. It was the visible sign of an entire country, a *massive* country of *well-organized* cannibals. After all the battles they'd fought against endless tides of barbarians on K'Vaern's Cove's continent, the thought of what "civilization" meant on *this* continent was horrifying.

"Civilization is either great, or truly terrible," he said, putting his thoughts at least partially into words. "Mediocre doesn't enter into it." He gazed out over the valley for a moment longer, then shook his head and looked over at Pedi. "Now on to the next battle," he said.

Pahner nodded and walked around the line of *turom* to touch Pedi on the arm.

"Ms. Karuse, could you join us for a moment?"

Pedi looked around at the Marine, then at the medic, who shrugged.

"I'll keep an eye on him," Dobrescu told her. "Right now, the best thing for him would be for us to stop. But that's not going to happen anytime soon."

"Very well," she said. She patted the covering over the shaman, then turned to Pahner and Roger as the ambulance moved on. "What can I do to help?"

"You know we're heading for the hills," Roger said. "What can you tell us about the route?"

Pedi obviously had to stop and think about that.

"What I know is all from traders and raiders. I've never traveled the hills myself." She paused until the prince nodded understanding of the qualification, then continued. "There's supposed to be a broad road to the town of Thirlot, where the Shin River drops through the Seisut Falls from the Vales to the valley of the Krath. There is a road up along the Shin, but it is closed by the citadel of Queicuf, and the town of Thirlot itself is walled, very heavily defended. You would have to take the gates, at least, and I don't think that's possible."

"You might be surprised," Roger told her. "We could probably take out the gates, but then we'd still have to fight our way through the city."

"And we probably don't have enough forces to do that," Pahner said. "We took the Krath in Kirsti by surprise, but fighting our way through a fully prepared town is something else."

"You could call upon them to surrender," the Shin said, rubbing her horns in thought. "If they refused, and you took them by storm, they would be liable for total destruction. If you created even a small breach, they would almost automatically have to surrender."

"That's a recognized law of war?" Pahner asked. "It sounds like it."

"Yes," the Shin answered. "The satraps fight all the time, and they don't want to destroy the cities. So they have elaborate rules about what is and isn't permissible, and what cities should and must do. Fortifications, also, but those are considered much harder to take. But even if Thirlot surrendered, you'd also have to fight your way through the stronghold of Queicuf, and that would be much harder."

"Two fortifications." Pahner pulled out a piece of *bisti* root and cut off a slice. He slipped it into his mouth and chewed thoughtfully, then shook his head. "If this were a purely military party I could see it. But we've got a swarm of hangers-on and the human noncombatants to worry about, too. I'd really rather not risk it, under these circumstances."

"What kind of alternative do we have?" Roger asked.

"Up the mountains," Pedi replied, with a gesture to the east. "There's a small track that leads to the south side of the Mudh Hemh lands; it comes out near Nesru. The Krath have a curtain wall there to prevent Shin parties from taking the Shesul Pass, but the position is only lightly defended from this side."

"So you think we could punch them out of our way?" Pahner asked.

"Having witnessed your warriors in action, I feel sure of it," she replied. "But there are Shin raider parties on the other side of the wall, from Mudh Hemh and elsewhere. Those from Mudh Hemh, I can talk out of attacking us, if they announce their presence in advance. Those from other Vales might or might not recognize my authority, and there are other hazards. The route is lightly used, so it hasn't been cleared of *nashul* and *ralthak.*

"And what," Roger asked, "are *nashul* and *ralthak*?"

"*Nashul* are . . . burrower-beasts. They look like rock and attack by surprise. Very large, very hard to kill. *Ralthak* are fliers, very large. They both eat the high-*turom*, the *tar.*"

"And if we take the route by the Shin?" Pahner asked.

"We will be headed directly to the Vale of Mudh Hemh," Pedi said with a gesture equivalent to a human shrug. "We will have to pass through the Battle Lands, and I have no idea what the traders in Nesru will think of that, but they're all under the control of Mudh Hemh, more or less. We shouldn't have trouble on that route. Not from Shin, at any rate. Thirlot and Queicuf are considered impregnable, though."

"I'm sure we could take them," Pahner said. "If we used plasma cannon to take down the gates."

"Not," Roger said. "Overhead."

"Precisely, Your Highness," Pahner said dryly. "That was in the nature of sarcasm."

"Oh," the prince replied with a smile. "And there I was thinking it was a test." He shrugged. "Whichever, the mountain route it is."

CHAPTER TWENTY

Semmar Reg stepped out of the Place of Justice and looked up at the monster towering over him. It was a two-legged beast, with vicious talons and an obviously wicked disposition. The rider on its back, however, was even more terrifying. His weapons and accouterments were different from those of the Valley Guards—armor of leather and fine-linked mail, a lance, and a long weapon like a thin arquebus. Reg bowed low as the apparition drew up at the head of a column of similarly equipped riders and dismounted. Whatever else the stranger might be, Reg noted, he carried more pistols than anyone the mayor had ever seen.

Reg had hurried to the town hall as soon as he heard the sound of a firefight from the south. From Sran's bell-tower, he could easily see the Guard checkpoint on the Kirsti Road on a clear day. Of course, today was far from clear, despite the recent rainstorm which had washed much of the ash out of the air, and the current visibility conditions had made it difficult to make out details. But when he reached the tower's top, he saw a small amount of smoke from arquebuses and bombards still drifting around the fortification. He'd also seen this column of riders, well on its way to the town, and if they'd taken many casualties from the Guard, it wasn't apparent.

What *was* apparent was that a formed military unit was just about to descend upon Sran. And that hadn't happened in two hundred years.

Rastar looked around at the town and felt a distinct glow of pleasure. It climbed up the mountains at its back, with one house piled practically on top of another. On the south side, a mountain stream tumbled out of a knife-edged gorge and was gathered for use by several mills that seemed to be the main source of local income.

It was evident that at least some of the place's citizenry had once been more prosperous than they were today, for several large one-time manors had been converted into housing for workers. But if the manor houses' previous owners had fallen upon hard times, the workmen living in their homes today appeared to be doing well enough. For that matter, the entire town seemed relatively prosperous, which was good. Prosperity mattered to the humans, since they felt so very kindly towards town-living *turom*. Rastar, on the other hand, was Vashin. The Vashin had settled into their northern fortresses barely three generations before the Boman overran them, and the long tradition of raiding was bred into their bone and blood. It might have become somewhat muted in the last generation or so, but they certainly weren't "townies."

Thus it was that Rastar saw the town from the uncomplicated perspective of a cavalry leader on a long march. Which was to say, as a chicken waiting to be plucked. Of course, there was no need to be impolite about it.

"Good day to you, kind Sir," the former Prince of Therdan said in truly vilely accented Krath with a gesture of greeting. "It's lucky for you I got here first!"

Reg bowed again, nervously.

"It is a great honor to meet you . . . ?" he said.

"Rastar Komas," the armored stranger supplied. Or, at least, that was what Reg *thought* he said. Between the outlandish name and the even worse accent, it was very difficult to be certain. "Prince of Therdan," the stranger went on, with a false-hand gesture of expansive good-will. "It would seem that a caravan, of which I am a member, is about to pass through your town and into the Shin Hills. Unfortunately, we're just a tad short on supplies."

"I believe you are the party from over the seas?" Reg said delicately. "I was informed of your presence. However, the High One has decreed that you are not permitted to leave Kirsti. I . . . wonder at your presence here. Also, the Shesul Road is closed to all but military traffic. I'm afraid that you're not authorized access."

"Oh, trifles, my good man. Trifles, I'm sure!" Rastar said with a human grin. It was not a normal Mardukan expression, since Mardukans, like any sensible species, regarded the baring of teeth as a sign of hostility. Not even Eleanora O'Casey could fault him for smiling so cheerfully at the local mayor, but Rastar was pleased to observe that the expression had exercised the proper effect upon him.

"I'll admit that there was some minor unpleasantness when we left Kirsti," he continued. "But surely no rational government would hold you responsible for our presence when half the Kirsti Guard is dead at the *Atul* Gate."

"Oh." Foreign accent or no, Reg had no problem understanding that last sentence. He tried not to flinch as he absorbed its dire implications, but he was fairly sure where the rest of the conversation was going. "I agree with your assessment," he said, after a moment. "What can the town of Sran do for you?"

"Well, as I mentioned, we're terribly short of supplies," Rastar said with another smile which just coincidentally happened to show a bit more tooth than the last one. "But you're in luck, because I got here before those barbarians from Diaspra or . . . even the worse, the *humans*. So I'm thinking that we can get clear with, oh, say one measure in five of your storehouses. And, of course, some little trinkets. Purely to satisfy the wanton lusts of those Diaspran infantry barbarians. We'll *try* to keep the humans from burning the town down, but you know how they are. Perhaps if everything was assembled, on carts, ready to go, when they arrived it would be easier to restrain them. And now that I think about it, if we could distract them with a feast outside town, we might actually be able to keep them in check.

"Now, I suppose we *could* pay for some of it," he added with a gesture expressive of anxious consideration. "But then we'd be here all day negotiating, and they'd probably arrive before we were ready for them. What do you think would be best?"

"I'll go get the head of supply," the mayor said.

"God, I love good subordinates!" Roger said as he looked around with a sigh of pleasure.

"They are a treasure, aren't they?" Pahner agreed with a laugh.

A long column of *turom* carts was lined up beside the road. Some of them were still being loaded, but most were already piled high with sacks of barleyrice and other less identifiable merchandise. On the other side of the road there was a large tree-park, apparently a source of firewood for the town, and scattered amongst the trees was a mess line. Several cauldrons of barleyrice steamed over fires, and two *turom* were turning on a spit just beyond several long tables covered with fruit and fresh vegetables. The meat was going to be a little rare, but . . .

"Tremendous, Rastar," Roger said as he trotted his *civan* up to the Vashin prince, who was gnawing on a *basik* leg. "I'm surprised you were able to do all this so easily."

"Oh, it was tough," Rastar assured him, then belched and tossed the leg bone over his shoulder. "The local mayor was a tough negotiator."

"What's it going to cost us?" Pahner asked as he walked up to them, still pointedly refusing to ride one of the *civan*.

"Oh, as to that," Rastar said airily, "it seems the locals were so impressed with our riding form that—"

"Rastar," Roger growled, "you were supposed to *pay* for the supplies."

"I *tried* to press payment upon them," the Therdan said. "But they absolutely refused. It was truly amazing."

"What did you threaten them with?" Pahner asked.

"Me? *Threaten?*" Rastar demanded with a Mardukan hand gesture eloquent of shock. "I can't believe you could accuse me of such a thing, when we Vashin are so universally known for our humility and boundless respect for life!"

"Hah!" Roger laughed.

"Well, I *will* admit that the reputation of humans for boundless cruelty and wanton slaughter had, unfortunately, preceded you."

"Oh, you bastard," Roger said with another laugh. "I'm going to have to govern these people some day, you know."

"As well they sense the iron hand inside the glove, then, Your Highness," Pahner said. "Until their society is stable and they themselves are educated enough for democracy to take hold, a certain rational degree of fear is a vital necessity."

"I know that, Captain," Roger said sadly. "I don't have to like it."

"As long as you *follow* it," Pahner said. "The difference between the MacClintock Doctrine and the fall of the ISU was a lack of respect for the ISU and its thinking that it could 'nation-build' on the cheap, which left the cupboard bare when it came up short on credit and couldn't pay cash with its military."

"I'm aware of that, Captain," Roger sighed. "Have you ever noticed me trying to use 'minimal force'?"

The Marine looked at him thoughtfully for a moment, then shook his head. "No, I haven't. Point taken."

"I've become more comfortable than I ever wanted to be with calling for a bigger hammer," Roger said. "I don't have to like it, but the past few months have provided all the object lessons anyone could ever want about what happens when you're afraid to use force at need."

He started to say something more, then closed his

mouth, and Pahner saw him look across to where Nimashet Despreaux rode her own civan beside the line of ambulances. For just a moment, the prince's eyes were very dark, but then he gave himself a shake and returned his attention to the Bronze Barbarians' commander.

"Since you—and Rastar—seem to have everything thoroughly under control, I'm going to go check on Cord and the other casualties. Ask somebody to bring me a plate, would you?"

Roger dipped his head under the leather awning and looked across the litter at Pedi.

"How is he?"

Most of the wounded were being transported in the leather-covered *turom* carts that looked not much different from Conestoga wagons. Roger had spent some time in similar conditions on the march, so he knew what it was like to be bounced and bumped over the poorly maintained roads while regrowing an arm or a hand. Unpleasant didn't begin to describe it. But until they got back to "civilization," and convinced civilization that there was the hard way, and then there was Roger's way, there wasn't a great deal of option.

What option there was, though, had been extended to Cord. His litter was suspended between two *turom,* which had to be at least marginally better. At least he wasn't being shaken by every bump in the road, although whether or not the side-to-side motion was actually all that superior was probably a matter of opinion. At the moment, however, it was the best Roger could offer his *asi.*

He had seldom felt so inadequate when he offered someone his "best."

"He still won't wake up," Pedi said softly. "And he's hot; his skin is dry."

"Afternoon, Your Highness," Dobrescu said. The medic climbed down from one of the carts to stand beside the litter and gestured at Cord. "I heard you were checking on the wounded and figured I'd find you here."

"How is he?" Roger repeated.

"He's not coming out of the anesthesia," the medic admitted. "Which isn't good. And as Blondie here noted, he's running a fever. That isn't anything I've run into before; they're cold-blooded by nature, so a fever isn't normal with them. It's not all that *high* a fever, but he's about three degrees above where I think he should be, based on the ambient temperature."

"He's . . ." Roger paused, trying to decide how to put it. "He's sort of a . . . warrior monk. Is it possible that he's unconsciously . . . ?"

"Using *dinshon* to increase his body temperature?" Dobrescu finished for him. "Possible. I've seen him use *dinshon* a couple of times to control his metabolism. And the fever might be whatever metabolic remnant lets him do it reacting to the infection. There's a reason people develop fevers; the higher temperature improves the immune response. So fever, under certain circumstances, might be normal in Mardukans. But he's still in a bad way."

"Is there anything else to be done?" Roger asked. "I hate seeing him like this."

"Well, as far as I know, I'm *the* expert on Mardukan physiology," the medic said dryly, "and I'm afraid I can't think of a thing. I'm sorry to put it this way, Sir, but he's either going to pull through, or he isn't. I've given him the one antibiotic I know is usable in Mardukans, and we're pumping him with fluids. Other than that, there's not much we can do."

"Got it," Roger said. "I'll get out of your hair. Pedi?"

"Yes, Your Highness?" the Shin said miserably.

"Wearing yourself down caring for him isn't going to bring him back any sooner," the prince said pointedly. "I want you to rotate with those other slaves we 'rescued' and get some rest when you can. I'm going to need you up and ready to deal with the tribes as we're moving. If we get overrun because you're too tired to wrap your tongue around the words to get us through, it's going to kill him deader than dead. Understand?"

"Yes, Your Highness. I'll make sure I'm available. And capable."

"Good," Roger said, then sighed. "This is going to be a long trip."

"What?" Dobrescu said darkly. "On Marduk? Really?"

"Rastar, we also need intelligence on what we're heading into," Pahner said, after the prince had left. "Pedi has never used this route herself."

"I've talked with the locals," Rastar replied. "The language problem is pretty bad, but I got Macek to use his toot to check the translation for me. According to the locals, the road to the pass is steep and apparently of poor quality. It's maintained for *turom* carts from here to the pass itself, but past the keep, it's nothing more than a track. I don't think we can use the carts after that. Or, at least not very far after that."

"Well, if your Vashin are rested, head up the road, slowly." The captain shook his head. "I never thought I'd be back to the days when my idea of good intel was some vague descriptions of the road and cavalry a couple of hours out ahead of me."

Roger's *civan* balked at what passed for a crossroads. The road through Sran had been steep enough, but just the other side of the town, it went nearly vertical. It was paved with flat stones and had obviously been maintained, but a fresh Mardukan gullywasher had just opened up, and the roadbed had turned instantly into a shallow river of racing brown water laced with yellow foam.

"This is insane, Captain! You know that, right?" Roger practically had to scream over the thunder of the rain and the bellowing of panicky *turom*. After the caravan had passed, the roadbed would be awash with more than rain.

"It is, indeed, Your Highness!" Pahner shouted back. He'd been in conversation with the Vashin cavalry scout who'd been left at the intersection, but now he turned and crossed the road to look over the far side. There was a sheer drop to the white water fifty meters below. "Unfortunately, it's the only route. If you have any other suggestions, I'd be happy to hear them!"

"How about we click our heels together three times and say 'there's no place like home, there's no place like home'?" Roger suggested, and the captain laughed.

> Theres a wheel on the Horns 'o the Morning,
> An' a wheel on the edge of the pit,
> An' a drop into nothing beneath you,
> As straight as a beggar can spit . . .

"Kipling again?" Roger said with a lift of an eyebrow.

" 'Screw Guns,' " Pahner informed him.

Roger grinned through the pounding rain, then kneed his mount back into motion once more, ascending into the storm. After another hundred meters or so, the road flattened out a little, going from a twelve- or fifteen-degree slope to one of a mere six or seven. The prince began to relax just a bit . . . only to have the *civan*'s foot slip. Roger threw his weight against the saddle as the *civan* skittered on the slick paving stones, searching for footing. After a moment, it recovered, and he kicked it in the side.

"Come on, you bastard! Onward and upward!"

Krindi Fain grunted and heaved at the wheel of the *turom* cart. For a moment, nothing happened, and then someone else shouldered in beside him. Erkum Pol's massive muscles flexed, and the cart lurched upward, lifting out of the crevice hiding under the knee-deep water roaring down the roadbed. Fain straightened his aching back and watched the cart move farther up the hill, then turned as someone tapped him on the shoulder.

"Captains don't, by and large, push carts up mountains, Captain," Armand Pahner observed.

The line of carts was barely moving—not too surprising, perhaps, given the steep slopes they'd encountered since leaving Sran. The first three had been bad enough, but the fourth was the worst so far, nearly two hundred meters long, and climbing at a constant fifteen-degree angle. Virtually everyone, human and Mardukan, had a shoulder into the carts, and the *turom* had been unhitched from the rearmost carts and doubled up on the lead ones to make the ascent.

As Fain turned towards the human, a ripple of lightning struck, jumping from one side of the gorge to the other with a sound like an artillery barrage. It started a small landslide, and the *turom* went berserk—or tried to, straining at their harnesses and slipping on the stones of the road as boulders careened about their feet.

"Well, I'm not a commander at the moment, Sir!" Fain shouted over the tumult, jumping forward to throw his shoulder back into the cart beside Erkum's as it started to slide backwards. "And I don't have any significant duties. So it seemed to be the best use of my time."

Pahner grabbed a chock and threw it under the right wheel as one of the *turom* slipped to its knees.

"Just don't get yourself killed, okay?"

"Not a problem," the former quarryman panted. "What is it you humans say? 'Caution is my middle name.' "

"To the winds," the Marine laughed. " 'Captain Krindi Caution-to-the-Winds Fain.' "

"Maybe so," the Mardukan captain grunted as the cart slipped again. "But at least 'caution' is in there somewhere!"

"This isn't going well," Roger said, "but at least we don't have company."

The reason the road was so little used had become only too evident. The column had made less than twenty kilometers since leaving Sran, and the long Mardukan day was well into its equally lengthy afternoon. It was hard to estimate how fast the Kirsti forces could react, but all of them were surprised that nothing had come up the road after them already.

"It's possible that the High Priest's death has kicked off an outright civil war," O'Casey pointed out. "Unlikely, but possible. In which case the lack of reaction is because everyone is consolidating their positions and they don't have any forces to spare for something as unimportant as chasing *us* down."

"It's more likely that they're simply taking their time,"

Pahner said. "I'd guess that the raiders really are out of it, though. They probably could've reacted before this, unless there was some specific reason not to. Like, for example, if Sor Teb was in enough trouble to possibly get a personal introduction to the Fire."

"We can always hope," Roger said sourly.

"But hope is all," O'Casey pointed out. "And even if he *is* dead—or, at least, in serious disfavor—*someone* should be chasing after us by now, unless something is distracting them closer to home."

"Don't rely too much on the delay," Pahner cautioned. "I'm sure the Scourge could move quickly enough to have overtaken us by now, but a conventional unit is going to want all its logistics in place before it moves. And speaking of logistics—"

"—we've got too much, for once," Roger finished.

"Not precisely, Your Highness. What we have is too few carts, or too few *turom*, for the stuff we've got. We need to reduce the load. Probably to about half of what we're pulling now."

"If we do t'at we won't have 'nough to make it to t'e port," Poertena pointed out.

"And if we try to drag it all with us, we won't live to get there, anyway," Pahner said. "If we can't trade with the tribes for what we need, we'll never make it through, period. Dump it."

"Aye, aye."

"The Vashin say that there's another forty or fifty kilometers of this," Pahner continued. "They're at the pass, though, or close enough to see it. We need to be to their position by tomorrow evening, or we're going to be in deep trouble."

"Of course, if we can't take the pass after we get there . . ." Roger pointed out.

"Oh, thank you so very much for reminding me of that, Your Highness."

"Good gods," Honal said. "That's not a curtain wall— that's a bloody fortress."

He and Rastar were perched on a ridgeline with a good

view of the pass. The opening was narrow, not much more than a wide canyon with nearly vertical sides. A stone wall and gatehouse had been thrown across it, and a series of structures were under construction or complete along the nearer side of the wall. On the southeast side of the pass, a wooden palisade and keep were being converted to stone, and on the western side a bastion was being laid out. The keep had been tied into the curtain wall, and it was apparent that in the long run the Krath intended to fill the pass with fortifications.

"I'm not going to underestimate the humans," Rastar said. "Maybe they can do this. Send a messenger. We're not going to take this place with cavalry."

"We might as well get dug in and get some fires going," Honal commented, looking at the angle of the sun. "It's going to be a long day."

Roger reined in his *civan* and slid to the ground, handing the reins to one of the waiting Vashin. He started to turn away, but he caught Dogzard's warning growl just in time, and backhanded the *civan* as it tried—again— to take a chunk out of his arm.

"It's not time for dinner yet, you beast," he said. "And you'd better be glad, or I'd shoot you and have you spitted."

"They just have to know who the boss is, Your Highness," Honal said with a gesture of humor.

"That's usually not a problem," Roger said. "Where's your position? I take it you're not standing out in the open so they can all watch you checking out their little fort."

"Up on the ridge," Rastar said, gesturing over his shoulder. "We're pretty sure we've been spotted, but we're not making our presence, or numbers, known."

"Have they sent out a patrol?" Roger asked as he started to climb the hill.

"Two of them," Honal said with a grunt of laughter.

"And?"

"We captured both groups," Rastar said. "We're holding them in a side valley. It looks like the garrison is composed almost entirely of lowland peasants, too. They certainly aren't mountain boys, anyway! They didn't even see our ambush until we'd sprung it, and they gave up almost immediately. The second patrol had ten in it, and we took it with only two Vashin."

Roger chuckled as he topped out on the ridgeline and increased the magnification on his helmet visor.

"What's so funny?" Rastar asked.

"What you just said is the punchline to a very old human joke. It's in a lot of cultures, but the punchline is always the same: 'It's a trap! There were two of them!' "

"I'd like to hear it sometime," Honal said. "You humans have good jokes."

"Yes, it's surprising how many points of congruence there are between humans and Mardukans," Roger said. "More than between us and the Phaenurs, that's for sure! Those people are *weird*. Of course, humor is one of the qualities that has the hardest time translating across species lines. That's what I meant about points of congruence."

"We laugh at the same stuff? That's a big thing?" Honal asked.

"Bigger than you can probably guess, yet," Roger assured him as he peered out across the valley. Then he zoomed his helmet back and removed it so he could run his fingers through his hair.

"Not a problem," he announced.

"Really?" Honal grunted a laugh. "If you think *this* isn't a problem, maybe we have fewer 'points of congruence' than you thought!"

"No, I'm serious," Roger assured him with a grin.

"Oh, I don't doubt we can take it," Honal said. "But we're going to lose a lot of people doing it."

"No," Roger said. "Or, rather, we probably would lose them if the garrison knew we were coming. Or where we're coming from."

He regarded the fortress for a few more moments, then shook his head.

"Send a messenger back. Ask Captain Pahner to

expedite getting a team from Julian's squad up the road. I've got a little project for them."

Roger wiped his hands as Julian rode into the encampment. The sun was barely down, but the Vashin had already broken up into squads across the ridgeline, lighting fires against the mountain cold and settling in for the night. The cold-blooded Mardukans found it nearly impossible to move when the temperature dropped below what humans considered sweltering. The humans, on the other hand, including the small guard detachment with Roger, thought the nighttime temperatures were balmy.

"Cold enough for you, Julian?" Roger asked, as the Marine climbed off the *civan*. With the sunset, the temperatures had dropped to what could be considered a pleasantly warm fall day in Imperial City.

"Just great, Sir," the sergeant said sourly. "Except for the saddle sores, that is. I can't believe you made us ride these things!"

"I suspect it's just going to get cooler," Roger said, looking to the north. "And as for the saddle sores, I'm afraid I didn't have much choice. We're going to be on a tight timetable, and as the temperature drops, it's going to get even harder to move for the Mardukans."

"On that, I've got a message for you," the squad leader said uncomfortably. "Captain Pahner dropped half the carts and doubled up the *turom* on the rest. So they're moving better."

"Good! Will they be here in time?"

"Probably, but they had some problems. They ran into something like a 'mountain *atul.*' Some of the *turom* panicked, and one of the carts ran back over . . . Despreaux."

"*What?!*"

"She's fine! Just a broken arm," Julian said, raising a hand as Roger shot to his feet and turned towards the picketed *civan*. "And the captain asked me to point out that you've got a job here."

"Yes, but—" Roger began in a semi-frantic tone.

"And Despreaux said for me to tell you that if you

come rushing back to see 'your poor hurt girlfriend' *you'll* have a broken arm, too."

"Yes, but—"

"And you called me all the way up this frigging road on one of those ass-busting *civan*," Julian finished. "So you can damned well tell me why, Sir."

Roger thought about that for several moments, then drew a deep breath and turned back around.

"Ah, hell," he sighed.

"Let's just get on with the job, Sir." Julian patted him on the shoulder. "Life's a bitch, and then you die. Right?"

"Right." Roger sighed again, then gestured into the darkness. "All right, then. I've got a job for you. And, I have to admit, not one that could wait while I went back to check on Nimashet. Take a look at the target."

They walked to the crest of the ridge, and Julian jacked up his helmet's light-gathering and zoom.

"Big pocker," he remarked, gazing at the wall. "Any idea on the garrison?"

"About two hundred," Roger said calmly.

"Be a bitch to take by frontal assault, even against swords and arquebuses," Julian observed. He looked up both flanking ridges, and grimaced. "Are you thinking what I think you're thinking?"

"You and Gronningen are our high-country experts," Roger said, with a smile in his voice.

"Sure," the sergeant grumped. He didn't mention that that position had previously been occupied by Dokkum. The native of the planet Nepal had been an expert at everything involving "elevation." Unfortunately, "had been" was the operative term. He'd died just before Ran Tai.

"This isn't going to be a short movement," the NCO went on after a moment. The carpeting Mardukan jungle had given way to a more open, deciduous forest, but even that stopped well short of the tops of the ridges. There was a faint track, a trail left by the local equivalent of goats, along the ridgeline, but getting to it would be difficult. The ridge was at least five hundred meters above their present position, and those meters were damned near vertical.

"We'll get the Vashin moving by just before dawn, one way or the other," Roger said. "I need you in position by then."

The Mardukan night was eighteen hours long, which would give the squad at least fifteen hours to effect the move. Julian thought about it for a few seconds, then nodded.

"Can do, Boss." He shook his head in mock sorrow. "I need to get less competent, or something."

Roger chuckled and clapped him on the back.

"Just imagine the stories you'll be able to tell in the NCO club. You'll never have to buy a beer again."

Julian looked back up at the trackless mountain and nodded.

"Now there's a motivator. Free beer. Free beer. I'll just keep repeating that."

CHAPTER TWENTY-ONE

Macek spat over the edge of the ridge and shook his head.

"You look into the abyss, and the abyss looks back," he muttered.

"Less philosophy, more climb," Gronningen growled back from where he'd paused on a wide spot at the base of the second peak.

The squad was strung out along a knife-edged ridge, the top of the saddle between two mountains. The "flat" surface was no more than a meter wide, with sheer drops on both sides. And the assault team would have to cross a nearly vertical shoulder of the second peak to get into position above the citadel.

"There was a shelf," Julian said, puffing slightly. The ridge was nearly five thousand meters above Mardukan sea level, which meant that even with the slightly thicker atmosphere, oxygen was in short supply. More than that, Julian had let Gronningen set the pace, knowing the indomitable Asgardian would push them to the limits . . . and he had. "About another hundred meters up and to the northwest," the NCO added with another pant.

"I think I see it," Gronningen agreed. He dialed up the zoom on his helmet and studied the terrain feature.

"Narrow," he opined, then removed his helmet and wiped at the sweat on his forehead. The night had gotten downright cool, and there was a strong wind blowing up from the valley, but the pace had everyone sweating as if they were still in Marduk's jungles. "Really narrow."

"Best His Nibs could spot before sundown," Julian replied, checking his toot for the time. "Four more hours until we need to be on the walls."

"We can make that easily," Gronningen said, replacing his helmet and picking up his pack. "If we keep going, that is."

"Lead on, Mule," Julian said. "Onward and upward."

Julian leaned out from the narrow ledge and sent a laser sweep across the top of the fortress far below.

"Two thousand meters."

"Right at The Book's outside drop limit," Macek said with a dubious headshake. "Long way to fall."

"It is that," Julian agreed unhappily.

The ledge was, indeed, narrow—a thin shelf of slightly harder granite intruded into the surrounding matrix. Some latter-day earth movement had shifted and folded the mountain, thrusting the horizontal dike outwards, exposing it to erosion. Over time, the remnants had become a half-meter wide section of granite, suspended over a two thousand-meter drop.

"It's the only choice we have, though," the squad leader added. "I want everyone to spread out. It looks like we're right over the inner battlements. Watch your distribution, and for God's sake, don't get entangled—this damned spider-wire'll slit you in half if you give it a chance."

"Yeah, but it works," Gronningen said as he surreptitiously attached a clip to the sergeant's descent harness. The combination of his voice and the night wind concealed the tiny sound it made as it clicked home . . . and then he pushed Julian off the cliff.

There wasn't a thing Julian could do—the blow to his back was too unexpected. He was thrown well out from the cliff, and found himself almost automatically shifting into a delta-track, a sky-diving position for maneuvering. His brain ran frantically through a list of ways to survive the drop, but nothing came to mind, nor could he understand why one of his best friends had just succeeded in killing him.

Macek spun in place, his bead rifle level, but Gronningen held up one hand with a screaming spider reel in it. It was obvious that the other end of the wire was attached to Julian.

"What the pock are you *doing,* Gron?" the corporal snarled. "You've got about two seconds to explain!"

"Just this," Gronningen said, with a rare smile. He attached the reel to the wall with a mag-clamp and laid on the tension. "I mean, now we know it works, right?"

Julian gazed down at the battlements, a hundred meters below him. He'd been observing them fairly carefully for the last several minutes, since the spider-line had slowed him to a halt. There wasn't much else he could do; the line had him suspended almost head-down.

He heard a faint rattle of rock, and then Gronningen appeared next to him, fully inverted.

"Gronningen, what are you dicking around at?" Julian asked with deadly menace.

" 'I love you, too, man,' " the Asgardian quoted. "You remember in Voitan, I said 'You gonna pay'?"

"Oh, you son-of-a—"

"Ah-ah!" The Asgardian grinned. "I pull this clamp, and it's really gonna smart when you hit the top of that thing."

"Oh, you son-of-a . . . ." Julian stopped and sighed. "Okay. You got me. Jesus, did you get me. I promise, no more jokes. Just . . . don't do something like that again, okay?"

"You should have seen Geno," Gronningen said with another grin, as he handed a fresh spider-spool across to the squad leader. "I think he nearly burst a blood vessel."

"Well, I'm proof positive that you don't die of fright

on the way down," Julian said. "Jesus. This isn't a truce, though. I'm gonna get you. Just you wait."

"I tingle with anticipation," the Asgardian told him with a chuckle. "You got a good grip on that reel?"

"Yeah. Why?"

"Good," Gronningen said, and flicked off the clamp that was holding the sergeant suspended.

Julian tried not to scream as he dropped into empty air again.

Macek looked around the top of the battlements with an expression of disbelief. Except for the eternal sighing of the wind, there wasn't a sound to be heard, and there was no one in sight.

"Okay, I'll bite," he whispered. "Where's the guards?"

"I don't know," Julian said. "Not here."

The top of the gatehouse was about thirty meters across, with a trap door at either end. The gate filled the pass from side to side. On the southeast side, a narrower walkway led to the top of the secondary keep, apparently a barracks or headquarters. Gronningen walked back from there, shaking his head, while Macek grimaced.

"Don't tell me they don't post sentries," he said. "That's . . . insane."

"It's freezing," Julian pointed out. "I mean, it's only about ten degrees out here. If they were out in this, they'd be catatonic, maybe dead."

Gronningen consulted his toot, then nodded with a remote expression.

"Fifty or so, Fahrenheit, yes?" he said. "Not cold, but brisk."

"More than just brisk for scummies, man," Julian said.

"So they just don't guard at all?" Macek asked. "Still not too smart."

"They're used to fighting Shin," the squad leader replied, "and I don't think they can move in this, either. Look at the Vashin. They're all huddled around fires being torpid. This kind of cold can *kill* Mardukans."

"So they're all inside waiting to hit us on the heads

as soon as we stick 'em in there?" Macek asked. "It's a clever plot to lure us to our deaths?"

"No, that was the recruiter who got us to join the Marines," Gronningen said. He walked over to the nearer trap door and pulled at the handle. The door was outsized, designed for Mardukans, and Gronningen was probably the only man in the company who could have lifted it. It didn't even quiver, though, and he knelt down to examine it more closely. Light seeped up around the edges, and he grunted as he found the darker shadow where a latching bar cut across the light.

"Not a problem," Julian said, kneeling beside him. The sergeant slipped a device from his belt and slid the incredibly sharp, flexible ribbon-blade into the crack. It sliced through the half-meter ironwood bar as if it hadn't even been there.

Gronningen was ready, and air hissed in his nostrils as he heaved upward. The door rose a few centimeters, and Julian got under it and threw his own weight against it. Between them, they raised it shoulder high, and Macek propped it up with a piece of wood.

There was no ladder, but it was a simple enough proposition—after climbing the mountain—to lower themselves into the room below. The chamber was about fifteen meters on a side, with a high, domed ceiling, and a stairway in the west corner. It, too, was deserted, with a dead coal fire in a hibachilike affair in the middle of the room.

"That's a quick way to asphyxiate," Macek observed in a whisper.

"Out?" Gronningen murmured, pointing to a door on the east side. "Or down?"

"Down," Julian whispered back promptly, although his expression was puzzled.

The spiral stairs led to a passageway—high for the humans, but low and narrow for Mardukans—that went both right and left, towards the gates and the barracks, respectively.

"Right," Julian said, and led the way.

The passageway turned, apparently following the

shoulder of the hill, and opened onto a large room with barred windows through which a cold wind blew. The room was at the base of the gates, and stairs disappeared upward into the gloom where the gate controls were presumably located.

Other than some litter in one corner, the room was empty.

"This is getting silly." This time, Macek didn't bother to whisper.

"We'll try the barracks," Julian said. "There has to be *somebody* around here."

They followed the same passage back in the opposite direction, towards the barracks. They had to deal with two more barred doors along the way, but finally they entered the main hall of the keep. It was a vaulted monstrosity, with a huge fire pit in the middle and the ubiquitous cushions that served Mardukans for chairs scattered around the pit.

No one was using any of the cushions, however. Instead, the middle of the pit was filled by a group of Mardukans, arranged in a fairly neat pile. Half-burned logs and ash had been dragged out of the center and pushed to the side. Obviously, the Mardukans had set a fire in the pit during the day so that they could sleep on the warmed rock underneath at night.

And every one of them was in the semi-hibernation torpidity that extreme cold induced in their species.

"Oh, puhleeease! " Macek exclaimed in disgust. "This is *it*? I rode all the way up here, played mountain goat, and then jumped off a damned cliff for *this*?"

"I think these guys must've taken the short airbus to school," Julian said. "The Vashin at least try to keep *one* guy per squad awake. This is idiotic. Geno, get up to the roof and signal the prince. Tell him we've taken the 'fortress.' "

"Will do," Macek said with a sigh. "But this really bites."

"What? You wanted a fight?" Gronningen asked, looking at the heaped Mardukans. The entire garrison's weapons were stacked neatly along one wall, and all of their armor was laid out in ranks. Obviously, they were ready to get up in a few hours, when things warmed up, and start banging horn with the best of them. "*I* think this is great," the Asgardian announced.

"Whatever," Macek grumped. "It just offends my sense of professionalism."

"And Gomer here pushing me off the cliff didn't?" Julian asked.

"Nah," the corporal replied with a grin. "In fact, that was about the most professional payback I've ever seen!"

The column rounded the last corner of the interminable track just after dawn. It had started to rain again, but with the increased elevation, it was a cold, miserable rain that ate into the Marines' uniforms like acid. The chameleon uniform was, technically, all-environment—capable of handling anything from jungle to arctic. But the Marines had been slogging across a hostile world for nearly six months, and it showed.

The uniforms were a tattered patchwork of different cloths. There were whole sleeves and legs of *dianda*—the silklike flax of distant Marshad—as mute testimony to the terrible battle at Voitan. The *dianda*, in turn, was patched with the fine sedgelike cloth of K'Vaern's Cove and Diaspra. All of the patches were of faded dark cloth, which had the virtue of low visibility but blended poorly with the changeable chameleon cloth.

The Marines looked as faded as their uniforms. Their faces were drawn and pale, from the ascent into the mountains, from the cold, from the ongoing low-level vitamin deficiencies of their *coll*-oil supplements substitute, and from the omnipresence of war. All in all, Roger thought, the company looked on its last legs.

He walked to the front of the column and waved an ironic salute at Captain Pahner.

"I make you a gift of the Fortress of Shesul Pass, with fifty *turom*, one hundred and twenty rather questionable soldiers, and a rich booty of small arms," he announced, and Pahner chuckled.

"I think you're getting too into this, Your Highness."

"Just trying to make like a Roman, Captain," Roger replied with a grin. "Seriously, we should probably rest up for a day or two before we move on."

"We can't discount pursuit," Pahner pointed out.

"No," the prince agreed. "But when you get a good look at this place, I think you'll agree we can also leave a nonexpendable rearguard to hold any pursuit off." He waved to O'Casey as she joined them.

"Ms. O'Casey." He greeted her with a nod. "The mountain air appears to agree with you," he said, and it was true. In many ways, the academic looked better than the Marines about her.

"That's a long walk to force on an old woman," his chief of staff replied.

"Well, the captain has almost convinced me to let you take a break," Roger joked. "The Krath must've had plans for this pass; the facility's area is far larger than necessary for the garrison. There are sufficient quarters to house all of us in relative comfort, although they don't appear to have discovered the chimney, so the fires fill the rooms with smoke."

"If you don't mind, Captain," Doc Dobrescu said, dropping down from one of the passing carts, "I have to agree. We've got a lot of wounded and injured, and these carts are pure hell on them. Give them a couple of days under a roof and warm, and they'll be able to heal much faster."

"All right," Pahner said. "We'll stay. Two days. Your Highness, I assume the Vashin are down from the cold as well?"

"They're not doing well," Roger agreed. "Actually, they're more used to it than I expected, probably from being from the northern plains, but the most they can do is to maintain sentries."

"We'll let them rest as well," Pahner decided. "We should be able to go down to about ten percent security. I'd really prefer to put out a sentry group down the valley, but we'll settle for putting them up on the walls. Sergeant Major!"

"Yes, Sir," Kosutic replied. The carts had reached the

open bailey of the fortress and were now stopped in a line. Roger noticed that most of them were being driven by Marines, and the handful of native teamsters driving the rest had small charcoal braziers burning under their seats.

"We're stopping here for a day or two," Pahner told Kosutic. "Leave the carts mostly packed; there should be stores in the castle, and we'll live off of them. Ten percent security, Marines only. Get everybody bunked down and working on gear."

"Yes, Sir," Kosutic repeated, making no effort to conceal her obvious relief. The sergeant major was like iron, but she knew when a unit was on its last legs. Now she looked up and shook her head.

"Speak of the devil," she said, and grinned as Julian walked towards the command group. But the intelligence sergeant didn't grin back, and her own smile faded as she absorbed his expression.

"Sirs," he said, nodding at the officers, then held up a small device. "I found this in the commander's quarters."

Pahner accepted it, turned it over in his hands, and frowned at the maker's mark.

"A Zuiko tri-cam?" he mused.

"I think they must have been in contact with the port," Julian said darkly. "We may have a real problem, Sir."

"Maybe," Roger said. "And maybe not. We need to find out where it came from. Get some of the locals functional and find out."

"Yes, Sir," the sergeant said. He turned towards the fortress' main entrance, then stopped. "Or, maybe not."

One of Rastar's Vashin was walking slowly towards them, trailing a plume of smoke. One of the ways the cavalry coped with the cold was by toting small braziers of charcoal around with them like incense censors.

"Captain Pahner," the cavalryman said slowly when he finally reached the group, and saluted. "Marine. Gronningen. Has. Found. A human." The sentence seemed to have taken everything he had, and he dropped his salute and stood like a statue.

"We have *got* to get lower. Soon," Kosutic said to fill the gap in the conversation.

They'd all known that this moment would come, but this was the first "new" human they'd had contact with since crashing on the planet. And while the Mardukans *might* have stopped them from getting off-planet at any time, the humans *could* stop them if they realized what they faced. How to handle the local humans had been considered and debated at vast and exhausting length, but it had been impossible to make any clear plans without more information than they had. Now the moment of reckoning was upon them.

"Well, I guess we'd better go meet him," Pahner said finally.

Harvard Mansul wished he had his camera. Of course, he might as well have wished he were back at Society headquarters on Old Earth, while he was at it. As a matter of fact, he *did* wish that, too, but he was a realist. He would have settled for getting the tri-cam back intact. The Zuiko was tough—it had to be, to survive around him—but it wasn't invulnerable, and sooner or later they would open it up to find out how it worked.

At which point, it would stop. Working, that was.

When he wasn't worrying about his tri-cam, he passed the time in his rather dank cell by wondering how long it would take the Society to mount a rescue. If they ever bothered. He'd reached the point of regretting his habit of disappearing for years at a time. Considering his stint on Scheherazade, the Society might not start looking for *decades*.

He sighed and banged on the door again. Usually the horned-ones roused before now, and he looked forward to the morning exercise time. But so far, there'd been virtually no sound filtering down to his little stone cube today.

"Hellooo! It's *morning*! Would you kind gentlemen mind letting me out?"

"I felt it was best to let you handle it, Sir," the private said. "I didn't know how you wanted to play it,

or even if you wanted him to know we were here, so
I sent one of the Vashin down to check on him. He's
been . . . kind of loud."

"Okay, come on," Roger said. "Let's find out what they
caught."

"I wonder if they were keeping him tucked away in
the larder for munchies later?" Kosutic mused.

"I doubt it," O'Casey said. "I haven't seen a trace of
any religious items here in the fortress. I think they probably just picked him up somewhere and stashed him until
they were told what to do with him."

"Given our own experience, I can guess what that
would have been," Roger snorted, leading the way down
the flight of stone steps and along the narrow—for a
Mardukan—passageway. They reached the cell door, and
he threw back the bolt and pulled it open.

"And who might you be, Sir?" he asked cheerfully.

Mansul looked up at the human confronting him and
frowned in puzzlement. Judging by the remains of the
uniform, the person was an Imperial Marine. Given the
rest of his appearance, he was probably also a deserter,
because no Marine of Mansul's acquaintance who *wasn't*
a deserter would ever have allowed his uniform to get
into such a state.

The man in the cell door was not just a full head
taller than Mansul. He was also either very clean-shaven,
or had almost no facial hair. Good bone structure, a hint
of pre-Diaspora Asian around the eyes, but otherwise very
classically Northern European. Great hair falling in a
golden mass, too. He'd make a wonderful picture all
around, the photographer decided. Then there was the
odd rifle—chemical propellant, by the look of it—and the
long sword tossed over his back. Quite the neobarb.
Absolutely perfect. Even the lighting was good.

It really made him wish those horned barbarians hadn't
taken his camera.

Mansul took another look, and it was actually the family resemblance that caught him first. One of his last
assignments before Marduk had been to cover the

Imperial Family when Her Majesty had celebrated the Heir's birthday. Mansul couldn't remember having seen a shaggy, broad-shouldered, sword-toting barbarian standing around to help cut the cake or pour the punch, yet the young man before him had the distinctive MacClintock brow. So who—?

"Good God!" he heard himself exclaim. "I thought you were *dead*!"

Roger couldn't help himself. The astonishment in the prisoner's expression and voice was simply too great, and a trace of his own recent classical reading came to mind. Despite the response he *knew* it would elicit from O'Casey, he simply couldn't resist.

"I am happy to say that the news of my demise was exceedingly exaggerated." He waited for the groans to stop behind him, then held out his hand. "I'm His Highness Prince Roger Ramius Alexander Chiang MacClintock. And you are?"

"Harvard Mansul," the man replied in a voice which was still half stunned. "Imperial Astrographic Society. You've been *here* the whole time?"

"I've been on Marduk, yes," Roger said. "The rest is a somewhat long story. And I believe we've gotten hold of some of your property." He held out a hand to Pahner for the tri-cam, then passed it over.

Mansul gave the item for which he had so passionately longed for more than a week barely a glance, then flicked the lenses open.

"Smile."

Roger knocked on the door, waited for the quiet voice from the other side to respond, then opened it, looked around, and grinned.

"Private room, I see," he observed. "Very nice."

"Quite the little love nest," Despreaux replied. She was propped up on a pile of cushions on the floor, her arm immobilized in the force-cast. Her face was slightly gray, she was still covered in mud from the trek, and bits of leaf and dirt were caught in her hair and on her pants.

Any other woman would've looked like hell, Roger thought, but Nimashet Despreaux managed to come across like a tri-dee star made up to look like a maiden in distress.

"I'm really upset with you," Roger said, sitting down and taking her good hand. "You're supposed to take care of yourself better than this."

"I tried," she said, and leaned against him. "God, I'm tired of this."

"Me, too," Roger said as he wrapped an arm carefully around her.

"Liar. You're dreading getting back to court, aren't you?"

Roger paused for a moment, then shrugged.

"Yes," he admitted. "Marduk is . . . uncomplicated. We make friends, or we don't. We negotiate, or we kick ass. It's black and white, most of the time. Court is . . . all negotiation. It's all gray. It's all who you pissed off last, and people jockeying for position. There's nobody to . . ."

"To watch your back?" she finished for him, leaning into him. "I will."

"You've never had to deal with the court ladies as a 'person,'" he replied. "You were just a Marine; you didn't count." He shook his head, eyes troubled. "It'll be different now, and their knives go right through armor."

"So do mine, love," she said, twisting carefully around until she could look him in the eye. "And, Roger, the Marines see *everything*, they *hear* everything. And you're going to be supported in a way that I doubt even another MacClintock ever was. *We're* going to be at your back."

He picked a bit of leaf gently out of her hair.

"I love you," he said.

"I look like hell," she snorted. "You're just trying to make me feel better."

"You look great," he said huskily. "Absolutely beautiful."

She looked at him for a moment, then pulled his head down to hers. The kiss lasted a long time, while Roger ran his fingers up and down her back. But finally she drew back with a snort.

"So that's it," she said. "You just like me when I'm immobilized!"

"I *always* like you. I was in love the first time I saw you out of armor, although I'll admit I was a bit . . ."

"Intimidated?" Despreaux supplied.

"Yes," he admitted. "Intimidated is probably the right word. You're a bit overpowering, and I really didn't want to get into a relationship. But . . . you're as good as it gets."

"Your mother is going to go spastic," Despreaux said. "I mean, completely ballistic."

"I don't really care about Mother's reaction," he replied. "Frankly, after what we've gone through, Mother is going to owe me, big time. And it's not as if I were the heir, so I'm not exactly a great dynastic match. Mother can kiss my ass before I'll give you up."

"I love it when you talk dirty," she said, and pulled him down for another kiss.

Roger ran his hands up her sides, leaving a trail of goosebumps in their wake. After a moment, the hands migrated around to the front, as if by their own accord, and ran across her midriff in subtle fingertip touches. She writhed to the side, pushing up her T-shirt, and—

There was a discreet knock on the door.

"*Shit,*" Roger muttered with intense feeling. Then he sighed, sat up, and raised his voice. "Yes?"

"Your Highness," Corporal Bebi said from the far side of the door, "Captain Palmer wants a command confer ence in seven minutes in the fortress commander's office. Sergeant Despreaux is excused on account of her injury."

Roger didn't have to see the private's face. His tone alone made it eloquently clear that butter would never melt in his mouth.

"I told you the Marines know everything," Despreaux whispered, pulling her top down with a moue of disappointment.

"*Seven* minutes?" Roger asked.

"It . . . took a few minutes to find you, Your Highness," Bebi explained, and Despreaux took the opportunity to run her hands up Roger's back.

"I'll—" Roger cleared his throat. "I'll be right there."

"Yes, Your Highness."

"Two minutes to run from here to the commander's office," Despreaux said. "Now, where were we?"

"If I turn up out of breath and rearranging my clothes, everyone will know where I was," Roger said.

"Rogerrr," Despreaux said dangerously.

"On the other hand," he said, leaning back down towards her, "they can kiss my ass, too."

She smiled in delight as he ran his hands up her back once more. He leaned even closer, her lips parted, and—

There was a discreet knock on the door.

"Bloody . . . *what?*"

"Your Highness," Dobrescu said diplomatically, "I know you have a conference in a minute, but I'd like to talk to you about Cord."

Roger shoved himself to his feet, shaking his head and breathing heavily, as Despreaux rearranged her clothes again.

"Come!" the Heir Tertiary to the Throne of Man said grimly.

"What now?" Sergeant Despreaux whispered.

Most of the supplies the Krath had laid in were stored in boxes of boiled *turom* leather. At first, going over the collection in the citadel's storerooms had been a bit like a very leathery Christmas. But after a few hours of opening boxes and cataloging contents, Poertena and Denat were getting worn out.

"Dried and salted fish." Denat slammed the top of the box closed and resealed it. "More damned dried and salted fish! I'm surprised these Krath didn't grow gills."

"T'ey needed to grow some damned brains," Poertena said. The company was still chuckling about Julian's find. "You scummies are frigging weird when it gets cold."

"Well, at least we don't go around bitching about a decently warm day," Denat snapped back. "How many times have I seen one of you Marines writhing on the ground over a little heat?!"

"Hey, I t'ink t'at was Pentzikis, and heatstroke's no

joke!" Poertena protested. "I was only kidding! Get a pocking grip—we're almost done here."

"Well, pock you, you shrimp!" the Mardukan snarled. "I'm done. *You* finish. If you can even lift the boxes!"

"Denat, what's eating you?" Poertena asked, and there was genuine alarm in his tone. The Mardukan was trembling, as if he were having a fit. "We can quit t'is if we need to. You don' look so good."

"I'm *fine!*" Denat bellowed. He grasped his horns and yanked furiously at them. "I'm *fine*. I'll . . . *aaaarh!*"

Poertena thought very hard about keeping his mouth shut, but he'd just noticed something, and it was really bothering him.

"Uh, Denat?" the armor asked carefully. "Did you know t'at t'e bases of your horns were swelling?"

Roger smiled and accepted the candied apsimon from O'Casey.

"Ah, for the days of kate fruit!" he sighed.

The main command group had gathered, and he turned to the newest member of their party.

"So, Harvard. What in hell are you doing here?"

The IAS journalist set down his *basik* leg and wiped his hands fastidiously.

"It was a routine assignment, Your Highness. Not much has been done on Marduk, since there's not a regular passenger line that stops here. There was an IAS piece back in your grandfather's time, when they were first planning on opening the planet to colonization, but since then, nothing. And that piece just covered the Krath capital. At the time, the Shin were more or less at peace with the Krath, and a sidebar about the Shin in the article caught my editor's eye. He sent me out to get a story about the 'mountain tribes.' "

He took a sip of wine and shook his head.

"I knew as soon as I landed that things had changed. The only information on the planet available was the earlier IAS article and two studies of Mardukan sociology and planetography. They didn't say much, but there were obvious sociological changes in the Krath capital.

Among other things, when I tried to get updated photos of their religious celebrations, I was barred from their temples."

"Updated?" O'Casey asked. "The previous IAS team had gotten pictures? And *included* them in its article?"

"Yes, the Krath were very open about their ceremonies," Mansul said. "It was a highly ascetic religion, similar in some ways to Buddhism, stressing personal restraint and meditation. The ceremonies involved small sacrifices of grain and meat to the God of Fire. Most of the contributions actually went to the priests, who were also the primary researchers and archivists, to pay for their upkeep. I don't know what they're doing now, but the rate of sacrifices has certainly gone up, if the smoke from the fires is any indication."

"You might say there have been a few . . . liturgical changes," Roger said darkly. "I wonder what bright person introduced them to the concept of human sacrifice?"

Mansul choked on his wine.

"*Human sacrifice?*"

"Well, Mardukan, mostly," Roger said. "Cannibalism, too." He took another bite of apsimon and grimaced at the taste.

"I take it you find their transition . . . unusual?" O'Casey asked Mansul.

"To put it mildly." The IAS photographer wiped daintily at the spilled wine. "All of the source material on the Krath religion insists that it's an ascetic faith, similar in some respects to Taoism in ancient China. Or, at least, that was the case when the original IAS team came through. Its sacrificial aspects were personal: meditation, and acts of generosity. They didn't even sacrifice *turom!*"

"Well, they sacrifice their slaves, now," the chief of staff said flatly. "And then they eat them. We saw the inside of the temples. And the kitchens and the bone pits."

"Are all the slaves from the Shin?" the journalist asked.

"I don't know," O'Casey admitted, "and our local Shin guide seems to be missing."

"She's tending to Cord," Roger said. He glanced at Mansul. "It's a long story."

"I like long stories," Mansul admitted. "Once they're boiled down, they make excellent articles. Why don't you tell it to me?"

"Where to start?" Roger asked.

"Start at the beginning," Pahner advised. "Go to the end—"

"—and fill in all the stuff in the middle." Roger nodded. "Okay."

"But maybe later," the Marine added. "We need to determine what happens next. Mr. Mansul, you came from the port?"

"Yes, and there are problems there, too."

"Saints," Roger said.

"Really? That I hadn't noticed. What I did notice was that the governor did *not* want any humans drifting out of the compound. He hadn't been apprised of my visit, and he acted like I was an Imperial spy. Frankly, I was starting to wonder if I was going to be an 'accidental death' when one of the locals offered to smuggle me out. I fell in with the Shin, and I was with a village south of Mudh Hemh when a Krath raiding party fell on the group I was filming. They took the Shin with them to Kirsti, but left me here, presumably for repatriation. Or maybe to wait for the governor to recover me. And then you happened along."

"How were you 'smuggled out'?" Pahner asked.

"There are breaks in the defenses," Mansul replied. "Contraband moves in and out." He shrugged. "I was just one more package."

"Now that's interesting," Roger said.

"Isn't it, just?" the captain agreed.

"Oh, there's more," Mansul said. "There's a small . . . colony, might be the right word . . . of humans living among the Shin. Others who have run afoul of the governor's bully boys. There's about fifteen or twenty of them, and supplies are funneled to them from somewhere."

"From where?" Julian asked.

"That I don't know, although I think the local chieftain does. These people aren't given to charity. He'd only be supporting the refugees if there was a reason."

"Satan," Kosutic sighed. "Complicateder and complicateder."

"Yeah," Roger said. "And no. The basics are the same, maybe even easier, if their security is so lax smugglers can move in and out at will. We need to get to Mudh Hemh and make contact with this Shin leader."

"Pedi Gastan," Mansul inserted.

"Pedi Gastan?" Pahner repeated sharply.

"Why, yes." Mansul looked surprised. "You've heard of him?"

"You might say that." Roger's expression was a cross between a grimace and a smile. "Truth being stranger than fiction, we rescued his daughter from pirates." Mansul blinked, and the prince chuckled. "But what I don't quite understand," he went on, "is why we didn't hear anything about this 'colony' of humans from *her*." He gazed at the photographer with just an edge of suspicion. "She's been very open with us, as far as we can tell, and she's never even *heard* of humans, much less anything about any refugees her father might be shielding."

"I don't know why she wouldn't have," Mansul said slowly. "I only met the Gastan briefly, and my understanding is that the refugees' existence is kept very secret. In fact, none of us are allowed in Mudh Hemh at all. Instead, he keeps the 'colony' hidden away in one of the really remote vales under the eye of a very small clan. I was on my way there when my escorts and I ran into the Krath. I suppose it's possible that even his daughter might not know what he was up to."

"I guess *anything* is possible," Roger allowed slowly. Then he snorted. "Of course, some things are more possible than others, and keeping a secret from Pedi strikes me as one of life's more difficult endeavors!"

"But it *is* possible," O'Casey said. "And if the Krath are in contact with the port, and if the Gastan knows it, then he'd have every imaginable reason to keep the Krath from finding out that *he* was, too."

"But could he really keep it so secret that Pedi hadn't even heard about humans at all?" Roger asked a bit skeptically.

"Probably he could," O'Casey replied. "Don't forget that this is a pre-technic society, Roger. I know there's a trading interface between the Krath and the Shin, but every bit of information has to be passed by word-of-mouth, and I doubt very much the there's anything like a true information flow between the Shin and the people who keep slaughtering them as religious sacrifices. So even if the Krath know about the human presence here on Marduk, they probably don't discuss it with the Shin. Anyway, it's obvious from the way most of the Kirsti population have reacted to us that the existence of humans isn't general knowledge even among them."

She shook her head.

"I'd say that it's entirely possible that the very existence of humans is restricted to the uppermost levels of Krath society this far from the port itself. In which case, it's probably entirely possible that the Gastan could keep the secret even from his own people. Of course," she frowned thoughtfully, "I'd *love* to know how this human managed to contact him in the first place."

"You may have a point," Roger conceded, and nodded to Mansul. "You were saying before we interrupted?" he invited.

"Well, if you've rescued the Gastan's daughter, that should work out well," the reporter said, trying not to show his relief as the hard light of suspicion dimmed just a bit in the prince's dangerous green eyes. "I think he's on our side, anyway, but—"

There was a knock at the door, and then Poertena stuck his head in without waiting for permission.

"Beggin' you pardon, You Highness, but I need Doc Dobrescu right pocking now! Somet'ing's wrong with Denat. I t'ink he going nuts!"

"Go," Pahner and Roger said simultaneously. Then they looked at each other for a moment before Roger gestured at Pahner.

"I think we're about done here," the captain continued smoothly. "Doc, you go. Julian, wring everything you can out of the prisoners about the rest of the route to the Shin lands. Sergeant Major, everyone else is on full rest and refit. I want us to be in good condition when we leave. Let's get to it."

"And I'll go find out what's wrong with Denat," Dobrescu said.

"Any ideas?" Roger asked.

"I haven't even looked at him yet, Your Highness," the medic protested. "And I'm a shuttle pilot, not a psychologist. I'll keep you posted, though."

Warrant Dobrescu followed Poertena into the small supply office that the Pinopan and Denat had taken over and shook his head at the Mardukan.

"What have you been sniffing, Denat?"

"I'm fine," the Mardukan said. He was shivering, his body sliming heavily, and a reddish bulge had appeared around the base of each of his horns. "I'm sorry I snapped at you, Poertena. But I'll be fine. This will pass."

"What is it?" Dobrescu asked, setting down and laying out his med-scanner. The scanner could pick up a lot even from a distance, and it showed Denat's heart and metabolic rate off the scale. The Mardukan was actually at an elevated temperature compared to ambient, which was very unusual. "Poertena said you'd been grouchy lately, and he told me about what just happened. I need to know what's going on."

"It's . . . a Mardukan thing," Denat said. A shudder ran through his massive body.

"I kind of need to know a little more than that," the medic persisted. "I have to tell Captain Pahner something. That's a human thing."

"It's nothing!" Denat shouted, banging all four fists on the massive, ironwood desk so furiously that the eight-hundred-kilo piece of furniture leapt into the air.

"Denat, according to my instruments, you're coming apart at the seams," Dobrescu said mildly. "Why not tell me what's wrong?"

"Because nothing's *wrong*," the Mardukan ground out. "This is perfectly *normal*."

"Then what is it?" the warrant officer asked reasonably.

Denat looked at him, rubbing his hands together in distress. Then he sighed, and told him.

Pedi removed the rags from around the injury and dropped them into the solution the healer had given her, then reached for fresh dressings. She and the two other released slaves had been caring for Cord ever since the injury. The wound itself was mostly healed, but he still wouldn't awaken, and he was getting even more restless and warmer. Lately, though, she'd at least been able to get him to take a little food, and he'd been muttering under his breath. She'd picked up a few words of his home language before he was wounded, but not enough to recognize much of what he was saying, although the word "*banan*" was close to "*benan*," so perhaps he was talking to her.

She opened a jar of lotion and began smoothing it on the dry patches in his skin. She'd picked up some of his background, more from talking to the humans and Denat than from him, and she realized what a valued person he must have been in his home country. To come to such knowledge as he had developed was hard for the sort of backcountry village from which he'd sprung, and men—warriors especially—who gathered that much training and understanding were extremely valuable to any tribe. She suspected that the human prince, surrounded as he was by a plethora of warriors and scholars, didn't know what a wrench it must have been for both Cord and his people to lose him.

And she had to admit that it would be a wrench for the human to lose him. And for her. The old shaman was one of the finest men she'd ever met; strong, yet gentle and wise. Knowledgeable, but physically brave, and often humble to a fault. It was hard to find such qualities anywhere, and she had to admit that they were even harder to find amongst the Shin than most places.

Because the medic didn't know if the increased body heat might cause mental damage—surely a horrible thought!—they had been wrapping the shaman's head in cool cloths. She started to replace the current cloths, then stopped with a gasp.

She laid her hands on the swellings at the base of the shaman's horns and felt a shudder pass through her body. She had to fight conflicting emotions, but finally she drew a deep breath, pulled back the light sheet that covered him, and took a peek before she quickly dropped it back again.

She sat back, thinking hard, and many things fell abruptly into place. She remembered what Light O'Casey had said about the language similarity, and she thought about the ramifications of the situation. She thought about them very carefully, and then, last of all, she thought of the sight of Cord coming over the railing of the pirate ship.

"Oh, Pedi, this is *such* a bad idea," she whispered as she pulled the sheet all the way back.

"What we have here is a failure to communicate," Dobrescu said with a chuckle.

He'd asked Captain Pahner, the sergeant major, and the prince to meet him in the stores office. They had—and they'd also reacted predictably to the sight of Denat's trembling body and bulging forehead.

"What the hell does that mean?" Roger demanded. "Denat, are you okay?"

"Aside from wanting to kill you, I'm fine," the Mardukan grated. "And that has nothing to do with your being a prince. You just spoke to me, is all."

"Is it a good idea to do this here?" Pahner asked.

"He should be fine," Dobrescu said soothingly. "And we'll leave in just a second. But the actual problem is fairly simple: he's in heat."

"In what?" Kosutic asked. "That's a . . . Oh, yeah."

"That's right. Mardukan 'males' are functionally and technically females, by our standards," Dobrescu said. "And vice versa. Denat's sex produces the eggs, the other sex produces the sperm. When the time comes, and the two, ahem, 'get together,' Denat's sex use their . . . notable organs to implant their eggs in the other sex.

"He's currently ovulating. Which means, evolutionarily speaking, that he should be battling other 'males' for a chance to mate. Thus the horn prominences and other signs. Unfortunately . . ."

"I have no mate here," Denat growled. "And I won't simply wander around, howling into the wilderness while I look for anything to couple with."

"In a way, he ought to," Dobrescu said. "Mate, that is. From a population standpoint, it's a bad idea to take one of these guys out of the equation."

"The problem of conservation you were talking about a while back," Kosutic said.

"Yes, because the sex that produces the eggs only does so twice per year. If they don't implant the other sex, they lose the chance for a long period, statistically speaking," Dobrescu said. "The reason the Kranolta took such a beating *after* they overwhelmed Voitan was that their egg-producers were scattered all over hell and gone."

"Can the—I have to think of them as females," Pahner said. "Can the *females* accept the eggs at any time?"

"Yes. They maintain a sort of 'sperm sac,' equivalent to the *vans* in humans," Dobrescu said with a slight smile for the captain's obvious discomfort. "The eggs are implanted by . . . well, we've all seen the ovipositors. Once implanted, they're joined by the sperm in the region, and become fetuses. I've been looking forward to watching the development, but we've always missed that stage. There were some in development in Marshad, but I didn't get much of a look at them."

"I didn't see them at all," Kosutic said. "Pregnant Mardukan females?"

"Yeah," the medic said. "The fetus sacs form what look like blisters on their backs."

"So . . ." Pahner began, then paused. "I just discovered that I don't want to know the details. Or, at least, while I'll be interested in reading your report, I don't want to discuss it at the moment. Is this important to the mission?"

"Just from a medical perspective," Dobrescu said. "The only military consideration I see is that I wouldn't expect them to be much use from a military point of view during their heat."

"Are *all* of them going to start acting like this?" Kosutic asked. "Denat is a fairly controlled fellow, but if the Vashin and Diasprans get hit, we're going to have some big-time fights. I don't want to even try to imagine what Erkum Pol would be like, for example."

"I don't know what their season is," Dobrescu admitted. "The Vashin and Diasprans, I mean. It could happen, and when it does, it will probably happen all at once. Denat's from a different area, and it seems to be seasonally affiliated. Which is probably all to the good at the moment. He's the only Mardukan from that area with us."

"Wrong, Doc," Roger said. "Cord and Denat come from the same village."

"Ouch!" Dobrescu grimaced and shook his head. "Good point, Your Highness. I need to check him out and find out if he's got the same condition. If he does, it might explain some of the strange stuff that's been going on with him since he was hurt."

"Please do," Roger said, and stood up. "Denat, sorry, man. Wish there was something we could do."

"It's all right," the Mardukan said. "Now that I know what's going on, I can focus on controlling it." He gave a gesture of rueful humor. "I wish that I were in Marshad, though."

"What was her name?" Roger asked. "The spy girl in Marshad?"

"Sena," Denat whispered.

"Well, if you're still . . ." the prince paused, looking for the right term.

" 'In season,' is probably the easiest way to refer to it," Dobrescu said with a grin.

"If you're still 'in season' when we take the port, we'll see what we can do," Roger said with a sigh. "Otherwise, I guess you'll just have to grit your teeth."

"I've always recommended cold showers, myself," Kosutic said with a grin. "But that's probably contraindicated for a Mardukan, huh?"

"We need to consider the ramifications of this long-term," Pahner said. "Doc, as soon as you check Shaman

Cord out, I want you to try to determine how soon the rest will go . . . into 'season.' We need to be able to plan around that."

"Yes, Sir," the warrant officer said. "Personally, though, I plan on taking that week off. These guys can be downright touchy."

CHAPTER TWENTY-TWO

"Tell me again what you heard," the Gastan said. He peered at the fortress through the device, the *binoculars,* the humans had given him.

"The merchants all quit Nesru at once," the Shin guardsman said. "All at once. A messenger arrived from Queicuf with word that Shesul Pass was under attack from the rear, or that it had fallen. He said at first that a small force had arrived and taken it with demons. But no one believes him."

Of course no one believed him, the Gastan thought wryly. After all, only a tiny handful of the Shin knew about the humans. Most of his tribesmen believed that his binoculars had been produced by Krath craftsmen from far up the great valley, and none of them recognized the enormous difference between the artisans who could produce them and the most skilled craftsman the Krath had ever produced. But any Shin who ever saw human weapons used would have every right to believe he looked upon demons.

"And now Queicuf heats its oil," he mused aloud, trying to get more detail out of the image the binoculars showed him. He and the guardsman stood on the edge of an ash cone to the north of Mudh Hemh. It gave an excellent view of the Krath stronghold without going to the trouble and danger of crossing the river. Of course, a view was all it gave him, and the way things were going, the time might come when he would have to carry his banner to Nopet Nujam. Which would be . . . inconvenient.

The danger which might impel him to do that was that the Krath seemed to have found a way through the Fire Lands. It was obvious that whatever path they had found was difficult and not suited to the movement of large numbers, but the Scourge raiding parties which had used it had inflicted painful losses. Very painful ones.

The problem was that the discovery seemed to have convinced the Krath that it was time to take Mudh Hemh at last, while the Vales were distracted by the knowledge that the Scourge had found a way into their rear. If they were determined to make a fresh attempt, the main thrust would come—as always—through the Battle Lands, and he would have no choice but to oppose that attack.

Yet if he took his banner to Nopet Nujam, he would face two problems. The first was that the motley mass of raiding parties that always gathered around Mudh Hemh would feel constrained to follow him, which would make the trip a logistic nightmare. But in many ways, that would be better than the alternative, because if they indicated a willingness to stay behind, he would have to assume it would be to do some casual raiding and looting in his own lands during his absence.

Unfortunately, if they chose to follow his banner, he would face his the *second* problem. He would have to leave the Vale too lightly covered against the Krath who might creep through the Fire Lands along their new, secret path, because he would need his clan to control the hangers-on among his own "allies." And that didn't even consider the possibility that the clan would get into a feud with one of the Shin raiding groups, resulting in who knew how much bloodshed and who knew what political headaches with other clan-chiefs.

Being the "king" of the Shin was like juggling live coals.

Not for the first time, he felt sorrow for the loss of his daughter Pedi, and not just the natural grief of a father whose daughter had gone to the Fire. She'd been headstrong and stubborn as the mountains, but if he'd sent her to Nopet Nujam to be his eyes and ears, she would have returned with a concise and correct report. He really didn't have anyone else he could trust to do that; they all "embellished." And not one in a hundred of them could read. It was like pulling teeth to get them to study anything but raiding and hunting.

He felt a stronger pang of grief—and guilt—as another thought crossed his mind. Grief that he had lost her . . . and guilt that he wished he had lost Thertik instead.

He raised the binoculars once more, using them to hide his eyes from Nygard lest they reveal too much, but he could not hide the truth from himself. Much as the Gastan loved all of his children, it was . . . unfortunate that only Thertik and Pedi survived out of their litter and that Thertik was male. Perhaps even worse, his eldest son was the perfect model of a Shin warrior. Fearless in battle. Skilled with every weapon. Able to drink the most hardheaded of his fellow tribesmen under the table.

And utterly devoid of any trace of imagination. If only Pedi had been his heir! Or if only Thertik had been a weakling he could have convinced the clan to set aside in favor of Pedi or a consort carefully chosen for her. But she hadn't been, and Thertik wasn't. And so at a time when the very existence of the Shin hung from a thread, he dared not trust his own heir's discretion sufficiently to tell him about the clans' one, slim chance for survival.

But he could have told Pedi. If she'd been his heir. Or if he had been willing to betray Thertik by trusting his daughter with information he dared not entrust to his son.

I should have told her anyway, he thought. *Not that it would have made any difference in the end.*

"So Shesul Pass might be under attack," he said aloud, letting no trace of his thoughts shadow his voice. "Or may be fallen. Any word who the enemy was? Aside from 'demons,' of course!" he added with a grunt of laughter.

"No, Gastan," Nygard said. "The messenger from Queicuf didn't know."

"Who could have penetrated to the Shesul?" the chieftain mused. "None of the raiders that I know of could scratch those walls." He thought about that statement for a moment. It was true enough, as far as it went, because he *didn't* know of any 'raiders' who might have taken the pass. And if he could think of anyone else who it might have been, this was not the time or the place to share that thought with Nygard.

"Enough," he said instead, with a gesture of resignation, "I have too many other problems to worry about to consider this one in depth."

He straightened and took a sniff of the air, heavy with the scent of brimstone, wafting down from the Fire Lands to the north. It was one of the Vales' many products. Brimstone for gunpowder, ores, hides, gems, and raw nuggets of gold—all of them flowed out of the Vales and through Mudh Hemh. And everyone wanted it. The other Shin, yes, but especially the Krath. Mudh Hemh was the most populous Vale, since the fall of Uthomof, and it was also the richest, acting as a conduit for trade with the entire eastern half of the Shin Range. Which was why it was the Vale above all Vales the Krath wished to seize.

They had tried at least a dozen times, from as many directions, to invade the Shin Range and wipe out the Shin once and for all. The destruction of Uthomof had been the result of one such war, and he could smell a change in the air, a danger as faint and sharp as the hint of sulfur on the wind, but just as real . . . and growing stronger. War was coming; he could feel it in his bones.

But until it did, he had heads to crack and disputes to settle. It generally came down to the same thing.

Roger swung up onto the *turom* cart and waved at the valley spread out before them.

"Tell me what I'm seeing, Pedi."

It was obvious that the Vale of Mudh Hemh was a pretty complicated place, geologically, as well as politically. The valley was at least partially an upland glacial cirque, with some evidence of blown volcanic caldera. The various geological catastrophes had created a sort of paisley shape, broken by regular hills and surrounded by rearing volcanic mountains. The Shin River cut across the valley almost due east and west, and its course was flanked on both sides by a mixture of fields and fortifications.

To the east, on the nearer side of the river, two massive fortresses faced each other across a large, torn sward. Each was easily as large as the main temple in Kirsti, and each sealed off the entire width of its respective vale from mountain to river. The fields in between them were large—it was at least ten kilometers from the nearer fortress to the further one—and they'd clearly been cultivated until fairly recently. At the moment, however, they were occupied by an army.

The nearer fortress had a new, raw look to it, as if it had been thrown up in haste, but it was holding its own against the force spread out before its walls. The army (it could only be the Krath regular forces) spread across the fields, filling the vale from side to side. A tent city to the rear was laid out in widely spaced blocks, while massive squares of infantry closer to the fortress awaited their orders to assault the Shin walls. They were moving forward against the nearer fortress in regular waves, but reinforcements for what Roger assumed were Shin defenders could be seen crossing a covered causeway behind the fighting and moving down side roads in the protected lee of the fortress.

Both fortresses had companion forts on the far side of the river, or perhaps they could more accurately have been considered overly large outer works, protecting the farther shore. There was no open ground on that side, just a broken mass of rubble, fallen basalt, and flood ravaged shore. But neither side seemed to consider it uncrossable.

To the west, behind the fighting but on the nearer side of the river, lay the ruins of what had once been a fair sized city. It might not have been much compared to Kirsti or K'Vaern's Cove, but it had been larger than Voitan. Now it was a tumbled ruin, clearly being mined for the stone of its buildings.

On the far side of the river there was a large embayment, or secondary valley, with a walled town built into the side of an ash cone. The ash cone, in turn, was the outrider of a large area of geothermal activity. A small stream, tinged bright blue with minerals, flowed down from the ash cones, geysers, and fumaroles.

A massive bridge, wide enough for four *turom* carts abreast, crossed from the town to the ruined city. Obviously, it was the conduit for the majority of supplies and reinforcements for the newer fortress.

"The two main forts are Nopet Nujam and Queicuf," Pedi told him. "The area between them is usually a trade city, Nesru, full of Krath and Shin traders. The far forts are Nopet Vusof and Muphjiv."

Roger nodded. He still didn't know why her father might have concealed any contact he had with the human at port from her. Which was fair enough, since she hadn't been able to think of any reason, either. Although it was probable that O'Casey was right about the reasons the Gastan felt impelled to keep it a secret, but why conceal it even from Pedi? She might be stubborn, impulsive, and personally reckless, but Roger and the rest of the *Basik*'s Own had seen more than enough of her to realize that she was also highly intelligent and possessed of an iron sense of honor. Her father should have trusted her with his secret.

Then again, Mother should have trusted me instead of finding trumped-up excuses to send me away from court, he thought. *Not that I'd ever given her the sort of proof that she could trust me that Pedi must have given her father.*

He shook the thought aside and returned his attention to Pedi.

A part of him wished that she'd conducted this briefing
sooner than this, but she'd been very little in evidence
since the sojourn at Shesul Pass. Part of that was because
of how much of her time had been devoted to nursing
the now clearly recovering Cord, but she'd been nearly
invisible even when she wasn't attending to the shaman's
needs. In fact, she'd spent much of her time sleeping
in the back of a *turom* cart, which Roger put down to
recovery from all the time she'd spent with the ailing
Cord. She'd certainly earned the downtime, at any rate,
and she appeared to be on the mend as well. Her energy
levels seemed to be up today, anyway, and at the
moment, happiness at being home was written in every
line of her body language.

"The city across the way is Mudh Hemh, and the
closer one, the ruined one, is Uthomof. It fell to the
Krath in the time of my great-grandfather, and they
passed on to besiege the walls of Mudh Hemh itself. But
in my grandfather's time, we drove them back to Queicuf
and built Nopet Nujam. They lost heavily in that battle,
and they've rarely sent great forces against us since."

She looked down at the attacking army and shook her
head in one of the human gestures she had absorbed.

"I fear we have, as you humans would say, 'ticked
them off,' " she added. "May I borrow your binoculars,
please?"

Roger handed them over. They were clumsier than his
helmet systems, but they were also more powerful, and
Pedi observed the nearer fortress through them for several
moments. Then she nodded.

"My father's emblem is on the walls, along with those
of virtually all the clan-chiefs. I wonder who defends
Mudh Hemh?"

"I imagine we should go find out," the prince said,
updating his map to reflect her information and dumping
it into the network. Pahner had decided that the humans
could make use of the low-powered, low probability of
intercept, inter-toot network. It was unlikely that the
standard communications and recon satellite that was
parked over the port would be able to pick it up.

"Father is not going to be happy about any of this," Pedi warned him.

"Not even about having you back?" Roger asked lightly. Then he smiled. "Well, in that case, we'll just have to see if we can't persuade him to be happier."

It took nearly three hours to arrange the meeting. The sun was on its way down by the time Roger, Pahner, and a cluster of Marines and Mardukans—including Pedi and an adamant, if barely ambulatory, Cord—were brought into the presence of the Gastan.

Pedi's father was short for Mardukan, not much taller than an average Mardukan female, but broad as a wall. The double swords which were the customary armament of a Shin warrior were slung across his back, and between those and the gaggle of trophy-covered chieftains at his back, he was quite the picture of a barbarian war chief.

Roger waved Pedi forward, and she stepped in front of her father, a leather bag in one hand, and bowed her head.

"Father, I have returned."

"So I was told." The Gastan spoke quietly, sparing the humans barely a glance. "*Benan,*" he added.

"*Benan,* Father," she agreed. "And allied to the *humans.*"

No one could have missed the emphasis she'd placed upon that final noun, or the ever so slight edge of challenge in her body language. But if the Gastan noticed either, he gave absolutely no sign of it.

"I suspect you have something for me in the bag?"

Pedi bowed again, slightly. Then she reached into the bag and removed the head of the Kirsti high priest. She held it out by its horns, and a whisper ran through the mass of chiefs like a wind in the pass. The Gastan contemplated it for a moment, then reached out and took it from her.

"Taken by you?"

"Yes, Father."

"I have an army at the gates, I'm holding the reason,

and I have a daughter who confesses to the crime. You know that we are—were—at peace with the Krath. The penalty for such an offense is to be given to the Fire Priests."

"And what of their offense against us, Father?" she snarled. "What of the taking of my party, of the attack upon Mudh Hemh?"

"A price we accept to prevent . . . that," he said, gesturing with one false-hand in the direction of the surflike sounds of combat. Roger suddenly realized that they were very near the top of the wall, probably in the upper levels of one of the bastions flanking the main gate.

"What do you think I should do, Daughter?" the Gastan asked after moment.

"I suppose . . ." She hesitated for a moment, then inhaled and raised her head proudly. "I suppose I should be turned over to the priests. If it will end the war."

"Over my dead body," Roger said conversationally, and smiled.

"Perhaps, human," the Gastan said. "And we have yet to deal with you. In fact, it is not my daughter towards whom the Fire Priests bend their malice, but one 'Baron Chang.' Would that be you, human?"

"It would," Roger replied. "And you won't be handing me over like a lamb to the slaughter, either."

"Baron," the Gastan mused. "That is a noble of your human lands, yes?"

"Yes," Roger agreed.

"You are responsible for the good of others, 'Baron'? You hold their lives in your hand and feel the weight of that?"

"Yes," Roger replied soberly.

"I have lost over four hundred Shin warriors since this war started, 'Baron.' Including Thertik, my son and heir." Roger heard Pedi inhale sharply, but the Gastan's attention never wavered from the human. "That is the price my people and I have already paid. And you think that I would quail at the thought of turning you over to the Krath if it ends this slaughter?"

"I don't know," Roger said. "I would ask you this one thing, though. If they came up to you and pointed to one of your warriors and said 'Give *him* to me. We will sacrifice him to the God and devour him, and that will end this war,' would you?"

The Gastan regarded him levelly for a long moment, then made a gesture of ambiguity.

"Would you?" he responded.

"No," Roger said. "That was the choice put to us, and I rejected it. Pointedly."

"Hmmm. But just who are you responsible for, 'Baron'? This group? These ragged mercenaries? Humans seem to have such in plenitude. Why not give one, if it saves others?"

"Because humans, and Mardukans, aren't pawns," Roger said, then sighed. "I can stand here debating this all day if you like, I suppose, but it's really not my forte. So are you going to try to kill us, or not?"

"So quick to the battle," the Gastan said with a gesture of humor. "Do you think you would win?"

"That depends on your definition of 'win,'" Roger said. "We'll make it out of this citadel alive, some of us, and we'll collect our group and leave. You'll get overrun by the Krath while you're trying—and failing—to kill us, and while that happens, we'll keep right on heading for the spaceport. It's nothing that we haven't done before. It will, however, tick off my *asi*'s *benan*. I have to consider that."

"Hmmm," the Gastan said again. "You're just going to walk to the spaceport, 'Baron'?"

"Of course," Roger said. "We're humans, after all. They'll accept us."

"I see that you've fallen into evil company," Pedi's father said. One of Roger's eyebrows arched at the apparent *non sequitur*, and the Gastan gestured at the IAS journalist who had been quietly recording the entire meeting. "We have warning from the Office of the Governor that this man is a wanted criminal, a dangerous traitor and thief who should be returned to the port for trial," he said.

"I'm *what*?" Mansul lowered the Zuiko and glared at the Gastan.

"I have other such messages, as well," the Shin continued as if the journalist had never spoken. "One of them mentions a group of humans, ragged mercenaries who may attempt to pass themselves off as Imperial Marines. They are to be considered very dangerous and should be killed on sight and without warning. There is a reward—a very attractive one, in fact—for their heads. What do you think of *that*, 'Baron'?"

"Gastan, you know that's a lie about me, at least!" Mansul protested. "So you must realize the rest of it is lies, as well!"

"Must I?" the Gastan asked easily. "Softly, Harvard Mansul. I want to hear the answer of this human noble. This 'Baron Chang.'"

Roger regarded the Gastan for a long slow moment, then nodded.

"My name," he said, clearly and distinctly, "is Prince Roger Ramius Sergei Alexander Chiang MacClintock. And I am going to wipe the floor with the governor. And with anyone else who gets in my way."

"Roger," Pahner growled, and his hand dropped to the butt of his bead pistol.

"Softly, protector," the Gastan said, raising his own hands in placation of both the Marine commander and of his own chieftains, who had shifted at the human's movement. "Softly, Armand Pahner. Softly, humans, Shin. Friends. Friends I think, oh yes."

He hefted the head of the High Priest. The climate of Marduk had not been kind to it, and he regarded the loathsome object coldly for a moment, then looked over his shoulder at one of his guardsmen.

"Bring me my sigil."

He waited until the trophy staff was brought forward, then strode to the outer door. The humans followed at his gesture, and as they stepped onto the walls, the bull-throated roar of the Shin and the howling of the Krath forces arrayed against them pressed against their faces like the overpressure waves of distant explosions.

A large horn, longer than Roger was tall, had been laid upon the walls, obviously in preparation for this moment, and the Gastan first blew into a side valve. A mournful hum cut through the sound of the battle noise, and faces turned towards him from below. He gave them a few moments, then opened a speaking tube built into it.

"*Krath!*" he bellowed, and the megaphone effect sent his voice echoing across the valley like thunder. "Here is the head of your High Priest! We have the humans who took it within our walls! And here is the answer of the Vale of Mudh Hemh to your demands!"

He raised the head high in both true-hands and spat upon it, his motions broad enough to the observable across the entire battlefield. Then he attached it to the highest point of the staff, raising it for all to see, and set the iron shod foot of the staff into a socket atop the battlements.

He left it there and strode back into the conference room without so much as another backward glance, his shoulders set, while the ear-splitting shouts of the Shin on the walls bayed jubilant defiance at the Krath. Roger and his companions followed, and the Gastan turned to them grimly.

"And so my daughter's allies are mine, as well, it seems," he said. "But, Prince Roger Ramius Sergei Alexander Chiang MacClintock and Captain Armand Pahner of the Bronze Battalion, if you think you are scurrying off to Marduk Port without helping us out of this mess my daughter has gotten us into, you are sorely mistaken."

"There is a human group, the Imperial Bureau of Investigation," the Gastan said as he passed over a flagon of wine. "You know it, yes?"

"Yes," Roger agreed, pouring a glass of the wine. The meeting had been narrowed down to the main staff and a few of the tribal leaders. The IAS photographer had managed to shoehorn himself into the group and was discreetly recording in the background, and Roger was—

inevitably—accompanied by Dogzard. But for once, the size of Roger's entourage wasn't completely out of hand.

As their commanders settled down to talk things over, both groups of subordinates were weighing each other and wondering who was bringing the most to the table.

There were certainly more of the Shin. At the first sign of the Krath attack, the Gastan had gathered the tribes, and every segment of the Shin Mountains was represented. There were at least three distinctly separate groups, distinguishable by their armor and weapons, as well as their features.

The most numerous group seemed to be the one associated closely with Pedi's father. They were of about normal height for Mardukans, armed with a motley of weapons—mostly swords and battle axes—and wearing armor that ranged from light boiled leather to heavy plate. Their horns, like Cord's, were high and rounded, with prominent ridges along the sides. Many of them had elaborate decorations on their horns, and helmets designed to display them to best advantage.

The second group appeared to be displaced Krath officers. They were equipped almost exactly like Flail commanders, armored in heavy plate with mail undershirts, and armed with long swords and square shields. They also had the haughty bearing that Roger had come to expect from the Krath.

As it turned out, they were clan leaders from "lowland" vales, where the influence—and money—of the Krath was strongest. They were heavily raided, so they tended to be unflinching in battle, but they were also ready to negotiate if battle could be avoided.

The last group seemed to be the poorest, and was armed with spears and not much else. Physically, they were shorter than the average Mardukan, and their horns were strange—very dark in color, and curving sharply back along the skull. Their senior clan leader wore light chain armor over boiled leather and bore a huge and obviously ancient battle ax. From a combination of Pedi's previous briefings and overheard comments, Roger knew that these were clans from the very back of the high

country; Shin that were seen only once in a generation—
so seldom that many of the *Shin* considered them to be
little more than a legend.

"There is an agent of the IBI in the port," the Gastan
continued. "He is presently out of communication with
his superiors, but he has been acting against the governor, waiting for one of his contacts to turn up. It was
he who contacted me and began sneaking humans he
believed to be at risk out of the port. He was asking
for some rather extraordinary help in your regard, so I
forced him to tell me why. He told me much—not all,
I'm sure, but much—and gave me this." The Gastan
handed over a data chip. "Your 'Empire' is in sore straits,
Prince. I fear I have very bad news."

"What?" Roger asked. He shrugged and took a sip of
wine. "As bad as it's been on this planet, how much
worse can it be at home?"

"The port is closed to you. The governor has sold his
soul to your enemies, the 'Saints.' They aren't always in
the system, but they often are, and no Imperial spaceship has come to here in nearly a year. As far as anyone
can tell, everyone here has been forgotten by the Empire.
Without a ship, even after taking the port, there is no
way off the planet, and if the Saints detect that their
bought governor has been overthrown, your lives will be
worth nothing."

"We've gotten that far in our own assessments," Roger
told him. "On the other hand, *your* analysis of just
exactly how piss-poor our chances are brings a question
rather forcefully to mind. If our odds are so bad, and
if the Saints are going to rain down so much grief when
they swat us, why should you risk helping us?"

"The governor has allied himself with the Krath. He
has not yet used your human weapons against us, but
if the Krath do not overwhelm us with this attack, it
will be only a matter of time until he does. He has
already done so in support of the Son of the Fire closer
to your port. Sooner or later he will do so here, as well,
and when he does, we will be unable to resist. The IBI
agent promised me that if we aided him, he would

ensure that we were supported when the planet was retaken. It is a slim hope to cling to, but better than none."

"Well, in that case, let me fatten it up for you," Roger said. "We don't begin to have time for me to explain to you exactly how many of our laws the governor and his cronies have broken here on Marduk. Let's just say that the conditions he's created, alone, would force the Empire to step in to repair the damage. But in addition to that, I personally guarantee that the gratitude of House MacClintock will follow, as well. If it's the last thing I do, the Krath and their depredations *will* be stopped."

"But for that to happen, one must assume that Her Majesty can be bothered to find Marduk on a map," the Gastan sighed. Roger stiffened slightly, and the Mardukan made a quick gesture of negation. "I question neither your laws, your word, nor your honor, Prince Roger, but at times even the most honorable of leaders must look first to problems closer to home, and there is worse news than I have already given you."

Roger sat very upright on his cushion, gazing at the Mardukan war leader narrowly, and the Gastan raised both false-hands in a complex gesture of sympathy.

"There was an attempt to overthrow your mother, the Empress," he said levelly. "Units of your Marine Raiders attacked the palace. They were repulsed, but not without heavy loss of life and much damage to the palace."

"Mother?" Roger was stone-faced, all expression locked down in almost instant reaction, but the cold of interstellar space swirled suddenly through his heart and belly, and for all his formidable self-control he knew his voice was flat with shock . . . and fear. He felt the sudden, frigid silence of the other humans behind him, but he never looked away from the Gastan. "My mother is alive?" he asked in that same, flat, level voice.

"She is," the Gastan said, "although she was injured in the fighting. But there is worse, Prince. Much worse. I grieve to tell you that your brother and sister are dead. So also are your brother's children. He and they were

killed in the attack upon the palace; your sister's ship
was destroyed in an ambush in space."

"Bloody *hell*," Julian whispered into the stunned stillness. "Does that mean what I think it means?"

"I think not," the Gastan said. "Not, if you mean what
I believe you do, at any rate. Because the word of the
Empress is that the plotter who was central to the
attempt is none other than her youngest son, Prince
Roger MacClintock. And for his crimes, he and all with
him have been outlawed for treason."

"The general outline is the same as the one the Gastan
gave us," Julian said as he transferred the data from his
pad to the others' systems. The Marine meeting had really
been narrowed down for this one; everyone but the core
command staff had been excluded. Decisions had to be
made based on the information on the chip, and the
nature of those decisions would determine the actions of
what remained of Bravo Company for the foreseeable
future.

"If anything," the intelligence sergeant continued, "the
details are worse.

"The coup appears to have been an attempt by the
Fleet to take control. That's the official analysis, anyway,
but the reasoning is really nebulous, and no one has
actively taken responsibility for any of the actions. All
of the Raiders were killed, either in the assault, or in
a response drop by Line Marines. As nearly as I can tell,
virtually the entire Empress' Own was wiped out holding the attackers until the line beasts could take them
from behind." He looked up from his pad, grim eyes
meeting those of the other Marines. "It looks like we're
effectively all that's left of the Regiment, Skipper," he
told Pahner.

"I'd already assumed as much," the captain said quietly. Silence hovered for a moment as he and his subordinates thought of all the men and women they would
never see again. The men and women they had assumed
were safe at home while they battled their own way
across the steaming hell of Marduk.

"Go on, Sergeant," Pahner said finally, his voice still quiet but unwavering.

"Yes, Sir." Julian glanced back at his notes, then resumed. "This IBI agent—Temu Jin—included a group of articles from various e-news outlets, as well as analysis articles from *Jane's*, *Torth*, and *AstroStrategy*, as well as full e-news loads from the top outlets. They're all indexed, and he highlighted some of them. I've only skimmed those.

"Apparently, the coup caught the IBI flat. A flier bomb was set loose in IBI headquarters—it's a pile of rubble, now. The head of the IBI was at Home Fleet headquarters at the time. It was also struck, but it managed to survive and launch a counterattack, including calling down a drop by the Marines of Home Fleet. Nefermaat, the IBI's second-in-command was off-planet at the time, and he's now wanted for questioning. There's a note on that from Jin. He thinks Nefermaat's disappearance is probably an indication that he's dead rather than linked to the coup in any way."

"Reason?" Pahner asked flatly.

"It turns out that Nefermaat was in Jin's line of control. Jin's orders to lie low came in about two days after the coup, along with a note that said basically that the real legal situation was unclear, and that all agents were to ignore orders from *any* higher authority, unless they could verify that they were valid."

"That could just be Nefermaat cutting out a section of the IBI," O'Casey mused. "Or this could be disinformation directed at Roger."

"What in the world makes you think that?" Roger asked. "How would anyone even know we're here—that *I'm* here—to be disinformed in the first place?"

"I don't know," O'Casey said. "But when you start getting into these labyrinthine games of empire, you have to be aware that some of them are very deep and very odd. And that some are just odd, but look deep and mysterious because the people running them are so confused."

"For now, until something else presents itself, we'll take

Jin's data as valid," Roger decided. "Just keep in mind that it could be wrong."

"Very well, Your Highness," Julian agreed. "We'll get to Jin's speculation in a moment, but for right now, I'll just say that I agree with it. And if he's right, that means Nefermaat is a scapegoat. A dead one. Or, at least, on the run and in hiding."

He referred back to his pad once more and nodded.

"Your mother is alive, Your Highness, but according to the reports, she was injured. It's only the last article in the queue which has her back in public at all . . . accompanied by Prince Jackson and the Earl of New Madrid."

"My *father*?" Roger stared at him in stark disbelief.

"Yes, Your Highness," Julian confirmed. "He's now established as a pro-consort, engaged to your mother."

"Holy shit," Roger said very, very quietly. "I can see why you think there's something fishy in Denmark."

"According to the news accounts, we were all reported dead, along with Roger, when the *DeGlopper* failed to arrive at Leviathan on schedule," Julian continued. "It looks like our 'demise' made quite an impression on the news services . . . until the coup attempt came along and pushed us to the back of the queue."

"I thought the story was that I'm behind everything," Roger said.

"Yes, Sir, but that's a recent development. A *very* recent one, in fact. It's only turned up in the last news from Sol, and it represents an entirely new twist on the original story.

"In the immediate aftermath of the coup, our disappearance was linked with Alexandra's death, as part of the general attack on the Imperial Family, but that didn't last. I can't tell from the data where the suggestion first came from, but eventually someone pointed out that we'd disappeared well *before* the rest of the Family was attacked. The new theory is that what really happened was that we dropped out of sight as the first step in a deep, complicated plan on Roger's part to kill off everyone between him and the Throne." He grinned tightly at his silent audience. "At least we're no longer dead; now they want all of us for treason."

"Standard protocol," Pahner said. "How much?"

"Lots," Julian told him with an even tighter grin. "There's a forty-million-credit reward on your head, Captain."

"I hope I'm around to collect it." Pahner grinned back, but then his expression sobered once more. "You're right, though. This doesn't add up. What are the fleets doing?"

"Prince Jackson ordered all fleets, with the exception of Home Fleet, away from the Sol System. In fact, he ordered most of them into his sector of control, but that's also along the Saint border, so it makes some sense. Sixth Fleet hasn't been able to move yet, though. According to reports, they're having trouble scaring up the logistic train they need to shift stations so radically. Especially with every other Fleet command moving at the same time and scrambling to meet its own logistical requirements. For now, they're still in the Quarnos Sector."

"Admiral *Helmut* can't find the lift capacity he needs?" Roger stared at Julian for a moment, then snorted harshly. "Oh, yeah. *Right!*" He shook his head. "And what are the Saints doing while all this is going on?"

"As far as I can tell, nothing. And that has me worried."

"Why would they sit this out?" Roger wondered aloud. "I'd expect them to pick off a few systems, at least. Like, well, Marduk."

"From what Julian's saying about Prince Jackson's redeployments, plenty of Fleet units are headed this way," Pahner pointed out. "Presumably, they know that, too. So maybe they're lying low, figuring that now is a bad time to attack."

"And maybe they were told that if they lie back now, they can have a concession later," Roger said harshly.

"And maybe that, too," Pahner admitted.

"Okay." Roger drew a deep breath. "We won't make any assumptions about their motivations for the moment, simply note that they haven't moved—yet—and hope it stays that way." He looked back at Julian. "That still leaves a few dozen other burning questions, though. Like who's in charge of the Fleet? What happened with Home Fleet? And what the hell happened with the IBI to let them blindside Mother this way?"

"General Gianetto has been given the position of High Commander for Fleet Forces," Julian said.

"Ah," Pahner said with his first real smile of the meeting. "Excellent!"

"Uh," O'Casey cut in. "Maybe not so excellent."

"Why is it excellent?" Roger asked. "And why maybe not? Armand first."

"I've known Guy Gianetto on and off for nearly half a century," Pahner said, frowning at O'Casey. "He's ambitious, but he's also solidly in favor of a strong Empire, a strong imperium. He would never betray the Empire." He started to say something more, then made himself visibly change his mind. "What does Eleanora have to say?" he asked instead, his tone half-challenging.

"That you're entirely correct," she replied. "General Gianetto would never betray the Empire. As he sees it."

"You're saying he might feel that some action is necessary to save the Empire from itself?" Roger asked. Pahner opened his mouth, but the prince raised a hand gently. "Let her speak."

"He and Prince Jackson have gotten closer and closer over the last decade," O'Casey said. "Both of them favor a strong defense, although Jackson's interest in such questions is . . . complex. For one thing, his family fortune is closely tied to defense industries. For another, he's the most prominent noble of the Sagittarius Sector, so he's constantly aware of the threat from the Saints. That gives him two reasons to favor a strong defense, which is why he's so consistently found on defense-related committees."

"What's wrong with wanting a strong defense?" Pahner asked. "It's a big, ugly galaxy out there, Councilor."

"Preaching to the choir here, Captain," O'Casey said seriously. "But there are inevitable questions. There's a *lot* of corruption in the procurement process—you know that even better than I do—and Jackson and his family have fingers in all the pies. He's also cultivated very friendly relationships with the majority of the senior officer corps. *Very* friendly relations. He not only hosts them to parties and junkets, but he's even gone so far as to countersign loans for some of them. Even covered some of them when they defaulted."

"That's against Fleet Regulations," Pahner said. "If it's true—I'm not saying it isn't, mind—but *if* it's true, where the hell has the IG been? And why didn't *I* get invited?"

"At a guess, you didn't get invited because you were too junior until you took this command," O'Casey said. "And, yes, where *was* the Inspector General?" She looked Pahner straight in the eye. "What was Gianetto for the last seven years?"

"Oh," the captain said in a flattened tone of voice, and his mouth twisted bitterly.

"Gianetto is considered a paragon of virtue," the chief of staff went on. "That's why he was made IG in the first place. And, okay, he's a much . . . smoother guy than Admiral Helmut. And Her Majesty initially trusted him. But over the last couple of years, she's been getting more and more indications that— Well, let's just say that I'm not surprised to see him in this. Saddened, but not surprised."

"So what do we think is happening?" Roger asked. "Julian."

"I think the coup succeeded, Your Highness," the sergeant said flatly. "I think Jackson is either directly or indirectly controlling the Empress. I think Gianetto and your father, at least, are in on it."

"Who's got Home Fleet?"

"That's still Admiral Greenberg, Sir," Julian said after a quick reference to his notes. "Commodore Chan, his chief of staff, was fingered as the local planner of the coup. He was 'killed resisting arrest'. . . ."

"And you can believe as much or as little of that as you like," Roger added bitterly.

"At any rate, Greenberg managed to retain command and acted as his own chief of staff for at least a few days, maybe a week or two. It's hard to tell. Eventually, though, Chan was replaced by Captain Kjerulf, the fleet Operations officer," Julian added.

"Greenberg is a snake," Pahner said. "Unless you have something countervailing to add, Ms. O'Casey?"

"I concur entirely," the chief of staff said. "Snake. I recall that Chan was well thought of, on the other hand."

"He might have fallen in with bad companions," Pahner said with a grimace of distaste. It was clear he was still unhappy and unsure about Gianetto. "But it's more likely he was a convenient scapegoat. But Kjerulf, now. That's an interesting datum."

"You know him?" Roger asked.

"Oh, I know just about everyone, Your Highness," Pahner told him with a bleak smile. "Maybe not all of them as well as I *thought* I did, I suppose. But Kjerulf is Gronningen with five years of college, then Staff School and Command College, plus thirty years of experience."

"Hmmm," Roger said. "So what does that tell us?"

"He was probably a ready pick," O'Casey replied. "They couldn't justify letting Greenberg operate permanently without proper staff backup, and he was the first person logically available, whether the real conspirators wanted to use him or not. If that's the case, it tells us the coup isn't fully spread through the Fleet. And that not everyone may be quite as convinced by the 'party line' as they'd like. Not if they need to worry so much about window dressing and allaying suspicion that they've put a man like Kjerulf into such a sensitive position."

"Everyone agree with that?" Roger asked, looking around his advisers' faces. "There was a successful coup. Its control may not be entirely solid yet, but it's heading that way. And Mother's under duress." Heads nodded around the table, and he grimaced. "Wonderful. Because if it was, there's just one problem."

"It can't last," O'Casey supplied for him. "Eventually she'll either break their control, or—if it's a direct drug or toot control—it will get found out."

"So what does that tell us?" Roger said again. "Assume they think I really am dead."

"I think it's obvious that that's exactly what they think, Your Highness," Kosutic put in. "*DeGlopper* was the first bead in the magazine, and they obviously think they got us. What I don't know was whether they intended to make you the fall guy all along, or if this was some sort of *ex post facto* brainstorm." The sergeant major snorted a bitter laugh. "You know, from a purely tactical viewpoint, you gotta love it. Look at it—they've got the perfect Overlord of Evil! They can keep right on chasing you for decades as a way to maintain the 'threat' that justifies whatever 'emergency measures' they decide to take, and they know they can never catch you, because you're *dead!*"

"The sergeant major is right," O'Casey agreed. "And if they think you're dead, and they're worried about the Empress slipping out of their control, they have to be angling for an Heir. Probably another one by New Madrid."

"And if they don't get an Heir and mother suffers a tragic accident anyway?" Roger asked. "Uncle Thorry, right?"

"The Duke of San Cristobal, yes," O'Casey agreed. "But—"

"But he's damned near senile, and never bothered to have children," Roger completed. "And after him?"

"At least a dozen claimants," O'Casey said. "All with more or less equal claims."

"Jackson's not in that group," Roger amused. "But he's close. And given his position of advantage . . ."

"It's probable that the Throne would fall to him," O'Casey said. "But whether or not he could hang onto it would be another matter. Given all of the other competing heirs, it's almost as likely that the Empire would simply dissolve into warring factions. The rival cliques are still out there, you know, Your Highness."

"Arrrgh." Roger closed his eyes and rubbed his face. "Julian, what's the dateline on the first news story that said Mother was something like 'alive and recovering'?"

The sergeant did a quick scan and pulled up an article.

"Nice word choice, Sir. 'Alive and should fully recover from her wounds.' Two months ago. *Three days* after the attack."

"Now those must've been some tense days," Roger said

with a lightness which fooled none of them. "And I thought being on Marduk was a *bad* thing. We have seven months."

"Aye," Pahner agreed. "The child must be born of her body."

"Which means she at least has to be alive when the can is cracked," Roger said.

"Well, technically, yes," O'Casey said. "But, it's possible—"

"Under other circumstances, maybe," Roger cut her off. "But not these. If she dies before they have an acknowledged Heir to the Throne, then—like you just said—odds are the entire Empire could fall apart on them." He shook his head. "No, Eleanora. For right now, she's their trump card. With the child born and well, proven to be of her genetics, while she's still alive to confer legitimacy on their regime, they're covered. *Then* Mother dies, Jackson becomes Regent, and from there he can do as he wishes. But she has until the child is born to be relatively safe. Which means we only have seven months until my mother's life probably isn't worth spit."

"Agreed," Pahner said. "At the same time, Your Highness, we have to get through our other problems before we can do anything about that one. We'll just have to cross that bridge when we come to it."

"Indeed, Captain. Indeed." Roger sighed sadly. "Well, if it were easy, they wouldn't pay us the big bucks."

CHAPTER TWENTY-THREE

Harvard Mansul was lurking just outside the conference chamber when the meeting broke up.

The journalist rarely asked the prince any questions, preferring to pump the junior Marines and the Mardukan mercenaries, who were more than willing to share their stories. And, of course, he had *not* been invited to attend the command staff meeting, itself. But he was getting hours of video of the prince, and it was beginning to bother O'Casey.

She stepped out of the meeting room just as Mansul started to dart off after Roger, and she stuck out an arm and grabbed him before he could get away. He looked at her in some surprise, but the chief of staff had developed remarkably sinewy arms during the trek across Marduk, and he was wise enough not to resist as she dragged him back into the now empty room.

"We need to talk," she said pleasantly.

"Yes, Ma'am," the photographer said. "I'm trying to stay out of the way."

"And you're succeeding," she noted. "And I know that this is a heck of a story. But it's not necessarily one the IAS can publish when we get back."

Mansul sighed and nodded.

"I understand that. But do you know what the prince

365

intends to do? Is he going to contact the Empress when we return? How are we *going* to return?"

"That's . . . not settled yet," O'Casey temporized. "But . . . You do understand why we've got to start excluding you from some meetings?"

"I understand," Mansul repeated. "But this isn't just a good story, you realize. This is history unfolding. And *what* history! I mean, this is the best story in a thousand years! He could play his own leading man!"

"What do you mean?" the chief of staff asked.

"Come with me," Mansul said, and took her arm. "I want to show you something."

He led her out of the door and towed her down the corridor, asking the occasional guard for directions to the prince.

They finally found him out on the battlements, conferring with the local Shin leadership. The skies, as always, were gray, but the brilliant pewter cloud glare of Marduk's powerful sun was near zenith and the day was bright—hot, and almost dry at this altitude. The prevailing wind in this area came down from the glaciers up-valley, and on some days it built up to a near-gale. Today it was running about thirty kilometers per hour, and the prince's hair had come unbound. It streamed sideways in the wind as he and the native leaders conferred, gesturing at the distant battle lines.

"There," Mansul said.

"What?"

"That's what I brought you to see," he replied. "*Nobody* sees it. I want you to look at the prince and tell me what you *see*. Take your time."

"I'm very busy, Mr. Mansul," the chief of staff said. "I don't have time for games. It's Prince Roger."

"This isn't a game, Ms. O'Casey," he said seriously. "Now look."

O'Casey looked at Roger. He was talking with the Gastan and one of the other Shin warlords, accompanied by Pahner and Kosutic, the still barely mobile Cord, a group of Vashin and Diaspran bodyguards, and Dogzard.

"I see Roger and company," she snapped. "What about it?"

"Describe him," Mansul said quietly. "As if *you* were writing the article."

"A tall man . . ." she began, and then, suddenly, stopped.

A tall man, darkly tanned by alien suns, a sword on his back and a pistol at his side, his unbound blond hair streaming in the wind. He was surrounded by a group of powerful, intelligent, capable followers who were not just willing to follow him anywhere, but already had— and would again, at a moment's notice, even knowing the impossible tasks they faced. His face was young, but with almost ancient green eyes. The eyes of a man who had already strode through a dozen hells. . . .

"Oh . . . my . . . God," she muttered.

"Now you understand." The journalist's whisper was an odd mix of delight and something very like awe. "This isn't just the story of a lifetime. This is the story of a *century*—possibly a millennium. You couldn't pry me off with a grav-jack."

"That's . . ." She shook her head, trying to clear the vision. "It's just *Roger*."

"No. It's not," the journalist said. "And, trust me, you aren't the Ms. Eleanora O'Casey I had a passing view of at the palace. You've *survived*, Ms. O'Casey. Sure, you were protected, but are you ready to tell me you're the same person you were before this tremendous trek?"

"No, I'm not." She sighed at last, and took one more look before she turned away. "But it's still silly. I don't care what he's become, he's still *Roger*."

"This is silly," Roger muttered. "I take it back. There *is* such a thing as too much overkill."

They were observing the Krath siege lines from the top of the western wall, trying to determine if there was anything Roger's force could add to the defense. Pahner had dragged all the senior commanders, along with the main "battle staff," up to the battlements with them for a good hard look. And it didn't look good.

"Yes," the Gastan said with a gesture of amusement. "It is a bit overwhelming, isn't it?"

It looked very much as if Kirsti had moved its entire
army in toto up to the plain. From the mountains, standing beside Pedi's *turom* cart, that army had looked like
a large ant mound; from the walls, it looked like . . . an
immense ant mound.

The tent city at the rear measured nearly four kilometers on a side, broken into three distinct camps with
regular roads and well laid out garbage and personal
waste management. The latter seemed to be primarily
trucked out, rather than simply dumped into the river,
which struck the humans as the best field hygiene they'd
come across yet. On the other hand, it was apparent that
the majority of the forces weren't spending much time
under canvas.

A regular siege had been laid on in front of the Shin
citadel. Dozens of separate zig-zagging communications
trenches led forward from the area of the Krath encampment to a much larger trench parallel to the walls. The
parallel trench was covered by stout wooden palisades,
and bombards fired occasionally from emplacements along
the parallel. But the bombards in use were on the small
side; they were still far enough from the fortress that
they were barely in range; and there weren't very many
of them. Coupled with their low rate of fire, their impact
on the defenses was marginal . . . so far.

Despite the indications that the Krath were here for
the long haul, they seemed quite prepared to settle things
more quickly if the opportunity offered. And they
obviously considered that they had the manpower to
explore . . . more direct and straightforward alternatives to
battering a way through stonework with artillery. A frontal assault—or, more precisely, *another* frontal assault—
had obviously been tried earlier in the day, and the dead
hadn't been cleared away from the base of the walls
yet.

The forces arrayed against the Shin were enormous.
Between the rear of the siege works and the tent city,
there were blocks and blocks and blocks of infantry. So
many that all most of them could do was sit on the
ground, awaiting their next orders. There literally wasn't

room to use more than a fraction of them against the fortress at any given time.

"There are at least two hundred thousand troops *in view*," Julian said, consulting his toot. "It looks like that could be another sixty thousand in Quericuf and the wing forts, and an unknown number in the tents."

"Worse than the Boman," Rastar muttered. "These bastards are *organized*."

"The majority of them return to the tents at night," the Gastan said. "They're as much for warmth as for cover, and they have to clean their pretty armor, don't they?"

"I suspect that they wait until they return to do their business, as well," Honal commented. "Otherwise, they'd be up to their knees in shit by now."

"If they just charged all at once, they'd overwhelm you," Pahner said, ignoring the side conversations.

"Possibly," the Gastan replied with a gesture of resignation. "And possibly not. Moving them all forward at once is . . . a bit of a challenge. It takes a lot of tricky coordination. And they'd have to stack themselves on top of each other to get to the top of the wall. We're the Krath's prime source for any number of raw materials, including wood, so they're having a bit of trouble finding sufficient materials for enough ladders. Then, even if they took the fortress, they'd have to manage the groups that were in it. They've taken *sections* of the wall before, but those Krath who seize them just mill around on top, wondering what do next until we counterattack and kill them or drive them off. They're perfectly willing to keep trying assaults on the off-chance that one may work—they've certainly got the manpower for it!—but they've also fallen back on more complicated means."

He waved at the palisaded parallel . . . and at the trenches zig-zagging forward from it. It was obvious that the smaller trenches had perhaps another fifty to seventy-five meters to go to reach the point at which the next parallel would be cut, that much closer to the walls.

"They've been moving the siege lines forward steadily," the Gastan said. "They won't have to get a lot closer to bring their bombards into effective range. When they do, they can pound us hard enough to cause a breach. Then they'll pour their troops through, and it will all be over."

"Not much I can add," Fain said. He'd been doing a few calculations on the back of the wall, and now he dropped his piece of charcoal and dusted his true-hands, body language distinctly disgruntled as he contemplated the figures he'd scrawled across the stone. "Each of my fellows would have to kill fourteen hundred of them. I can't guarantee anything over a thousand, unless we get more ammunition."

Pahner had been rubbing his chin in thought. Now he pulled out a piece of *bisti* root and cut off a sliver.

"I'll tell you the truth," he told Pedi's father. "We need to take the spaceport, and from what you've said, it's not all that long a trek from here. If we took it, we could come back with all the firepower we need to clear out the Krath."

"It's a point," Roger agreed. "A couple of cluster bombs would be a treat on these guys."

"That would be . . . difficult," the Gastan said coldly. "I have a hard enough time convincing my people that it's worth fighting the Krath at all, especially given the reason that they sit on our doorstep. If you were to go, for whatever reason, I doubt I could continue to ensure your safety. Or that of my other human guests."

Pahner sighed, nodded, and slipped the slice of root into his mouth. He chewed thoughtfully for a few seconds, then shrugged.

"I suspected it would be something like that. Okay, let's try a few 'old-fashioned' remedies first. If those don't work, we'll think about alternatives."

"I guess that's about our only option," Roger agreed. "On the other hand, sooner or later, we're going to have to move on the port, anyway. I truly hope taking it won't be as tough as it could turn out to be when we do get around to it, and I think we need to think about that simultaneously. Armand, you and I need to concentrate on ways to deal with the Krath. But while we get fully up to speed on the local situation and the balance of forces, Julian, you need to start massaging the data Jin gave us. We need a way into the port."

"Yes, Your Highness," the NCO said doubtfully. "If there are any of us left to take it."

Roger tried not to let his amusement show as he watched Pedi and the still limping, very slowly moving Cord jockey for precedence through the door. The Marines had already swept the other side, and even including Despreaux and Pedi, Roger was probably the most dangerous person present. But the precedence of security was everything.

"I'm sure we're all friends here, Pedi," he said, placing a hand on her back as she passed him. Then he drew his hand back and looked at it oddly. Her back had felt . . . lumpy. If she'd been a human, and if it had been her front, instead of her back, he would have thought he'd accidentally put his hand on a breast. But the feel had been firmer, like a large blister. Or a tumor.

Whatever it had been, Pedi shied away from the touch. Then she seemed to recover her customary poise.

"And we were sure the High Priest would never have your party attacked in his presence, Your Highness," she said. "My duty to my *benan* is clear. It is *my* responsibility to ensure the room is safe. Not the Marines'."

"And it is mine to ensure that it is safe for you, Roger." Cord's voice still wheezed alarmingly, and Roger shook his head.

"You need rest, old friend," he said. "You can't guard me if you're as weak as a day-old *basik*."

"Nonetheless, it is my duty," Cord said, trying unsuccessfully to conceal how heavily he was forced to lean upon his spear for support.

Roger paused in the doorway and turned to his *asi*. He looked up into the face that now seemed familiar, rather than alien.

"Cord, I need you for your advice more than your guarding. And I need you *well*. Respect my opinion in this; you need to rest still. Get your strength back. I hate to mention it, but you're not as young as you used to be, and you need more time to recover. That was a bad wound, so rest. Go to Mudh Hemh. Have a mud bath. Get some sleep. I have the Marines to cover me, and I'll come to Mudh Hemh myself, as soon as the last of these negotiations are complete."

Cord regarded him impassively for a long moment, but then made a gesture of resignation.

"It is as you say. I cannot perform my duties as I should in this condition. I'll go."

"Good!" Roger clapped him on the arm. "Recover. Build up your strength. You'll need it soon enough."

"Good morning. My name is Sergeant Adib Julian, and I will be giving the first briefing on suggested tactics for relieving the Krath problem," Julian said, looking around the room. The hall was near the center of the Shin citadel and was large enough to accommodate all of the prince's commanders and the senior Shin warlords.

The latter were an extremely mixed bag. Some of them were from groups that were in long-term close contact with the Krath, and those were fairly "civilized." They'd turned up wearing well polished armor and seemed to be following the briefing with interest. They seemed especially fascinated by the hologram of the force structure the NCO had thrown up. However, many of the other chieftains were obviously from "the back of beyond." The latter were notable for their lighter and less well maintained armor, and the wide separation the Gastan had instituted between the groups—and between some of the clans *within* each group, for that matter—suggested that some of them would rather beat on each other than on the Krath.

"A short analysis of relative combat strengths of the Krath and the Shin/Marine alliance indicates that direct assault is unlikely to be effective," Julian continued, bringing up a representative animation of a Shin/human assault. "The inability of the human forces to use their plasma weapons, coupled with a lack of powered armor, means that any direct assault, even with human,

Diaspran, and Vashin support, is liable to be swallowed without a burp."

As he finished speaking, the short, holographic animation ended with the "good guys" dead on the field and the Krath flag flying over Nopet Nujam.

"Alternatives to this may be viable, however," he continued, and brought up a new animation. "The Krath have had only very limited experience with a *civan* charge, and have no equivalent at all of the pike wall."

In the animation, a unit of *civan* quickly ran down one flank of the Krath forces, causing the rest to redeploy. As they did, the animation drew back, showing a hazily outlined "blue" unit of pikemen and assegai troops, supported by conventional Shin forces, on the slopes above the Krath tent city.

"If this attack is simultaneous with an attack on the tent city by a stealthed armor unit, sufficient chaos may be created to permit a major sortie, supported by Diaspran and Marine infantry, to retake the siege lines and destroy the palisades and the majority of their bombards before they ever get them into effective action."

The "blue" troops on the slopes swept downward, butchering the surprised Krath in their path, and the animation ended with the wooden palisades of the siege lines, the tent city, and the bombard emplacements all sending up pillars of black smoke as they blazed merrily away.

"And then what?" one of the more barbaric chieftains asked, looking up from the design he'd been carving into a tabletop with a dagger. "You think they'll turn and run after a single defeat? We need to take Thirlot! We'll cut them off from food and retreat as we always have, and it's good loot, besides!"

"Thirlot is well defended," one of the lowland chieftains said, buffing his polished breastplate. "They left a good portion of their force there on the way up, and another is in Queicuf. If your scruffy band thinks it can take Thirlot, more power to it."

"Scruffy?! I'll give you *scruffy*!"

"Enough!" the Gastan barked, and his guards banged

the floor with their ceremonial spears. "Shem Cothal, Shem Sul. Taking Thirlot was considered and rejected. Sergeant Julian?"

"We might be able to take Thirlot," Julian said, looking pointedly at the chieftain in the breastplate. His toot, taking its cue from the Gastan, flashed the name Shem Sul across his vision. "Certainly we could enter the city. With our aid, you could probably destroy the forces that the Gastan's spies indicate are in the city. Our non-plasma heavy weapons could smash the doors, our armor could open up any hole necessary to get you inside the walls, and a force of Shin and Marines could enter the city and roam almost at will."

He held the eye of the more polished barbarian until the latter made a gesture of agreement.

"What we could not do is *hold* it," he said then, turning to the other chieftain, Shem Cothal. "And if we can't hold it, we can't cut their supply lines. The Krath would turn their army to the rear and assault Thirlot by swarming the walls. Those walls are barely ten meters high; they could stand on each other's shoulders and come right over them. And they can march back down the road on the rations they have right here in camp—it's barely two days to Thirlot. When they got there, our force in the city would be overrun. It would certainly be forced out with severe casualties, possibly cut off and destroyed. Other plans involving putting a blocking force on the Queicuf-Thirlot road have also been rejected for the same reason. We simply don't have sufficient forces to hold anything other than Nopet Nujam against the Krath army."

"All of that is no doubt true," Shem Sul said. "But I have to agree with my colleague." He gestured at the hologram. "You're discussing a spoiling attack, nothing more."

"It's the best we can do at this time," Julian said. "And it's a spoiling attack we can replicate almost at will."

"They're not so stupid," the other chieftain said. "They'll change their dispositions. 'Tis but a tithe of them

that attack at anytime. All they have to do is pull some
of their other troops back, and your raiders are going
to be useless."

"Then we'll change tactics," Roger said. "The point is
to wear them down."

"As opposed to us being frittered away," Sul replied.
"You'll take casualties on each raid, and they will *win*
a battle of attrition. I have to agree with Shem Cothal;
we have to cut their supply lines. Cut those, and their
army withers on the vine. Nothing else, short of a human
superweapon, will work."

"We can't use our superweapons until we've taken the
port," Pahner said. "And you're correct, this is an attrition
battle, with the addition of trying to break their will. At
some point, we might take Thirlot, if only to burn it to
the ground, but only if it helps with our objective, which
isn't to *beat* them so much as to convince them to go
away. We don't have the numbers to kill them all—our
arms would fall off before we were done—so we're
looking at ways to convince them victory would simply
be too expensive. We'll look at other options, as well,
but for the time being, we need to discuss the briefed
plan."

Roger had been listening carefully, but now he sat up
straight, picked up his pad, and started rotating the
hologram, zooming in and out on the region around
Queicuf. He zoomed in on the road just to the east of
the fortress, where the valley narrowed down to the gorge
of the Shin River, pinching the road bed between the
valley walls and the deep, broad river.

"Julian, is this map to scale?"

"No, Your Highness. The vertical exaggeration is at one
to three."

"Hmmm . . . fascinating . . ."

"What, Your Highness?" Pahner asked. He eyed the
prince thoughtfully, wondering what the youngster was
up to now. Whether it was *practical* or not, it should
at least be interesting as hell, the Marine thought,
because at some levels, Roger was a much more devi-
ous tactician than he himself was.

"There might just be an exploitable weakness here," the prince said, rotating the image again so that he was looking at the battlefield from ground level. "Captain Pahner, Lords of the Shin, we probably should try the briefed plan, if for no other reason than to put them a bit more on the defensive. But there might just be another way. Oh, my yes. Quite a weakness."

Cord turned back down the corridor, still leaning heavily on his spear for support, as the door closed on the prince. Pedi started to take his arm, then snatched her hand back as he jerked away.

"I am not so weak that I need your support, *benan,*" he said harshly.

"I ask pardon, *benai,*" she said. "I had not realized that contact with your *benan* was so beneath you."

"Not beneath me," Cord sighed. "Perhaps I should not snap, but . . ."

"But?" Pedi opened the door and checked the hallway beyond. The Gastan had placed guards along the corridor, and they nodded to her as she passed. She had known some of them for years, grown up with them. But she could feel the distance that now separated them, a gulf that was hard to define, yet as real as death itself. All that she knew was that either she had grown away from Mudh Hemh, or it was somehow rejecting her.

"But . . ." Cord began, then inhaled deeply, and not just from the pain of moving with his partially healed wound. "I know that I'm your *benai,* not your father," he growled. "But in the *asi* bond, the master has certain responsibilities. Although in my culture, females cannot become *asi,* if they had . . . problems, it would be the . . . responsibility of the master to deal with them."

"Problems?" Pedi asked archly as they came to their shared chamber. "What problems?" she asked as she opened the door and swept the room.

"Don't play with me, Pedi Karuse," Cord said firmly as he lowered himself onto the pile of cushions within. The fact that he barely managed to stifle a groan as he settled into them said a great deal about how far from recovered he truly was. "I'm in too much pain to play games. I can see your condition clearly, as can anyone with eyes. It is only the humans who are confused. I would have expected your father to be fuming by now."

"It is not my father's place to 'fume,'" she said sharply. "As *benan*, I am beyond the strictures of my family."

"Then it *is* my responsibility to investigate the situation," Cord said. "I am furious about this, you know. No true male would do this and then leave you to bear the burden."

Pedi opened her mouth, then shut it.

"It is my burden to bear," she said, after a moment. "It was my choice."

"It takes two to make such a choice," Cord pointed out, grimacing as he tried to find a comfortable position. "There is a male, somewhere, who has much explaining to do. A male who would impregnate you and then refuse to acknowledge that fact—such a male is without honor."

"It's not his fault," Pedi said. "I cannot—I *will* not— say more. But this is my responsibility to bear."

Cord sighed in exasperation, but made a gesture of resignation.

"As you will. I cannot imagine you lying with a male without honor. But let it be your secret, your 'cross,' as the humans would say. I shall raise any of the brood as if they were my own."

"I wouldn't hold you to that," Pedi said, getting the balm the human physician had made. "It is . . . It isn't your fault."

"I, however, am a male of honor," Cord said, then sighed in relief as she rubbed the salve into the inflamed wound. "I thank you for that," he told her, then shook himself and looked at her sternly. "But to return to what truly matters, I will not let your children be raised as bastards, Pedi. I will not. It will be as if they were mine."

"I understand, *benai,* but I can handle it," she said woodenly. "And the situation with the father is . . .

complex. I wish that you would let me manage it in my own way."

"As you wish," he said with another sigh. "As you wish."

"I wish this didn't look so easy," Julian muttered.

"What?" O'Casey asked. "Something about this god-forsaken mess strikes you as 'easy'?"

She sat up straight on the camp stool, rubbing her back, and grinned at the sergeant. It was a very crooked grin, because both of them had been perusing their separate "slices" of the intelligence data from the IBI agent for the last couple of hours. While Julian concentrated on Marduk itself, she had been wading through the data about the coup, and she was coming to the conclusion that Julian was right about that information's reliability. And about the implications of that reliability.

There was too much data on the disk, and it was too consistent, and from too many known sources, to have been entirely generated locally. But if it had been generated by a central authority, if either the Empire or the Saints knew that Roger was alive on Marduk, the planet would have been crawling with searchers. Since it wasn't, the data was probably genuine, and the IBI agent was probably on the level. In which case, whatever happened here on Marduk, "just going home" was no longer an option.

"If you have good news, I could use some," she went on, leaning back from her own pad.

"That's just it—I don't know if it *is* good news," Julian said. "The problem is that this governor is either a complete and total idiot . . . or else subtly brilliant. And I've been working on the premise of subtly brilliant, looking for the dastardly plan."

"I haven't even looked," O'Casey admitted. "Who is the governor?"

"Ymyr Brown, Earl of Mountmarch," Julian said, then looked up sharply as O'Casey let out a rippling peal of laughter before she slapped her hand over her mouth to restrain the follow-on giggles.

"You know him?" Julian asked. She nodded, both hands over her mouth, and the sergeant's eyes glinted wickedly. "Okay, I can see from your reaction that you *do* know him, and that he's probably not all that great. But you have to give him a break—growing up with a name like 'Ymyr' couldn't have been all that much fun."

"You're being much too kind to him," O'Casey assured him. Another giggle slipped out, and she shook her head. "And take my word for it, whatever you're looking at is *not* a deeply laid plan. However stupid it seems."

"I almost wish it was," the sergeant said. "I just *hate* relying on the bad guys' stupidity. Even idiots have a bad habit of slipping up and doing something reasonably intelligent every so often, if only so Murphy can screw with your mind. Besides, *nobody* could really be this dumb."

"What did he do?" O'Casey asked, looking over his shoulder at an indecipherable schematic. After a moment, it resolved itself into a map of the port.

"Well, he set up an intelligence network in all the satraps of Krath," Julian said. He touched a control and brought up a picture of the continent, with data scrolling along the sides and political boundaries mapped in. "That much isn't dumb. But he has all these reports coming in, and he didn't want the spies just walking through his front gates. So he set up *cleared lanes* in the *defenses*!"

O'Casey grinned again, this time at his expression. Disbelief mingled with professional outrage on the sergeant's face, until he ended up looking just plain disgusted.

"That's Mountmarch all over," she said. "He's a brilliant media manipulator, and thinks his brilliance at that extends to everything. There's nothing in the world for which he doesn't have a better, and much more brilliant, plan. Of course, the reality is that the vast majority of them backfire—often badly."

"Who is he?" Julian asked. "Other than the governor of the colony, that is?"

"He used to be a power at court," O'Casey said as

she leaned back. She hadn't bothered to store her files on the Earl of Mountmarch in her toot, so they'd been lost along with most of her reference works and papers when *DeGlopper* was destroyed. Now she delved deep into plain old, biochemical memory for as much as she could recall about the earl and frowned thoughtfully.

"That was back in Roger's grandfather's later days," she went on. "There's not much question that he really was a brilliant example of a 'spin merchant,' and the old Emperor was very fixated on public opinion. Even though he wasn't elected, he felt that the will of the people should be observed. Which is all well and good, but ruling based on opinion polls, especially ones pushed by narrow agendas, is never a great idea. It's one of the reasons that the Empress is still having so many problems. Or was, before the coup, at any rate."

Their eyes met grimly for a moment. Then she gave herself a shake and resumed once more.

"The approach of the Imperial bureaucracy—that it's either completely untouchable, or that its function is solely to act in accordance with the will of opinion polls (which actually means at the will of skilled manipulators like Mountmarch who *shape* those polls)—is a tremendous drag on getting anything fixed," she said. "It's that holdover of bureaucratic and senior policy officer inertia, coupled with the iron triangle of senatorial interests, the interests of the bureaucracies, and the special interest groups and polls that combine to drive the senatorial agenda, that have made it nearly impossible for the Empress to get any real change enacted or to replace the worst of the bureaucrats with more proactive people.

"But I digress," she said, pausing to inhale, then cocked her head as Julian broke out in laughter. "What?"

"Well, to tell you the truth, I don't think I've heard you say that much about the situation back home this entire trip."

O'Casey sighed and shook her head.

"I'm *familiar* with preindustrial societies, and plots and

plotters seem to be the same on Earth as on Marduk. But it's modern Imperial politics that are my real forte."

"I can tell," Julian said with another chuckle. "But you were saying about Mountmarch?"

"Mountmarch," she repeated. "Well, he excelled at taking the interests that were brought to him—whatever they were, but they tended to be on the 'Saints' end of the political spectrum—and turning molehills into mountains. He knew just about everyone in the media, and no matter who paid him, or for what, before you could say 'it's for the children,' whatever was going to end the universe this time would be the number one headline on all the e-casts and mags. And suddenly, with remarkable speed, there'd be committees, and blue ribbon panels, and legislation, and opinion polls, and nongovernmental charity organizations—all of them with lists of contacts and almost identical talking points, sprouting up like mushrooms. It really was quite an industry.

"And the leaks! He had access to everyone in the upper echelons of His Majesty's Government, either because they were afraid of him, or else because they wanted him to do the same thing for them. And whenever there was a tidbit of information that worked for the interest he was pushing at the moment, it would be major news the day he got it. Then along came Alexandra.

"Roger's mother had been watching him basically push her father around for years, and she didn't care for it one bit. In general, Alexandra tends towards the socialistic and environmentalist side of the political spectrum herself, but she's also aware of the dangers to society of going too far. So when the newest item Mountmarch was pushing was over the Lorthan Cluster, she pushed back—hard."

"Lorthan?" Julian asked. "You mean the Lorthan Incident?"

"The very same," she said. "Mountmarch was given the information that a task force had been sent out to lie doggo and try to catch the Saints red-handed raiding the Lorthan colonies. They'd been insisting that it was nothing but pirates, and offering 'military assistance in our need,' but all the indications were that it was a Saint force or forces that were trying to drive humans, and their 'contamination,' off of the Lorthan habitables."

"So was it Saints, or pirates?"

"Well, officially, no one knows," O'Casey said. "The task force was the ambushee rather than the ambusher, and officially, there was no information one way or the other on whether it was Saints or pirates. Of course, a pirate fleet that could take on an Imperial task force is pretty unlikely. And then there were the two *Muir*-class cruisers that were captured nearly intact."

"I hadn't heard that," Julian said.

"And you still haven't. But when we get back and I get situated, I'll take you out to Charon Base and you can see them. The point is that the leak cost nearly four-teen *hundred* Fleet lives, and Alexandra was *not* pleased."

"So she pinned it on Mountmarch?"

"He was the most common facilitator of such things. Whether he did it, or someone else, she really didn't care. She used administrative actions to remove most of his titles, but as a sop she must have posted him to Marduk. The most out of the way, barren, forsaken, and useless post in the Empire. And he's under Imperial law, so if he so much as sneezed, he'd be dealing with IO and the IBI, instead of local officers and the IC Authority. He can manipulate those; he still has people who, for some godforsaken reason, think he has a clue. But the Inspectorate and the IBI are another thing entirely."

"Remind me not to get on her bad side," Julian said. "Of course, I think that with a little training, Roger's going to be nearly as nasty. Maybe nastier. The tough part will be keeping him from killing anyone who pisses him off. But for right now, at least I can give him some good news—the local commander is an idiot, if a good manipulator of the media, and it looks like the port is going to be a cakewalk."

"Let's not get cocky," she said warningly.

"Oh, we won't," Julian said. "Two of the plasma can-non are listed as off line, but Item Number One will be to take them out anyway, just to be on the safe side. We'll send the armor in first to remove the wire, in case it's really there, then the mines. There's other bits. We'll get it right."

"And then grab a ship and go home," she said.

"To what?" Julian asked. "That's not going to be so easy."

"No," she admitted. "Everything in this download is hanging together, so I think Temu Jin is on the up and up. All the usual suspects in something like the 'attempted coup' are saying all the usual things. In fact, they're being so 'normal' that I've got the very definite feeling of either excellent information management, or pressure from behind the scenes. Although the *Imperial Telegraph* has called for a 'full and independent medical review of Her Majesty' with 'all due deference to the Throne.' On the other hand, they're being castigated by most of the major news outlets for 'pressuring her in her grief.' "

"As if that matters when the safety of the Empire is on the line?" Julian asked.

"Well, it does to some, or at least the polls will say so," O'Casey said with a thin smile. "Only the Commons can call for a vote of confidence on Her Majesty, and that's what it would take to force an independent medical exam, if our suspicions are correct. And we're not the only ones voicing them; there's a broad rumor that the Empress is being mind-controlled by Roger's father, with Jackson barely even mentioned. The problem is, that its being spun into a 'conspiracy theory' tying back to the death of the Emperor John and everything up to an invasion by implacable alien bugs from the Andromeda Galaxy."

"Thank goodness for the Andromeda Galaxy!" Julian laughed. "Without it, there'd be no science-fiction at all!"

"Indeed," she smiled. "Well, one wag does have it as the Andromeda *System*, but he's probably talking about Rigel."

"Probably," Julian agreed. "Another favorite."

"But if—when it turns out that she *is* being controlled, we're going to have an uphill climb to convince people that she was. In this case, something which happens to be the absolute truth is being successfully tied to every silly, paranoid fantasy floating around loose. Which means that it's undoubtably in the process of being dismissed by every 'serious-minded' person in the Empire."

She shook her head.

"I wish I could be convinced that it was just happening to work out this way, but I don't think it is. *I* think what we're looking at is a carefully organized defense in depth. First, the people really behind the coup are counting on 'sensible people' to reject such crazy rumors out of hand. That will undercut any effort to force an independent exam of the Empress which might prove that she's being controlled, which is bad enough. But even worse, if Roger turns back up and claims he's been framed and that his mother's being mind-controlled, it's going to be really, really hard to convince anyone that he's telling the truth.

"But at the same time, I think Jackson is deliberately setting New Madrid up as the fall guy—the 'evil manipulator' the 'good Regent' can discover and pin all the blame on if the wheels start to come off. He can hammer New Madrid under any time he has to, and look at the other advantage it gives him. New Madrid is Roger's *father*, whether Roger can stand him or not. So who would be a more natural 'evil manipulator' than the father of that arch traitor, Roger MacClintock? Obviously, father and son thought the whole thing up together!"

She sighed, and shook her head again.

"I'm sure he believes Roger really is dead, so the whole thing is designed to use New Madrid as a scapegoat and a diversion if he needs one. I suppose I could even argue that the fact that he thinks he may need a diversion badly enough to concoct this new story blaming it all on Roger is a sign that his control is a lot shakier than it looks from here. But even though he's setting it up for an entirely different set of reasons, it's only going to make things look even worse for Roger if Jackson 'suddenly discovers' that New Madrid has been controlling the Empress all along. And it's going to be a lot tougher for us to deal with *that* than it's going to be to get through Mountmarch's defenses here on Marduk."

"Oh, I'm sure you'll figure something out," Julian said. "And the good news is that if you can't, it's just as likely we'll all be dead long before the problem crops up."

CHAPTER TWENTY-FOUR

"I wish we could use the pocking radios."

Roger peered through the battlefield smoke and cursed. The Krath army used about one arquebus for every ten soldiers, and between those, the Marines on the right, the Diaspran infantry on the left, and the occasional bombard firing from either side, the fields were covered in a veritable smokescreen. His helmet visor's systems gave him far better vision than any unaided eye could have provided, but that wasn't saying a lot. Worse, the billowing waves of smoke made it impossible to use visual signals in place of the radios. He could punch the occasional communications laser through, but enough gun smoke deprived him even of that.

"Tough, isn't it, Your Highness?" Pahner asked. "The fact is, up until we hit the Krath, you were spoiled as far as emissions discipline is concerned. When you don't have a complete monopoly on it, there are plenty of times when you don't have the luxury of using radio. Doesn't do to let the other side hear you, whether they can understand you or not. Then there's direction-finding. Or the battle could be taking place across lag distances where the turnaround time on transmissions just makes it impractical." He looked out across the smoke-covered fields between the two citadels and nodded. "At least this time you can *almost* see what's happening. That gives you at least a chance of judging what's going on."

Feet pounded on the stone steps behind them, and Roger turned to the runner who'd just arrived from the left wall. The sound in that direction had switched back to regular platoon volleys, he noted.

"How goes it, Orol?"

"Captain Fain says the enemy is off the wall and in retreat," the runner replied, rubbing blood from a cut at the base of his horns out of his eye.

"Bad?" Roger asked.

"Not really, Your Highness," the Mardukan said with a grunt of laughter. "They're not much as individual fighters; not a patch on the Boman. They barely got to the top of the wall, and we counterattacked with steel. We had a good killing."

Roger laughed and slapped him on the shoulder.

"Go get your head looked to, you old coot," he said. "There's more where those came from."

"Aye, and they'll be back tomorrow," the Mardukan replied. Then he saluted and headed back down the stairs, and Roger turned to Pahner.

"It sounds like the action on that side is pretty much the same as what's happening on the right. Time to sally?"

"I think so," Pahner replied. "Gastan?"

"If you think it wise," the Shin king said. "They could get bogged down and trapped, though," he added, looking just a bit dubious.

"Time to find out," Roger said, and walked to the rear of the wall. His position overlooked the courtyard directly behind the gates, which was currently packed with *civan*. The aggressive, bipedal omnivores were stamping their great three-toed feet and snapping at each other restlessly. The older of them recognized the conditions and were ready for action; it often led to a really good feed.

"Time for you to earn your damned pay, Rastar!" he shouted.

"Just make sure you're around to cover it!" the last Prince of Therdan shouted back, then looked at the commander of the gate tower. "Open the gates!"

The cavalry unit headed out in column of fours, crossing the double moat system and bypassing a bit of ruined siege tower from the Krath's farthest advance until they reached the outer works. Then they shook out into a single column, riding down the road and away from the castle at a walk. As the last rider cleared the outermost fortifications, the entire column began to pivot until it had turned into a line faced at right angles away from the roadway.

The instant the maneuver was completed, the *civan* broke into a long, bounding canter towards the left flank . . . and disappeared almost immediately into a fog bank of smoke.

"Blast!" Roger glared in disgust as the smoke overloaded his helmet's thermal sight capability—easier to do with the cold-blooded Mardukans than with most species. "The hell with this, I'm heading down to Fain's position. Maybe I can see something from there!"

"Very well, Your Highness," Pahner said, and gestured with his head to the collection of Marines and Diasprans, headed by Julian, who had remained behind to guard the prince's back. "But please keep firmly in mind that you are now Heir Primus."

"I will," Roger sighed. "I will."

Captain Fain looked up from a brief conversation with Erkum Pol and nodded as Roger loomed out of the smoke billowing up from the Diasprans' rifle fire.

"Good afternoon, Your Highness. How is it going with the rest of the wall?"

"They seem to have come in most heavily over here," Roger said, peering through the smoke towards the enemy trenches. "Is it just me, or do they seem to still be up and about?"

"As a matter of fact, they appear to be contemplating another attack, Your Highness," Fain replied. "I would consider that unwise, were I their commander, particularly given how disordered they are. But . . . nonetheless."

"They won't be contemplating it for long," Roger told the captain with an evil chuckle. "I'd hoped that they wouldn't have regained their trenches; it was too much to hope that they'd actually be getting ready to try again."

"Ah, are we going to witness a *civan* charge?" Fain asked, then gave a grunting Mardukan laugh when Roger nodded. "I'm sure Honal is just *hating* that!"

"I can't see a blasted thing!" Honal cursed.

"Well, if we stay on this heading, we should find something to attack . . . eventually. Even if we can't see it," Rastar said calmly, consulting the tactical map on the human pad Julian had programmed for him. "According to this, we're about two-thirds of the way to the forces opposite Fain."

"If that bloody Diaspran even knows where he is," Honal said as his *civan* stumbled in a hole. A Krath who appeared to be lost stumbled out of the fog of smoke within the sweep of Honal's sword and promptly died. "Come on, Valan!" Honal snarled as he flipped blood from his blade. "Give us a *breeze!*"

"Rain coming," Roger said as the sky darkened slightly. "That should finish off any visibility."

"Breaks of the game, Your Highness," Fain replied. "Of course, rain could lay some of the smoke, too, which wouldn't hurt." The native captain shrugged, never taking his eyes from the field before him. "I do believe that the Krath have dressed their lines. Perhaps you should consider moving back to the central keep."

"Hell with it," Roger said, leaning out and peering into the smoke himself. "I'm safe enough here."

Fain sighed and looked over his shoulder for Erkum Pol.

"You're safe enough *for the time being,* Your Highness. But if I ask you to retire, I must insist that you accept my judgment. I will not explain to Captain Pahner why I got you killed."

Roger looked at him with an expression very like surprise, then burst into laughter and nodded.

"All right, Krindi!" he said, wiping his eyes. "I'm sorry, but you sounded *exactly* like Pahner there."

"That wasn't my intention, Your Highness," the officer said, looking towards the Krath lines again. "But I don't consider it an insult. And, I have to add, that time might be soon."

The Krath used human-sized signs, held on long poles, as their unit guidons. The signs were marked with complex color patterns that designated unit and rank. In a culture without radio or any of the other adjuncts of high-tech civilization, such extremely simple visual signals were the only way for units to maintain cohesion in the smoke and confusion of a battlefield. The Krath had no option but to use them—or something very like them—if they wanted to hang on to any sort of organization, but the system also made it easier for the Diasprans to estimate when they had really reconsolidated. And they seemed to have gotten their act back together in record time.

"Just a bit more," Roger said. "Then I'll leave." He looked towards the Krath citadel, which had just disappeared behind a wall of silver. "Rain's almost here anyway. Won't be able to see a thing in a few minutes."

Even as he spoke, the blast of wind that precedes a storm tore aside the smoke, revealing the battlefield in all its detail.

"Oh, my," Roger said.

"Ho! My prayers are answered!" Honal said, as a breeze caressed his cheek. Then, as the smoke cleared, he grimaced. "Maybe it was better the other way."

The Krath hadn't simply reconsolidated the units which had just assaulted; they'd brought up reinforcements, as well. The new units had been deployed in blocks to either side of the original assault group, and the last few were moving into position as the smoke blew aside. Which left the Vashin barely two hundred meters from the nearest Krath battalion . . . which was just starting to dress its lines.

"Too late to worry about that!" Rastar snapped as he glanced in both directions. For a wonder, the cavalry had more or less kept its dress. "Now, for Shul's sake, don't get so carried away you get cut off or something; I'm tired of having to come to your rescue. Bugler, sound the charge!"

"The kazoos, the kazoos of the North,' " Roger muttered. The Vashin used a short metal and bone horn that sounded remarkably like a kazoo, to a human.

"Now that is pretty," Pahner commented over Roger's shoulder.

"I thought you were staying by the gates," Roger said, glancing back at the Marine. Then he returned his attention to the field. "And, yes it is."

The pennon-fluttering Vashin lances had come down as one, and the *civan* had burst into a gallop, heads down and legs pumping. The species was similar in appearance to the extinct Terran velociraptor, and nearly as dangerous. At the moment, laid flat-out, tails whipping to maintain their balance, they looked like the most dangerous thing in the galaxy. Coupled with the Vashin on their backs, they were certainly the most deadly shock melee force ever evolved on Marduk.

"What's that quote?" Roger asked softly. "Something about it's good that war is so terrible?"

" 'It is good that war is so terrible, else we might grow too fond of it.' An American general named Lee in the early industrial period. He had a point."

"It's beautiful," Roger said. "But the Krath are going to swallow them without a burp."

The battalion the Vashin were charging contained at least three times as many men as they had. And it was but one of at least twenty drawn up in front of the walls.

"After fighting the Boman, the one thing Rastar knows is when to disengage," Pahner pointed out.

"Let's hope," Roger replied.

Rastar tried to withdraw the lance which had just transfixed the Krath infantryman, but it was stuck fast. He hated to give up the weapon's reach advantage, but he also knew better than to make himself a stationary

target trying to recover it. And so he kept right on moving while he drew his sword and slashed at one of the swarming locals just as his *civan* stamped at another. The wicked, iron-shod claws shredded their target's torso even as the sword bit into flesh, but it was obvious they were getting bogged.

It wasn't that the locals were trained to receive cavalry. Indeed, the battalion that they'd struck at first was gone, shattered and scattered to the winds. But there'd been another behind it, and still more forces pouring out of the trenches. At this point, the Vashin were almost surrounded simply because of the sheer inertia of the Krath forces on either flank of their penetration. The terrified infantry *wanted* to get out of the way, but there was nowhere for them to go.

He looked around for the bugler and realized he was almost all alone.

"Bloody hell," he muttered. It was a curse Honal had picked up from the human healer, and it was appropriate for the moment. The ground in every direction was covered with bodies. "I really need to get us out of this."

He began waving at nearby units, gathering them about him as he headed to the rear and the rain began to fall. At first, the drops were scattered, but in moments the storm had become a real Mardukan gullywasher. Water pounded down like a hammer—or a waterfall—and quickly formed puddles nearly knee deep to a human.

Rastar slashed down a few of the locals on the way out, especially when they were delaying his forces, but his main objective now was to withdraw his men intact, not to run up his body count. He'd only drawn his pistols once, but when he saw a cluster around a group of dismounted Vashin, all four came out. The Vashin, including Honal, were hunkered down behind their dropped *civan,* slashing and firing at a group of about twenty Krath who obviously wanted their weapons and harnesses.

Rastar pressed the *civan* into a gallop, and it responded wearily. He could tell the beast was badly fatigued, but its feet spurned the bodies of the fallen and it leapt over

the occasional *civan* body until it finally bounded into the midst of the Krath attackers. Rastar laid down a curtain of revolver fire all around himself, while the *civan* kicked and bit in every direction, until a dozen of the other troopers he'd rallied came charging in to finish the enemy off .

"Rastar!" Honal protested as he drove his sword into one of the wounded Krath. "You're not leaving any for me!"

Rastar leaned over and offered his cousin an arm up as one of the other troopers dismounted to retrieve the bugler and the flag of Therdan.

"And what the hell was the colors group doing following you, and not me?" he demanded.

"You bloody idiot! You ran ahead of us. And you complain about *me* being headstrong! We got bogged down, and there you were, charging into the distance like some kid!"

"Oh, sure, blame it on me," Rastar said. He took the bugle from the bugler, who was clearly too cut up to wield it, and put it to his lips.

"Sounds like they're withdrawing," Pahner said, stepping back under an awning as the skies opened up.

"I wonder if the Krath will advance in this?" Roger asked.

"Probably, Your Highness," the Gastan said.

"What is this, 'Follow Roger Week'?" Roger asked with a smile he hoped the Gastan interpreted correctly.

"The buildup on this flank was easy to note," the Gastan said. "I'm not sure the sally was worth the loss of your riding beasts."

"I don't think it was," Roger agreed. "And even if the raiding party in the rear started any fires, they've been put out by the rain."

"Time for Plan B," Pahner mused. "If we had one. But the only one I can think of is to take the spaceport first. Gastan, I won't argue for that plan, but how long would it take for a force to make it to the port from here?"

"No more than twenty days," the Gastan replied. "Less

for runners. I can have a message to Temu Jin in less than nine, and a reply in twice that."

The brief, intense rain squall was already clearing, and Roger gazed at the distant fortress.

"It's slightly lower than us, but we don't have any effective artillery to destroy it," he mused.

"They were starting to cast real siege cannon in K'Vaern's Cove," Julian said. Then he grimaced apologetically. "Sorry, just brainstorming. Too far, too long."

"And what would we do if we destroyed the walls?" Roger asked, gesturing at the Krath. The good news was that it seemed the combination of rain and the sally had caused the enemy to withdraw for the day, but— "They still outnumber us forty-to-one," he observed.

"We broke up their formations when they came at us by targeting the leadership," Fain said. The concept of brainstorming had been explained to him, and he found it a valid idea. "It was a technique I'd considered against the Boman, but I was never able to implement it at the time; my men weren't good enough shots. All the target practice since made the difference."

"The French introduced that technique during the Napoleonic wars," Pahner commented. "Congratulations on rediscovering it. I should have suggested it."

"But we can't snipe them to death," Roger said, looking up at the mountains looming above the citadel. The mountains to the north and south had relatively shallow slopes, and the Krath fortress had been cut into them. But beyond that, the valley necked down to the gorge of the Shin River. From there, it dropped over a thousand meters to the town of Thirlot. "We could drop teams on them, but even with armor, that would be pinpricks."

"Assassinate the leadership?" Julian suggested.

"They're relatively civilized," Pahner pointed out. "They're fighting by policy, not personality, and they have a solid chain of command. If we kill the current leaders, their replacements will step into their positions with hardly a ripple. Otherwise, that would work."

"We could roll rocks down the hill on them," Julian said. "Gronningen can handle the boulders."

"Pinpricks again," Pahner objected. "Even a large land-slide onto the citadel or the army wouldn't do enough damage. Even if we did it several times, they'd just give up the slopes. And we *still* couldn't move them."

"Do it enough, and it might break their will," Julian argued mulishly. " 'The objective is to break the will of the enemy.' "

"A combination of all of them?" Fain mused. "Marines and my fellows sniping, the Shin to take to the heights and start rockslides, the occasional sally and raid . . . over time, we might be able to wear them down to the point they'd quit the field?"

"No." Roger shook his head, still looking at the distant ranges. "Not a battle of attrition; we need a battle of check-mate. Gastan, how long, again, to get a message to Jin?"

"Nine days." The Shin king gave Roger a sidelong glance. "What are you considering?"

"I'm going to make them wish they'd never pissed me off," Roger said. "I'm going to get them to surrender, without the need for a single battle. I'm going to send them home without their arms, their food, their bedding, or their pretty little tents. And with virtually no loss of life. I'm going to humiliate them."

"And how, exactly, are you going to do all that, Your Highness?" Pahner asked.

"I'm going to introduce them to geology," Roger said with a feral smile.

Pahner looked at him, then up at the mountains, and then up at the end of the valley. The intensity of his speculation was obvious, but, finally, he shrugged with a puzzled expression.

"The salient point to the plan is that this entire val-ley was once a lake," Roger said, looking around the steam-filled room.

The conference had been moved to the town of Mudh Hemh for a multitude of reasons, but the main one was that Roger wanted input from Despreaux. Since all the wounded had been moved to Mudh Hemh, the confer-ence had to be moved to follow them.

The shift was beneficial on another level, as well. Although the town was filled with the sharp smell of rotten eggs from the nearby geothermal area, it was also surprisingly pleasant for the humans—which, of course, meant unpleasantly chilly for Mardukans. The Shin of Mudh Hemh maintained their movement ability by bathing in the warm waters from the Fire Lands, and the town was half-barbarian village, half-sybaritic spa.

Indeed, since the conference had been pushed into evening, it ended up being held in the primary bathhouse of the Gastan; and most of the Mardukans were submerged up to their necks in the steaming hot water. In any other circumstances, the thought of a major war-planning session being held in a spa would've been ludicrous. But to the Bronze Barbarians, who had held them in pouring thunderstorms, swamps, mountains, and flooded plains over the last half-year, this was infinitely better than many alternatives. The sight of Dogzard, paddling from person to person to mooch treats, and of the IAS journalist, discreetly filming the entire conference, simply added an amusing counterpoint.

But the prince had to admit that the sight of Nimashet, half-undressed to submerge in the water, was a tad distracting.

"The geology of this region indicates that during the last glacial period, the valley was first carved by a glacier, and then the glacier was slowly replaced by a deep upland lake," he continued, and threw up the first picture, a representation of the valley with the lake sketched in. He hoped that it was clear enough that the Shin, unaccustomed as they were to representations, would understand what they were seeing.

"Somewhere around the vicinity of Queicuf, there was once a massive dam—probably half volcanic debris, and half ice; you can still see some of the traces of it in the slight prominence that Queicuf is established upon.

"It's the sediment from that upland lake and the ash from the volcanoes that gives you the rich soil you till. But the most important point for us right this minute is that it's possible to create the lake again."

"You're not going to flood the valley!" one of the chieftains protested.

Roger had sketched out the plan for the Gastan before the conference, and he more than suspected that the wily Shin monarch had planted that particular question. The chieftain who'd "spontaneously" blurted out the protest was one of the Gastan's personal retainers, and Pedi's father had very carefully gone over the points which might be expected to create concerns among his followers when he and Roger first discussed the possibilities. The human prince was beginning to appreciate how skillfully the Gastan manipulated his meetings. It was an important point to retain for his own later use, and also one to keep in the forefront of his mind now. If the Gastan decided that he didn't like a human plan, he was going to be a dangerously capable opponent.

"No," Roger said now, with a grin and a wave of his arms that replicated, as well as the under-equipped, two-armed humans could, the Mardukan gesture for intense amusement. "No, not the entire valley—just the bit the Krath are standing on."

A wave of ripples spread out from the chieftains gathered in the steaming water, and by the way some peered at the hologram and rubbed their horns, he could see that they understood the representation just fine.

"Even if we wanted to flood the entire valley, we don't have the materials," Roger told them. "What we propose to do is to drop a portion of the mountainside above the Shin River where it exits the valley. Please send messages to our contacts in the spaceport requesting that they send us as much octocellulose as possible. That's a very strong conventional explosive, and we'll use it first to drill holes in the slopes above the exit, and then to blow out a large chunk of the mountain.

"This chunk will create a temporary dam. We should be able to drop enough material into the river to raise the level to a point which will force the Krath to move out into the open, under our walls. The alternative will be drowning, or at least standing in cold water up to their groins. Their army will have no choice but to surrender."

"Or to charge the walls," one of the other chieftains said darkly.

"The water is going to rise *fast*," Pahner interjected. "They'll have, at most, two hours to decide what to do and to do it, and all the indications are that they're pretty incapable of reacting to surprise. I'd be astonished if they could even get a decision *made* in two hours, much less implement it."

"But if they realize what we're planning," Roger said, "and the preparations will of necessity take place in plain sight, they'll have ample time to plan a response. So we'll have to have a deception plan. We'll make it look as if the forces emplacing the charges are actually building a fortress to threaten their logistics line."

"What if we can't get the explosives?" Despreaux prompted.

"In that case, we'll use gunpowder," Roger said. "There's a powder mill here; Mudh Hemh is a primary supplier. It will take longer, and more materials, but it'll still work."

"I could make some nitro," she mused. "They have everything I need."

"I'd prefer you in one piece," Roger told her with a grin. "Nitroglycerin is far too volatile. If we can get the octocellulose, let's go with that."

"You said a temporary dam," the Gastan said. "How 'temporary'?"

"It will last at least two days," Roger said confidently. "It may last for years, depending on how the material falls."

"It could be made semi-permanent, if you wish," Fain interjected. "We Diasprans are quite familiar with such structures; with a few days' work, we could insure that it stays up for weeks. With a few weeks, we could make it permanent. That assumes that the subgrade is good—I'd need to look at that. But I concur on the couple of days, minimum. The material of the mountain appears to be a mixture of this black rock—"

"Basalt," Roger said.

"This 'basalt,' and the fine ash. The basalt will create

the structure, and the ash—which is notably nonporous— will fill the gaps. I suspect that it will make an excellent dam all by itself."

"I have seen dams like this," one of the highland chiefs offered. "They're scattered throughout the mountains. This . . . this could work. If you can 'drop' enough of the mountain."

"If we can get the octocellulose, that's not a problem," Roger said with a shrug. "A piece of octocellulose the size of your thumb has the explosive power of a keg of gunpowder. The material is hard to describe, but it's a very tight packing of eight carbon molecules associated with nitrates, such as your saltpeter that goes in gunpowder. It's a common explosive among my people."

"We can't just lay it on the surface, Your Highness," Doc Dobrescu interjected. "We'll have to dig the charges in. Dig 'em in deep, if you want the sort of material movement you're talking about."

"That will be a challenge," Roger said. "I spoke with Krindi about it, and we can either blow out a sort of mining cavity by hammering in a spike and then blasting out the cavity, or we can try to produce very long steel drills that can be hammered in over time."

"Nah," Julian said. "Despreaux, can you make a shaped charge?"

"Sure," the sergeant replied, then grimaced. "Well, supervise," she amended, shrugging her arm. "There are field expedient shaped charges you can make out of hammered iron. Why?"

"I had a buddy who was an engineer," Julian said with a thoughtful expression. "He said that when they were in school, they made craters by first blowing a hole with shaped charges, then filling the cavity with explosives. I don't know the size of the shaped charges, though, or how much to put in."

"Well, if we blow a series of holes, then pack them with a combination of octocellulose and gunpowder, not having the materials for a decent ANFO slurry, it should work," Despreaux said, her face lighting up.

"I think that your paramour likes explosives more than

you, Prince Roger," the Gastan commented dryly, and Roger shrugged as grunting Mardukan laughter filled the room. His relationship with Despreaux had become widely known.

"She likes it hot, what can I say?"

"We still have to assume that the Krath will become aware of our plans," the Gastan said.

"Even if they do, they'll find it difficult to attack the workings," Roger responded. "Your forces—and ours—fight better on the heights."

"Still, I think they'll try," the Gastan said. "And when they fail to take them, they'll come here, instead."

"They've come before!" one of the chieftains protested, dipping into the sulfurous water and coming back up blowing bubbles. "We'll stop them as we have before!"

"If they all come at once?" the Gastan asked. "Desperate in their fear of the rising waters?"

"You'll have to be prepared to offer them a truce, you realize," Roger said. This, too, was something he and the Gastan—and O'Casey—had discussed, and so he was prepared to look around mildly as the bellows of protest arose. One serendipitous advantage of having the conference in the bath chamber was that the chieftains were unarmed. Of course, it still looked as if they were willing to tear him limb from limb with their bare hands.

"No quarter for the Burners of the Shin!" "Death to the Krath!" "Blood! *Blood!*"

"What?" Roger shouted back, waving his hands at them. O'Casey had helped the Gastan set this part up, and the prince could see her trying not to smile.

"You can't kill them all!" he continued. "I don't mean 'you shall not'; I mean you *can*not! You'd have to cut throats until your arms fell off! And that assumes they lined up to have them cut! No, you're going to have to *feed* them, instead, which means bringing in food from the upper Krath and across the Shesul Pass, so the first thing to do is put them to work repairing that road. You *do* realize that you're going to be disarming them all, right? And that all their weapons and armor are going to be spoils?"

He looked around at the suddenly silent chieftains and saw the credit signs dancing in their eyes.

"Yep. For that matter, you can probably squeeze the Krath for tribute. This is Kirsti's primary field army. If they don't have it, the next satrap up the line can take all the territory he wants—they're probably holding him back by an agreement to refrain while they crush you. If you crush them, instead, they're going to be between a rock and a hard place. Tributes galore. Control of Queicuf again, control of all the trade routes, tribute— hell, an end to the slave raids and sacrifices. 'When you have them by the balls, their hearts and minds will follow.' "

"You make it sound so easy," one of the chieftains complained.

"Ah, well, that's my job," Roger said with a grin. They laughed again, but then he allowed his grin to fade. "Easy? No. They'll probably hit Nopet Nujam hard. They might hit Nopet Vusof. But they won't have much time to do anything, unless someone goes tattling from this meeting. If we use cratering charges—and that sounds like the best plan—we can drop the mountainside the day after we reach the heights. Two hours after it goes down, the water will be up to their tents."

"We must be ready to face a heavy attack, though," the Gastan said. "We will need every warrior ready, either on the walls or resting for their time. With the aid of our human allies, we may yet win the day—win it fully, and for all time. But there is hard battle ahead of us still, and we must steel ourselves for it. The Shin! Death to the Krath!"

"DEATH TO THE KRATH!"

CHAPTER TWENTY-FIVE

Roger sank into the water and sighed as the chieftains filed out.

"That went well," he said, hooking an arm around Despreaux.

"Perhaps," the Gastan said. "Perhaps."

"What's wrong?" Roger asked. "I think the plan will work. Things will go wrong, but we should be able to implement the basics, no matter what."

"My father fears for our people," Pedi said. She and Cord had remained silent throughout the meeting, but they'd been a presence nonetheless—the adviser to the prince and the Light of Mudh Hemh, who was now his *benan*. There was something else going on there, as well, but Roger was unsure what it was.

"We'll take fierce casualties in the final attack, if it comes," the Gastan said finally. "The deaths of warriors. That is what concerns me, because it is only through warriors that the people can continue, that . . . new life comes into the world.

He glanced over at his daughter, then away.

"I'm missing something here," Roger said.

"I think I've got it," Dr. Dobrescu said. "It's like the Kranolta, Your Highness. Gaston, pardon me if I'm blunt. What you're afraid of is that whereas females, like Pedi,

403

can carry many children, it's only through the warriors—
the males—that children can be made. Is that correct?"

The Gastan sighed and gestured.

"Yes. When a male lies with a female, only a few pups
are produced. But if two males lie with the female, more
are produced. A female can carry . . . oh, maybe six or
eight, with difficulty. But a male can never . . . give more
than three or four. So if the males fall in battle, from
whence comes the next generation?"

"You have to remember, Your Highness," Dobrescu said,
after carefully deactivating his toot's translator program,
"that Mardukan 'males' are technically females."

"And they implant eggs rather than injecting sperm,"
Roger said, also in Imperial. "Got it. And since they only
come into season twice a year . . ."

"We have lost more warriors than females to the raids,"
the Gastan said, "and we already feel the effects of this
long war. If we lose as many as half of our warriors—
and in a great attack, that is possible—we may be
doomed even if your plan succeeds. The Krath will just
outbreed us."

"Co-opt them," Eleonora suggested. "Let them 'immi-
grate.' The Krath are overcrowded. Let them trickle up
into the mountains. Have them rebuild Uthomof."

"Perhaps," the Gastan said with an edge of doubt. "It's
been suggested before. There are outer villages that have
been so stripped by the raiders that they're empty. We
don't want the Krath Fire Priests, though."

"Priests can be . . . adjusted," Fain said. "You may be
faced in the near future with more prisoners than you
have population. Before they leave, ask the best of them
if they want to move up here. Make them Shin, not
Krath. If they keep their religion, make sure it renounces
sacrifice. You should make that a condition of the peace
treaty, anyway."

"I'm still confused about that," Kosutic said. "According
to Harvard, it's a recent innovation, and it doesn't fit
his data on their religion at all. I'm guessing that it's
human cultural contamination, but from where and why
is the question."

"It started in the time of my father's father," the Gastan told her. "Initially, it was solely among the Krath, but in my father's time, they started raiding us for Servants of the Fire. Part of that may have been because the warriors of Uthomof had raided all the way to the outskirts of Kirsti. The first of the Shin Servants were taken in punitive raids, but it has grown steadily ever since."

"It was among the Krath, at first?" Kosutic asked. "They didn't start by raiding you?"

"No, not at first. Later . . . it's more from us than from them, now."

"Eleonora?" The sergeant major looked at O'Casey. "Human sacrifice and cannibalism?"

"In civilizations? As opposed to, say, tribal headhunters?"

"Yeah," the Armaghan said, slipping deeper into the water. "Aztecs. Kali . . ."

"Baal, if you count ritual infanticide," the chief of staff said with a quizzical expression.

"Baal!" Kosutic sat upright and slapped her forehead. "How could I forget Baal? I bet that's it!"

"What's 'it'?" Roger demanded.

"Where to start?" sergeant major asked.

"Start at the beginning . . ." Pahner suggested with a slight smile.

"Gee, thanks a lot, Sir!"

The priestess settled back in the water once more, frowning thoughtfully.

"Okay," she said finally. "The worship of Baal is *old*. Baal is an only slightly 'mixed' god; he's mostly a cattle god, and he only added a human form later. The Minotaur is probably related to his worship, and there are some very significant pre-Baal religious motifs in pre-Egyptian culture.

"One of the major aspects of the worship of Baal is ritual infanticide. Children, infants younger than eight weeks, are wrapped in swaddling clothes and put in fires that burn within a huge figure, usually that of a bull but sometimes of a minotaur-looking human. These are frequently children of high-caste couples.

"Prior to the development of civilization in the Turanian and Terrane regions, the area was a hunter-gatherer paradise. But a tectonic shift—a change in Terra's axial inclination, actually—in about 6000 B.C.E., caused a severe climate change. The Sahara was created, which was a desert where the Libyan Plains are now. Civilization developed rapidly in response, as the hunter-gatherers were forced to change their lifestyles to adjust to the climate changes.

"Now, the first evidence of the cult of Baal arose practically in tandem with civilization. Aspects of it were found in very early Egyptian society, although the sacrificial aspects are ambiguous. But it was definitely found in the proto-Phoenician cattle herders and fishermen in the Levant. The Phoenicians, of course, carried it far and wide, and it might have influenced the shift from Tolmec self-sacrifice to Aztec human sacrifice. Certainly they were in contact with the Tolmecs, as well as the proto-Incans and the Maya; the Phoenician logs that were, ahem, 'recovered' from Professor Van Dorn in 2805 proved that conclusively."

"One of the classics of ideological bias," O'Casey said with a laugh. " 'Analyzing them for authenticity' indeed! If his research assistant hadn't called the authorities, he would've destroyed *all* the tablets."

"Exactly," the sergeant major agreed. "But at least it finally ended the two hundred-year reign of the Land-Bridge Fanatics in anthropology. Now, the rationale for infanticide is still occasionally debated. Infanticide is practiced by every society, and it's often supported more by women than by men . . ."

"Excuse me, Sergeant Major," Despreaux said with a frown. "*Every* society? I don't think so!"

"Ever heard of abortion, girl?" the Armaghan snapped back. "What in hell do you think *that* is? I'm not arguing for or against infanticide, but it's the same thing. The point being that there's a widespread human drive towards it. But that doesn't explain the ritualization, which is only found in certain cultures, and most notably in the cult of Baal. In 2384, Dr. Elmkhan, at the

University of Teheran completed the definitive study of the rise of Baalism. He analyzed results from over four thousand digs throughout Terrane and Turania and came to the conclusion, which to this day is hotly debated, that it was a direct response to population problems in the immediate aftermath of the climatic change."

"Ah, bingo," Roger said. "The Krath population problem!"

"The Krath population problem" Kosutic agreed. "My guess is that it *was* cultural contamination—and not accidentally, either. There was a satirical piece by an early industrial writer about the Irish. . . . What was his name? Fast? Quick?"

"Swift?" Pahner asked. " 'An Elegant Solution' or something like that. 'Let them eat their young.' "

"Yes," O'Casey agreed. "But what Swift didn't realize was that there were societies where, for all practical purposes, that was what *happened*. In fact, one of the major factors influencing the rise of Christianity in Roman culture was its proscription against infanticide. There *is* a drive towards it, but it is *not* widely supported. Roman matrons, given the choice of saying 'My God forbids it' jumped on board by the thousands. It was that proscription, along with the acceptance of the Rituals of Mithras as the standard Mass, that *created* the Catholic church."

"The Rituals of *what*?" Despreaux asked plaintively. "You're going too fast."

"I'm just sort of sitting here with my jaw on the table," Roger told her with a snort. "I'm not even trying to understand half of it."

"The Rituals of Mithras," Fain put in, lifting up so that more than just his ears and horns were out of the steaming water. "One of the conversations the Priestess and I had. As a political ploy to gain the support of the Roman Army, the early Christians took the entire series of rituals from a religion called the Mithraists and turned it into their Mass."

"If imitation is the sincerest form of flattery, the early Christian church was very impressed with the Mithraists," Kosutic said sourly. "But at that point the Christians had

two of the major political forces in Rome on their side:
the Army, which switched to Christianity in droves as
soon as they saw that it was just Mithras in another
guise; and the matrons who no longer had to throttle
their excess children. The rest is known history—the
Emperor converted, and it was all over but the shouting. And let me tell you, that was ferociously argued—
and occasionally warred over—for nearly two thousand
years *after* it could be debated in public. But in the end,
the preponderance of evidence pointed to that being the
pattern, rather than his mother telling him he had to
do it.

"On the other hand," she noted, "it has little or nothing to do with the Krath, other than as an example of
the intersection of religion and politics."

"Can I ask one thing that's bothering me?" Roger said.

"Ask away, Your Highness," the sergeant major replied.

"You used the *present* tense a *lot* when discussing the
cult of Baal and its sacrifices," Roger said carefully. "And
I recall you saying something about 'the Brotherhood of
Baal' among the Armaghans . . ."

"The Brotherhood does not practice human sacrifice,"
Kosutic said, then waggled her hands. "As far as I know.
Although they do have the occasional death under the
'enhancement' rituals, which might count. They certainly
do *not* practice ritual infanticide. The Church of Ryback,
on the other hand, has a variety of Baalian influences."

"The Saints," Pahner said. "I wondered when you'd get
to the point."

"The Saints," the sergeant major said with a nod.
"There are various . . . word choices and phrases in the
Church of Ryback that indicate to comparative theologians
that it was influenced by the New Cult of Baal, which
was formed—and died—during the Dagger Years. Also,
the Rybackians have various sub-cults, which are, ahem,
more 'fundamental' than others."

"I notice that you say 'ahem' when you're trying not
to say something," Roger observed. "What was *that*
'ahem'?"

Kosutic sighed and shook her head.

"There are . . . rumors that are generally discounted about some of the sub-cults of Ryback eating their young. Personally, I don't put much faith in them. You hear that sort of thing about all sorts of hated sub-groups. But . . . I also wouldn't put it past them, either. Anyway, you can imagine *their* reaction to the overcrowding of the Krath. Never prove it, though."

"And we could be wrong," O'Casey pointed out. "There's the whole influence of the spaceport, the original survey team, the previous group of archeologists . . . It could have been any of them, or spontaneous serial development, for that matter."

"Oooo, like pyramids?" Kosutic asked with one eyebrow arched.

"Well . . ." O'Casey blushed faintly and actually wiggled in the water. "In this case, it's at least possible. I know that archeologists still have a bad reputation from that, but in this case it's *possible*. Cannibalism is endemic in every culture except the Phaenurs."

"Who don't even have *wars*," Despreaux whispered to Julian.

"Oh, they have them," the intelligence sergeant replied. "They just don't get noticed."

"They're empaths," she protested quietly. "How could *empaths* have a war?"

"You've obviously never had a Jewish mother-in-law," Julian told her under his breath.

"Sergeant Major, you're clearly having fun," Pahner interjected. "But I'm not sure that knowing where the Krath got the idea for sacrifices gets us. I think we need to concentrate on the tactics for a little bit, here."

"I think that's straightforward," Roger said. "We'll write a message to Jin. The Gastan sends it via his runners. When we get the explosives, Nimashet builds the shaped charges, we blow the mountain, and then we call for the Krath's surrender."

"And in the meantime, Your Highness?"

"Well, in about five or six days, we start assembling teams and training," Roger said. "And until then, I intend to drink some wine and sit in a hot tub with my girlfriend. I suggest you do the same. Well, except the girlfriend part. You can abstain from that."

"Thanks so very much, Your Highness," Pahner said.

"No problem," the prince replied. He held out a flask and cup. "Wine?"

Temu Jin looked at the message, then at the messenger.

"Do you know what they're going to do with it?" he asked.

"I don't even know what 'it' is, human," the Shin runner replied curtly. The runner appeared to be almost a different species from the Gastan. He was as tall as any Mardukan Jin had ever dealt with, and had weirdly long fingers and shortened horns. Combined with the four arms and widely spaced eyes, it made him look like a mucous-covered insect. "All I know is that there are four more of us waiting. And we are to take packages from you. We wait until the packages are prepared."

"Come on, then," Jin said, with a gesture.

The meeting was taking place at the back of the spaceport, as usual. Now Jin descended the slight slope from the edge and headed to the nearest Krath hamlet, a tiny burg called Tul by the locals. The majority of the few off-planet visitors stayed on the port reservation. The few who didn't usually exited by the main gates, and thence down the road to the Krath imperial city, called, with surprising imagination, "Krath." Very few humans, or any other visitors, for that matter, came to Tul.

On one level, that made it a bad place to hide purloined materials. The sight of a human face there was a dead giveaway that something was going down. On the other hand, the bribes were lower, and the local farmers and craftsmen reminded him of home. As long as he kept up the payments, they were unlikely to go squealing to the taxmen, who were their only contact with the central government.

And it was convenient for the purpose—which was to build up a cache against the day he needed it.

Originally, the caches had started as insurance against the possibility that Governor Mountmarch might decide he could dispense with the services of one Temu Jin. Jin was well aware that he was deep into the "knows too much; not close enough to the inner circle to be trusted" category. Life on the frontier was cheap, and the only law was the governor. If Mountmarch wanted him dead, it was a matter of a nod. Against that almost inevitable day, he'd started smuggling the odd weapon or ammo pack out of the port. And when he'd realized how easy it was, he'd upped his depredations to using whole pack teams of Mardukans to smuggle material out.

As far as anyone would be able to tell, it was just a regular black-market operation. He sold Imperial materials to the Mardukans, and in return he had a nice Mardukan servant and trade goods, which he used to purchase materials from docking spacers. In reality, the majority of materials weren't being sold, but stored in bunkers. Each time he sent stuff down, he also sent along payments to the mayor—either human goods, or Krath coin. And each time he pulled stuff out, he paid more. He had backup caches in the hills, including a full set of armor, for which he had the codes, and a heavy plasma gun. If he had to fight to get the rest, he could. But he'd never had any trouble with Tul. He thought of it as his little war-bank.

And now it was time to make a withdrawal.

They came into the village the back way, through the *turom* fields, stepping carefully around the round balls of horselike dung. Like much of the continent's architecture, the mayor's house was a squat construction of heavy basalt rocks. It was built more like a fortress than most, and its back door was constructed of half-meter thick planks that didn't respond well to a standard knock. Which was why Jin drew his bead pistol and pounded on the door with its handgrip, swinging the gun like a hammer.

After a few moments, the door swung open to reveal a wizened old Mardukan female. Jin had never been sure if she was the cook, or a mother-in-law, or what. It probably didn't matter, but it nagged at his sense of curiosity. She was *always* the one to answer the door, no matter if he was early or late.

She looked at him, looked at the Mardukans with him, made a motion to wait, then closed the door. After a few moments more, it was opened by the local Krath leader.

"Temu Jin, I see you," he said. "You bring Shin to my door?"

"I need to get a few things."

"Of course," the mayor said with a gesture of resignation. "I fear that the authorities are becoming too interested in this affair."

"I'll do my best not to let you get caught up in it," and Jin said. "I treasure your security as much as you treasure my gold."

"Perhaps," the mayor muttered, then beckoned for Jin to follow him and led the way through the darkened town.

The route took them to an abandoned basement which had been hollowed out and reinforced on one side. The hollow, in turn, had been packed with boxes, and Temu Jin started checking packing lists.

"Cataclysmite," he muttered, shaking his head. "What in *hell* does he want two hundred kilos of cataclysmite for?"

Despreaux waved the cup of wine away as Julian filed out of the door.

"Not for me, either."

"Don't make me drink it all alone," Roger said. "Besides, it's good for healing bones. It's got calcium in it."

"That's *milk,* you goof," Despreaux said. She chuckled, but then she sobered. "Roger, we have to talk."

"Uh, oh. What have I done now?"

"I think . . ." She stopped and shook her head. "I think we should stop seeing each other."

"Look, you're my bodyguard," Roger said. "I have to see you."

"You know what I mean."

"If it's the fraternization thing, we'll handle it," he said with a frown. He was beginning to realize that she was serious. "I mean, we've been . . . well . . . friends for this long. If it was going to go wrong, it would have before now."

"It's not that," she said, shaking her head. "Let's just leave it, okay? Say 'thanks,' and shake hands and be friends."

"You're *joking*," he spat. "Tell me you're joking! What ever happened to 'eternal love' and all that?"

"Some things . . . change. I don't think we're right."

"Nimashet, right up until we got to Mudh Hemh, you thought we were as right as— Well, I can't think of a metaphor. *Very* right. So what's changed?"

"Nothing," she said, turning away and getting out of the water.

"Is it one of the Marines?"

"No!" she said. "Please don't play twenty questions, all right?"

"No, not all right. I want to know what's changed."

"You did, *Your Highness*," she said, sitting back down on the edge of the water and wringing out her hair. "Before, you were prince Roger, Heir Tertiary to the Throne of Man. Now, you're either a wanted outlaw, or the next Emperor. And you're not willing to settle for wanted outlaw, are you?"

"No," Roger said balefully. "Are you?"

"I don't know," she sighed. "There's been so much death, I'm afraid it's never going to end. Not even get better."

"Hey, yo, Sergeant Despreaux," he smiled. "You're the one who carried me out of the battle in Voitan. Remember?"

"Roger, I haven't fired a shot in combat since . . . Sindi. Yeah, I think that's it. That little 'holding action' of yours before the main battle."

"*What?*"

"Remember when we were coming out of the temple in Kirsti? Who was the only person with ammo?"

"You were," Roger replied. "But . . . I thought you'd just been very conservative with your fire."

"I hadn't fired *at all*!" she snapped. "Not even when that bastard almost took your head off on the back stair!"

"But—" Roger stared at her, stunned by the revelation. Then he shook himself. "Kosutic had me covered," he said. "Besides, what does *that* have to do with never seeing me again?"

"Nothing," she admitted. "Except that you're not going to just let bygones be bygones. You're going to go charging back to Imperial City with blood in your eye. And you'll either overthrow Jackson, or die trying. Right?"

"Damned right!"

"So, you're either going to be dead, or the Emperor, right?"

"Well, Mother is probably competent—"

"But when *she* dies, or abdicates, you're the Emperor, right?"

"Oh."

"And do you think that the Emperor can just marry any old rube farm girl from the back of beyond?" she asked. "Sure, when you were just Prince Roger, it was like a dream come true. I figured I'd be a nine-day celebrity, and then we'd find some out of the way place to . . . be Roger and Nimashet. But now you're going to be Emperor, and Emperors have *dynastic* marriages, not marriages to girls from the out-planets."

"Oh," he repeated. "Oh, Nimashet—"

"You know I'm right," she said, wiping at her eyes. "I saw the way O'Casey was looking at me. I'm willing to be your wife. I'm even willing to be your girlfriend. I'm not willing to be your mistress, or your concubine. And those are the choices available to Emperor Roger and Sergeant Nimashet Despreaux."

"No," he said, wrapping his arms around her knees. "Nimashet, I'll *need* you. Even if we succeed, and that's not a given, I'll need you to be there. I . . . you're always at my back. Maybe you're not shooting anymore, but you're still there. Even when Cord isn't, *you're* there. You're like my right arm. I can't make it without you."

"Hah," she snorted through the tears. "You'd still be cursing your enemies with both arms and legs hacked

off. And drown them in blood to kill them. *You* don't
know when to quit. Me? I do. I quit. When we get back
and everything is done, I'm turning in the uniform. And
until then, I'm going to see Sergeant Major Kosutic about
putting me on noncombat duties. It's beyond combat
fatigue, Roger. I just can't focus anymore. I may be at
your back, but that's because you're wiping everything
out in front of you, and at your back is the safest place
to be. The only problem is that I'm supposed to be *your*
bodyguard, not the other way around."

"You've saved my life . . ." He thought about it. "Three
times, I think."

"And you've saved mine as many," she replied. "It's
not a matter of keeping score. Just, let it go, okay? I
can't marry the Emperor, I can't guard you worth a
damn, and I'm not much good for anything else. I'll head
back to Midgard, buy a farm, find a nice stolid husband,
and . . . try not to think about you. Okay?"

"No, it's not 'okay'! I can see your logic, sort of. But
if you think I'm going to release you to go hide on a
farm, you've got another think coming. And unless there's
a clear reason for a dynastic marriage, I'm still going
to marry you, come hell or high water. Even if I have
to drag you into the church, kicking and screaming!"

"You and what army, Mister?" she asked dangerously.
"If I say no, I mean no."

"Look, none of this is settled until we get to Terra,"
Roger said. "Let's just . . . bank it right now. We'll pull
it out and look at it again when things settle down. But
I don't care if you're not one hundred percent in close
combat. Who's making the shaped charges?"

"Me," she sighed.

"And who's going to be managing the demolitions?"

"Me."

"And when we get back to Terra, can I trust you to
hang in there and do whatever needs to be done to the
best of your ability, as long as you don't have to kill
anyone?"

"Yes," she admitted.

"Can I go get any old joker off the street that I can

trust? Or any of the Marines on Terra? No. I'll need every single body I can trust. And you're a body that I can both trust and admire," he finished with a leer.

"Gee, thanks." She smiled.

"You told me a long time ago that we might not get to retire to Marduk. That Mother might have other plans for us. Well, the same goes for you. Unless we're all killed, I'm going to have things I need you to do. Only one of them involves marrying me, and we'll discuss that when the time comes. Okay?"

"Okay."

"Does this mean I can't wrestle with you in the water?" he asked, running his hand up her side.

"If you get this cast wet and short it out, Dobrescu will kill you," she pointed out.

"It's okay. I'm a faster draw than he is."

"Well, since you put it that way," she replied, and slid down into the water and leaned forward to kiss him.

"Your Highness," Bebi said, leaning in the door. "Captain Pahner's compliments, and he'd like to see you in his quarters."

"I think I'm beginning to detect a pattern here," Roger snarled under his breath.

"Once is happenstance, twice is coincidence, and three times is enemy action," Despreaux replied huskily. "So far, it's just coincidence."

"So far," Roger replied. "But I have to wonder."

CHAPTER TWENTY-SIX

"You are a cruel human, Adib Julian," Kosutic said.

"It's an art," he replied, tapping the pad. "Despreaux's blood pressure and heart beat both increase, they're having an argument. Heart beat increases, and blood pressure drops, and they're . . . not."

"What about Roger?" the sergeant major asked.

"To tell you the truth, he's scary," Julian said. "The whole time, his heartbeat never changed within any sort of standard of variation. Steady fifty-two beats per minute. That's the lowest in the company, by the way. And his blood pressure barely flickered. You can't tell *anything* about what he's thinking or feeling from biometrics. Spooky."

"He gets angry," Kosutic said. "I've *seen* it."

"Sure," the sergeant agreed, flipping the pad closed. "And when he does, he's *still* got ice water running in his veins."

"Hmmm. You know, I think we're just starting to understand why you *don't* want to pock with a MacClintock."

Thousands of years before the coming of the race called Man, the mountain had been fire. Molten rock and ash spewed from the bosom of the world, laying down interleaving layers of each as the mountain grew higher and higher. Side openings occurred, and the red rock flowed from them like a steaming avalanche, occasionally breaking loose whole sides of the mountain in a semiliquid, fiery hot gel called pyroclastic flow.

Eventually, the fierce nuclear fire that was at the core of the local hotspot passed on, and the mountains began to cool. Water brought its beneficence of cooling to the steaming mountain, scouring its flanks and bringing growth where there had been molten rock. In time, the black, smoking wasteland became a fertile slope of trees and flowers.

Time passed, and the sun of the planet called Marduk flickered. For a time that was short for a sun, or a planet, the sun became cooler. To the sun itself, the effect was barely noticeable. But on the sole life-hugging planet that orbited it, the effect was devastating.

The rains stopped. Where there had been steaming jungles, there were sunbaked plains. Ice came. Where there had been liquid-drenched mountains, the water fell as snow and compressed, and compacted, and stayed and stayed, until it became mountains—walls of glacial ice.

Species died, and the nascent civilizations of the higher latitudes fell. Survivors huddled around hot springs while the white walls drew ever closer.

Along the side of the mountain, the white ice grew and grew. The hot spots to one side kept a continual melt in place, and the runoff water—dammed up behind the terminal moraine of the glacier—filled the valley from end to end. Regular floods laid down layers of lighter and darker materials on the valley floor, improving the already excellent soil. The glacier brought with it loess, the fine dust that was left when ice crushed its enemy rock. The glacier also brought massive boulders that it laid down in complex, swirling patterns that later residents would often use as roadbeds and quarry for building stone. And everywhere, it crushed the sides of the valley, hammering at the walls of the mountain and tearing at its stone and ash foundations.

Finally, in a short time for a star, the sun restarted

and turned its thermostat all the way back to high. The rains came. Jungles regrew. And the ice . . . melted.

It started slowly, with more floods each spring than there'd been the spring before. Then the glacier started to break up, and the terminal moraine, the dam at the head of the valley, became intermingled with chunks and blocks of the ice. For a time, the dam grew higher, as the floods carried the silt and debris of four thousand years of glaciation to it. But finally, inevitably, the dam at the head of the valley burst. First came a trickle, then a flood, then a cascade, and finally, a veritable tsunami of water, crashing down the gorge in a flash flood to end all flash floods. It scoured the gorge wider than a hundred thousand years of lesser floods. It wiped out the small village that had been recently founded at the base of the gorge. And it drained the Vale of the Shin, leaving a fertile pastureland that simply begged for colonization.

And the mountain slept.

Erkum Pol wielded the machete like a machine, hacking away at the undergrowth while holding on to the rope to prevent himself from sliding back down the slope. It was also wrapped around his waist; it was a very steep slope.

" 'Set a few charges,' he said," Julian muttered as he slid sideways and stopped himself by grabbing a tree. Unfortunately, its bark was well provided with long spines, one of which jammed itself into his hand. "Aarrrgh! 'Blow up the side of the mountain,' he said. 'No problem,' he said."

"We have the explosives," Fain said, sliding down the rope beside him. "We have the 'shaped charges.' What's the difficulty?"

"Maybe emplacing them on a sixty-degree slope? We're going to have to dig out pits for the charges and hold them down with pins hammered into the rock. They have to have a bit of something holding them down. Usually, it's just the charge's case and the weight of the material, but in this case, we're going to have to anchor the cases, since they're pointing sideways. And I'm not sure any weight of cataclysmite is going to be enough to cut *out* from the bores."

"A trench," Roger said, coming hand-over-hand along the slope through the undergrowth. "We'll dig a shallow trench and fire them directly down. From this height, we should get plenty enough material to seal the river."

"We can do that," Fain said. "Like starting a new quarry."

"Exactly. In fact, if you can scratch out a trench in the loam, we can put in a line of det-cord which will practically make it for us."

"That will give away our position, Sir," Julian pointed out. The top of the Krath citadel was vaguely visible from their position, or, its northern bastion was, at least.

"They'll spot us up here before long anyway," Roger pointed out in return. "And they'll definitely notice when we blow the shaped charges."

The latter were waiting up the slope on the narrow track a local guide had "found" over the mountain. It was obvious that despite the best efforts of both the Gastan and the local Krath to restrict all commerce between them to Trade Town, and thereby tax it, plenty of smugglers moved through the hills around it.

"Captain Fain, put out some security teams and let's get to work," Roger said.

"Yes, Your Highness. It will be like old home week."

"What in the Fire do they think they're doing up there?" Lorak Tral wondered aloud.

The Sere's commander had envisioned the entire plan in a single instant when word of the High Priest's death reached him. For too long, the Shin, and the Scourge which pursued them, had been a thorn in the side of the Krath. But with the High Priest's death at the hands of humans (humans presumably allied with the Shin, judging from their actions), the stage had been set at last for the elimination of the Scourge. For two generations, the Scourge—most of them little more than jumped up Shadem and Shin themselves—had been on the upsurge. If they were permitted to continue to grow, the

Krath would fall under the sway of slave-raiders. Better to use this opportunity to cut their legs off. By crushing Mudh Hemh, the Sere would show its importance to the council and the utility of the Scourge would be cut in half.

And it didn't hurt that it would leave *him* as High Priest.

"Perhaps they're planning to cut the supply line," Vos Ton said. The fortress' commander rubbed his horns nervously. "Even a slight stoppage in resupply will make our position difficult. I could wish you'd brought fewer troops."

Tral gazed up at the position and shook his head.

"Even with their rifles, they'll have a hard time stopping us from using the road. And they cannot stop us from taking Mudh Hemh."

"If we ever do," Ton groused. "Nopet Nujam is not a simple proposition. I warned you of that when you came up with this scheme."

"It's important to show that no one can simply walk in and kill our High Priest," Tral replied. "We must show them the error of their ways."

"Each day we laboriously besiege them gives them another day to try something new," Ton pointed out. "That's all I'm saying."

"No matter what they do, they are too few to truly affect us," the Sere replied. "Unless you think they can call the God of Fire down upon us?"

"No," Vos Ton replied, looking up at the figures, mostly hidden by trees. Even if they rolled rocks down, they wouldn't fall on his castle. "No, but I wonder what they *are* going to call down on us."

A moment later, a tremendous boom bellowed down the mountainside. A towering cloud of dust and smoke reared up, and then, as quickly as it had arisen, it rained down rocks and severed trees. They bounced and tumbled, battering downwards, and although most were captured by the trees below the cut, many made it all the way to the base, leapt off the last ledge, arced across the road, and ended up in the Shin River.

The roadbed at the narrows was cut into a shallow natural ledge that wended its way about ten meters above the river, higher than almost any reported flood. The few rocks and trees that made it to the river raised the water slightly, but the increase was only a fraction of the difference between its normal surface and the roadway.

"Are they trying to block the road?" Ton asked in a puzzled voice. "Or raise the river to block it?"

"Whichever it is, if they get enough into the river to become a problem, we'll send out a working party," Tral replied. Then he grunted in laughter. "Look," he added as the deep, rushing water broke up the shallow dam and carried it away. "The river does our work for us."

"Perhaps," the fortress commander agreed dubiously. "But I wish we had some reports from our spies. I would like to know what their conference was about. I want to know what they think they're doing up there."

"Hmmm . . ." Tral said. "We're almost ready for the great attack. We can move it up by a few hours; then, whatever it is, we'll have taken their fortress before they're able to use it."

"What about the Scourge force?"

"They were to attack as we did," the Sere leader said. "And, really, they were never to be anything more than a distraction. Whatever happens, it will be the Sere that breaks the back of Mudh Hemh for all time. It is *that* which will be remembered."

"From your mouth to the Fire God's ears," the fortress commander said.

"You know," Roger said, stepping into the narrow trench, "I bet they really are wondering what we're doing up here."

"Well, in about six more hours, it won't matter what they think," Despreaux said. She'd gotten out of her force cast that very morning, and she waved her newly liberated arm enthusiastically, pointing to spots along the trench even as she elbowed Roger out of the way with the other arm. "Here, here, here . . ."

"Hmmm," the prince murmured. After a moment's

thought, he threw his rifle to his shoulder and zoomed up the gain on the telescopic sight. "Interesting."

"What?" Julian asked. His rifle had no scope at all.

"Just . . . some of the groups down there," Roger muttered. He walked to the end of the trench, where a tree had been uprooted, sat down behind it, and laid the rifle across the trunk. "Most of them are just scurrying around. But there's a couple of groups that are clearly watching us. And one of them looks like a batch of commanders . . ."

"We discussed this, Your Highness," Julian said repressively. "We're not supposed to shoot."

"I know," Roger sighed. "But I'm still pissed at them over the thing in Kirsti."

"Let me worry about that," Despreaux said. "And the demo. We've only got about fifteen minutes until the shaped charges are in place; you need to be heading for the crest."

Roger gathered up his rifle and stood with manifest regret.

"I think one of them is that senior war leader, Lorak Tral. One shot wouldn't hurt anything, would it?" he sounded so much like a little boy trying to wheedle a special treat out of his tutor that Julian smiled. But the sergeant also shook his head firmly.

"Go with the plan, Your Highness. You promised."

"Okay, okay." Roger looked up the hill and grimaced. "That's a long damned climb."

"And when you get there, you might as well keep going," Despreaux said. "I'll be pouring the slurry fifteen minutes after the shot. By the time you climb back down here, it'll be time to retreat, and if you're in my way then, I'll leave boot prints all over you. I, for one, don't intend to be on the mountain *at all* when we shoot this one."

"I get the point," Roger sighed. "And you're to come directly to Mudh Hemh, understand? You're in no condition to be in Nopet if they assault."

"I will," she said with a smile. "Now get going, Your Highness."

✧   ✧   ✧

Roger slid off the *civan* and gave Pahner a casual salute.

"It's hard to consider a group that can build something like this 'barbarians,' " he said, waving at the massive walls above them. The back gates to Nopet Nujam weren't as large as the front gates, but their protective towers and bastions still made an imposing edifice.

"Local craftsmen, sure," Pahner said. "But it was Krath engineering. Your Highness, you're not supposed to be here."

"Anything going on?" Roger asked.

"No," the captain said stolidly. "The Krath got some small forces up on the mountain after you left, but the Diasprans beat them off. No injuries on our side. The emplacement team is on the way back, and the security team has retired to the back of the mountain. We're going to fire the shot anytime now, and it would really please me an immense amount to have you back in Mudh Hemh when that happens."

"I've got the picture," Roger laughed. Then he sobered. "Remember to send Despreaux back, as well. With that bum arm, she's not in shape for combat ops yet."

"Nor will she be even after the cast comes off," Pahner observed, looking him straight in the eye. "As I believe you're aware."

"When did you find out?" Roger asked after a long moment of silence. "I . . . She told me the other night."

"Oh, I started to suspect back around Sindi," Pahner said. "It was to be anticipated in most of the Marines— that's one of the reasons I've been trying to shift them to leadership positions, rather than shooting. Despreaux's not the only one. About the only squad I have full confidence in any more is the Third; Julian's maniacs are relentless."

"That . . . makes things difficult," the prince said quietly. "What about me? Or the Mardukans?"

"I think you're one of those guys who doesn't really peak, Your Highness." Pahner shook his head. "Dobrescu's been pointing out your vitals to me lately. Your heart-beat and respiration hardly changed the whole time you were in the Temple; that's unusual, in case you hadn't been aware of it."

"Oh, I'm getting that feeling," Roger said. "But what are we going to do at the spaceport?"

"If we can get this one licked, I think the rest will be a walkover," Pahner told him. "From Jin's data, the way Mountmarch has compromised his own security should make taking the port itself easy. And taking an arriving ship with modern equipment, which just happens to be stockpiled at the port where we can get at it, shouldn't be too hard. If we can just deal with this little problem. Which, I might add, brings us back to you. Specifically, to your presence at this particular locus of space-time."

"Okay, already," the prince said, pulling himself back onto the *civan* and kicking it on the snout as it turned to take a piece out of his leg. "I'm sure we'll muddle through somehow. See you after the surrender."

"Yep," Pahner agreed, with a waved salute as casual as Roger's own. He waited until the prince and his Mardukan guards were well down the road before he shook his head.

"Whose, Your Highness?" He murmured then. "Whose?"

Roger tapped on the door and entered at the grunted reply.

He'd returned to Mudh Hemh accompanied by a bare minimum security detail, but when he reached the town and found only two guards on the entire front wall, he'd realized the extent to which it had been stripped of defenders to reinforce Nopet Nujam. So he left his three Diasprans at the gatehouse to reinforce the Shin guards, and he was accompanied only by two Vashin. Those he left outside as he entered the dwelling the Gastan had turned over to Cord.

The interior was dark, but high for a human. Stone benches along two of the sides were covered in pillows, and the back side of the chamber was occupied by a cooking hearth and a large, low bath.

Cord was dangling his feet in the latter with his back to the door, while Pedi and the two serfs they'd liberated from the Lemmar rubbed his back.

"It looks like you've fallen into a good pond, Old Frog," Roger observed with a chuckle.

"I'm glad you've returned safely," the shaman said, and Roger carefully hid his concern as Cord clambered laboriously to his feet. Officially, his wound was well on its way to healing, but the old warrior wasn't snapping back the way he had after he'd been wounded at Voitan. Indeed, Roger was beginning to worry, very privately, that his *asi* might *never* snap back. Not all the way, at least.

"And I'm ashamed of my weakness," Cord went on, almost as if he'd read Roger's thoughts. "An *asi* should have been at your side."

"I have plenty of bodyguards," Roger remarked. "I have far fewer counselors I trust. Although, come to think of it, I'm running low on bodyguards, as well. It doesn't really matter, though. You need to get healed up; worry about the rest later."

"So why are you here?" Cord asked, limping over to one of the benches.

"Despreaux's on her way here from Nopet, which means they must be about to put off the shots. It should be spectacular, even from here. I thought you'd like to watch."

"Oh, that *would* be fun to watch," Pedi said. "You're taking off the whole face of Karcrag, yes?"

"Pedi should not be exerting herself," Cord said, lying back on the bench. "We will stay here."

"*Pedi* should not be exerting herself?" Roger repeated. "What in hell does that mean?"

"Nothing," Pedi answered angrily. "Nothing that he has any right to make a decision about."

"You are my *benan*," Cord said coldly. "It is my responsibility to ensure your welfare as it is yours to ensure my safety."

"*Welfare*, perhaps" she spat back. "But not *safety*. I will be fine, thank you!"

"Whoa," Roger said. He glanced at the other two

former slaves, who were huddled in the corner, clearly unhappy about the argument. "I don't want to cross this whole planet just to die in a domestic disturbance. Cord, you need to get out in the fresh air . . . well, as fresh as it gets around here. We'll head up to the walls, watch the shot, and come back. And while we're walking, both of you can be thinking about what you want to tell me about what's going on."

"It is none of your responsibility, Prince Roger," Cord said.

"As you've pointed out to me before, Old Frog, I'm responsible for the success or failure of everything in this band. And we *will* have that talk. After we watch the shots."

"They're getting nervous," Pahner said. The Krath had sent another group up the mountain, using a different path from the one their own people had used. Since the security team had pulled back, it was just as well that the Krath would be too late arriving. They'd also pulled most of their forces out of the tent city, however, and seemed to be preparing for a large-scale assault.

"Yes," the Gastan said silkily. "Isn't it lovely?"

"You have your daughter's approach to handling enemies," Pahner said with a laugh.

"Fortunately, I don't have her approach to handling friends," the Shin king replied in a tone which was so suddenly exasperated that Pahner looked at him in genuine surprise.

"And I thought we were welcome," he said. "Or is there something I'm missing?"

"No, you're welcome, even chased by an army," the Gastan said. "It should be obvious to your Light O'Casey that this war has permitted me to consolidate my power as no Gastan has in three decades. And your support has been invaluable in that. But I could wish that my daughter had made better personal choices."

"Okay, now you've really got me confused," Pahner said as the Krath began filing into the assault trenches.

The Gastan looked down at him and made a gesture of confused resignation.

"I wish that I understood your human body language better. Are you jesting? Or do you really not see the signs?"

"Signs of what?" Pahner asked. In the distance, the Krath assembly horns began to sound as the entire host started to move forward. The troops in the assault trenches would seek to pin the defenders in order to clear the way for the mass assault of the walls.

"You really don't see them, do you?" the Gastan said. Pahner gazed back up at the Shin's ruler and shook his head.

"She's pregnant," the Gastan said as the explosives on the hillside detonated and the mountain came apart.

By luck, more than knowledge, the amount and spacing of the explosives was almost perfect—not too hard, and not too soft. At first, the only sign of the impending disaster was a series of muffled thuds and a dust-jet mushroom shape above each of the boreholes. Despreaux had set them to detonate sequentially, instead of simultaneously, and the series went off like a very large machine gun as the sixteen charges exploded in under three seconds.

For a moment afterwards, there was stillness, and Pahner feared that all the planning had been for nothing. Then, slowly, the face of the mountain started to slide. The giant faux-teak trees were the first to show the movement, swaying back and forth as if tossed by a heavy wind before they began to slide. Then dust began to rise, and finally the whole mass began sliding towards the valley floor to impact in a gigantic crash that was felt as far away as Mudh Hemh.

At which point, the blocked waters started looking for an outlet. And looking and looking . . . and rising and rising.

"Cool," Roger said, gazing at the neat divot that had been taken out of the side of the mountain. He and

Despreaux had moved to the wall of the Shin town, and now they stood watching the battle from the safety of the southern parapet.

The town's walls weren't very much compared to the mighty ramparts of Nopet Nujam. In fact, they were simply double wooden palisades with a stamped earth fill, and the works flanking the gates were open on top, with small guard rooms underneath. The walls of the town were designed to stop the occasional Scourge or hostile Shin raiding party, not to beat off the sort of serious attack that was directed at Nopet Nujam. And for the former purpose, they had worked just fine. They also made a dandy viewing platform.

From a distance, it looked as if some giant had taken an ice cream spoon and scooped out a serving of basalt and ash. The massive Krath fortress obscured anything but the column of dust rising into the air behind it, but it was clear that most of what they'd intended to do had worked.

"Now to see if it blocks the water," Despreaux said.

"You did good, Nimashet," he replied, slipping his arm around her waist.

"We'll see."

"Pessimist," he chuckled.

"I always keep in mind what can go wrong."

CHAPTER TWENTY-SEVEN

"This isn't going well," Pahner said.

"Tell me something I don't know!" the Gastan yelled back as he stuck one of the short Shin swords through a spear slit and drew it back red.

The Krath had started a full-court press, and unless something changed drastically very soon, it was going to work. The assault groups had come hollering out of the trenches, piling up bodies on the already blood-soaked ground. They'd barely made it to the walls before dying, but in doing so, they'd absorbed enough of the defenders' fire to permit the main Krath force to come in behind them in successive waves. The frenzied assault had concentrated on the main gates and the walls to either side, and the third wave had managed to smash the Shin defenders on the battlements and take three sections.

The humans' contribution had mostly been to remove the leadership, and they'd done a good job. Krath companies that had made it to the wall with any officers still on their feet were rare, but even that hadn't stopped the assault. The pressure from behind each wave had driven even the most cowardly into the defenses and up the walls. Now the gates' defenders were down to holding the gate-flanking bastions and doing their best to keep any battering rams away.

"Poertena, what do you have on your side?" the captain called.

"Krat', Krat', and more Krat', Sir," the Pinopan called back even as he took aim and fired through a slit. "T'e other bastion is holding out, though."

"Captain!" Beckley shouted from one of the front slits. "You can see water coming up out of the river! On this side of the fortress!"

"Where?" the captain demanded as he stepped across to a slit beside Beckley and zoomed up the magnification on his helmet. "Never mind." After a moment, he chuckled. "Now if we can only point it out to *them*."

"Look behind you, you stupid bastards!" the Gastan yelled out his slit. "The river rises! *The river fights for the Shin!*"

"Get it unplugged!" Tral shouted. "Break that dam! *Now!*"

"How?" the fortress commander asked. He'd already considered the problem, and he was preparing rafts loaded with gunpowder. He had his doubts about their efficacy, yet they were the only possibility he saw. Unfortunately, even if they had any chance of success of all, they would have to be guided into place, and in another hour—less— the water would be up over the work area. It was rising faster than the boatbuilders could finish their craft.

"I don't know!" the Sere commander snarled. "Figure it out!" He glared at the distant Shin fortress and waved both false-hands in a gesture of furious anger. "We have forces on the wall. All they have to do is take Nujam and we can move in there. That's *all* they have to do!"

"Tallow!" the Gastan ordered, never looking away from the slit. "*Look behind you! The river rises!*" he bellowed as the boiling fat was poured onto the Krath troops swarming atop the battlements outside the bastion. "*Go cool off there!*"

"They are," Pahner panted over the rising chorus of screams that greeted the splashing fat. The Marine had just returned to the slit beside the Shin king after dealing

with another threat. A Krath assault group had forced
the bastion's lower doors, and it had been hot work stopping them and then throwing up a barricade. The long
climb back to the top hadn't done anything for his
breathing, but he could clearly see the enemy army
starting to stream from the walls. It was unraveling from
the rear, where the remaining forces could see the river
rising to overwhelm all their worldly goods. But those
on the walls could see it as well, and they were scrambling down faster than they had come up. Already the
water was halfway into the tent city; by the time those
on the walls reached it, the entire area would be
underwater.

"All we do now is wait for them to come to the
inevitable conclusion," Pahner continued. "And conserve
our own people in the meantime."

"That's it." Roger dialed back the magnification of his
helmet. "There are no Krath on the walls. It's all over
but the negotiating."

"That should be complicated enough to go on with."
Despreaux shook her head. "That army is going to come
apart when it realizes its predicament."

"I'm sure the captain can handle it," Roger replied, and
turned as Cord and Pedi climbed up into the small,
wooden bastion, followed by the two freed serfs.

"You sat this one out," Cord observed with a grunt.
"Good."

"Are you up to this, Cord?" Roger asked. The shaman
still had a pronounced limp and hunched to one side
when he moved, and Roger didn't much care for the
sound of his breathing.

"The healer Dobrescu tells me I need to start to move
around," Cord replied. "I am moving around. The ladder, I admit, was unpleasant."

"Old fool," Pedi muttered under her breath.

"And you're looking better, as well, Pedi," Roger noted.
The Shin female's step had a spring that he hadn't seen
in quite some time.

"Thank you, Your Highness," Pedi replied. "It's amazing

what a little sleep and some *wasen* can do for a female's outlook."

Despreaux snorted and shook her head.

"I could never get into the whole cosmetics thing. I'm totally challenged that way."

"It's like any other weapon or armor," Pedi said with a gesture of humor. "You must practice, practice, practice."

"Oh, like sex," Despreaux observed brightly, then grinned at Roger's stifled gasp.

"That is . . . different with us," Pedi said somewhat primly. "We do not engage in it as . . . entertainment."

"Too bad." Despreaux grinned again. "You don't know what you're missing."

"Well, isn't it a nice day out?" Roger waved to the north, where a darker patch of clouds indicated approaching rain. "Volcanoes smoking, smell of sulfur on the wind, Krath army surrendering . . ."

"They've surrendered?" Pedi demanded excitedly.

"We haven't received a message yet," Roger admitted. "But they're off the walls. The war appears to be over."

"I look forward to slaughtering *them* for a change," the Shin female said darkly.

"Ah, we were intending to offer them terms," Roger pointed out. "I think it would be . . . difficult to kill them *all*. And we can probably get more for them if they're alive."

"You humans are so silly that way." Pedi's gesture bordered on contempt. "I say chop off all their heads and float the bodies down the river. They'll get the message that way."

"Well, there are alternatives," Roger said. "We could simply blind and castrate them all and then have them walk back. All except one in twenty or so that we can leave with one eye to lead the rest. Or we could fire them out of cannon; you could load them all the way to the hips in the bombards. Or we could lay planks over them, then put tables and chairs on top of the planks, sit down, and eat our dinner while they were all crushed to death. Or, best of all, we could go retake the spaceport, come back with assault shuttles, and drop jellied fuel weapons on them. They want fire, we'll give them fire."

"Roger," Despreaux said.

"Those would do," Pedi agreed. "But I can tell you're joking."

"The point is that humans quit doing that sort of thing because we're too damned good at it," Roger said. "We can do it efficiently or baroquely, using a million different methods, culled from our entire history. I doubt that Mardukans can exceed our inventiveness, although they might equal it. But taking that route never gets you anywhere; you get trapped in an eternal round of massacres and counter massacres. It's only after you break the cycle and create strong groups—nations—that enforce the laws and demand some sort of international standard of acceptable behavior, that things start to improve."

"Fine, but we're here. And it's now," the Shin protested. "And when you humans leave, the Krath will still be there. And their soldiers will still be there, and the Scourge will still be there."

"All part of the negotiations," Roger replied. "They've lost their field army. If they don't get it back, they're dead meat for the other satraps. We'll strip them of their treasure, make them pay tribute, and have them sign binding treaties against slave-raiding. We won't take the tribute to 'punish' them, but to weaken them so that they're not death threats to you. The conditions might hold, and they might not. But humans who are friendly to the *Shin* will also be in control of the spaceport, Pedi. If the Krath get out of hand, we *can* send an assault shuttle. And we will."

"What about the Scourge?" Slee asked.

"What about them?" It was the first time Roger had heard one of the released serfs ask a question, so it caught him a bit off guard.

"I don't care about the Sere, My Lord," the serf replied. "But it's the Scourge that has burned our homes and taken our children. Do they go free?"

"I doubt we'll be able to specifically target them," Roger said, after a moment. "But they'll be out of a job."

"Which means they'll go back to being bandits," Pedi said. "So be it. The Shin are better bandits than the Scourge any day."

"Not exactly something that I'd aspire to," Roger sighed. "But if that's what floats your boat."

"Your Light!" the sole Shin guard called. "There's a message from the north tower. A group has been spotted on the edge of the Fire Lands!"

"How large?" Pedi asked. She moved to the bastion's parapet and craned her neck, trying to get a glimpse beyond the northern defenses of the town.

"I don't know," the guard replied. "The message was simply 'a group.' " He pointed to the northern bastion, where a red flag with a complex design had been raised.

"Time to switch positions, people," Roger said. He turned and headed for the ladder. "I don't like this timing."

"Shit." Roger dialed back the magnification on his helmet. "Unless I'm much mistaken, that's a Scourge raiding party. How the hell did they get around our backside that way?"

"We knew that the Scourge had found a way through the Fire Lands," Pedi told him almost absently, straining her own eyes as she stared out over the wall. "We should have remembered that. *I* should have remembered, since it was how I came to be in their hands before the Lemmar captured me. But all of their captives were hooded on the way through the lava fields, so I was unable to tell Father where their route lies." She snorted bitterly. "It would seem they have chosen to use it again."

"Roger, we're . . . way outnumbered." Despreaux put in. She'd been doing her own count, and she didn't like her total. "We've got about fifteen guards in the town, and there are over a hundred Krath."

"It's not good," Pedi agreed. "But it's not quite as bad as it seems, either. Many of the clan leaders brought their families, and many of them are trained as I am. And we have the walls. I will go organize them, get them up here. Can you send a message to Nopet Nujam?"

"I can," Roger said. "But it's an hour's ride from there. Even if they sent the Vashin *now,* they'd be here too late. Get your battle-ladies. I'm going to find my armor."

"What are you going to do, Roger?" Despreaux asked nervously.

"Try to politely dissuade them," the prince replied.

"Sor Teb, as I live and breathe."

"Good afternoon, Prince Roger Ramius MacClintock," the head of the Scourge replied, walking up until he was within arm's length.

The Scourge raiding party had stopped and deployed just out of dart range from the walls. There were perhaps a hundred and fifty of them—a mixture of Krath and Shadem raiders. They were lightly armed and armored, but given what they were up against, that probably wouldn't matter.

Except for Roger.

The prince had donned his battle armor and packed along a heavy bead cannon. They hadn't gotten much in the way of ammunition from the spaceport yet, because they'd used most of their carriage for the explosives required to demolish the mountain. But they'd gotten a few rounds for the bead cannons, and his magazine was loaded first with shot rounds, then with solid. If he opened fire, he was going to cover the field in bits and pieces of Krath and Shadem.

"Well, if you know who I am, you ought to know that I don't bluff or negotiate very well," Roger told Teb calmly, and felt a trickle of amusement as the Scourge commander stiffened ever so slightly. Obviously, the Mardukan had hoped that the shock of knowing he'd been identified would throw Roger at least a little off stride.

"You're here on a fool's errand, Sor Teb," the prince continued. "The Sere have been stopped butt cold, and our reinforcements will be here in no time at all. Your army's trapped between our walls and a rising river, and it's surrendering *en masse*. Any captives you take will be returned, or you won't get your field army back. And if you don't turn around right now, as part of the negotiations we'll add your head to our demands."

"Very brave, Your Highness," the Scourge said with a grunting laugh. "But there are three things you're unaware of. First, given the situation that you and your people created in Kirsti, my head isn't worth spit in the Fire, anyway. Second, we're not here to take captives; we're here to kill everyone we can and loot the town to the ground, then return to the Shadem. I'm not *going* back to the Krath."

"Well, in that case my last point is that if you don't turn around, I'm going to turn you into paste," Roger said, hefting the bead gun. "I can kill at least half of you before you can make it to the walls. And then I can track down the rest and tear your arms out of their sockets. Oh, and you can't count—that was only two points."

"But I can, Your Highness." The Krath brought his hand around. "My third point is that I have a surprise for you."

Roger had never actually seen an example of the device in the Scourge commander's left true-hand—not in the flesh, as it were. But he recognized it instantly. It was no larger than an old, prespace flashlight, and the principal upon which it worked was almost as ancient as its appearance. Very few things could actually penetrate ChromSten armor, but there were ways around that. Essentially, Sor Teb's "surprise" was a last-ditch, contact-range weapon specifically designed to knock out battle armor or lightly armored combat vehicles. Known as a "one-shot," it consisted of a superconductor capacitor, a powerful miniaturized tractor beam, and a hundred-gram charge of plasticized cataclysmite in a ChromSten-lined channel.

If a one-shot could be brought into physical contact with its target and activated, the capacitor-powered tractor locked it there like an immovable limpet. Then the cataclysmite was driven at high speed down the weapon's hollow shaft in a wad with the consistency of modeling clay. When it hit the armor's outer surface, it spread over it, then detonated. The contact explosion couldn't blow a hole *through* the ChromSten . . . but it could transmit a shock wave through it, and the inner surface of the armor wasn't made of ChromSten. It was made of plasteel, far tougher and stronger than any prespace alloy, but far less damage resistant than ChromSten. It supported the ChromSten matrix, on one side, and the host of biofeedback monitors and servo activators which lined every square millimeter of the armor's insides, on the other. And the detonation of that much cataclysmite was perfectly adequate to blow a "scab" of plasteel no more than a centimeter or so across off the armor's inner backing.

With more than sufficient power to blast the scab right through whoever was wearing the armor it came from.

It was, in many ways, a suicide weapon. The maximum range at which the tractor could be activated with any chance of a successful lock-on was no more than five or six meters, and the odds against a successful attack rose sharply as the range rose. That meant that just getting it close enough to hurt someone in powered armor was problematical, but there were more than enough other drawbacks to it.

The one-shot's grip was specifically designed to contain the late cataclysmite's explosion, but it often failed. And even if it didn't, if the tractor failed to lock tightly to the target, back blast from the face of the target's armor would normally kill any unarmored human in the vicinity. Not to mention the fact that when the tractor lock *completely* failed, the one-shot became an old-fashioned chemical-fueled rocket with all the thrust it would ever need to blast right through a human body, or at least rip off the odd hand or arm. But when it worked, it let someone without armor take out an armored opponent.

Sor Teb had proven how fast he was in Kirsti. Whether or not he was actually faster than Roger was no doubt

an interesting point, but not really relevant at the
moment. He had the advantage of surprise, and unlike
him, Roger was trying to do two things at once. He'd
already begun to raise the bead cannon when he recognized the one-shot, and his own weapon's movement
distracted him ever so slightly as the Mardukan brought
the one-shot flashing towards him. Even if it hadn't, the
physics were against him.

CHAPTER TWENTY-EIGHT

"*Fuck!*" Despreaux threw her rifle to her shoulder. "*ROGER!*"

She tried to find Sor Teb, but as soon as he'd fired, the entire Scourge party had started sprinting for the walls. And Teb was no fool. He'd disappeared into the mass, vanishing beyond her ability to pick him out of it. So she chose one at random in frustration and put a round through his chest.

"*Modderpockers!*"

"What happened?" Cord shouted. "What happened?!"

All he'd been able to see was that there'd been a bright flash, and that Roger was on the ground. His armor appeared intact from this distance, but he wasn't moving.

"One-shot!" she snarled. "It's a short range anti-armor weapon. No good above a few meters' range, and a bitch to use, but if you hit, it can take out armor." She scanned the oncoming Scourge, this time looking for someone who seemed to be in charge. She found someone who was waving, which was good enough for her, and punched out another round. Her target went down and disappeared under the charging feet of his fellows, and she took an instant to fix her bayonet as the attackers reached the palisade.

"Is he alive?" Cord demanded, then shook his head and raised his spear. "We should have gone to negotiate, not him!"

"Too late for that," Despreaux shot back, and lunged across the palisade. The Shadem had leapt onto the shoulders of two other Scourge, but he tumbled backwards as the half-meter of steel punched through his throat. She spun in place as another head came over the wall. This one let go and grasped at his face as her slash opened it up from side to side, but it was the butt-stroke that got rid of his ugly mug.

She worked the bolt and fired from the hip, blowing a third raider back from the top of the palisade.

"Too late for that," she repeated, "but if he lives, I'll kill him!"

"Worry about whether or not we'll be here *to* kill him," Pedi advised as she took off the head of a Shadem who'd been pinned against the inner face of the parapet by Dogzard. Cord might not be able to move with his wonted speed and power, but at least he was wise enough to admit it to himself, and he moved behind his *benan,* covering her back without getting into her way.

"Good point," the Marine muttered, as she sought out a target further down the wall. "Damned if we're not going to have to kill them all."

"I'd heard you were having problems with that," Cord said through a grunt of self-inflicted pain as he drove his spear into the throat of a veiled Shadem who'd tried to sneak around Pedi's flank.

"I just got over it!"

"Mudh Hemh is under attack," the Gastan told Pahner evenly.

The two commanders had moved to the battlements to observe events. For a time, the battlefield had been absolute chaos as the Krath army mutinied *en masse.* Now its commanders were restoring some order, and a formal parley had started. The initial negotiations had been unspoken; groups that were armed and came within weapons' distance of the walls were engaged. Those who threw down their arms were allowed to huddle near the walls, still at a distance, but well away from the rising floodwaters.

Other groups, more foolhardy or desperate to retrieve their belongings, had been caught by the rising water. A few of them huddled on scattered outcrops of higher ground, but most had been swept away by the flood. The total who'd been lost in that fashion was small, but it had been intensely demoralizing, and it was after the first groups disappeared into the hungry waters that the Krath had actively started to surrender.

With the first recognized heralds on their way, and the Krath throwing down their arms, it seemed the war was over. Before the walls of Nopet Nujam, at least.

"Talk about snatching victory," Pahner said, looking to the rear. The red distress flags above the town were evident . . . as were the struggling figures on the walls. "Damn it."

"We can't get word to them to surrender," the Gastan said. "That will take too long."

"Roger will be fine," Pahner replied. "Despreaux will make him put on his armor, and nothing the Krath have will get through that. But the rest . . ."

He leaned over the edge of the battlements and looked around until he spotted a human.

"Turner! Find Rastar. Tell him to take *all* the Vashin to Mudh Hemh; it's under attack! Spread the word!"

"This is most unpleasant." The Gastan lowered his binoculars. "They're burning my town. If they think this is going to improve negotiations, they are sorely mistaken."

"Worry about that after we find out who's alive and who's dead," Pahner muttered.

"Erraah!" Despreaux butt-stroked the Krath so hard in the face that it smashed her rifle, but it didn't really matter. She was flat out of ammo . . . and just about out of time.

"Son of a *vern!*" Pedi yelled as she blocked a strike from a Shadem staff. She drove forward in a windmill of steel that ended in a kick which sent the Shadem stumbling back over the edge of the wall. His intestines slithered after him.

"*Pedi!*" Despreaux gasped, and threw her broken rifle past the Shin like a spear.

Sor Teb blocked the missile with one of his swords and snarled.

"I'm going to enjoy sending you to the Fire, you Shin witch!" the Scourge commander told the Gastan's daughter. He was just about the last Krath on the battlements. But, then again, they were pretty much alone, as well.

"You'll have to manage it first," Pedi said, and darted forward.

From Despreaux's perspective, the engagement was nothing but a vortex of steel. The sound of the swords grating on each other sounded like so many sharpening steels in action, and neither combatant was paying attention to any of the other battles going on around them. They were in a focused, private world of steel and fury, and as Despreaux watched the deadly, flashing blades, she realized to her amazement that Pedi's reflexes were just as extraordinary as Roger's or Sor Teb's.

They broke apart for moment, as if by mutual consent, just as Cord limped up to them, and the shaman shook his head.

"Wrist! Keep your wrist straight!"

"Thanks," Pedi panted. "I'll keep that in mind."

"No, I was talking to him," Cord said. "His technique is awful. *Your* wrist is perfect, darling."

"Darling?" Pedi looked over her shoulder at him.

"I'm sorry," he said. "It just slipped out."

"I'm going to feed you, your boyfriend, *and* your get to the Fire," the Scourge panted.

"You talk big," Pedi replied, focusing once more on the task at hand. "We'll see who's going to the Fire today."

"Yes, we will."

Sor Teb gestured with his left false-hand. Pedi's eyes flicked towards it for just an instant, and that was when his *right* false-hand moved. It threw a handful of dust into her face, and he drove forward right behind.

Pedi flung up a false-arm. She managed to stop most of the powder, but some of it still took her in the eyes and mouth, and she buckled as instantaneous pain and nausea ripped through her. But she still managed to drop to one knee, and she drove upward with both swords as the Scourge's downward cut sliced into her shoulder.

Sor Teb looked at the two swords buried to their quillons in his stomach and coughed out a gush of blood.

"No," he muttered, raising his off-hand sword.

Cord raised his spear, but before he could drive it forward, Dogzard—who'd had enough of this stupid single-combat and fairness stuff—crashed into the dying Krath's chest and settled matters by ripping out his throat.

Despreaux darted forward and caught Pedi as blood from her shoulder poured out.

"Damn it, why is Dobrescu *never* around when you need him?" she demanded of the universe.

"Pedi?" Cord went to his knees beside her, ripping at his hated clothing until he tore off a strip and wadded it into an impromptu bandage. "Pedi, don't go away from me."

"I . . ." She shuddered. "It hurts."

"The healer Dobrescu will be here soon," Cord said. "He's a miracle worker—look at me. Just hold on. Don't . . . don't leave me. I don't want to lose you, too."

"You won't . . . darling," she grimaced a smile. "I have too much to live for. You . . . and your children."

"Mine?" he repeated, almost absently. Then grabbed his horns in frustration. *"Mine?* How?"

"I . . . I'm sorry," she said with a sigh. "You were so hurt, so needing. You came into your season while you were injured. I couldn't stand to watch you in such agony, and you were calling for your . . . for your wife. I— Ahhh!" She panted in pain. "I love you. . . ."

"Look, this is touching and everything, but are you going to let me work on her shoulder, or not?" Dobrescu demanded.

"What?" Cord looked up as the medic tapped him with a foot, then stood. "Where did you come from?"

"I said I don't have much use for *civan*," the warrant

officer replied. "Never said I didn't know how to use one," he added as the first of the Vashin appeared on the walls.

"Oh," he added. "The cavalry's here."

Roger opened his eyes and groaned.

"Crap," he muttered. His ribs hurt like hell.

"Water?" Dobrescu inquired sweetly. The medic had dark rings around his eyes, but he looked as mischievous as ever.

"Well, since I'm alive, I take it we won." Roger took a sip from the proffered camelback, then grimaced. "What was the egg breakage?"

"Pretty hefty, Your Highness," a new voice said, and Roger turned his head just as Pahner sat down beside his bed. The captain looked as if he hadn't slept in far too long, either.

"Tell me I look better than you two," the prince said, and winced as he levered himself very gingerly into a sitting position.

"Actually, you probably do," Pahner replied. "Doc?"

"Four broken ribs and contusions, mainly," the medic said. "Which is no big deal with His Highness." He grinned tiredly at Roger. "I kept you under for a day just to keep you out of the way and give your nannies a chance to begin the repairs," he added. "You can start moving around whenever you like."

"It hurts like . . . heck," Roger noted.

"That's good," Dobrescu told him, and stood. "It might keep you from doing stupid things."

He tapped the prince lightly on the shoulder and walked out, leaving him with Pahner.

"You're alive," Roger said, returning his attention to the Marine. "That's good. How are we doing otherwise?"

"Just fine," Pahner replied. "The breakage was bad for the Shin, both in Nopet and Mudh Hemh. But they'll survive. The Gastan is talking about letting some of the Krath settle in the valley, since the Shin own both citadels again."

"The company? Diasprans? Vashin?"

"Low losses," Pahner reassured him. "We didn't lose any Marines, not even Despreaux—who, I note, you *haven't* asked about. We lost two Vashin, and a Diaspran. That's it."

"Good," Roger sighed. "I was going to ask about Nimashet as soon as I'd asked about business."

"I won't tell her about your priorities," the captain said with a rare smile. "But I'll note that I approve. And at least we've solved the whole problem with Cord and Pedi."

"What problem? I knew something was going on, but I couldn't tell what."

"Ah, you were asleep for that." Pahner's smile segued into a grin, and he shook his head as he pulled out a *bisti* root and cut off a slice. "The Gastan wasn't all that happy, either, although he wasn't showing it. It turns out she's pregnant."

"Pedi?" Roger asked. "When? How?" He paused a moment, then shook his head, an almost awed expression on his face. *"Cord?"*

"Cord," Pahner confirmed. "While he was recovering. He didn't have any memory of it."

"Ouch. Oh, and the whole 'I cannot use my *asi* that way' thing . . . Oh, man!"

"Yes," the captain said. "Which was why she couldn't tell him whose child—children—they were. He assumed she'd had . . . a fling, for want of a better term. Add to that that she was considerably less than half his age but that he was . . . interested in her anyway, and—"

Roger laughed, then clutched at his chest in pain.

"Oh, my. May-December romance, indeed!" he got out, almost crying between the laughter and the pain.

"So now the Gastan has a new son-in-law, who's older than he is," Pahner acknowledged. "And from what Eleanora and I can figure out, it's even more complicated than that. Since the Gastan's oldest son, Thertik, managed to get himself killed, Pedi is his legal heir. But a *benan* can't inherit his position. There have been a handful of female Gastans in the history of the Shin, although they're very rare. It's more common for a female heir's consort to inherit the title. But a *benan* is required to follow his—or her—*benai* wherever that leads, so he can hardly stay home to rule the tribes. Unfortunately, a *benan*'s children *can* inherit. So Cord's children—the Gastan's *grand*children—are the legal heirs to the overlordship of the Vales."

"And since Cord insists on following me off-planet . . ."

"Precisely," the captain agreed with a thin smile. "I hope you'll pardon me for pointing this out, Your Highness, but the three of you have a positive talent for leaving chaos in your wake. Well, to be fair, I suppose I shouldn't include Cord in that. Not, at least, until we met the Lemmar and his sense of honor got him into all of this!"

"I think you're being too hard on him," Roger said with a laugh. "As far as I can tell, he fought the good fight to resist his attraction to Pedi. It's not his fault that he lost in the end—especially not with her taking such unscrupulous advantage of him when he was unconscious and unable to resist her advances!"

"You *would* come up with something like that," Pahner told him, shaking his head in resignation. "And I suppose it actually is sort of funny, in a way. But don't you dare laugh when you see them. They're like a couple of teenagers. It's worse than you and Despreaux."

"Oh, thank you very much, *Captain*," Roger said, and chuckled. Then grimaced as the chuckle claimed its own stab of pain.

"Or Julian and Kosutic. Or Berent and Stickles. Or, God forbid, Geno Macek and Gunny Jin, for that matter." The Marine sighed, rubbing his head.

"I'm sorry, Armand." Roger reached out to his bodyguards' commander. "I know we've laid burdens on you that were unnecessary, and for that, I apologize."

The captain looked down at the hand on his arm, then patted it and shook his head.

"Command challenges just make life more interesting," he said with a faint smile. "Although, after a certain point, they do tend to drag you down." He shook his head again. "For example, I would really appreciate it if you could stay out of one-shot range for the foreseeable future."

"Sounds like a good idea to me," Roger acknowledged, settling back against his pillows and feeling very carefully of his chest. "Of course, it never occurred to me that the bastard might *have* one."

"It wouldn't have occurred to me, either," Pahner admitted. "And I can't say that the fact that he did makes me very happy. But at least he didn't drill you clean."

"I don't understand why he didn't," Roger said thoughtfully. "I thought once one of those things locked onto your breastplate, you were pretty much screwed."

"Pretty much," Pahner agreed. "But from the looks of your armor, you managed to twist sideways just as he hit the tractor-lock. It didn't lock squarely. Instead of depositing the explosive charge at right angles, it hit you obliquely and a lot of the force of the explosion leaked sideways across the face of the plate. It was still enough for the shock damage to break your ribs, disable about sixty percent of your armor systems, and knock you unconscious. But it never managed to blow a scab loose, and you were lucky, Your Highness. Your anti-kinetic systems lasted long enough to keep it from doing anything worse than pounding your ribs—hard. Doc Dobrescu wouldn't have been quite so cheerful about the state they were in if you didn't have an even better nanny pack than the Corps gets issued. I know they still hurt like hell, but they're rebuilding fast."

"I know I was lucky," Roger agreed, still exploring his chest gently. "It just doesn't *feel* that way."

"Maybe not," Pahner said somberly. "But if he'd manage to blast that scab loose, all the anti-k systems in the galaxy wouldn't have helped you. And if *they'd* failed, the concussion alone should have turned every bone in your torso into paste." He shook his head. "No, Your Highness. You definitely *were* lucky. That's all that saved you—well, that and those souped-up reflexes of yours. I don't know if anyone else could have turned enough to take it at a survivable angle."

"And what about Sor Teb?"

"He was lucky, too . . . for a while," Pahner said. "The tractor must have gotten a good enough lock to at least stay put, instead of blasting right back through him. And the angle must have been oblique enough to direct the back blast away from him. I'm sure he figured you really were dead, since he had a *second* one-shot on him and he didn't use it on you to make certain. Unfortunately for him, he encountered Pedi on the parapet and suffered a mischief."

"God, I bet she enjoyed that!"

"You could put it that way. Especially since it was what pushed Cord into declaring his feelings for her," Pahner agreed with an evil chuckle.

"But to return to you and Sor Teb's little surprise," the Marine continued, "he may not have managed to kill *you*, but he certainly did manage to kill your armor."

"Which isn't good," Roger said with a grimace. "It's not like we had all that many operable suits to begin with."

"Oh, it isn't all that bad," Pahner reassured him. "In fact, Poertena ought to be able to take care of the problem without too much difficulty. Assuming, of course, that we take the spaceport before he implodes."

"Poertena?" Roger quirked an eyebrow. "What's his problem?"

"He just found out that Mountmarch has a complete Class One manufactory at the port," Pahner said, standing up. "Can you imagine Poertena with a full-scale manufacturing plant at his mercy?"

CHAPTER TWENTY-NINE

Temu Jin picked up his cup and sipped. His attention—obviously—was entirely focused on the coffee, and he kept it that way as the timer clicked over to just past Mardukan noon.

There were normally two com techs on duty in the communications control center, but at lunchtime, they went off duty, one at a time, to get something to eat. There were still the two guards, of course, but they were stationed in the vestibule just inside the blast door that was the only possible way in, not in the center itself. On this particular day, it was the other tech's turn to go to lunch first, which left Jin as the only person actually in the room. Which worked out just fine for him. Especially since the com center also doubled as the control room for the security perimeter.

He watched the schematic from the corner of one eye and nodded internally as the first notation of a possible perimeter breach popped up on his screen. Right on time. It was nice to deal with professionals for a change.

The com center guards were supposed to be cycled off together just before noon, instead of one of them at a time going to get something to eat, but their relief was late. That wasn't particularly unusual—the relief was *usually* late on Marduk, and they would be late in their turn. But it meant they were suffering just a tad from low blood sugar, which made them more surly than usual with the Mardukan messenger.

"What do *you* want, scummy?"

"I have a message from the governor," Rastar said, in carefully badly accented Imperial as he held his message up in front of the security cameras. He stood there in the poncholike garment the peasants in the area around the spaceport habitually wore, and made himself look as much like one of the local rubes as he could.

It must have worked.

"Okay, we'll give it to the geek," one of the guards said, and keyed in the code to open the door.

"Thank you," Rastar said in his horrible Imperial, and stepped inside to hand over the folded message as the door finished opening. Then he reached under the "poncho" once more.

"And if you'll be good enough to take me to the communications center," he continued in suddenly flawless Imperial, as four polymer-bladed knives closed like scissors on the guards' necks, "I'll let you live."

"Rastar and Jin have the communications center," Julian said. "Fain's team has taken down the guards on the main gate. The Shin are through the wire on the spaceport, and they've seized the vehicle park. I've got the code that the plasma towers are off-line."

"I'll believe it when we're in," Pahner growled, and wiggled his body, writhing up through the chunks of ore in the back of the *turom* cart.

The main difficulty in taking the spaceport was that the sensor net extended well beyond its perimeter. Besides increased radar sweeps from the geosynchronous satellite, there were micrite sensors scattered all over the surroundings. Those tiny sensors sent back readings on power emissions, nitrite traces, metal forms, and a variety of other indicators that could mean a potential attack by either low-tech or high-tech foes. Defeating them wasn't really hard, but it was time-consuming and complex.

One of the things the sensors looked for was evidence of ChromSten or high-density power packs. To cloak both of those, the armored personnel had been secreted in piles of metallic ores after tests had shown that the ores were sufficient to hide them from the Marines' own sensors.

The facility routinely purchased bulk materials from the Krath and the Shin, and, once again, the IBI agent had been invaluable. He'd spent his time and limited resources suborning various persons in the facility, which gave him all sorts of interesting handles when he needed them. In this case, he'd not only convinced the chief of supply that he needed to order "a little early," but had even given him a list of what to order. If the chief hadn't chosen to comply, certain pictures that he had on his personal system would have been turned over to the governor. Amazingly, an order for six carts of iron ore and ten of mixed foodstuffs had been placed within a day.

Now, with the sensor net and—hopefully—the plasma towers under the control of "friendly" forces, the time had come to knock on the front door.

"Well, let's find out what's going to go wrong," Kosutic said as she dropped out of the bottom of a *turom* cart into a spider-crouch. She looked up at the open gates and shook her head. "Look out for one-shots; we know there are some around."

There was virtually no other conversation as the Marines poured out of the carts and through the gates. They broke up into teams of three and four, and spread out through the facility.

"Commo secure," Julian chanted, trotting after Pahner as they both headed for the governor's quarters. "Armory: a Diaspran took a hit there, but the Marine team has it secured." A burst of firing sounded from the left, and he checked his pad. "Barracks are holding out, but the situation is secure."

"Send the second wave of Vashin there," Pahner said. "Diasprans to remain on call. Shin to the spaceport."

"Secondary control tower secured," Julian continued. "Nobody there. Maintenance and repair: no resistance."

They rounded the Armory and pounded across the

manicured lawn of the governor's quarters. Two humans by the front doors were being securely trussed up by Diasprans dressed as lawn maintenance "boys."

"Servants are secure, Sir," Sergeant Sri said as he yanked one of the human guards back to his feet. "The governor's in his quarters."

Pahner followed the schematic, helpfully forwarded from Temu Jin, to the rooms marked on the map, and stopped outside the main doors.

Julian stepped forward and swept the interior with deep radar. Since Roger's unpleasant interaction with the one-shot, they'd all started getting back into "stuff can hurt us even in armor" mode. It took some adjustment—the armor had been the absolute trump card in so many previous encounters—but they were getting there.

"No high-density weapons," Julian reported as he swept the sensor wand back and forth. "A twelve-millimeter bead pistol. That's it."

Pahner considered the door's controls for a moment, then shrugged and kicked at the memory plastic until he'd inflicted sufficient damage to encourage it to dilate. He stepped through it, then cursed as a bead round bounced off his armor.

"Oh, *this* is lovely," he snarled.

Julian followed him through and shook his head as he saw the naked, trembling boy in the middle of the bed. The boy—he couldn't have been much more than ten—had grave difficulty just holding up the heavy bead pistol, but his expression was almost as determined as it was terrified.

"Put that thing down, you little idiot," Pahner told him severely over his armor's external speakers. "Even if you manage to hit me again, it'll only bounce off and hurt somebody. Where's the governor?"

"I'm not telling you!" the boy yelled. "Ymyr told me not to tell you anything!"

"Bathroom," Julian said, and crossed to the bed. He reached out and thumbed the bead pistol to "safe," then yanked it out of the kid's hands. "Just stay there for a second," he told him.

Pahner strode across the bedroom. This time, he didn't bother kicking; he just put a bead cannon round through the upper part of the bathroom door after ensuring that his armored body was between the bed and any blow back that might occur.

The bead went through the door, through the wall beyond, through a section of barracks wall, and then headed for the mountains in the distance as Pahner stepped through the door and picked up the naked fat man inside the bathroom by what was left of his hair.

"Governor Mountmarch," he growled, tilting the official's chin up with the muzzle of the cannon, "it gives me distinct pleasure to place you under arrest for treason. We were going to add all sorts of additional items, but I think we'll just stop at pedophilia. You can only execute someone once."

"Damn." Julian grimaced at the sudden yellow puddle on the floor. "Cleanup on Aisle Ten."

"That's it?" Roger leaned back in the chair at the head of the conference table. "That's the big fight for the spaceport we've been sweating for the last six months?" He shivered and looked over by the door. "Speaking of sweating, or, rather not, somebody turn the thermostat up."

Pahner smiled. Then he tapped a control on the surface of the faux-teak table and an image of the planet blossomed above it.

"Well, Your Highness, we had two hundred Vashin and Diasprans," he said, nodding at Fain and Rastar, who were looking notably lethargic. Julian had set the thermometer at about thirty-five degrees, which was on the low side for Mardukans. "We also had inside help from Agent Jin and almost a thousand Shin."

"Who expect to be paid," the Gastan said. "I'll need various gee-gaws to placate the hill clans, but for me, I need weapons. Bead rifles, for preference."

"Not a problem," Roger assured him. "We'll get a shipment set up as soon as possible."

"We've got other needs, as well, Your Highness,"

Pahner pointed out. "The troops need to be refitted. We've got base stores on most of the materials, but they'll need to be set and the electronics fitted. That takes the manufactory."

"We'll set up a schedule," Roger said. "I hope no one minds if outfitting the troops takes precedence?" He looked around at the shaking heads and gestures of negation. "Good. I want the Vashin and Diasprans outfitted as well."

"Why?" Pahner asked. "I thought we'd agreed they were going to secure the port, not come with us?"

"Well, they still need uniforms," Roger replied. "Proper, antiballistic uniforms—I want them running around in better armor than those steel breastplates. And the temperature control will keep them from going into hibernation every evening, too."

"And there's the taking of this ship to consider," Rastar commented. "I know you think we can be of no use in that, but I have to differ. Our place is in battle with the prince and his Marines."

"Rastar," Roger said uncomfortably, "again, I thank you for the offer. But ships are . . . They're not good places for the untrained to be running around."

"None the less," Rastar said, "it is our duty."

"Well," Roger said after a moment's thought, "how about if you're backup? We're going to recover the assault shuttles, anyway. We can pack about sixty Mardukans into them, once we pull out all the extraneous gear. If we need you in the assault, we'll call you in. If we don't need you, sorry, you'd really just be in the way. Once we have a ship and you've had a chance to examine it, you'll understand."

"That's a good point, Your Highness," Pahner put in. "Actually, they could get a little off-planet training by lofting the shuttles; there's plenty of fuel on the base. And the manufactory can be programmed to fit them with chameleon suits and standard helmets. They won't have all the features of our stuff, but enough. Coms at least, and basic tactical readouts. And thermostats.

"Furthermore," he smiled thinly, "they can act as

bodyguards for *you*, Your Highness. You realize, of course, that you're not going to be in on the ship assault."

"Oh?" Roger said dangerously.

"Oh," the captain replied. "You're Heir Primus now, Your Highness . . . and there is no Heir Secondary or Tertiary. You can't be risked. And, frankly, many of the points you brought up about the Mardukans hold for you. You're not *trained* in shipboard combat. I'll freely admit that—leaving aside such minor matters as the imperial succession, a little matter of a coup, the need to rescue your Lady Mother, and my personal oath to protect your life at all costs—I'd take you in a Mardukan jungle over a squad of Marines any day. But not in a ship. Different circumstances, different weapons—and you're not trained for either. And it's not a time to let 'natural ability' take its course."

"So the Mardukans and I sit it out on the planet? While you and the Marines take the ship?"

"That's the right plan, Your Highness," the sergeant major interjected.

"But—"

"If you decide to overrule me, Your Highness," the captain said stoically, "I will resign before I'll attempt the action. I will not risk you at this point."

"Pock," Roger said bitterly. "You're serious."

"As a heart attack, Your Highness. You're no longer in a category that can be even vaguely threatened. You are *the* Heir. I can't stress that enough."

"Okay," Roger said, shaking his head. "I'll stay on the ground with the Mardukans."

"I want your word on that. And no weaseling."

"I'll stay on the ground . . . unless you call for reinforcements. And take note; if you *don't* call for reinforcements when you need them, you'll be endangering me. And if *you* are rendered *hors de combat,* all bets are off."

"Agreed," Pahner said sourly.

"So you'd better take the ship quick," Roger pointed out.

"That shouldn't be a big deal," the sergeant major said.

"Most tramp freighters are pretty coy about being jacked, for obvious reasons. But we'll have a shielded shuttle, and once we're through the airlock, there's not much they can do with a platoon of Marines on board."

"You're taking everybody?" Roger asked.

"There are enough suits in the Morgue to outfit all our survivors," Kosutic pointed out. "It's another thing to toss on Poertena's pile, but it's not like he's busy."

Julian strode down the hallway, twisting his shoulders from side to side. The issue uniforms were made of a soft, pleasant cloth, and should have been very comfortable. But the uniform he'd just carefully folded and put away had been on his body for almost eight months. The various cloths of which it was comprised had been worn in. No matter how well-made, or how basically comfortable its fabric, a new uniform always took a certain amount of breaking in.

He forgot his minor discomforts as he rounded a corner on the final approach to the Armory. Besides new uniforms, they were drawing new weapons and turning in the ones they'd wielded for the last half year. Given that most of the bead rifles and grenade launchers with which they'd arrived were suitable only for salvaging as spare parts, he'd simply packed the weapon up and headed for the Armory. Like the uniforms, it made more sense to throw the guns away than store them.

Which was why he stopped with an expression of surprise. Half the remaining Marines were lined up on the floor in the corridor outside the Armory, laboriously cleaning their weapons.

"Don't even bother, man," Gronningen growled. "Poertena's being a pocking bastard."

"You're joking."

"Go ahead," Macek said tiredly. "See for yourself."

Julian stepped through the blast doors and shook his head. The new weapons, many of them freshly manufactured, and all of them gleaming with lethal purpose, were arrayed on racks in the back of the Armory, with a mesh security screen between them and the main

administrative area. In the front of the large vault was
a counter, with a swinging gate on one end and a repair
area on the opposite end. Poertena had settled himself
behind the counter and was minutely inspecting each
weapon that was turned into him.

"Pocking pilthy," he said, and tossed the grenade
launcher back to Bebi. "Bring it back when it clean."

"Come on, Poertena!" the grenadier snarled. "I've
cleaned it twice! And you're just going to DX it anyway!"

"I'm not explaining to Captain Pahner why t'e pocking Inspectorate downcheck my pocking Armory," the sergeant growled. "Bring it back when it clean."

"We're planning on *overthrowing* the Inspectorate!" the
grenadier protested, but he left anyway. With the
launcher.

"Poertena," Julian said, "you've got too much to do
to be picking over guns with micro-tools!"

"Says you," the Pinopan replied, and snatched the bead
rifle out of Julian's hands. "Barrel dirty!" he said, as he
broke the weapon open and checked it. "Silica buildup
in t'e pocking discharge tube! Julian, you know better
t'an t'at! Nobody gets a pass in t'is Armory!"

"Goddamn it, Poertena, you've got thirty suits to get
online!" Julian snapped. "There's a week of solid day-
in-day-out work right there. More, probably! Not to mention reconfiguring the manufactory to outfit all the Vashin
and Diasprans!"

"I guess I'm going to be too busy," the armorer replied
with a grin. "I hear t'at t'e sergean' major is looking
for you, though . . ."

"Ah, there you are, Adib!" Kosutic strode into the
Armory. "Poertena, take the sergeant's rifle and find somebody else to clean it. He's going to be rather busy."

"Oh, no," Julian groaned. "Come *on*, Eva."

"Don't you 'Eva' me, Sergeant," she said with a grin.
"You're fully qualified out on a Class One—I checked
your records. And it's going to take a squad to get all
the work done, anyway. Fortunately, you're a squad
leader."

"Look," Julian said mulishly, "I can stand here and argue all day over whether you should pick me or somebody else. And do it well. To start with, I *am* a squad leader; I'm supposed to manage my squad. You're the one who told me that—"

"Hi, Poertena," Roger said, as he stepped through the blast door. "I need to turn in my bead pistol and—"

"I'm outta here," Julian announced, and darted for the exit. "I think you said something about setting up the manufactory, Sergeant Major?"

"What did I say?" Roger asked as Kosutic snickered her way out of the room in Julian's wake, and Poertena snatched the pistol from his hand.

"What? You call t'is po . . . You call t'is *clean?* You Highness."

"Okay, Captain Fain, welcome to Supply Central," Aburia said as she beckoned for the Mardukan to come through the door.

In deference to the locals' temperature sensitivity, the room had been set at nearly forty degrees. For most humans, it would have been sweltering, but after six months on Marduk, the Marines found it pleasantly cool. Which didn't prevent the corporal from wiping a drop of sweat from her forehead as she gestured to the platform.

"Sir, I'd like you to stand up here, please," she said. "We're going to measure you for your uniform."

"This is an odd way," the Diaspran said. The room was filled with sounds that the Mardukan classified as a triphammer, and also a peculiar rushing noise. The most prominent feature, though, was a low vibration through the floor that Fain found very unpleasant.

"Well, we do it a bit differently, Sir," the corporal replied. "Please, on the platform."

The captain complied, and the Marine triggered a code with her toot.

"The lights are harmless, Sir," she said, as lasers patterned the Mardukan's body in blue. "They're measuring you for your uniform."

After a moment, they winked off.

"And if you'll step down," the corporal continued as she removed a piece of plastscrip from the console, "this is your number. Stickles is in the other room, and he'll show you where to pick up your gear."

"That's it?" Fain asked, waving for Erkum to climb up onto the platform.

"Yep," the Marine said. "Back there, there's a big machine that's going to turn everything out. It's got imported material for the base on the uniform, and various imported and local materials will be used to make the helmet. It's just like the machines in K'Vaern's Cove," she finished, "only—"

"Much more sophisticated," Fain finished as Pol stepped down from the platform and accepted his own piece of plastscrip.

"Yes, Sir," the human said with a grin. "We've got a few thousand years of technology on you, Sir. Don't take it badly."

"I don't," the captain said as he left. "I'm just glad you're on our side."

"Well, it's not always perfect," Aburia admitted. "And just being able to make stuff doesn't always mean it works the way you planned."

"Oh?"

"Look, you stupid beast. If you want to go with me on the ship, I have to get this on you."

Roger appreciated the time it must've taken Julian to design and build the custom-made suit for Dogzard. He considered that the sergeant's efforts were a nice compliment, especially considering all the other duties he'd fitted it in around. Dogzard, however, failed to share his appreciation for the final product.

The Mardukan beast hissed as Roger tried to force one talon into the suit. Then she jerked suddenly backwards, twisted away, and darted into a corner.

"It's state-of-the-art," Roger panted as he leapt across the compartment in an effort to pin the monster down. "It's even got little thrusters, so you can maneuver in zero-g, and . . ."

Dogzard writhed in his grip until she managed to twist loose, then raced for the door. Showing a startling level of sophistication, she hit the door release and dashed out.

"Well," Roger said, sucking a cut on his hand. "I think that went well."

CHAPTER THIRTY

"I think this is going pretty well," Pahner said as he watched a Vashin cavalryman try out his new plasma cannon. For any human not in powered armor, the heavy weapon was a crew-served mount, but the Mardukan stood on the range, holding the cannon and firing it "off-hand." Not only that, he was putting a round a second down range. Then he stopped for a moment, flipped the selector to "auto," and began putting out bursts of plasma that ate into the cliff being used as a backstop until the power magazine discharged itself and automatically popped out. At which point, the cavalryman used a false-hand to pop a new one into place . . . and resumed fire in under a second.

"We still can't use them inside the ship," Kosutic said, grinning as the hillside started to smoke from the target practice. "They do too much damage."

"Agreed," Pahner said, and cut himself a fresh slice of *bisti* root. It had struck him that Murphy was working overtime when it turned out that there wasn't a single stick of gum left in the entire compound. He'd nearly shot one person who was chewing his last stick when Mountmarch's personnel were rounded up.

"We can't use them on shipboard if we want it intact, at any rate," he continued as he began to chew.

"Although . . . when we load them, we'll outfit most of them with bead cannons. Maybe one plasma cannon in three. And instead of loading with beads, we'll load flechette packs. That way they won't be a cataclysm just waiting to happen."

"You're thinking you might actually use them?" the sergeant major asked with a frown.

"I'm thinking that if you're going to have a backup, it might as well be a backup you can use," the captain replied with a sigh. "And it's the little details that are crucial."

He was right about that, the sergeant major reflected. And it had been a fortnight for details. Besides refitting and rearming all the Marines and their Allies, there'd been a billion other "details" to handle, all of them as quickly as possible.

The first order of business had been to determine just how deeply the Saints actually had their hooks into the planet. As it turned out, the governor had partially covered himself by getting permission for "occasional welfare and socialization visits" from passing Saint warships. His request had pointed out that he was on the backend of nowhere, with no naval backup, and that refusing requests might be a good way to start a war.

But his personal files, helpfully cracked by the ever-useful Temu Jin, had revealed the other side of the story. The steadily growing accounts in New Rochelle banks would have been hard enough for Mountmarch to explain, but the electronic communications records were damning. It was clear that he'd been in the Saints' pocket almost from the day he arrived on Marduk. Indeed, some references in the correspondence raised the very real possibility that he'd been a Saint operative even while he was a centerpiece of court intrigue. One reply from his Saint handler—identified in the messages only as "Muir"—indicated that the Saints had used a combination of money and blackmail, probably about his illegal predilection for young boys, as a means of control. When the Bronze Barbarians returned to Old Earth (and assuming they managed to both survive the trip and then get the various warrants against them dropped) the database would make interesting reading at IBI.

For the moment, however, what was more important was that the data gave them a good read on Saint visits, and the next warship wasn't scheduled for over two months. Furthermore, it indicated that activity overall would be cut back for the foreseeable future. Prince Jackson's coup had all the other star nations surrounding the Empire on high alert, and the majority of the Saint fleet had been pulled to more important systems.

While Julian and Jin had been tickling the electronic files, a team made up of Third Squad and augmented by Eleanora O'Casey for political interaction had been sent out to cover their back trail and pick up the shuttles. Harvard Mansul had requested and been granted permission to accompany them, and they'd visited most of the Company's waypoints. They'd retraced their entire six-month journey in less than a week, and insured that the various societies they'd passed through had survived. Mansul, in the meantime, recorded interviews with many of the Mardukans who'd experienced the Company's passage. Besides laying the groundwork for a series of fascinating articles and one heck of a docudrama, his records were intended as evidence for Roger's defense when the time came, since they made it clear he and Bravo Company had been far too busy surviving to be involved in any plots against the Throne.

K'Vaern's Cove's was well on its way to a major industrial revolution, and dragging Diaspra kicking and screaming along behind it. The flotilla's ships' captains had returned, and the Cove had been very much in two minds about precisely what to do about Kirsti. Public attitude had been hardening towards sending a follow-up military expedition, but O'Casey had been able to inform them that by the time a fleet could make it back to Kirsti, the Fire Priests would have had their attitudes adjusted and be waiting for a *friendly* visit.

Marshad was experiencing some political instability, and had been mauled in two minor wars. The team "counseled" everyone involved, but O'Casey recognized that it would take a full soc-civ team to get the city-states cooperating, rather than competing for territory. Marshad did still have control of the lucrative *dianda* trade routes to Voitan, however, and the revenues from that were helping it recover from its near demise at the hands of its former overlord.

Denat had accompanied the team, but rather than return to his home tribe, he had decided to remain in Marshad until their return trip.

Voitan was in a renaissance, as well. It had developed a lively merchant class that traded wootz steel ingots and finished weapons to Marshad for *dianda,* then shipped the *dianda* south to the city-states. New trade routes had been opened all the way to the Southern oceans, and the market in the south was hungry for both Voitan steel and Marshad cloth. Voitan was having some trouble with an influx of workers fleeing the war in the south, which sounded something like the worst of the city-state wars in ancient Italy, but given the shortage of labor with which the reborn city had started, the influx was mostly to the good.

Q'Nkok was flourishing as a side benefit of the rebirth of Voitan. In many ways, the first town the Marines had visited was the least changed by their passage. It supplied raw materials from the mountains and jungles to its west and north to Voitan and the other, larger city-states, and the only real change seemed to be the increased clearing on both sides of the river. With the shift of the People to materials suppliers, rather than hunter/gathers, their need for extensive forests had dwindled, and a new treaty for extended lands had been signed, ending for the time being any rationale for conflict between the two groups.

The shuttles were virtually untouched. All they needed for liftoff was fuel, and on the way back the team stopped to pick up Denat, along with T'Leen Sena, who had accepted his proposal of marriage.

The shuttles, and the port's other aircraft, had also sufficed to pick up the Vashin and Diaspran dependents, along with spare *civan* and even a few *flar-ta,* including

Patty. They'd found that they could just fit one *flar-ta* to a shuttle, and as long as they kept the beasts sedated, the trip was a piece of cake.

In addition to all that, the Mardukan members of The *Basik*'s Own had been put through a brief course in shipboard combat. They'd been taken into orbit aboard the assault shuttles and shown how to move in free-fall. After a brief period of total disorientation, most of them had taken to it well, and it turned out that the locals' four arms were incredibly helpful in zero-gravity combat.

After their initial exposure to micro-gravity, they were put through a few maneuvers and finally exposed to vacuum in their new uniforms. After that, there wasn't much more to do. The best the humans could do with the materials at hand was to familiarize the locals with space combat in its most basic sense. If it came down to it, the Mardukans would have to learn the ins and outs as they went, which was rarely a path to long-term survival.

Cord had not joined them in their training. Despite the old Shaman's sulfurous protests, Roger had decided that his *asi* had no business in any potential boarding actions. It looked more and more as if Cord would be at least partly disabled permanently from his wound, despite all Dobrescue could do. Even if he'd been in perfect health, Roger had pointed out ruthlessly, nothing Cord could have done in battle would make much difference one way or the other to the protection of someone already in powered armor. But he *wasn't* in perfect health, and that was that.

What Roger very carefully had not mentioned was his conviction that his *asi* had no business in combat under any circumstances when he stood on the brink of finally becoming a parent. Pedi had been equally careful to stay out of the entire discussion, but Roger had recognized her gratitude when Cord finally grumpily accepted that his "master's" decision was final.

With the Mardukans' training as close to complete as it was going to get, they'd hidden the assault shuttles away, reloaded with fuel and ammunition, in the jungle on the edge of the Shin lands and settled down to wait for the right ship. When the time came, the main force would loft in one of the port shuttles, suitably stealthed, while the Mardukan "backup" waited on the ground in the much more threatening assault shuttles.

One ship had come and gone already, but since it was a tramp freighter flagged by Raiden-Winterhowe, they'd passed it up. Hijacking ships under the protection of one of the other major interstellar empires wasn't a good idea. What they were looking for was a ship flagged by the Empire, or even better, one that was *owned* by an Imperial company but under a flag of convenience. They might be returning to attempt a counter-coup, but they didn't want to start an interstellar war in the process.

It had been a hectic two weeks, but now, with all the preparations in place, all they had to do was wait and train. And if a ship didn't come soon, they'd either have to cut back on the Vashin ammunition allotment—which might lead to a mutiny—or else find a new hill for them to shoot up.

Pahner chuckled at the thought, then keyed his helmet com in response to a call from the com center. He listened for a moment, then nodded, and turned to Kosutic.

"All right, Sergeant Major. Tell the troops to quit their fun and suit up."

"Ship?"

"Yep. A tramp freighter owned by Georgescu Lines. Due in thirty-six hours. I doubt they can detect plasma bursts from more than twenty hours out, but I think we should start shutting down the ranges and getting our war faces on."

"Georgescu? That's a New Liberia Company, isn't it, Sir?" Kosutic asked, and Pahner frowned. He understood the point she was making, because New Liberia definitely wasn't a part of the Empire of Man.

"Yes," he said, "but the company's owners appear to be Imperial. Or maybe a shell corporation. And it's not like New L is going to go to war with the Empire, even if we do cop one of their ships."

"No, I don't guess so," Kosutic agreed.

New Liberia belonged to the Confederation of Worlds, which was a holdover from the treaties which had ended the Dagger Wars. The Confederation was a rag-picker's bag of systems none of the major powers had wanted badly enough to fight each other for, and the treaties had set it up primarily as a buffer zone. Despite the centuries which had passed since, however, it had never progressed much beyond subsistence-level neobarb worlds, most of them despotisms, of which New Liberia was by far the most advanced. Which wasn't saying much. Even that planet wasn't much more than a convenient place to dump an off-planet shell corporation, or register a ship at a minimum yearly cost. As for New Liberia itself, the planet had a population under six million—most of them dirt poor—and a few in-system frigates that were play-toys for whatever slope-brow bully-boy had come out on top in the most recent coup. They were unlikely to charge the Empire with piracy, especially of a freighter which was owned by an Imperial corporation skating around the tax laws.

"We'll call on them to surrender, try to keep casualties to a minimum, and pay Georgescu off when we get back," the captain said. "I suppose we *could* simply say that we're commandeering the ship and ask the captain to come down to the surface to surrender, but then there's the little issue of there being a price on our heads.

"If I thought there was a chance in hell that we'd do anything but get ourselves disappeared when we returned, I'd turn us over to the first authorities we found," he continued with a frown. "But there isn't one. Jackson couldn't afford *not* to make us disappear."

"Do you think he was the one who put the toombie on *DeGlopper*?" Kosutic asked. They'd lost so many Marines on the trip that she had a hard time even coming up with all the names, but she remembered shooting Ensign Guha as if it had happened yesterday. Killing a person who was acting under his own volition was one thing. Shooting that toombie—a good junior officer who'd desperately wanted to do anything but what the chip in her head was telling her to do—still made her sick to her stomach. Even if the shot *had* saved the ship.

"Probably," Pahner sighed. "As the head of the Military Committee in the Lords, he had the contacts and the knowledge. And he was no friend of the Empress."

"Which means he also killed the rest of the Family," the sergeant major said. "I'd like some confirmation, but I think that he's one person I'll take active pleasure in terminating with as much prejudice as humanly possible."

"We *will* require confirmation that the Empress isn't in full and knowing agreement with his handling of the situation," Pahner said. "I don't think there's any doubt that she isn't, but getting hard proof of that will be . . . interesting. I have a few ideas on the subject— where to begin, at least—but before we can do anything about it one way or the other, we need a ship." He waved to Honal, who'd been overseeing the training. "Round them up, Honal. We're expecting company."

"Good!" the Vashin said. "I'm looking forward to ship combat. And I like the thought of seeing all those other worlds you keep talking about."

"So do I," Pahner said quietly. "And especially to seeing one that's not Marduk."

"Captain." Roger nodded in greeting as the Marines walked into the command center. "It looks like everything is prepared to receive visitors."

"It had better be," Pahner growled. "We've only been getting ready for the last two weeks."

"I was thinking. You have any major plans between now and when we launch the shuttles?"

"Nothing I'd classify as *major*," the Marine said. "Why?"

"In that case, I was thinking it would be a good idea to have a party," Roger said with a smile. "I've done up a few suitable awards. . . ."

Roger had been a bit put out to discover that he hadn't originated the concept of the dining-in. But after he watched Pahner and Kosutic put together the plan for the evening in less than five minutes, he was less upset.

The sun was setting over the mountains in the west as the majority of the group that had fought its way to the spaceport gathered around tables arranged under awnings. The spaceport's mountain plateau was much higher and drier than most of Marduk, which gave a rare clear sky and a view of both of the moons. It was also much cooler, but the Mardukans' new uniforms finally made them immune to the torpor which set in with the evening's chill.

Supper was a seven-course dinner. It started with fruits gathered from their entire trip, and everyone agreed that the winner was either the K'Vaernian sea-plum or Marshad's kate fruit. The wine was a light white from a vineyard in the Marshad plain that came highly recommended by T'Leen Targ. The second course was wine-basted *coll* fish flown in from K'Vaern's Cove—small, tender ones, not steaks from giant *coll*—accompanied by nearpotatoes skillet fried with slivered Ran Tai peppers. The wine for the second course, a light, sweet sea-plum vintage which had been recommended by T'Seela of Sindi, was perfect for cooling the palette after the peppers.

The third course was a fruit-basted *basik* on a bed of barleyrice. Roger's table was presented with a very large platter. Several normal *basik* had been clustered around a sculpture of a very large, very pointy-toothed *basik* made out of barleyrice. The wine for that course was a kate-fruit vintage from the new vineyards around Voitan.

The fourth course was the *piece de resistance*. Julian had gone out and single-handedly downed a damnbeast, using nothing more than a squad of backup and a bead cannon, and his prize was served roasted as whole as possible. A certain amount of careful rearrangement had been required to cover up the enormous hole in its neck, and it was delivered on a giant platter carried in by six of the local Krath servants. Julian personally officiated over the carving of the steaks, which were served along with *peruz*-spiced barleyrice and steamed vegetables. The

wine was a vintage from Ran Tai that the company had
come to like during its sojourn there.

The remaining courses were desserts and niblets, and
the feast culminated with everyone sitting around on the
ground, picking bits of damnbeast out of their teeth while
they tried to decide how much wine they could drink.

Finally, as the last course was cleared, Roger stood and
raised his wine glass.

"Siddown!" Julian called.

"Yes, sit, Roger," Pahner said. "Let's see . . . I think . . .
Yes, Niederberger! You're to give the toast."

The designated private took a hasty gulp of wine, then
stood while Gunny Jin whispered in his ear. He cleared
his throat and raised his glass.

"Ladies and Gentlemen, Her Majesty, Alexandra the
Seventh, Empress of Man! Long may she reign!"

"The Empress!" The response rumbled back at him,
and he tried not to scurry as he settled back into his
chair in obvious relief.

"*Now* you stand up, Roger," Pahner said.

"Shouldn't it be you?" Roger asked.

"Nah. You're the senior officer, *Colonel*," the captain
said with a grin.

"No rank in the mess!" Julian called.

"I was just pointing it out," Pahner said. "Your turn,
Roger."

"Okay." Roger got to his feet again. "Ladies and Gentlemen, absent companions!"

"Absent companions!"

"Before we get into any more toasts," Roger continued, waving Julian back down, "I have a few words I'd
like to say."

"Speech! Speech!" Poertena yelled, and most of the
Vashin joined in. The armorer had taken a table with
them, even though they'd made it clear that they didn't
want to play cards.

"Not a speech," Roger disagreed, and held out his hand
to Despreaux. She handed over a sizable sack, then sat
back down with a smile.

"On the auspicious occasion of us almost getting off

this mudball," Roger said. "Sorry to all you people who were born here, by the way. But on this occasion, I think it's fitting that we distribute a few mementos. Things to remember our trip by."

"Uh-oh," Kosutic whispered. "Did you know about this?"

"Yep." Pahner grinned. "Or, rather, I found out just in time."

"Lessee," Roger said, pulling out a piece of plastscrip and a small medallion. "Ah, yes. To St. John (J), and St. John (M). A silver 'M' and a silver 'J,' so that we can frigging tell you apart!"

Roger beamed as the twin brothers made their way up to accept their gifts, then shook their hands (Mark's had regenerated quite nicely since Kirsti) as he handed over the mementos.

"Wear 'em in good health. Now, what else do we have? Ah, yes." He reached into the sack and pulled out a wrench no more than three centimeters long. "To Poertena, a little pocking wrench, for beating up on little pocking bits of armor!"

He continued in the same vein through the entire remaining unit of Marines and many of the Vashin and Diasprans, showing that he recognized their individual quirks and personality traits. It took almost an hour of mingled laughter and groans before he started wrapping up.

"To PFC Gronningen," he said, holding up a silver badge. "The unsleeping silver eye. Because you *know* Julian is going to get you, sooner or later."

He handed the badge to the grinning Asgardian and punched him on the shoulder.

"You're doomed. You know that, right?"

"Oh, yeah."

"Lessee. We're getting near the bottom of the bag. . . . Oh, yes. To Adib Julian, a marksman's badge with a 'no' symbol over it. The marksman's bolo badge for always being second in any shooting match!"

Julian accepted it with good grace, and the prince turned to the sergeant major, Pahner, and the senior Mardukans.

"I'd considered the unsleeping eye for Rastar, as well," Roger said, and the wave of human chuckles was swamped in grunting Mardukan laughter as the Marines and the Vashin alike recalled their first meeting and Roger's ambush of the sleeping Rastar. "But in the end, I decided on this." He reached into the bag and withdrew an elaborately chased set of Mardukan-sized bead pistols. "May you never run out of ammo."

"Thank you, Your Highness." Rastar accepted the gift with a flourishing bow.

"No rank in the mess," Roger reminded him, and turned to his next victim. "For Krindi, a set of Zuiko binoculars. It seems you're never able to fight at long range, but what the heck."

"Thank you, Y—Roger," the Diaspran said, and took the imaging system with a slight bow of his own.

"To Eva Kosutic, our own personal Satanist," Roger said, with another grin, and handed her a small silver pitchfork. "The silver pitchfork medal. She was always there to prod buttock; now she has something to prod with. You can feel free to put it anywhere you like."

"And yours was always a nice buttock to prod, Roger," she told him with a grin as she accepted the award. Roger laughed with everyone else, then turned to Cord.

"Cord, what can I say? You've stuck with me through thick and thin, mainly thin."

"You can say nothing and sit back down," the shaman replied.

"Nah, not after I went to all this trouble," the prince said, and winked at Pedi. "Okay, we have: a package of baby formula Dobrescu promises me will work for Mardukan kids just fine. A package of disposable diapers—I know you guys stick your kids in your slime, but when we get among humans, that might not always be an option. A set of four baby blankets—what can I say, do you *always* have to have quartets? And last, but most certainly not least, a set of earplugs. Just for Cord, though. He's going to need them."

"Oh, thank you very much, Roger," Cord said, accepting the items and sitting down.

"Don't think of it as a roast," Roger told him. "Think of it as a baby shower."

"What is that?" Pedi asked Despreaux quietly.

"Normally," the Marine whispered back, "it's when you give gifts that can help with an expected baby. In this case, though, Roger is twitting Cord."

"And here comes Dogzard," Roger said, looking under the table.

The beast raised her head as she heard her name, then she leapt to her feet when she saw her master's body posture.

"Dat's a good Dogzard," Roger told her, and pulled a huge leg of damnbeast off the table. "Who's a good beastie, then?"

The semi-lizard snatched the bone out of Roger's hand and retreated back under the table. Her meter-and-a-half-long tail stuck well out from under it, lashing happily from side to side, and Roger waved his hand.

"Ow, ow!" He counted his fingers ostentatiously, then sighed in relief while everyone laughed. But then the prince lowered his hands, and turned to the last person on his list.

"And so we come to Armand Pahner," he said seriously, and the laughter stilled. "What do you present to the officer who held you together for eight horrible months? Who never wavered? Who never faltered? Who never for one instant let us think that we might fail? What do you give to the man who took a sniveling brat and made a man of him?"

"Nothing, for preference," Pahner said. "It really *was* my job."

"Still," Roger said, and reached into the now all but empty bag to pull out a small badge. "I present you the Order of the Bronze Shield. If I can, I'm going to have Mother turn it into an order of knighthood; we need at least one more. For service above and beyond the call of duty to the Crown. Thank you, Armand. You've been more than you've needed to be at every turn. I know we still have a long way to go, but I'm confident that we can get there, together."

"Thanks, Roger." The captain stood to accept the gift. "And I have a little present for you, as well."

"Oh?"

"Yes." The Marine cleared his throat formally. "Long before the ISU, before the Empire of Man, in the dawn of the space age, there was a mighty nation called the United States. As Rome before it, it rose in a pillar of flame and eventually fell. But during its heyday, it had a few medals to reckon with.

"There were many awards and ribbons, but one, while common, perhaps surpassed them all. It was a simple rifle on a field of blue, surrounded by a wreath. What it meant was that the wearer had been where the bullets flew, and probably shot at people himself, and had returned from the fire. It meant, simply, that the wearer had seen infantry combat, and survived. All the other medals, really, were simply icing on that cake, and like the ISU before it, the Empire has maintained that same award . . . and for the same reasons.

"Prince Roger Ramius Sergei Alexander Chiang MacClintock," the captain said, as he took the newly minted badge from Sergeant Major Kosutic and pinned it onto the prince's uniform, "I award you the Combat Infantryman's Badge. You have walked into the fire again and again, and come out not unscathed, but at least, thank God, alive. If your mother gives you all the medals you deserve, you're going to look like a neobarb world dictator. But I hope that you think of this one, sometimes, because, really, it says it all."

"Thank you, Armand," Roger said quietly.

"No, thank you," Pahner replied, putting his hand on the prince's shoulder. "For making the transition. For surviving. Hell, for saving all of *our* asses. Thank you from all of us."

The party had descended to the point at which Erkum Pol had to be dragged down before he hit someone with a plank, and Roger had gotten Despreaux off to one side. She'd been quiet all night, and he thought he knew why.

"You're still insisting that you can't marry me, aren't you?" he asked.

"Yes, and I wish you'd quit asking," she replied, looking down the hills to the Krath city in the valley. "I'm short, Roger. I'll stick along to Earth, and I'll do what I can to get your mother out of danger. But I won't marry you. When we're settled, and things are safe, I'm putting in my discharge papers. And then I'll take my severance bonus and go find me a nice, safe, placid farmer to marry."

"Court is just another environment," Roger protested. "You've been through a hundred on this planet, alone. You can adjust!"

"I probably could," she said, shaking her head. "But not well enough. What you need is someone like Eleanora, someone who knows the rocks and shoals. Part of the problem is that we're too alike. We both have a very direct approach, and you need someone who can complement you, not enhance your negative qualities."

"You'll stay until Earth, right?" he asked. "Promise you'll stay until then."

"I promise," she said. "And now, I'm turning in, Roger." She stopped and looked at him with a cocked head. "I'll make an offer one last time. Come with me?"

"Not if you won't marry me," he said.

"Okay," she sighed. "God, we're both stubborn."

"Yeah," Roger said, as she walked away. "Stubborn's one word."

CHAPTER THIRTY-ONE

"We've never had a 'health and welfare' inspection *before*," the voice said suspiciously.

"Yeah, tell me something I don't know." Jin controlled his voice carefully, sliding just the right hint of exasperation into it. "We've got a task force with an IBI inspection team coming out, and we need to make a big show. Personally, I think they're operating on the theory that everyone needs a good shaking up after the coup attempt, but what do I know? According to The Book, we're *supposed* to do these things on every ship, not that anybody ever did it! But now we're under the gun, so we're trying to get a paper trail going."

There was a long pause, and Jin wished that he could see the other's face, but the freighter had supplied only a voice channel.

Emerald Dawn was a known ship. She'd passed through the system at least twice before, once since Jin had been inserted. She generally traded minor technological trinkets like fire-starters for local gems and artwork. In addition, she got a small fee for dropping electronic transfers in the system, which was the real reason for her visits. As a matter of fact, he'd talked with the ship on her previous run, and he hoped the familiarity of his voice would lull them to some extent.

"Okay," a new voice said finally. "This is Captain Dennis. One person can come aboard for your 'health and welfare' check. But this is the *last* time I'm coming to this port. I don't need this aggravation for a handful of cheap-ass gems, a mail chit that barely covers our air loss, and a cargo of scummy art-shit."

"Whatever." Jin let a bit of the peevish bureaucrat into his tone. "I'm just doing my job."

The shuttle was on autopilot, so he slid out of the pilot's chair with a nod at Poertena, and pulled his way aft. This was made somewhat difficult by the fact that the small craft was crammed with Marines in battle armor. Most of them had clamped onto the walls and floors, but a few were drifting, more or less at random.

He stopped opposite Captain Pahner, whose feet were stuck to the ceiling as he stood "head-down," perusing the schematics for the target.

"They're not real happy," the IBI agent said.

"I don't care if they're happy," Pahner said. "Just as long as they open their doors."

"One shot, and we're all vapor," Jin noted.

"And as far as they know, they're suddenly the most wanted ship in the Empire," Pahner pointed out. "It would be very bad form for a tramp freighter to shoot up an official Imperial inspection craft. They'll let us dock. After that, you just hit the deck."

"Why does this make my butt pucker?" Fiorello Giovannuci—known to the dirt-side com station as "Captain Dennis"—asked as he gazed at the viewscreen image of the approaching small craft.

"Because your butt always puckers when we get boarded." Amanda Beach, his first officer, shook her head in mock gravity. "Relax. It's got all the codes for an Imperial customs ship. Really, it's because your conscience isn't pure. You need to spend some time on the planets, reacquiring your oneness with Gaia."

Giovannuci glanced at her, then shook his own head and sighed.

"Your sense of humor is the reason you're out here,

you know. Just keep it up." He leaned forward, as if the viewscreen could tell him more if he only stared hard enough, and rubbed his cheek. "And you're wrong. There's something very much not right here."

"You want me to go down to the airlock?" Beach asked as the CO fell silent, watching the shuttle make its final approach. He continued to say nothing for several more seconds, but, finally, he nodded.

"Yes. And take Longo and Ucelli."

"My," she said, pursing her lips as she got to her feet, "you *are* nervous. Isn't that sort of overkill?"

"Better over than under," Giovannuci said. "Go. Fast."

Jin waited until all the telltales turned green, then opened the airlock door and swung forward through it cautiously. The three people waiting for him represented a fair percentage of the total crew for a tramp like this, and their presence in such numbers indicated just how uncomfortable they must be.

He'd have been just as nervous in their shoes. The profit which could be made from "jacking" ships like this were enough to make them high-priority targets. Even a tramp as old and beat up as *Emerald Dawn* was worth nearly a billion credits. So anytime one was parked anywhere but at a fully secured port—which did not, by any stretch, describe Marduk—its crew was always on the lookout for pirates. And it wasn't impossible to imagine the entire port being captured, or even that one Temu Jin would be in on it. Stranger things had transpired in the borderlands.

Besides, now that he thought about it, that was actually a pretty fair description, in a slightly skewed way, of what was actually going to happen.

The threesome had obviously been chosen with some care. According to her collar tabs, the woman was senior, a merchant lieutenant, so probably she was *Emerald Dawn*'s second-in-command. She looked a bit long in the tooth for that, and fairly beat up. Regen healed *almost* perfectly, but scars were inevitable—at least when a limb hadn't had to be completely regrown—and this one, for all her striking looks, had plenty. She'd been in more than one fight, and a couple of them must have been with knives.

The second most notable was the largest of the group, a hulking figure which outmassed even the redoubtable Gronningen. But something about him told Jin that he was one of those big, fast men people tended to underestimate on the theory that anyone that big had to be too slow to be dangerous. He would bear watching.

For that matter, so would the little guy. He was the calmest seeming of the lot as he leaned nonchalantly against a bulkhead, but the low-slung double pistols sort of said it all.

And all three of them wore light body armor.

Jin stepped forward carefully, keeping his hands in view at all times, and extended the pad.

"Pax, okay?" He tabbed the controls and gestured around. "All I want is a thumbprint saying that the 'inspection' was complete, and that you have no complaints. I'll put in all sorts of stuff checked, basically half the stuff on your manifest. And we're all happy. I'm happy, *you're* happy, the IBI asshole is happy, and everybody can go back to business as usual."

Beach took the pad and glanced at the document on its display. As the bullet-sweating geek had suggested, it showed a detailed inspection of an imaginary ship conforming to their class, with a list of cargo opened and checked. It was quite an artistic forgery, a masterpiece of the genre.

"Why, thank you," she said, giving him a thin smile as she annotated and thumbprinted the pad. "What's wrong? You look nervous."

"Yeah? Well, Mr. Gun-Happy over there looks like he's remembering the last baby he ate, and I ain't even gonna comment on Mr. Troll," Jin said with a nervous laugh.

"I don't eat babies," the gunman whispered. "They stick in your teeth."

"Ha. Ha," the IBI agent said.

"Done," Beach said, and handed him the pad.

"Thanks," Jin replied with a relieved sigh. His hand

was unaccountably clumsy as he accepted the pad, and it slipped out of his fingers. He swore, grabbed for it, then followed it to the deck, and as he did, he noted with the cool, professional detachment available only to the truly frightened that the threesome had reacted to the little ruse as if such things happened to them every day.

The fabric of his suit hardened under the kinetic impact of the first round just as the shuttle doors exploded open behind him.

"Shit," Giovannuci said, and hit the alarm button with a fist as he erupted from his seat. *"Jackers!"*

They couldn't simply announce that they were Marines who were commandeering the vessel in the name of the Empire. First, no one would have believed them, and, second, they were all wanted for treason. Somehow, they were pretty sure that "No, really. It was all a big mistake," wouldn't fly. So the plan was to secure the "welcome party" and try to keep casualties to a minimum in the assault.

The "plan," clearly, was a bust even before Gronningen did a flying leap out of the airlock. The undersized gunboy was pumping rounds into Jin as the IBI agent rolled across the deck to spread the hits across the protective surface of his uniform. The big guy, on the other hand, had produced a cut-down flechette cannon—from where was a mystery—and was filling the airlock with flechettes, while the leader type had produced a heavy bead pistol and had Gronningen perfectly targeted.

"Don't fire until fired upon" obviously wasn't going to work under these circumstances.

Gronningen hit the deck sliding, and targeted the little gunner first, but the gunman had taken one look at the Marine battle armor and decided the odds were against the home team. The heavy bead round clove through the bulkhead, but the gunner was already gone. Gronningen's next round, however, flipped the heavy gunner over backwards in a spray of red.

The woman was *fast*. Before he could reacquire her, she'd hit the deck exit button and was *out* of there. The inner airlock door slammed shut behind her, and Gronningen levered himself to his feet as Macek slid by and hit the door button.

"Sealed," Geno said. "Oh, well." He rolled out a slab of claylike substance and slapped it onto the hatch. "Fire in the hole!"

"Who in Muir's Name *are* these guys?" Giovannuci demanded. A security team was on the way to the command deck, but he wanted to be forward. The last thing he'd seen was a wave of heavy Imperial armor coming out of the shuttle, and that was not good news.

"I don't know," Beach replied over her communicator. "What kind of jackers wear battle armor? Or even know how to *use* it, for that matter? But if they're Empies, why don't they have a warship? And if there *is* a warship, where in hell is it?"

"I don't know," the CO replied, looking at his schematic. "But whoever they are, they're already through the lock. And moving down Deck C. It looks like they know where the morgue is."

"Do they want to *capture* us?" the second officer demanded. "I'm falling back to the Morgue, but I've only got a limited group. So far, only eight and the two commandos at the Morgue door."

"Well, I've got bodies, but *you've* got all the weapons," Giovannuci snapped. "Sidearms are useless against that armor."

"I know," Beach said. "I'm into the Armory. Now, if we can just match bodies to bullets!"

"I'll send groups through the side passages," Giovannuci said. "For once, the way they butchered this thing when they converted her will work in our favor."

"Oh, yeah? Well, next time, tell them to put the Pollution-bedamned Armory further away from the main hatch!"

"Will do. Giovannuci, out."

❖   ❖   ❖

"Lai, go with First Squad to Engineering," Pahner snapped. "Gunny Jin, you're with Second." As the teams headed out, the sergeant major snagged Jin and Despreaux. She peered into the squad leader's helmet visor, but its swirling mirrored surface made it impossible to see the younger woman's expression.

"Despreaux, I know you're not tracking too well . . ." Kosutic said.

"I'm *fine*, Sergeant Major," the sergeant replied.

"No, you're not," Kosutic contradicted calmly. "You're a basket case. So's Bebi and Niederberger. And Gelert and Mutabi, for that matter."

"Shit," Jin said. "Mutabi went?"

"Yes," Kosutic replied. "I've been trying to hold all of you out of combat as much as possible. This time, I don't have any choice."

"I'll be fine," Despreaux said desperately. "Really. I was fine in Mudh Hemh."

"Nevertheless, Jin's going along," Kosutic told her. "Let him run your squad; you just cover everyone's back."

"I can *handle* it, Sergeant Major," the sergeant said. "I *can*."

"Despreaux, just do what I say, okay?" the NCO snapped.

"Yes, Sergeant Major," she replied bitterly. "I'll go ahead and give up my squad to the Gunny."

"Trust the Gunny," Jin told her quietly, tapping her on the shoulder.

"It'll be okay," Kosutic said, as the deck shook with a distant detonation. "Somehow or another, it'll be okay."

"Who the pock *are* these guys?" Julian snapped. He'd narrowly missed being smeared by the hypervelocity missile that had just torn the bulkhead into so much confetti. For a "tramp freighter," *Emerald Dawn*'s crew had some heavy-duty hardware. And a lot of personnel.

"Captain Pahner, this is Julian. Third Squad is stuck on the approach to the Bridge. I'd estimate the defenders are in at least squad strength, with heavy weapons, and they're fighting hard. We tried to cut through bulkheads, but several of them are made of reinforced blast steel. We're having a hard time cutting that. We've eliminated two defense points, but we've also lost two suits to get here." He looked around at the four members of the squad behind him. "Frankly, Sir, I don't think we're going to get through without some reinforcements."

"Julian, hold what you've got. I'll see what I can scrounge up."

Pahner looked over at Temu Jin and raised an eyebrow. The IBI agent had been attempting to hack the ship's infonet for almost two minutes. It was clear that whatever they'd run into—smugglers, pirates, or whatever—this was no "tramp freighter."

"So, what did we just walk into Agent Jin?"

"Well, if it's a tramp freighter, I'm an Armaghan High Priest. No offense, Sergeant Major."

"None taken," Kosutic rasped. "We need to do something here, Captain."

"Yes, we do, Sergeant Major." Pahner looked over at her. "But we really, really need some information to decide what, don't you think?"

"Personnel, personnel . . ." Gunny Jin muttered, looking at the faded signs stenciled on the bulkheads. "Where's the crew quarters?"

"Kyrou, cover your sector," Despreaux snapped. The private had been glancing over at Jin as the gunny tried to navigate the unfamiliar maze.

"Yes, Sergeant," the plasma gunner replied, turning back to the right.

"Ah, crew quarters," the gunny muttered finally, then took a few steps and turned left into a cross-passage. "Oh . . . shit."

Despreaux froze as the gunny and Kyrou vanished in a ball of silver and the bulkheads to either side began to melt.

"Nimashet?" Beckley called. *"Sergeant?!"*

Despreaux felt her hands begin to shake. For just a moment, Beckley seemed kilometers away, and she closed her eyes. But then she drew a deep breath and opened them once more.

"Alpha Team, lay down a base of fire. Bravo, *move!*"

The sergeant major glanced at her schematic and grimaced.

"Lamasara's gone," she said bitterly. "We're losing people by the minute, Captain."

"Yes, we are," Pahner replied calmly. "But until I know to *whom*, we're just going to hold where we are. With one exception." He flipped to a different frequency. "St. John. Go, go, go."

St. John (J) looked over at his brother and smiled.

"Oh, goody. Time to take a little walk."

"I hate freefall," St. John (M) grumped, but he also tapped the controls of the Class A Extra-Vehicular Unit. The round EVU pack, more of a small spaceship than a suit, accepted the previously set up commands and released carefully timed puffs of gas that sent the two Marines on a course that hugged the surface of the globular starship. A course that would eventually intersect the first of two weapons hard points.

"Ah, just think of it as a stroll down to the bagel shop," St. John (J) said. He cycled his bead cannon to ensure that it was working in vacuum. "Or the Muffin Man."

"Them was the days, wasn't they, Bro?" Mark sighed. "Do you know the muffin man . . ."

"The muffin man, the muffin man," John replied.

"Do you know the muffin man," they chorused as the EVU packs picked up speed, rocketing them towards an anti-ship missile platform. A platform that probably would be heavily defended. "Do you know the muffin man, he lives in Drury Lane!"

"Got it," Jin called. He watched the data streaming out of the ship-sys and blanched. "Oh, no."

"Sergeant Julian, this is Pahner."

Julian leaned forward and sent a stream of heavy beads

down the passage to cover Gronningen. The big Asgardian darted across the opening and dove through a hatchway, barely avoiding a stream of plasma fire.

"Go ahead, Sir," the sergeant gasped.

"There's bad news and worse news. The bad news is that this isn't a tramp freighter. It's a Saint Special Operations insertion ship under the command of one Colonel Fiorello Giovannuci."

"Oh . . . pock. Commandos?"

"Greenpeace Division," Pahner confirmed. "And in case you didn't recognize the name, Giovannuci was the bastard in command of the Leonides operation a few years back. He's as good as they come . . . and a true believer."

"Oh . . . I—" Julian paused, unable to think, then shook himself. "Go ahead, Sir."

"This is where we get to the worse news," Pahner's voice said calmly. "Gunny Jin is down, probably gone, at what turned out to be the Armory, and not the crew quarters, ship's plans notwithstanding. Where Despreaux's squad is apparently blocking the majority of the commando *company* from making it into the Morgue."

"Oh. A *full* company?"

"Yes. They are, therefore, the current priority. If the Peacers get to the Armory, we are well and truly screwed, so we're just going to have to take care of them before we can reinforce *you*."

"Yes, Sir."

"Cover your back. Do not let reinforcements into the Bridge. By the same token, do not let the Bridge guards, who are almost the only ones with heavy weapons, out. Understood?"

"Hold what we've got. Nobody goes in, nobody comes out. Engineering?"

"Gunny Lai bought it there, so did Sergeant Angell. But Georgiadas has the situation under control; there's a security point there that they took, and they're covered in both directions. You're not, so hold on hard. Got it?"

"Got that in one, Sir. What's to stop them from taking off, Sir?"

"Nothing." Julian could hear the grim humor behind

that single word. "Georgiadas reports that the drive is warming up under remote from the Bridge even as we speak."

"Yes, Sir." Julian licked his lips and cursed quietly. "Sir, I'll be asked. What in the hell are we going to do? I think I'd rather face the Kranolta again."

"I'm going to do the one thing that I swore to myself I would not, under any circumstances whatsoever, especially if things were bad, stoop to."

"Go! Go! Go!"

"Your Highness, just wait!" Dobrescu snapped. "Thirty more seconds to lift. That's the optimal window. So just sit the hell down and shut the hell up."

"God*damn* it!" Roger almost punched the display, but he remembered all those centuries ago, the last time he'd been in a cramped little compartment like this one in powered battle armor and gently tapped a control panel. Yet it was hard to restrain himself. Hard. The display showed that the thirty Marines who'd lifted off to the "tramp freighter" had been reduced to twenty-four already. At this rate, there wouldn't be anyone to rescue.

"Prepare for lift," Dobrescu called over the all-hands circuit. "Helmets on! You sc—Mardukans get ready. You're going to feel *realll* heavy. Three, two, one . . ."

"Just hang on, Nimashet," Roger whispered. "Just hang on. . . ."

Four Marine assault shuttles, containing the Mardukan contingent of the *Basik*'s Own, lifted skyward on pillars of flame.

"All units, hold what you've got," Pahner called. "The cavalry is on the way."

"Satan, protect us," Kosutic snapped as a team of commandos rolled across the corridor. She winged one, but the other three got away. "We're getting outmaneuvered and outshot, Captain."

"I've noticed," Pahner said calmly. "Suggestions?"

"Let Poertena and me take it to them," Kosutic said. "Having a mobile force will force them to react."

"I'll have a mobile force here in—" He consulted his suit. "Seven minutes."

"Seven minutes is a lonnng time, Armand."

Pahner sighed and nodded.

"That it is."

"Aaaahhh!"

"Oh, calm down, Rastar," Roger grunted. The shuttles still had the extra hydrogen tanks installed, and the plotted intercept had been calculated based upon that almost limitless fuel supply. So they'd lifted at three gravities and would hit a DV-Max of almost seven. For Roger and the pilots, that was simply very unpleasant. For the Mardukans, who had never experienced more than a couple of gravities during their limited micro-gravity familiarization flights, it was a nightmare.

They'd put all of them through at least one lift, but nothing like this. The humans had managed to convince themselves that there was no conceivable situation in which the Mardukans would actually be used for a combat assault, so they hadn't subjected them to the real stresses of such a launch. And now the Mardukans, and their allies, were paying the price for that complacent gentleness.

"All hands, remember, *crunch!*" Roger gasped. "Squeeze your stomach like you're taking a dump, but plug your butt." He glanced over at the telltales. "There's only another . . . three minutes."

"I *hate* freefall," St. John (M) said as he hugged the hull of the ship.

Their EVU packs were gone, and the two Marines were now flat on their faces behind a tiny exterior catwalk. The first emplacement, a missile launcher, had been undefended. But by the time they made it to the second and last, a heavy plasma cannon, the Saints had suffered a rush of common sense and sent one of their few "free" heavy weapons to protect it. The ship-to-ship cannon itself couldn't depress far enough to engage the Marines, or they'd already have been reduced to constituent atoms, but the heavy bead gun that had popped out of the firing port had them well and truly pinned. Because of the angle it had, they couldn't even back up and swing around.

"Mom always said we'd come to a bad end," St. John (J) said.

"Don't go all heroic on me, Bro," Mark said. "There's got to be a smart way out of this."

"In about thirty seconds, the prince is going to come over the horizon, Mark." John readied his plasma cannon. "So you've got exactly twenty seconds to figure something out."

"Oh, that's not hard," Mark said . . . and stood up.

The first bead took him in the left arm. The heavy projectile smashed the ChromSten armor like tissue paper, severing the limb just above the elbow in a spray of gas and body liquids.

"Pock, not again," he gasped as he aimed his cannon one-handed at the base of the defensive platform and locked the trigger back.

"Pollution," Giovannuci whispered as he turned away from the display. The armored form had taken three bead rounds before the plasma platform went up, but it was still firing. Whoever it was *had* to be dead. But he kept firing until *Emerald Dawn*'s last space defenses turned into floating bits of wreckage.

"What does it take to *kill* these people? *Who the fuck are they?*"

"Sir," his com tech said, "you have *got* to hear this."

CHAPTER THIRTY-TWO

"Saint ship, this is His Highness Prince Roger MacClintock. Cease resistance to this legal boarding, and you will be detained for eventual repatriation as prisoners of war. Continue your resistance, and you'll be considered unlawful combatants under the laws of war. In two minutes, I will be performing a forced boarding with the remainder of Prince Roger's Own. You have until then to comply."

"Is there any indication which shuttle that's coming from?"

"Negative, Colonel Giovannuci. It's being rebroadcast from all four."

"Pity," *Emerald Dawn*'s commander murmured, then shrugged. "Put me on."

"Approaching shuttles, be aware that the prince is dead. He was killed in a shipwreck. So you're not him."

Roger looked at the communicator and shrugged.

"Believe what you will, but the report of my demise was exceedingly exaggerated. One minute, twenty seconds."

"If we surrender, they'll probably do what they say," Beach said over the discrete command channel. "These can't be jackers. Only Imperial Marines are this precise. Its Empies, all right."

"And that means it might *be* the prince," Colonel Giovannuci mused. "But it doesn't really matter. If we surrender and they repatriate us, the clerics will send us to the wall. The only real choice is to win."

He considered the situation, regarding the monitors covering the three main fights. He knew that Beach, like most naval officers assigned to SpecOps, resented the tradition which put Army officers in command of the ships assigned to them. He was even prepared to admit— privately—that the Navy's arguments against the practice might have a point when it came to naval actions. But this was *his* sort of fight, not Beach's, and he thought about his options for a moment longer, then looked up at the commando lieutenant at his elbow.

"I don't like them holding the Bridge passage. I want some freedom of movement. Take some of the Bridge guards and work around to the other side of them. Then we'll try to nutcracker them between us—clear them out and get ourselves some room to maneuver. While you get into position, I'll be dealing with this pompous oaf."

"Prince Roger, or whoever you are, thanks for the offer. But, no. I think we'll take our chances."

Roger shrugged again and flipped the schematic to show the approach vectors.

"Have it your way. See you in a few minutes." He changed frequencies and nodded at the image of Fain that appeared on the monitor. "Captain, when we dock, send one platoon to the Bridge, one to the Armory, and one to Engineering."

"As you command, Your Highness," the Diaspran said.

"I'll be going to the Bridge. I recommend that you take one of the other locations." Roger turned to the Vashin who shared the compartment and waved a hand. "Rastar, I want your guys to head for the boat bays, but other than that, just spread out and slow down these Saints that are trying to sneak their way to the Armory. Send one unit to Captain Pahner, though, for him to use as a reserve."

"Okay," Rastar said as the acceleration finally came off. "That's a relief," he added with a sigh of bliss as the shuttle changed to freefall.

"Don't get used to it," Roger advised . . . just as the deceleration hit.

"Aaaaaaahhhh . . ."

"Colonel, we're getting killed down here," Beach said. "I've slipped a few people through to the Armory, but they're just making up for our losses. We're stalemated."

She looked at her schematic and shook her head with an unheard snarl.

"And we've got somebody moving around. I just lost a team by Hold Three."

"I know," Giovannuci replied, watching his own displays. The internal systems hadn't been designed to handle a pitched battle, but he'd been able to use the monitors to follow at least some of the action. Not that very many of them were left; the invaders had been systematically shooting them out. He could more or less tell where they'd *been* from the breadcrumb trail of smashed pickups in their wake, but not, generally, where they currently were.

"The bad news is that they're about to receive reinforcements," he told his executive officer. "We need to break the stalemate before that happens, or at least to get some mobility going for us."

"Suggestions are welcome," Beach said tartly.

"About the only thing that might work is hitting one of the defense points and breaking out," the colonel said. "It will only take a couple of minutes to get set. We'll hit them simultaneously in five minutes."

"Works for me," Beach agreed laconically. "And I hope to hell it works for all of us. If the Empies don't kill us, the clerics will."

Eva Kosutic slid along the passage, using her turned-up audio and movement sensors to search for hostiles . . . and trying very, very hard not to let anyone on the other side know where *she* was. The majority of the Saints were in light body armor and skin suits, so fairly light weaponry was capable of penetrating it with carefully aimed fire. In her case, she'd loaded one of her dual magazines with low-velocity penetrator rounds. Designed to avoid damage to important systems in shipboard actions, they left a very small hole in their victim and didn't tumble or expand upon entry. But they were capable of defeating light armor points and portions of helmets. And for Eva Kosutic, that was all that was required.

Her sensors told her there was another group moving along the same passage, trying to infiltrate past the various Marine groups to the Armory. She looked around, and then lifted herself into an overhead position, holding herself in place against the deckhead with one hand and both legs planted.

"I'm going to send all these Pollution-damned Empies straight to Hell," Sergeant Leustean said. The commando NCO twisted his hand on the foregrip of his bead rifle and snarled. "Straight to Hell."

"Well, don't get us all kilt doin' it," Corporal Muravyov replied.

"We'll be doing the killing!" the sergeant snapped . . . just as the sergeant major opened fire.

The first three shots entered just below their targets' helmets, penetrating the light armor on the relatively undefended patch at the top of the neck and severing the cervical vertebrae. But by the third shot, the team was reacting, the highly trained commandos spinning and diving for cover. But good as they were, they didn't stand much of a chance up against a suit of combat armor, and an even more highly trained Imperial bodyguard who'd just gone through an advanced course in combat survival.

Kosutic dropped to the deck and walked over to prod the bodies.

"Not today, Sergeant." She sighed, then glanced at her telltales. More movement. "Not today."

✧   ✧   ✧

Roger double-checked the seal, then hit the hatch release, letting Rastar and two other Vashin precede him through the still-smoking hole in the ship's side.

Even freighters used ChromSten for their hulls. The material was expensive, making up a sizable fraction of the total cost of the ship. But given that it was proof against almost all varieties of space radiation, and an excellent system to protect against micro-meteor impacts, it was worth every credit.

Freighters did not, however, have warship-thickness ChromSten. The material on the outside of a freighter was generally less than two microns thick, whereas a warship's might be up to a centimeter. And it was that difference which had permitted the thermal lances on the assault shuttles to eat through the hull in less than three seconds.

The point Roger had chosen for his hull breaching was one of the vessel's innumerable holds, and its interior was filled with shipping canisters of every conceivable size and shape. Roger took a look around, shrugged, and waved the Vashin forward. Somewhere, there was a battle to be joined.

Rastar tapped the controls of the sealed portal, but it was clear that the hatch out of the hold was locked.

"I'll fix that, Your Highness," one of his Vashin said, lifting his plasma gun.

Rastar backpedaled furiously, but he still caught the fringes of the blast as the door shattered outwards.

"Watch those things!" he shouted, then keyed the radio to transmit as the luckless cavalryman flew back from the doorway, most of his mass converted to charcoal. "Watch those things. They're not carbines, for Valan's sake!" He looked around and then down at his suit. "Why is the suit hardening?"

"Damned scummies," Dobrescu growled as he clambered past the prince. Roger could barely hear him over the shrill wail of escaping atmosphere. The blast from the plasma cannon and the resulting overpressure had popped part of the temporary seals between the shuttle's hull and the hole blasted through *Emerald Dawn*'s skin.

"Watch your fire!" the warrant officer shouted over the Vashin frequency.

"Can we do anything about it?" Roger asked.

"Not unless I pull away and reseal," Dobrescu replied sourly. "We might as well wait until we repair the hole."

"Which brings up an interesting point. Do we have anyone who knows how to weld ChromSten?"

"Fine time to ask now, Your Highness," Dobrescu said with a harsh laugh.

"We weren't supposed to have been facing this much resistance," the prince pointed out.

"Begging your pardon, Prince Roger," one of the Vashin said as he trotted over through the increasing vacuum. "Prince Rastar's compliments, and we have no idea which way to go."

Roger chuckled and gestured at Dobrescu.

"Get going, Doc. Raise as much hell as you can while doing the minimum damage. Keep them from reinforcing the Bridge, Engineering, and the Armory. Pay attention to the shuttle bays, especially."

"Got it," Dobrescu acknowledged, adjusting his carbine sling. "Where are you going?"

"Bridge," Roger replied as four Vashin fell in with him. He arranged them so that the sole plasma gunner was in *front* of him. The others' bead cannons were loaded with shot rounds and couldn't penetrate his armor.

"Now we find out if I'm a genius, or an idiot."

Giovannuci flipped through screens, trying to get a handle on the battle. He was sure all four of the shuttles had managed to breach and board, and one was visible on an exterior monitor. Unfortunately, the holds were poorly covered at the best of times, and so far he hadn't been able to find out how many of the Marine reinforcements had come aboard.

He touched another control, then looked up as he heard Lieutenant Anders Cellini, his tactical officer, gasp.

"Sir," the tac officer said in a strangled voice. "Screen four-one-four."

Giovannuci keyed the monitor for Hold Three and froze in shock.

"Are those what I think they are, Sir?" Cellini asked with a pronounced edge of disbelief.

"They're scummies," Giovannuci replied in a voice of deadly calm. "With plasma and bead cannons. That resource-sucking, inbred cretin gave *scummies* plasma cannon. And he brought them aboard *my* ship!"

"Well, at least it's not more Empie Marines." The tac officer sounded as if he were trying very hard to find a bright side to look upon, and Giovannuci barked a harsh, humorless almost-laugh.

"You're joking, right?" he snapped. "Empie Marines would at least know not to blow holes in the side of the *ship*; that hold is *depressurized*."

When Harvard saw the yellow light above the hatch, he knew that volunteering to "help out" had been a bad idea. Not that he'd had a lot of choice. There were so few Marines left that, in the end, the prince had shanghaied every human he thought he could trust to assist the Mardukans. Now technicians from the port, and even complete civilians like Mansul, were running around the interior of a Saint Q-ship, trying to keep the scummies from killing themselves.

It was turning out to be a difficult assignment.

"The button won't open the door," Honal snarled, hitting the circuit again.

"Uh . . ."

For entirely understandable safety considerations, Harvard had wedged himself into the middle of the scummies' formation. Unfortunately, this meant he couldn't reach the Vashin nobleman before the light dawned.

"Aha!" Honal said. "The emergency release."

"Honaaalll!"

It was too late. Before the human could get the Vashin's attention, Honal had flipped out the emergency unlock lever and thrown it over.

As Honal would have realized, had he been able actually to read the information displayed on the lock-assembly, the far compartment wasn't totally depressurized. It was, however, at a much lower atmospheric pressure than the near side of the hatch. The result was a rather strong suction.

Honal was unable to let go of the hatch before it flew backwards, dragging him with it. However, the physics of its opening, rather than spinning him to slam into the bulkhead, combined with the blast of wind at his back to pick him up and pitch him violently down the passage.

All that Mansul could hear was a short, cut-off cry, the clang of the hatch hitting the stops, and a crunching sound. Then he was carried along by the stampede as the Therdan contingent rushed to the aid of its commander.

Harvard found him lying against a piece of radiometric monitoring gear, crumpled and twisted like a pretzel. His head was tucked under one armpit, and one of his legs was thrown over backwards, touching the deck.

"So, Harvard Mansul," he croaked. "What *does* a yellow light mean?"

"You're joking, right?" Beach had lost contact with Ucelli and was trying to round up more stragglers to feed into the cauldron around the Armory. She was also hunting Empies. A team had been ambushed somewhere around here, and she was determined to track down the Marines responsible. She'd sent Ucelli to block the passage leading up from Cargo Main, but now she wished she'd kept him around. The little gunslinger would've been good backup for facing down scummies. Although . . . maybe not scummies armed with plasma cannon.

"No, we're down to the wire, here," the colonel said. "If we can't get more people armed up and armored, I'm going to have to punch the ship."

"I'd really appreciate it if you didn't do that," Beach said. "I know we've had our differences over the One

Faith, but you have to admit that suicide generally isn't a good thing. Think of the resource waste."

Giovannuci smiled thinly at her over the monitor.

"No, Beach, we *are* different. You see, I *believe*, and you don't. That's why I'm in command, and you're not. If you can't break the deadlock at the Armory, I'll have to set the scuttling charges."

"Oh, grand," she whispered, after she'd cut the circuit. She thought furiously for a moment, but she couldn't really see a way out. The tactical officer had a second key for the self-destruct mechanism, so she was unnecessary; her absence from the Bridge wouldn't keep Giovannuci from doing exactly what he'd just said he would.

"Oh, Pollution," she whispered again . . . then slammed into the bulkhead as her uniform hardened under a savage kinetic impact.

She bounced back and spun in place, raising her bead rifle, but a whirl of silver smashed into the breech, crushed her left hand, and pitched the weapon from her grasp. She started to drop into a crouch, but the backswing caught her on the side of the helmet, and she rebounded off the bulkhead again, then slumped to the deck.

Poertena used the wrench to smash out the monitor, then dragged the unconscious officer into a nearby supply cabinet. Assuming they survived this goat-pock, they might need her, so he pulled off her communicator and weapons, then welded the door shut. The door had an air seal and was marked as an emergency life-support shelter, so as long as the ship didn't explode, she should be fine.

Rastar looked down the seemingly endless passageway, and then glanced at the human pilot.

"You're sure it's this way?"

"That's what the schematic said," Dobrescu replied shortly. "It's a ways yet."

"Very well." The Vashin prince lifted his arm into the air in a broad and a dramatic gesture. "To the shuttle bays!"

He continued down the high, wide passage. It was the first thing they'd found on the ship that wasn't made for midgets, and it was a vast relief. He and Honal had divided their forces in order to approach the shuttle bays from different directions in the hope that one of them might get through unintercepted. So far, neither of them had encountered any actual resistance, and that made Rastar very, very nervous. It was also one reason he was so glad to see this spacious corridor. All the Mardukans found the normal short, narrow passages, and the strangely close "horizon" caused by the curvature of the ship, very odd and alien, but his concern was much more basic. The farther ahead he could see, the less likely he was to walk into an ambush.

After about five minutes, they reached a "T" intersection, with signs leading to the Bridge and the shuttle bays. The Vashin noble waved to the left, then watched as the plasma gunner on point flew backwards with the entire back of his head blown out.

Rastar didn't even think about his response. He simply drew all four bead pistols and leapt across the relatively narrow intersection, guns blazing. He was surprised, however, to see only a single human figure in the passage. The human was standing with pistols in each hand, and they flashed upward like lightning as Rastar leapt. Despite the fact that the human couldn't possibly have known exactly where and when Raster would appear, four rounds cracked into the Vashin's suit before he landed on the far side of the intersection.

Fortunately, none of them penetrated, and Rastar slammed to the deck. He raised his hands to the group on the far side, motioning for them to stay put. Then he popped his head out and back, quickly, followed by a hand in a "wait a moment" gesture that was nearly as universal among Mardukans as it was among humans.

When that didn't draw any fire, he poked his head out into the corridor, as close to the deck as he could get it. This time the response was immediate and vigorous, and Rastar swore as he jerked back. One of the incoming rounds had missed completely, but the other had plowed a groove in the side of his helmet. Another half-centimeter to the side, and it would have plowed a hole clear *through* the helmet, which would have been most unpleasant.

The Prince of Therdan sat back, considering what he'd seen in his single, brief glance. The Saint was short, even for a *basik*—not much taller than Poertena. But the speed and lethal accuracy he'd already demonstrated told the prince that here was an opponent worthy of him. It wasn't as good as swords or knives, but it would have to do.

He thought for a few more moments, then grinned in the human fashion as he saw the sign on the bulkhead beside him. He didn't know where the passage the human was in actually led, but it *didn't* lead to the shuttle bays, assuming the bulkhead sign was correct. The little gunman must have chosen his position to take anyone headed for the shuttle bays in the flank as they passed.

"Dobrescu?" he said over the radio.

"Yes?"

"Go back the way we came. Link up with Honal."

"What about you?"

"I think this fellow is good enough that we'd all like him kept right where he is," Rastar replied.

As he spoke, he eased a bit closer to the intersection, then leaned out, spotted the human—half-concealed now behind what looked like a ripped-out hatch—and fired four rounds rapid-fire. His opponent ducked, but only for an instant, and then it was Rastar's turn to roll hastily further into cover as beads screamed lethally past.

"You go find Honal," he told the human healer cheerfully. "I'll stay here and play for a while."

"We've got to go," Giovannuci said, and sealed his uniform jacket. The material wouldn't be proof against the plasma and bead cannon of the Empie Marines, but it would at least give some protection from flashback and spalling.

"What about Beach, Sir?" Cellini asked.

Giovannuci only shrugged and gestured at the hatch,

but as the armored commando keyed the opening, he wondered himself. The first officer was one of only four people who could disarm the scuttling charges, after all.

"Captain Pahner, we've got a counterattack going!" Despreaux called. "They're attempting to break out from the Armory!"

"How are you doing?" Pahner asked. Captain Fain had been held up by a small group of wandering commandos, but he was nearly to the sergeant's position—no more than a minute out. Of course, in combat, a minute was a *long* time.

"Kyrou and Birkendal are dead, Sir," the sergeant replied. Pahner could hear the thump of fire in the background over her voice. Given that she was inside armor, that meant some heavy impacts. "Clarke's hit, but still fighting, and the St. Johns are out on the hull. I'm down to four people, Sir."

"Just hold out for another minute, Sergeant," the captain replied calmly. "Just one minute. Fain's nearly there."

"We'll try, Sir," she said. "I'm—"

Pahner shook his head as the communications system automatically dumped a feedback squeal. Something had filled the frequency with static. He knew what the sound meant, but that didn't mean he had to like it.

"Sergeant Despreaux?" He asked. Silence answered. "Computer, switch: Beckley?"

"Sir!" The Alpha Team leader was panting. "Despreaux's down! We're in bug-out boogie mode, Sir. The Armory is open!"

"Hold tight, Beckley," Pahner replied. "You just have to hold on!"

"I'd like to, Sir, but it's just me and Kileti functional. Kane bought it, Chio has Clarke, and I have Nimashet. We're going to try to pull back through the Diasprans and hand over the fight. We don't have a choice, Sir."

"Computer, switch: Fain!"

Gronningen ducked as a burst of plasma filled the passage with steam. A previous burst had penetrated the inboard bulkhead and cracked a gray-water pipe. Now the blast turned the gray-water to vapor and fecal plasma.

"Julian!" he called, lifting his own plasma cannon over the security station and blasting away in return. "They're trying to break out!"

"*All units,*" Pahner announced over the general frequency. "*General counterattack underway. Hold what you've got; the Diasprans are nearly there!*"

"Pocking hell," the squad leader snarled, sliding on his belly towards the plasma gunner's position. "Why couldn't they just wait for our reinforcements?"

"Because they don't want to die?" the Asgardian suggested. "You know—"

The second blast of plasma had been more carefully coordinated, with two plasma cannons and a bead cannon all aimed at the base of the security point. Although the security point was a "hard patch," a ChromSten plate which was not only secured to the bulkhead but anchored into the next deck, the concentrated blast from multiple sources first weakened the armored patch, then ripped it out of its frame.

The ChromSten plate, its backing of hardened steel melted in the intense heat, flew down the passage, catching Moseyev unawares and slamming him into the outboard bulkhead.

And all the coordinated fire the plate was no longer intercepting tore into Gronningen.

Julian ducked under the last blast of plasma fire, reached the stricken Asgardian, and rolled him over. The final blast had caught him just below the waist, and shredded the heavy body armor with effortless viciousness. Gronningen's eyes were screwed shut, but he opened them for just a moment, raising a hand to his squad leader. His mouth worked soundlessly, and the hand clamped on the sergeant's armored shoulder.

Then it dropped, and Adib Julian let out a scream of pure primal rage.

"Stay down!" Macek bellowed as he grabbed Julian

from behind and fought to wrestle him to the deck, but Julian wasn't interested in staying down.

"*Dead!* They're all *dead!*" he yelled, and swatted Macek away like a toy.

"Sergeant Julian," Pahner called. "What is your situation?"

"*I'm sending them all to hell, Sir!*" the sergeant yelled back, and picked up the plasma gunner's weapon.

Julian's toot, courtesy of Temu Jin, had been reloaded with all the hacking protocols available to military and civilian intelligence, alike. He used them now, diving deep into the central circuits of his own armor, ripping out security protocols until the system was down to bare bones. Although personal armor was designed to be partially mobile in zero-gravity, the jump system had never been designed for full-gravity combat. But by taking all the control systems off of what was, effectively, a small plasma cannon, the sergeant could create a jump capability that was actually worth the name.

Of course, there were drawbacks.

"Don't try this at home, boys and girls," he hissed, and hit the power circuit.

His leap carried him over the barricade and into the deckhead, and the howling plasma stream melted the bulkheads behind him.

Macek let out a yowl as the stream passed across his lower legs, heating the nearly invulnerable armor of his suit and jumping the internal temperature nearly a hundred degrees. The automatic systems dumped the heat nearly as fast as it went up, but for just a moment, the armor made Marduk seem cool.

Julian's armor smashed into the overhead, taking him partially into the upper deck, throwing him from side to side in an erratic pattern that was impossible for the Saint battle armor to track. Somehow, he managed to turn a bounce into a spin, bringing himself around as the last of the power was expended, and as the jump gear's last, spiteful bit of plasma bit into the overhead, he caromed from one side of the passage to the other until he landed on his feet *behind* the Saint defenders.

The four Saints were still trying to track in on him as his first blast hit them. He swept the weapon from side to side, low, ripping their legs out from under them. As the commandos fell, he continued to sweep the weapon back and forth, ignoring the screaming emergency overload indicator as he melted not only their fallen battle armor, but the deck underneath and the bulkheads to either side. He expended the cannon's power like a drunkard, but before the capacitor completely discharged, the overloaded control circuits let go.

The ball of undirected plasma picked the sergeant up and slammed him backwards into the armored command deck hatch. Since the door was made of ChromSten, like the armor, but much thicker, he hit and bounced.

Hard.

Krindi Fain shook his head as the human suits fell backward into the intersecting side passage and then rolled around the corner for shelter. The air in the other passage was silver and red with plasma bolts, and the bulkhead on the opposite edge of the corridor disappeared as the fire from the Saints punched through it into one of the innumerable holds before dissipating itself on the cargo.

His unit—twenty Diasprans, the captain himself, Erkum Pol, and the drummer—was approaching from the ship's west. The Armory ought to be about twenty meters up the passageway the humans had just tumbled out of. And, obviously, it was heavily defended.

"Ah, me," he muttered as he fumbled with the human radio controls. "SNAPU: Situation Normal, All Pocked Up. First Platoon will prepare to engage," he said, continuing to trot towards the intersection as he finally got the radio to work properly. The fire had slackened off to what the defenders obviously believed was enough to keep the Marines from reentering the passage. "Platoon will face right into the corridor, in column of threes, proceeding to the Armory by volley fire at a march. Platoon, quick time . . . *march*."

✧   ✧   ✧

"Sergeant, what's that?"

Private Kapila Ammann would have been just as happy to crawl back into his bunk. He'd long ago quit trying to figure out why he'd ever joined the commandos. It was days like this that made him count the number of hours until his ETS date, but the way things were going, he wasn't going to make it for another one hundred and twenty-six days, fourteen hours, and—he glanced at his chrono—twenty-three minutes.

"What's what?" Sergeant Gao snapped, then looked up in surprise from the casualty he was treating. "A unit . . . marching?"

"Holy Pollution," Ammann whispered as the Diasprans rounded the corner. *"They gave scummies plasma guns!"*

In the last few months, the Diasprans had gone through revolutions in weaponry that humans had taken millennia to achieve. They'd started off as untrained conscripts who had been turned into pikemen. Then they'd progressed to musketeers, then to rifle skirmishers, and now they were plasma and bead gunners. But much of their drill from the early days remained. And they used it now.

The first rank turned the corner, pivoting on the interior Mardukan, leveled their plasma cannon, and opened fire, stepping forward at a walk.

CHAPTER THIRTY-THREE

"Aaaaahh!"

Kapila hugged the deck as the air literally disappeared around him. The Mardukan fire mostly went over his head, but its intensity first superheated the atmosphere in the corridor, then expanded it to the very fringe of vacuum. He supposed he could return the fire, but there didn't seem to be much point. If he killed one or two of the scummies with a shot, the rest would turn him into drifting atoms for his efforts. Even if they didn't, a near miss would be sufficient to kill him. Flying fragments could easily punch holes in his standard ship suit, which would permit the intense heat to fry him to a crisp . . . which would at least save him from asphyxiation when his suit depressurized.

But so far, they seemed to be missing. He liked that, and he had no intention of doing anything to change it.

He rolled his head to look back up the passage behind him and saw that the entire unit was gone. One or two of them might have gotten back into the Armory, but he saw at least four carbon statues that indicated casualties. Graubart was still alive, though. He might even stay that way, if he got some prompt medical attention. Sergeant Gao, on the other hand, was just a pair of legs, attached to some cooked meat.

Kapila slid his bead rifle carefully to the side and spreadeagled himself on the deck, hoping that the scummies would settle for just capturing him.

Of course, he'd heard that scummies tortured their prisoners to death. But if it was a question of the possibility of torture, or absolutely buying it from a plasma blast, he'd go for the possibility any day.

"Cease fire," Fain ordered as he stepped around a gaping hole in the deck. His troopers' fire had opened the bulkheads on either side of the passage to the surrounding compartments, and the wrecked corridor sparked with electricity and finely divided steam. The ChromSten reinforced Armory had shrugged off most of the damage, and now most of one of its walls and its support structure—which had taken a beating—could be seen through the gaps in the bulkheads. All in all, they'd done quite a bit of damage, he reflected. But as long as they were in their suits, the environmental conditions were survivable. Actually, things were looking good; the Armory hatch was shut, and the passage was secure.

"Sergeant Sern, take four men and secure the far end of the hall." He fumbled with his radio some more until he managed to shift frequencies. "Captain Pahner, we have the corridor outside the Armory. The doors are shut, though."

There was a human—presumably one of the "Saint Commandos"—lying face-down on the deck. He didn't appear to be injured, but he had his fingers interlaced on the back of his helmet, and he wasn't moving. Fain gestured to Pol, who picked the wretch up by the back of his uniform and dangled him in the air.

"And it seems that we have a prisoner, too."

Roger rounded the corner to the bridge entrance and stopped, shaking his head in awe. The ship was trashed. Indeed, never in his worst nightmares had he ever imagined that a ship *could* be so trashed and still hang together.

More or less.

The deck looked as if it had been carved by a giant kindergartner who had somehow gotten his hands on an absentmindedly mislaid blowtorch. The heavy-duty plastic of the decksole had melted and splashed, leaving jagged splatters, like impressionistic stalagmites, on the bulkheads and huge dripping holes in the deck itself. The bulkheads had sustained major damage of their own, as well. Many of the holes blasted through them were large enough for battle armor to crawl through into the surrounding compartments. One of the larger ones led to what had once been the captain's day cabin, which was as thoroughly trashed as the passageway itself.

And the Bridge hatch was, once again, firmly shut.

Roger sighed as the drifting smoke and steam suddenly moved sideways and disappeared. He didn't have to look at the red vacuum morning light on his helmet HUD to figure out what had just happened.

"Memo to self," he muttered. "Giving Mardukans—or Marines, for that matter—plasma cannon on a ship assault is contraindicated."

Honal followed the first entry team into the shuttle bay, then dove sideways as a blast of bead-fire tore the three Vashin apart. Fire seemed to be coming from everywhere in the open bay, but the majority of the human defenders were on the far side, near the bay's huge outer hatches. It was easy enough to tell where they were, but doing anything about it was another matter, because they'd taken shelter behind a massive raised plate which undoubtedly did something significant when shuttles were parked in the vast, cavernous space.

Honal favored bead rifles over cannons, since the full-sized rifles—after suitable reshaping by Poertena—made a short, handy carbine for someone the size of a Mardukan. Now he used his to return fire, walking the beads along the top of the plate. Each hit tore a chunk out of the top of the device—whatever it was—but didn't seem to faze any of the humans crouched behind it.

The rest of the Vashin entered behind him, but the fire which greeted them was murderous. Beside the Saints by the main airlocks, there were more scattered on catwalks around the bay, and some sheltering by a second set of hatches. The combined crossfire had the Vashin pinned down in the open, without any cover of their own, and the defenders were methodically massacring them.

"The hell with this!" Honal snarled. He and the human Mansul were partially sheltered by a control panel. It had taken a few hits, but it was still functional, judging by the red and green flashing symbols above the buttons at its center. He contemplated the device for a moment, and then smiled.

"Mansul, can you work this thing?"

Harvard Mansul had been in a few tight situations in his life. He'd dealt with bandits on more than one occasion, and even done a small piece on them at one point. Then there'd been the pirates. He'd been on a ship once when it was boarded by pirates, but the head of the group had been an IAS reader and let him go. In fact, he'd been sent on his way with an autographed photo of the suitably masked pirate leader. He'd been shot at by inner city gangs, stabbed doing a shoot in Imperial City, and nearly died that time his team got lost in the desert. Then there'd been being picked up by the Krath and imprisoned by a batch of ritualistic cannibals. That had been unpleasant.

But being pinned down by a Saint Special Operations team raised "unpleasant" to a new high. Nothing else on the list of his previous life experiences even came close. So sticking his head up to look at the control panel was not high on his list of priorities.

But he took a quick peek, anyway.

"Hatches, grav, cargo handling, environmental!" he shouted, pointing to the appropriate sections of the panel in turn. "What are you going to do?"

"Play a practical joke."

"Here goes nothing," Honal muttered to himself, and hit a green button.

Nothing happened. He waited a heartbeat or two to be certain of that, then grimaced. Time for Phase Two, he thought, and lifted the clear, protective plastic box over the red button beside the green.

He depressed it.

The blast of wind from the half-melted hatch behind him shoved him into the control panel hard, but that was about all. The Saints on the far side of the bay, with their backs to the opening shuttle bay doors, were less fortunate. More than half of them were picked up and sucked out the opening portal before they could react. The rest, unfortunately, managed to find handholds and hung on until the extremely brief blast of pressure change stopped. Then they opened fire again.

"Well, *that* didn't work," Honal grumbled irritably. The brief delight he'd felt when the first humans vanished out the opening only made his irritation when the others didn't even more intense, and he contemplated the controls again. Mansul's description of their functions was considerably less than bare bones, he reflected. And he, after all, was only an ignorant Vashin *civan*-rider. It was unreasonable to expect him to actually understand what any of them did, so perhaps he should simply do what came naturally.

He started hitting buttons at random.

Lights went on and off. Panels appeared out of the deck and rose, and other panels disappeared, while cranes and pulleys and less readily identifiable pieces of equipment dashed back and forth on overhead rails. Honal had no idea what any of the fascinating, confusing movements and energy were supposed to achieve under normal conditions. But he didn't much care, either, when one of the buttons lowered the platform the Saints had been sheltering behind into the deck. And then, finally, the gravity itself disappeared.

Honal watched an astonished Saint commando spin over in mid-air—well, mid-vacuum, the Vashin noble corrected himself—when he fired his bead rifle just as someone snatched the shuttle bay's gravity away from him. The Saint sailed helplessly out into the open, propelled by the unexpected reaction engine his rifle had just become, and then exploded in a grisly profusion of crimson blood beads as a burst of someone's fire tore him almost in half.

"Now this is more like it!" Honal said with a huge, human-style grin as he drew his sword and gripped the top of the control center with his false-hands as if it were a vaulting horse. "Vashin! Up and at 'em! *Cold steel!*"

"Roger, what's your position?" Pahner asked.

For a wonder, it looked as if things might be stabilizing. Georgiadas had managed to kill enough of the Saints counterattacking his position to hold on until the Diasprans arrived. Now he had Engineering intact, and while there might (or might not) still be a few of the enemy inside the Armory, Krindi Fain's troops had it isolated and fully contained. The counterattack by *Emerald Dawn*'s bridge personnel had also been stopped, and the Vashin were running rampant. Pahner's own area was still pressurized, but two-thirds of the ship had lost pressure, and large portions of the internal gravity net had been shut down. The Northern cavalry had developed a positive liking for zero-g combat. Which was just . . . sick.

He didn't want to think about the hideous price his people and their Mardukan allies had paid, but the Saints were clearly on the defensive and well on the way to completely losing their ship. Now if they could only talk *Emerald Dawn*'s surviving officers out of the Bridge before they did irreparable harm.

"I'm at the Bridge security point. Gronningen's dead, and Julian is injured. About the only ones standing are Moseyev, Aburia, and Macek, and even they aren't in very good shape; I'd put their armor at no more than thirty percent of base capability. Max. I'm getting ready to negotiate with the Saint commander."

"Understood." Pahner waved for Temu Jin to stay where he was, monitoring the hacked infonet, then headed up the passageway at a trot. "Wait until I get there. I've seen the results of your negotiations too many times."

❖　　　❖　　　❖

"Saint commander, this is Prince Roger."

Giovannuci looked over at the sweating tactical officer. Sergeant Major Iovan, who'd been with the colonel since Giovannuci was a shavetail, stood with a bead pistol screwed into Cellini's ear. Having a gun in one's ear could make just about anyone sweat, but the tactical officer was looking particularly wan. It had taken a while to get him to give up his release codes, and even longer for the computer to accept them. Probably because of his stammering. But now he seemed more or less resigned to his fate.

"Well, Prince Roger, or whoever you are. This is Colonel Fiorello Giovannuci, Imperial Cavazan Special Operations Branch. What can I do for you?"

"You can surrender your ship. I gave you one chance, and now most of your crew, and commandos, are dead. Last chance. Surrender, and we'll spare the rest. Resist, and I'll give you all to the Krath. They're ritualistic cannibals, but they don't get squeamish about humans."

"Well, I'll give *you* a couple of choices, buddy," the Saint snarled furiously. "Get off my ship, or I'll blow it up!"

"Talk to me, Armand," Roger said, looking at the sealed hatch.

"I'm on my way to the Bridge. Engineering and the Armory are secured. Captain Fain just took the Armory. But we've got to figure out what to do about this scuttling threat."

"Do think he's serious?" Roger asked. "He sounds that way."

"*Most* Saints aren't true-believers," Pahner said. "Unfortunately, I've heard of Giovannuci, and he *is*. Hold one, Your Highness. Computer: patch Kosutic."

"Kosutic," the sergeant major acknowledged, peering over her bead rifle's sights at the Saints she'd captured. "I think we've got most of the actual ship's crew, Armand. They seem a lot less interested in dying gloriously than the commandos."

"Good, but we have a situation," Pahner told her. "Tell me what you know about Saint scuttling charges."

"I take it this isn't an academic exercise," she said with a grimace. "They're always timer-delayed. They require a code and a key to activate—two of them, actually; they can't be set by just one person. They require at least one key and code to deactivate, but any key and code will work. They work on the basis of positive action locks; if you don't have the code and key, you're not going to turn them off. Authorized code/key holders are usually the CO, the exec, the tactical officer, and the chief engineer."

"Okay," Pahner replied. "That's what I recalled, too. Computer: all hands. All Imperial personnel, begin evacuation of the ship. Computer: command group. Captain Fain? Rastar?"

"Here," Fain called.

"This is Honal," Rastar's cousin said a moment later. "Rastar is . . . occupied, but we've secured the shuttle bays. They're damaged, but secure."

"You need to start evacuating the ship," Pahner said. "Pull off as many of the Saint prisoners as seems practical."

"Armand," Roger said on a discrete frequency. "We can't let them go. If we do, my life isn't worth spit."

"No, but if we get our forces off, we might have a shot at the next ship," Pahner replied.

"Imperial commander," Giovannuci called. "You have thirty seconds to begin evacuation. After that, I'll start the detonation sequence, and there's no way to stop it."

Roger had automatically shifted back to the command group frequency, which meant that the Saint colonel's voice had gone out to everyone else patched into it with him. He grimaced, but then he shrugged. Maybe it was for the best.

"That's the situation, guys," he said.

"Not good," Honal said. "We're loading on the shuttles, but our assault did a certain amount of damage."

"Honal," Kosutic said. "Send a team of Vashin down to the southwest quadrant. I've got a group of crew that needs evacuating."

"Colonel Giovannuci," Roger called, this time making

certain that he wasn't putting it out over the command frequency, as well. "We're evacuating as we speak, but both sides have casualties, and there are depressurized zones all over the ship. It's going to take a little time."

"I'll give you two minutes," Giovannuci replied. "But that's it."

"Armand, I am *not* giving up this ship," Roger snarled over the discrete frequency. "If they're stupid enough to go ahead and blow themselves up after we evacuate, well and good. But if they just fly away, we're pocked."

"I know, Your Highness," the captain sighed.

"Captain Pahner," Poertena's voice interrupted. "Are we suppose' to evacuate t'e Saints?"

"Yes," Pahner replied calmly. So far, only the command group knew they were looking at a self-destruct situation, and he intended to keep it that way as long as possible. "The ship is in bad shape. We need to get the Saints off for their own safety, and as prisoners of war."

"Okay. I t'ink I gots t'e ship's exec tied up in a closet. I'll go get her."

"Wait one, Poertena," Roger interrupted. "Where are you?"

"In t'e southeas' quadrant," the armorer replied. "Deck Four."

"Sergeant Major," Roger instructed. "Head to the southeast quadrant and link up with Poertena. Do it now."

"Don't go off half-cocked, Roger," Pahner warned. He was nearly to the Bridge tunnel.

"Not a problem," Roger replied. "I'm cool as cold."

Kosutic took the proffered crowbar and inserted it into a crack between the door and its frame. Then she threw her weight on it, and the metal seal popped loose with an explosive "Crack!" The closet door sprang open, and she looked in at the female officer in a combat crouch and shook her head.

"I could probably take you *out* of the armor," the sergeant major warned her. "And we don't have time for games."

"I know we don't. We need to get out of here," Beach

replied. "That Pollution-crazed idiot is getting ready to blow up the whole ship."

"What happens if we take the Bridge?" Kosutic asked. "For general information, we already have Engineering and the Armory."

"Well, if you take the Bridge, it's *possible* that I could shut down the scuttling charges," Beach admitted. "It all depends."

"We don't have a lot of time to debate here," Kosutic said.

"Look, we're technically illegal combatants," Beach said. "You know it, I know it. What's your law in that regard?"

"Generally, you're repatriated," Kosutic told her. "Especially if we can trade you for one of our groups."

"And then, most of the time, we replace *your* group on a recovery planet," Beach said. "So I can die fast, here, when the charges go off. Or I can die slow, being worked and starved to death."

"Or?"

"Or, I can get asylum."

"We can't grant asylum," Kosutic said. "We can *try*, but we can't guarantee it. We don't have the authority."

"Is the guy leading you *really* Prince Roger? Because, according to our intelligence, he's dead, and has been for months."

"Yeah, it's really him," Kosutic replied. "You want his word on it or something?"

"Yes. If a member of your Imperial Family promises, at least it's going to be a big political stink if the Empies don't comply."

"You have no idea how complicated you're making this," the sergeant major muttered.

"Imperial commander, you have fifteen seconds to exit the ship," Giovannuci called. "I don't think you're gone yet."

"We're working on it," Roger said, just as his helmet flashed a priority signal from the sergeant major. "Hold one, Colonel Giovannuci. This may be from my people in the shuttle bay. Computer: switch Kosutic."

"It's the Saint second, all right," the sergeant major confirmed over the secure channel. "She's willing to give us the codes in exchange for asylum. She wants Roger's personal word."

"If she thinks that's going to help, she obviously doesn't know there's a price on my head, does she?" Roger said with a grim chuckle.

"I think we're dealing with intelligence lag," Kosutic replied. "She knows you're dead; she hasn't heard Jackson's latest version yet. Either way, what do I do? We're on our way, by the way."

"Tell her she has my personal word as a MacClintock that I will do all in my power to ensure that she gets asylum from the Empire," Roger replied. "But I want to be there when she finds out I'm an outlaw."

"Will do," the sergeant major said with a grin that could be heard over the radio. "About a minute until we're there."

"And I'm here already," Pahner said as he strode up behind Roger. "You need to get the hell off the ship, Your Highness. Sergeant Despreaux is already on the shuttle, and so are most of the wounded."

"Somebody needs to take this bridge, Armand," Roger said tightly. "And we need it more or less intact. Who's the best close-quarters person we have?"

"You're *not* assaulting the bridge," Pahner said. "Lose you, and it's all for *nothing*."

"Lose the *ship*, and it's all for nothing," Roger replied.

"There'll be other ships," Pahner said, putting his hand on the prince's shoulder.

"Yeah, but if this one leaves, they'll be Saint carriers!"

"Yes, but—"

"What's the mission, Captain?" Roger interrupted harshly, and Pahner hesitated for just a moment. But then he shook his head.

"To safeguard you, Your Highness," he said.

"No," Roger replied. "The mission is to safeguard the *Empire*, Captain. Safeguarding *me* is only part of that. If just Temu Jin makes it back and saves my mother, fine. If you make it back and do the same, fine. If *Julian* makes it back and performs the mission, fine. She can make a new heir. If she wants to, she can use DNA from John and Alexandra's dad. The *mission*, Captain, is 'Save the Empire.' And to do that, we have to take this ship. And to take this ship, we have to use the personnel who can do that most effectively and who can physically get here in *time* to do it. And that makes taking this bridge Colonel Roger MacClintock's best possible role. Am I *wrong?*"

Armand Pahner looked at the man he'd spent eight endless months keeping alive on a nightmare planet for a long, silent moment. Then he shook his head again.

"No, you're not. Sir," he said.

"Thought not," Roger said, and pointed his plasma cannon at the hatch.

Giovannuci looked at the tactical officer and nodded as the first blast shook the bridge.

"On three," he said, inserting his key into the console.

Lieutenant Cellini reached out slowly to insert his own key, but then he stopped. His hand dropped away from the board, and he shook his head.

"No. It's not worth it, Sir." He turned to face Iovan, pivoting in place until the noncom's pistol was pointed squarely between his eyes. "Two hundred crew left, Sergeant Major. Two hundred. You're going to kill them all for what? A corrupt leadership that preaches environmentalism and builds itself castles in the most beautiful parts of the wilderness? Kill me, and you kill yourself, and you kill the colonel. *Think* about what we're doing here!"

Giovannuci looked over at the sergeant major and tipped his chin up in a questioning gesture.

"Iovan?"

"Everybody dies someplace, Lieutenant," the sergeant major said, and pulled the trigger. Cellini's head splashed away from the impact, and the sergeant major sighed. "What a senseless waste of human life," he said, as he wiped the key clear of brains and looked at the colonel. "On three, you said, Sir?"

❖   ❖   ❖

ChromSten was almost impervious to plasma fire, but "almost" was a relative term. Even ChromSten transmitted energy to its underlying matrix, which meant, in the case of the command deck, to a high stress cero-plastic. And as the heat buildup from the repeated plasma discharges bled into it, that underlying matrix began to melt, and then burn. . . .

"Breach!" Roger shouted, as the center of the hatch buckled, and then cracked open. For just a moment, white light from the bridge illuminated the smoke and steam from the blazing matrix before it was sucked greedily away by the vacuum.

The approach corridor was just *gone*. The intense heat from the plasma discharges had melted the material of the surrounding bulkheads and decks, creating a large opening that revealed the bridge as a ChromSten cylinder, thirty meters across, and fifty high, attached to the armored engineering core.

Getting across the yawning, five-meter gulf between his present position and the breach was going to be Roger's first problem.

"No time like the present," he muttered, and triggered his armor's jump gear with a considerably gentler touch than Julian had used.

He sailed across the chasm, one hand supporting the plasma cannon while the other stretched out for the hole, and slammed into the outer face of the cylinder. The outstretched arm slipped through the breach, but his reaching fingers found nothing to grip. His arm slithered backwards, and for just a moment he felt a stab of panic. But then his fingers hooked into the ragged edge of the hole and locked.

"Piece of cake," he panted, and exoskeletal "muscles" whined as he lifted himself up onto the slight lip which was all that remained of the outer door frame. He braced himself and ripped at the hole, widening it. The matrix of the ChromSten itself had begun to fail under the plasma fire, and the material sparked against his armored hand, returning to its original chrome and selenium atomic structure.

✧　　　✧　　　✧

Giovannuci and Iovan stood with their hands behind their heads, with the rest of the command deck crew lined up at their stations behind them, as Roger entered the compartment behind his plasma cannon. All of them were in skin-suits against the soft vacuum that now filled most of the ship.

Roger looked around the bridge, then at the gore splattered over the self-destruct console, and shook his head.

"Was that strictly necessary?" he asked, as he walked over to the tactical officer's body and turned it over. "Who?"

"Me," Iovan said.

"Short range," Roger said contemptuously. "I guess you couldn't hit him from any farther away."

"Take off that fucking armor and we'll see how far away I can shoot," Iovan said, and spat on the floor.

Pahner clambered through the hole, widening it further in the process, and crossed to the prince.

"You should've waited for us to secure it, Your Highness," he said over the command frequency.

"And give them a chance to destroy the controls?" Roger replied over the same circuit. "No way. Besides," he chuckled tightly, "I figured they were probably down to bead guns after Julian's crazy stunt. If they hadn't been, they'd still be shooting at us in the passageway."

He switched back to the external amplifier, cranked up to maximum in the near-vacuum that passed for "air" on *Emerald Dawn*'s bridge at that particular moment, and looked at Giovannuci and Iovan.

"I can't read 'merchant marine' rank tabs. Which of you is Giovannuci?"

"I am," the colonel told him.

"Turn off the self-destruct," Roger said.

"No."

"Okay," Roger said, with an unseen shrug inside his armor, and turned to Iovan. "Who are you?"

"I don't have to tell you that," Iovan said.

"Senior NCO," Pahner said.

"Yeah, he's got that look," Roger said. "Not a bridge officer, so you can't turn it off, can you?"

"Nobody in here can," Giovannuci said. "Except me."

Roger started to replied, then half-turned as Kosutic crawled into the bridge.

"I've got that second officer out here," the sergeant major said over the command frequency. "She's ready to turn off the self-destruct, just as soon as we clear all these guys off the Bridge. She said to watch the CO. He's a real true-believer."

"So which one of you is Prince Roger?" Giovannuci asked.

"I am," the prince replied. "And I'm going to see to it that you hang, if it's the last thing I do."

"I don't think so," the Saint colonel said, calmly, and pulled the one-shot from behind his neck.

Time seemed to crawl as Roger started to lift his plasma cannon, then dropped it. If he fired it, the blast would take out half the ship controls . . . including the self-destruct console. So instead, he sprang forward, his hand continuing upward to the hilt of his sword even as the plasma cannon fell.

The prince was almost supernally fast, but whether he could have killed the colonel before he fired would remain forever unknown, since Pahner slammed into his suit, arms spread.

The impact threw the prince's armor to the side, sending it smashing into the tactical display and out of the Saint's' line of fire just as Giovannuci swung the weapon forward, catching Pahner dead center, and squeezed the button.

Roger lunged back upright with a shriek of pure rage and spun in place as Iovan produced another of the weapons and came at him. But this time there was no mistake, and the flashing Voitan-forged blade took off the sergeant major's head and hand in a steaming fan of blood.

The shot from the anti-armor device had spun Giovannuci backwards and on to the deck. Now he climbed back to his feet and raised his hands.

"I'm sorry I missed," he said tightly. "But we're all going to die anyway. Pollution take you."

"I don't think so," Roger grated. "We have your second-in-command, and she's more than willing to turn it off. *You* are going to, though, I promise you," he continued in a voice of frozen helium, and looked at Kosutic. "Sergeant Major, take the colonel to the shuttle bays. Make sure he doesn't do any more damage, but don't let anything happen to him on the way, either. We'll deal with him later, and I want him in perfect shape when he faces the hangman."

The sergeant major said something in reply, but Roger didn't hear her as he dropped to his knees beside Pahner. He turned the captain over as gently as possible, but there wasn't really much point. This time, the placement had been accurate. The one-shot had struck the Marine squarely on the his armor's carapace, and the ricocheting scab of armor had done precisely what it was supposed to do.

Roger bent close, trying to see through the flickering distortion of the captain's helmet. The readouts indicated that there was still brain function, but as the blood drained from the head into the shattered body, it was fading fast.

"I promise," Roger said, lifting the captain and holding him. "I promise I won't die. I promise I'll save my mother. You can depend on me, Armand. You can, I promise. Rest now. Rest, my champion."

He sat there, rocking the body, until the last display flickered out.

EPILOGUE

Roger tapped his display as the former Saint officer left the captain's office. All things considered, Beach had taken the news rather well. On the other hand, since she'd thrown her lot in rather definitively with the group around Roger, there wasn't much she could do but help. As it was, she was an outlaw under both Saint and Imperial law. If Roger succeeded, she'd be sitting pretty. If he didn't, she wouldn't be any worse off. Once they got near civilization, of course, he wouldn't be able to trust her. But until they got to wherever they were going to start the process of infiltrating the Empire, she really had only two choices: help them, or die. It wasn't much of a choice.

He looked up from the display and stood as the next person on his calendar entered.

"Sergeant Despreaux," he said. "I'd like to speak to you about near-future plans."

He sat back down and returned his attention to his display, then looked back up with an irritated expression as Despreaux came to a position of parade rest.

"Oh, hell, Nimashet. Would you *please* sit down?" he demanded in exasperation, and waited until she'd obeyed before he glanced back at the display and shook his head.

"I hadn't realized how short you really were when we left Old Earth. You should have ended your term while we were still in Sindi."

"I thought about that at the time," she replied. "Captain Pahner spoke to me about it, as well. Obviously, I couldn't just leave."

"I could probably find a way for you to leave now," Roger sighed. "Along with the four other people who are alive and over their terms. But there'd be the little problem of the price on your heads."

"I'll stay with you for the time being, Sir," Despreaux said.

"Thank you," Roger said formally, then drew a deep breath. "I . . . I have to ask a . . . I'd like to make a request, however."

"Yes?"

He rubbed his face and looked around the cabin.

"I—Nimashet, I don't know if I can do this . . ." He stopped and shook his head. "I—Damn it, I know I can't do this *alone*. Please, *please* promise me that you won't leave at the first opportunity. Please promise that you won't just go. I *need* you. I don't need your gun; I can find plenty of gunners. I need your strength. I need your sense of humor. I need your . . . balance. Don't leave me, Nimashet Despreaux. Please. Just . . . stay with me."

"I won't marry you," she said. "Or, rather, I'll marry 'Prince Roger,' but I refuse to marry 'Emperor Roger.' "

"I understand," Roger said with a sigh. "Just don't leave me. Okay?"

"Okay," she said, and stood. "Will that be all, Sir?"

Roger looked at her for a moment, then nodded.

"Yes, thank you, Sergeant," he said formally.

"Then goodnight, Sir."